Jo Thomas worked ~~~~~~~~~~~~~~~~~~~~~~~~~~~~~~~ producer, first
for BBC Radio 5, before moving on to Radio 2 ~~~ *Steve Wright
S.~~~~~~ ~~~~ Jo won the RNA Katie Fforde Bursary. Her d
novel, *The Oyster Catcher*, was a runaway bestseller in ebook
and was awarded the 2014 RNA Joan Hessayon Award and
the 2014 Festival of Romance Best Ebook Award. Her
follow-up novels, *The Olive Branch*, *Late Summer in the Vineyard*
and *The Honey Farm on the Hill* are also highly acclaimed. Jo lives in
the Vale of Glamorgan with her husband and three children.

You can keep in touch with Jo through her website at
www.jothomasauthor.com, or via @Jo_Thomas01 on Twitter and
JoThomasAuthor on Facebook.

Readers can't resist Jo Thomas's feel-good fiction:

'Romantic and funny' *Sun*

'A perfect pearl of a story. I loved it' Milly Johnson

'Well worth a read' Carole Matthews

'Jo's trademark warmth and wit sing from the page . . . I adored it!'
Cathy Bramley

'Perfect escapism' *Marie Claire*

'Sunny and funny' Veronica Henry

'Perfect summer read' Liz Fenwick

'An utterly charming read full of rustic romance and adventure'
Woman magazine

'Perfect for those who dream of a new life in the sun!' *My Weekly*

'A heart-warming tale' Ali McNamara

Jo Thomas

Sunset over the Cherry Orchard

REVIEW

First published in paperback in 2018 by
HEADLINE PUBLISHING GROUP

1

Cataloguing in Publication Data is available from the British Library

ISBN 978 1 4722 4597 7

Typeset in Caslon by Avon DataSet Ltd, Bidford-on-Avon, Warwickshire

Printed and bound in Great Britain by Clays Ltd, St Ives plc

HEADLINE PUBLISHING GROUP
An Hachette UK Company
Carmelite House
50 Victoria Embankment
London EC4Y 0DZ

www.headline.co.uk
www.hachette.co.uk

For my daughter Mali.
Your journey is just beginning . . . enjoy!
Love you always x

Hello all,

Come on in. My name is Jo Thomas. If you've read my other books, you know you're in for a story about food and love, with a splash of sun, a dollop of fun stirred in and a cast of characters I hope you'll fall in love with. If you're new to my world, you're very welcome. I hope you're here to stay!

I was once at one of my favourite restaurants in Puglia, Southern Italy, where I wrote my second book *The Olive Branch*. The owner brought around a bottle of *limoncello*, a wonderful Italian lemon liqueur, at the end of the meal with glasses for us all. As he pulled up a chair, he asked what kind of books I wrote. He didn't speak any English and I didn't speak much Italian, but I explained that my books were about food and love, because I have always felt that the two are intertwined. He told me that for him, life was all about the food that he and his family grew on the land, cooked in the kitchen and served on the table. He held out his arm to the olive grove surrounding us, gestured to the *forno* in the kitchen, where the burning wood was glowing orange and merrily pumping smoke out of the chimney, and slapped his hand down on the scrubbed, wooden table, *la tavola*. 'For the ones we love,' he told me as he held his hand to his chest over his heart. And this is *exactly* the kind of book I like to write: about the food we grow to cook and put on the table for the ones we love. So, pull up a chair at my table.

This time we're in Spain. I loved visiting Spain to research this book. It was spring when I visited with two other authors, Katie Fforde and AJ Pearce. On our second or third day there, everything suddenly burst into life, with all the colour, noise and vitality we think of when we imagine a Spanish fiesta. The sky was the most amazing cobalt blue the whole week we were there. The vines on the hillside all around us had sprung into life. What we thought were dead stumps when we arrived, suddenly had leaves unfurling. The many garden birds in the trees and shrubs courted each other loudly, flapping, flirting and arguing. The wisteria over the terrace blossomed and there were bees like bomber planes noisily flying from one bloom to another. Along the winding road to our villa, wild flowers all of a sudden splashed their colours, a riot of reds, purples and yellows. In the air was the lovely scent of the yellow broom shrub that covered the hillside we were on. The countryside around us looked like a flamenco dancer's dress, bright, flamboyant and breath-takingly beautiful. The perfect setting for my novel! I do hope you enjoy this trip to my Spanish table set amongst the glorious cherry orchards there.

Con amor,

Jo

xx

Acknowledgements

Thank you, firstly, to Katie Fforde and Caroline Sanderson for sharing their love of flamenco with me. And thank you for introducing me to your fabulous flamenco teacher, Vicki Clifford. We had a wonderful and inspiring evening of flamenco dance in Stroud. Thank you, Vicki, for letting me join in a class the following day. I loved it! Even if I did stamp on my own toe! Any mistakes about flamenco here are entirely my own! But I urge any of you, if you want a fantastic form of exercise, no matter what your age or shape, to find a flamenco class near you. It will make you feel fabulous!

I couldn't have written this book without a cherry expert. Thank you, Emily Livesey, fruit manager from Lower Hope Cherries in Hereford, for answering all my questions and letting me pick your brains. Once again, any cherry-growing errors in this book will be of my own making. But I hope it makes you go out and buy wonderful, dark, fat cherries in cherry season!

Thank you to James Villa Holidays for the beautiful villa in Cómpeta, Andalucía. It was utterly and blissfully peaceful there. The words certainly flowed at Casa Nobleza! The views were amazing and the pool, just heaven. It was the perfect place to soak up the atmosphere and find the inspiration for the Spanish hilltop town in *Sunset over the Cherry Orchard*.

A thank you, too, to my lovely hairdresser Xan from Xan's hair studio for the horse talk and inspiring the lovely stallion in this book. Oh, and for my pink streak! I love it!

And, finally, thank you to my lovely editor Christina Demosthenous. Thank you for continuing the journey with me. Good luck and lots of love as you continue on a journey of your own now! The bravest decisions are often the best ones!

Jo

x

Prologue

'So, let me check I've got that right.' I read the order back to the customer, who is dressed in a straw trilby, floral shorts and wraparound shades, despite it being mid-February. The airport is busy, noisy and positively buzzing with excitement, despite the rain coming down in stair rods against the big tinted windows, sliding down them like huge tears, almost masking the big white planes taxiing up and down the tarmac outside. But no one in the bustling terminal seems to be worried by the weather. Everyone is positively demob-happy, like the last day of school, as they prepare to jet off to some Mediterranean sunshine or some proper winter snow on sunny slopes where adventures await them.

Some people love the winter. But not me, despite my name being Beti Winter. I love the smiles that summer brings. The hope of what's to come. I love the feel of sunshine on my face, warming my skin. I look around at the excited, beaming faces of holidaymakers who will, in a few hours' time, be lying on beaches, catching sunny rays and feeling invigorated by it. Then I sigh. The sort of sigh that comes from deep inside. So deep you didn't even know a sigh could come from there.

'It's a triple cheeseburger with bacon and extra cheese, but hold the onions and no gherkins?'

'And extra bacon. No lettuce. Who puts salad in a burger anyway?' says the young man, late twenties, rummaging in his money belt under his flopping beer belly. 'Couldn't hold my pint, could you?' He holds out a tall glass of lager.

I glance up at the departures board clock. Only just eight o'clock in the morning. This is what constitutes 'getting into the holiday mood', I have discovered since working here. I take the pint as he struggles to retrieve his money.

'Come on, Tez! They've put up our gate!' calls one of the lads standing behind him. The whole group are dressed in similar shorts, hats and sunglasses, and are all wearing T-shirts emblazoned with *Al's Big Birthday Bender* on the front, and *Al's 30th* on the back. 'Come on!' they call, jostling like boisterous bulldog pups.

'Got to get some soakage in!' Tez banters back, finally digging out his bank card for contactless payment as I hand him back his glass.

'Birthday bash, is it?' I nod at the T-shirt.

'Yes. We do it every year on our annual bonuses. Top computer programming sales team around!' He raises his voice and his pint to his mates, who cheer raucously.

'Extra bacon, extra cheese, no onion, no gherkin and definitely no lettuce.' I smile as I hand over his order.

'Cheers, love!' He takes the burger, abandons the pint on a nearby table and greedily starts eating as his mates drag him towards the departure gate.

'Have fun!' I say. Despite wishing I was the one heading for a holiday, I can't help but smile as they bundle him off. I can just imagine the hot sun that will greet them when they land; the clear blue sky, the sparkling sea and the soft sand . . .

'Two kids' meals, with matching toys, please.' A harassed-looking Mum snaps my thoughts back to the here and now. She has two small children using her legs as a maypole, and is trying to keep them and the collection of bags around her feet close, like she's herding cats.

I quickly process her order and hand it over on a tray. 'I'll put in a couple of spare toys, just in case you've got those ones,' I tell her, ignoring the glares from my boss, Stacey, who's slightly younger than me, but with an extra star on her lapel reflecting her years of service.

'It's one toy per meal,' she whispers fiercely at me. 'No exceptions.'

'Of course, Stacey.' I nod, smile and chuck in the extra toys anyway, hoping it will bring the woman a bit of respite on her journey. Travelling with kids is exhausting. Not that I know first-hand. I don't have children, and at thirty-two I'm doubting that will ever happen for me now. But I've seen the families rolling up, stressed at the start of their holidays, every day since I started here three years ago. I only took the job while I waited for something more suitable to come along. But that seems to be the story of my life so far.

A roar swells above us and another plane takes off. I know the schedule practically off by heart. I look at the clock, counting the minutes until my break.

'A plain burger, with fries and water,' says a smartly dressed businessman, putting down his case, unplugging his earphones and reaching inside his jacket pocket for his wallet.

'Enjoy your trip,' I tell him as I hand over the paper bag.

'Thanks.' He smiles back. 'I'll try.' He puts his earphones back in and turns to leave. I sigh that deep sigh again as I watch him go, longing to escape this place for somewhere hot and sunny.

'You don't need to engage everyone in conversation,' says Stacey. 'It's fast food, not some bar in Benidorm. It's not our job to make sure everyone has a brilliant time.'

Frankly, I'd rather be working in a bar in Benidorm, I think as Stacey turns her attention to her clipboard. 'Oh, and you can take your break . . .' she looks at her watch, 'now.'

I rip off my hat, apron and name tag, grab my handbag and head out of the door at the back of the kitchen and into the crowded concourse. Everyone around me is carrying big bags or pulling cases on wheels. People are wearing bright colours, sparkling flip-flops and straw hats, and looking up at the departures board, eager to depart. There's a crackle of anticipation in the air. Then a cheer goes up as the next gate is announced. Like a swarm of bees, they all move noisily in the same direction.

It looks like everyone's heading somewhere on this school half-term break. Everyone except me. I'll be going back to the flat after my shift finishes, and the closest thing I'll get to foreign climes is wondering which takeaway menu to order off. The same as most nights these days. But it wasn't always like this. I look at the happy, eager faces around me. Will and I were like that with each other once. I'm just not sure when it changed. When he stopped noticing me.

I take the stairs at speed, down to the shops, and dive into the nearest newsagent's for a sandwich meal deal. I can't help but wander past the shelves of magazines, the glossy covers selling me all sorts of stories of hopes and dreams. I'd give anything for life to be different right now. For something to give it a much-needed injection of excitement. My eyes automatically scan the wedding magazines. But I've got them all already. I've got the engagement ring, even if it was just my nan's thin wedding band, the thick file of plans and the veil too. Just missing the crucial ingredient. A date.

I let my eyes wander to the top shelf. Should I try and be a bit more like the babe on the front cover? Is that what I need to do? Just for a moment, I wonder if I could recreate that pose. No, I've bought enough new underwear I tell myself, thinking of my credit-card bill. My eyes wander to the parenting magazines. But I know we're definitely not ready for that. In fact, I'm not sure it will ever happen for us now, especially as we practically live separate lives. I can't remember the last time Will came to bed before I've fallen asleep – we barely even cuddle these days.

As I scan the shelves, I'm drawn to an image of blue skies, wisps of white cloud, and toffee-coloured stone buildings spilling down a mountainside to the glorious beach and the sea beyond. A magazine about living abroad, a life in the sun, selling the dream. I pick it up as another plane roars into the sky overhead.

'This isn't a library, you know. You'll have to buy that now,' the sales assistant calls over.

'What?'

'There's nothing worse than buying a brand-new magazine that someone's already read in the shop,' he answers tartly, pushing his glasses up his nose. And actually, if he wasn't so sniffy, I'd probably agree with him!

I look at the price on the cover in horror. But even that can't put me off buying it. Just looking at the photo gives me the lift I need.

I pay for the magazine, and hug it protectively to my chest, along with a bag of wine gums and a meal deal, as I make my way to the seating area, where I plan to settle down to savour each and every one of its pages, pretending it really is me getting on a plane and going somewhere. I put my hat, apron and name badge down beside me and open my egg and cress sandwich, giving it a quick prod for freshness, then pick up the magazine, preparing to lose myself in its pages for the next twenty minutes. My sigh of sadness turns to one of contentment. I take a bite of the sandwich and slide down into the seat.

I'm only three pages in when I hear it: a voice I'd recognise anywhere, shrieking with laughter. A shrill voice that cuts sharply through the noise of excited travellers filling the airport. I freeze, then bristle, gripping the pages of my magazine more tightly, peering over the top of it to see the familiar figure walking through the concourse in the middle of a small group of women. They all look to be in their late twenties, early thirties, and are carrying oversized handbags over their forearms and wearing expensive fake-fur bobble hats that I know I've seen for sale in the airport shops. My worst fears are confirmed. It's my cousin Olivia and her friends. And they're coming this way. My heart drops like a stone.

I look around for a quick and easy escape. The loos are within sprinting distance. I start to stand and gather my sandwich, magazine and apron. But as I do, she spots me.

Damn it! Should have stayed hidden behind the magazine. Wrong call. But it's too late. There's nowhere to hide.

'Bet? Is that you?' she says, as if she is broadcasting through a megaphone.

Olivia and her father, my uncle Paul, always insist on calling me Bet, despite me explaining time and time again that I'd rather be known as Beti. Uncle Paul and my dad have a difficult relationship. It goes back years – my uncle has never forgiven my mum for picking my dad over him, and he takes every opportunity he can to get one up on them; which includes putting me down whenever the chance arises.

My heart thumping and my mouth dry, I stand up and hold the magazine to me, shielding my hat and apron. Olivia's friends are staring at me as if waiting for me to say something exciting or funny.

'Small world,' Olivia says, leaning in and bumping cheeks awkwardly with me. Hers are bony and sharp. Mine are cushioned and well hidden. 'This is my cousin Elizabeth, but we call her Bet,' she tells her friends.

'Hi!' I nod at the group of women, then we stand and stare awkwardly at each other. I'm desperate for Olivia not to ask what I'm doing here.

'What are you doing here?' she says with that familiar teasing glint in her eye. She flicks her hair over her shoulder.

'So . . . off somewhere lovely?' I ask at the same time. It's a ridiculous question. We're in the departures lounge of an airport. Of course they're going somewhere lovely. Everybody is. That's why the place is humming with excitement.

'Iceland! Reykjavik!' She doesn't need asking twice to step

into the spotlight. It's always been the same. We grew up together, were pushed together at every family celebration and holiday. But we're nothing alike. Olivia was always one of the popular girls, while I . . . well I wasn't. I never really fitted in.

She beams around at her friends, who all look exactly like each other. The long straightened hair, the fake-fur-trimmed collars, the thick foundation and outlined nude lips. At least the different-coloured bobbles on their hats are a distinguishing feature.

'It's Georgia's hen weekend!' Olivia says. The woman in the black hat with the pink bobble positively preens in amongst the huddle, like she's a precious jewel nestled in a bed of soft pastel-coloured feathers.

'Ah, the hen night,' I say. Of course. They've talked about nothing else on Facebook for weeks, ever since the last party, a baby shower in a Scottish castle.

'Hen *weekend*! No one does hen nights any more,' Olivia corrects me with pleasure.

With an effort, I stretch my cheeks into a smile. 'Well, have a great one. And congratulations!' I add, hoping I can walk away with what's left of my dignity.

'What? This is Bet, as in your cousin, the one who's been engaged three times?' says the woman in a fawn hat to match her foundation and a baby-blue bobble, pointing a gelled fingernail at me and looking me up and down. The others follow suit. My cheeks are suddenly burning, and I wish I could use the magazine I'm holding to fan at the flames.

'Ha, the very same!' I try to joke, but inside I'm dying,

actually dying. *It's not like that!* I want to explain, but I can't find the words.

'We've heard so much about you,' says a silver-bobbled hat, and I hear a snigger or two. Suddenly, I'm back at school, in the playground, being taunted by my cousin and her coven. I take a deep breath. I'm not going to let this happen.

'Have you? All good, I hope!' I joke.

'So, Bet, what about the mysterious Will? Have you set a date yet? How long have you been together now?' Olivia is practically licking her lips, like a cat teasing its prey.

'Er, let's see, well, about five years,' I say as casually as I can.

'Five years!' the gaggle repeat, practically in unison.

'And not so mysterious really. You have actually met him, Olivia,' I follow up firmly.

'Engaged! For five years! And no date set?' says the bride-to-be.

'Um, no.' My backbone wobbles a bit and I'm desperate for the flight to Reykjavik to be called. 'Not an actual date as such. Yet.' I swallow. 'Still planning it. You know how exhausting these things can be!' I straighten and appeal to the bride-to-be, who nods in agreement, like I'm a kindred spirit all of a sudden.

'Oh, Bet is always planning. She has whole folders of ideas. And she's had plenty of practice, with three engagement parties!' They all laugh. 'She knows every florist and wedding favour supplier around,' Olivia continues. 'My dad used to joke that she should have her own parking space at those wedding fairs – do you remember, Bet?' She laughs again, and this time a little bit of fury bubbles up in me.

That's the problem with living in a small town: everyone knows your business and no one ever forgets. Yes, I've been engaged before. But with Will, it's different. We hit it off straight away, and saw each other whenever we could, even though he was living in Bristol and I was still at home in West Wales. We just couldn't get enough of each other in those early days. He asked me to marry him in a round-about kind of way, and we just went for it. Despite everyone telling me it was too soon, it felt wild, exciting and impulsive. Just what I needed after my nan died, after all that sadness. Not long after that, I moved in with Will in Bristol, and I'm still there.

My first engagement was when I was just sixteen, to my first boyfriend Rhys. We got engaged at the end-of-school party and planned to marry in two years' time, after his A levels. I checked out the registry office and decided to have a barbecue in my parents' garden afterwards. Everything was to be done as cheaply as possible. But by the following summer, he was making plans for university and I was left in Swn y Mor, broken-hearted, the wedding plans hidden in a bottom drawer with my other childhood memories.

Then, in my early twenties, there was Tom. I thought he was the one. Tom was a chef, and was working in one of the big hotels on the seafront. We were happy. And I think that's what annoyed Olivia the most. I'd found happiness on my doorstep, and Olivia always wanted what other people had. So she took him, and when she realised she still wasn't content, she dumped him. We attempted a reconciliation after that, but it didn't work. I could never really forgive him. We tried, but in the end, we wanted different things. He wanted to run a restaurant in Glasgow, I dreamed of a bar in Spain, and we finally called it a day.

Then I met Will and realised that everything about him was just what I'd hoped for. Everyone loves Will. What's not to love about him? He's outgoing, friendly, funny, intelligent and holds down a good job. Not to mention his looks: dark-haired and fit . . . his arms just ripple. He even plays lead guitar in a band in the local pub. He's like Danny O'Donoghue from The Script. OK, he's not Irish, but he has that same twinkle in his eye. When he arrives at a party, it gets going. That's why he was such a great holiday rep when I met him. He made everyone feel special. And when he used to look at me, he made me feel like I was the only person in the world.

'Still no date set for the big day then?' Olivia cuts through my thoughts, her eyes sparkling mischievously.

'Well, we've had a lot on,' I lie quickly. We haven't had anything on, apart from get up, go to work, come home from work, eat, sleep. Somehow, despite being engaged six weeks after we got together, we've never actually finalised a date.

Will's mum was in hospital with pneumonia, and we went to visit her the first day she was taken in. It was all a bit touch and go. That evening, after a microwave macaroni cheese and a quick cuddle on the settee, Will asked me if it would be OK if he told her we were engaged. He thought it would help lift her spirits. I agreed. It felt spontaneous and exciting. And it did lift her spirits. He promised me a proper proposal once she was better, the full down-on-one-knee somewhere romantic, and I could have free rein planning the wedding.

I threw myself into wedding plans to reassure myself that it would actually happen. Keeping my file reminded me of the fun times that were to come, as real life slipped into a more mundane routine. His mum loved hearing about my plans, but the full proposal never actually happened, nor did setting the date. We just slipped into the 'engaged' zone. Will thought we should wait until we were 'sorted'. Whatever that meant. Now we are well and truly stuck in a rut. And I'd do anything to get us out of it.

Bing bong, goes the tannoy. I strain my ears, hoping for the Reykjavik call to come, but it's just a customer announcement. A passport left at security, no doubt.

'So, Bet, what *are* you doing here?' Olivia looks around expectantly, no doubt for signs of Will. 'You're not still working here, are you?' she practically snorts.

I can't tell her that yes, I am still working here. I'm thirty-two years old, for God's sake! Is this it? A job flipping burgers and watching everybody else's lives moving on, literally? I look up at the departures board and scan down the departing flights. Her friends are watching me like vultures waiting for roadkill.

'Working here? God, no.' My jaw tightens with my lie. 'Actually, I'm off to Spain. Malaga.' I nod up at the board. 'A um . . . research trip.'

'Don't tell me you're finally going to do it! You're going to get that bar of yours! Bet's always talked about living in Spain, owning a bar,' Olivia tells her friends. It's true. It's always been my dream, ever since I first holidayed out there. 'Where is Will?' she adds, looking around.

'Toilet,' I lie again, feeling my head begin to pound.

What am I saying? Just tell the truth!

'She keeps him well hidden,' Olivia says with raised eyebrows. And who could blame me after last time? 'She and Will met in Spain. He was a holiday rep,' she explains to the coven, who are hanging on her every word. 'I mean, you'd be great at running a bar.' She smiles at me and the flames of fury die down a little.

'Do you think so?' I reply, letting my guard down just a tiny bit.

'Bet really knows how to organise a party. Spreadsheets, costings, themes . . . well, with three engagements, she's had plenty of practice!' They all guffaw with laughter, and the flames of mortification in my cheeks and the ones of fury in my belly flare up again.

And then the call comes over the tannoy for the Reykjavik flight, and relief washes over me, despite realising my break's nearly over and I've barely started my sandwich.

'That's us!' the bride-to-be squeals, her shriek going right through me.

'Nice to meet you, um, Bee,' says another woman.

'Hope you get your bar sorted!' adds a third, and they all nod in agreement as they start to move towards the departure gate almost as one.

'Is that really where you're going now? To find a bar?' Olivia's eyes are wide with admiration and a fair amount of disbelief.

'I am,' I say firmly, surprising myself. I look up at the board, and a little spark of excitement lights up inside me. Why shouldn't it be my turn? I remember the young Beti, with her hopes and dreams, and a feeling of determination

13

rises in me like a bear woken from hibernation.

'Let us know on Facebook, we'll come and see you!' And with that they practically run in the direction of their departure gate, riding on the excitement of their next adventure, their lives moving onwards. 'Three engagements and never made it down the aisle?' I hear one of them ask Olivia, and then they all giggle.

I open the magazine, and there, right in front of me, is a list of bars and restaurants to rent in Andalucía. My name badge falls to the floor and rolls under the wheels of a cabin case. I look up at the departures board again, then back at the advert. What if I could just get on a flight and rent a bar? Isn't that what people do? Would my nan approve of me using the money from the china cow she left me? I was planning to use it as our wedding fund. I chew on my bottom lip. But without a wedding date, what's the point?

Isn't this exactly what Will and I need to get us out of our rut, remind us of the couple we used to be? A place of our own? A fresh start? Bugger the new undies and chicken biryani I was going to order tonight. What we need is an adventure. We need to go somewhere! And as soon as we get to Spain and get settled, we'll be able to set a wedding date and plaster it all over bloody Facebook, I just know it. This is what Nan would have wanted me to do. And it's what I'm going to do.

I stuff my apron and hat under my arm and watch as my name badge is spat out from under the wheels of the case, battered and twisted. I listen to the roar of another plane as it takes off, and the little spark in my tummy suddenly roars into life with it.

I look at the adverts in the magazine again. One in particular leaps out at me – the Butterfly Bar. It's right on the harbour, and within my budget too. I text Will and tell him to meet me after work. Will is good at his job, but really he just wants to play guitar in a band. And where better than in our own bar, in sunny Spain?

I bend down and pick up my name badge. Where I'm going, everyone will know my name. 'Are you going to Beti's bar?' I imagine holidaymakers asking each other. Yes, I am! No more flipping burgers for me. Beti Winter is finally going somewhere.

Chapter One

'So that's one Gut-Buster burger with no onions or gherkins, and extra cheese, is that right?'

'And a Diet Coke. I'll sling a Bacardi in it, or whatever this Spanish stuff is,' says the man at the counter, holding up a bottle of clear liquid. He's in his twenties and is wearing a straw trilby and floral shorts, and his sunburnt nose is the colour of a cooked lobster.

'OK. Here you go. Enjoy your breakfast. *Adiós!*' I hand him the paper bag, which already has grease spots spreading across its sides.

'Uh?' He looks at me.

'It means goodbye . . . in Spanish.'

'Oh, cheers!' As he turns away, he is already tearing into his burger.

'Can you sweep up?' nods Victoria. 'And then you can go on your break.' Victoria is tall, blonde and slim and comes from Clapham. She's ten years younger than me. It's her dad's burger bar, and she's helping out while he recovers from a mild heart attack. She finished university last summer, graduating with a 2:2 in media studies. I, on the other hand, managed to scrape a couple of A levels in art, and travel and tourism. Even then I loved the idea of living abroad.

Victoria tells me she is weighing up her options. In other words, she's applying for 'proper' jobs. She hooted with laughter when I asked her how long she intended to stay in Spain. 'God, it's not like I want to still be doing this when I'm in my thirties!' She's hoping for the BBC or Channel 4, to make it as a documentary producer.

I finish sweeping, then pull off my hat and apron. It may only be late March, but the sun is already warming up, like a sunny May day back home. I've been here for two weeks now, and working behind that counter in nylon uniform trousers is torture. I unbutton my shirt and slide it off to reveal my strappy top underneath, heaving a sigh of relief as the light sea breeze gently tickles my skin. The sky is a brilliant blue, like the colour of the poster paint I used to use when I was a child. The few wisps of cloud are clearing as the day heats up, and the holidaymakers are making hay while the sun shines. It's raining cats and dogs back home, according to my mum's latest text.

Grabbing my bag from the cupboard at the back of the bar, I make my way across the precinct, around the big palm trees planted in wooden barrels, swaying in the soft breeze, to the sandwich bar on the other side.

'Hey, Beti. The usual?' Craig's deep brown, highly moist-urised face breaks into a wide white smile, to match the colour of the tips of his spiky hair. He is wearing a sleeveless white T-shirt and denim cut-offs. His colourful friendship bracelets, of which there are many, slip around his wrists as he turns slices of crispy pink bacon on the sizzling grill.

'Yes, please, Craig.' Craig's floury white bacon baps with brown sauce are the best, made even better by the addition of a cup of Tetley tea. He has a small lock-up shop, a chiller cabinet, a grill and a tea urn, and when he's sold out of breakfast baps, he spends the rest of the day on the beach, topping up his tan.

'How's things?' He smiles before asking in a quieter voice, 'Any news?' He looks at me with a sympathetic cock of the head, and though he means well, I don't trust myself to reply, merely shaking my head and rummaging for my purse in my bag.

He hands me the bacon bap in kitchen roll. I take it like he's handing me the secret ingredient to mending a broken heart.

'And don't forget to come back for a top-up of that tea,' he reminds me firmly, just as he has done every day since I started working at Buster's Burgers a week ago, here in the heart of the precinct in the harbour. Lado del Puerto – Harbourside – is now known for its high-rise holiday apartments, British bars and long stretch of crowded beach much more than for its traditional market and dwindling fishing industry.

'Thanks, Craig.' I want to thank him for everything, not just the tea and bap, but his concern too. But my treacherous bottom lip won't let me. Instead I take my breakfast and sit in the shade of a raffia umbrella on the other side of the palm trees, as far away as possible from the hubbub of holiday-makers, some nursing hangovers and replaying last night's parties, some not even having made it to bed by the looks of it. I look out to sea at the few fishing boats coming in, then hold my face to the mid-morning sun, drinking in its rays, hoping it will revive my exhausted eyes and spirits.

I unwrap the bacon roll and draw in the smell, letting it fill my soul, reminding me with a stab of everything I've left behind. At least back in Bristol I had a home, a life, a job, and a wedding I was planning. I thought coming out here was going to make everything better, catapulting Will and me out of our rut. We'd have a new business, and a future to look forward to. I thought I was finally moving up life's ladder. Instead, I've lost the lot.

I take a sip of tea. Craig likes to make proper builder's tea, as my dad would call it. God, it's hot! Burning, in fact. But at least it takes my mind off the pain in my chest right now. I take another sip, followed by a tiny bite of the soft white bap and the salty bacon. It's funny how the smell can sometimes be more tempting than the actual taste. A bit like life, I suppose, where the thought of something can often turn out to be quite different from the reality, and you end up wondering why you bothered with it in the first place.

I thought coming to Spain was exactly what Will and I needed to break us out of the monotony of our life back home. Just the boost to rekindle things in the bedroom department and put us back on track wedding-wise. I mean, relationships are supposed to be worked at, aren't they? I thought once we were here, doing something together, he'd finally notice me and look at me like he used to. I'd tried everything else: sexy underwear, trips to the supermarket armed with the Hairy Bikers cookbook, and a new hairstyle – which I'm desperately regretting now – with blonde highlights over my natural mousy-brown colour. I'm growing it out and can just about tie it back in a scrunchie again now, thank goodness.

Will and I met in Spain when I was twenty-seven while I was on holiday . . . with my parents! Mum and Dad had had a small win on the premium bonds and thought I needed a break from looking after my nan. I'd been living with her since she had fallen and broken her hip. It was on that holiday too that I realised that one day I wanted to live here and run a place of my own. I could just see myself serving drinks and tapas and living each day in the sunshine. There was an empty bar there I used to see every day, and I would dream about what I would do with it: the colour schemes, the place settings. When I got home, I even started Spanish lessons with a four-CD box set. I wonder if that's why I ended up working at the airport. It was one step nearer my goal. All I had to do was get on a plane one day. And that day finally came.

Will, in fairness, was surprisingly easy to convince. He was fed up working in the holiday company's offices, selling holidays and insurance over the phone, and jumped at the chance. Work even offered him a six-month sabbatical and his job back at the end of it if he wanted it. What could go wrong? I thought I had it all sewn up. A summer out here, running our own place, and then a winter wedding on a beach somewhere hot. We handed our notice in on our dark, noisy rented flat, which was always supposed to be a temporary measure but had ended up being the rut we got stuck in.

The next few weeks were a whirl of decluttering and packing, wading through websites and making appointments to see bars, narrowing them down to a shortlist of those we thought could be 'the one'. We were spending more time together, enjoying each other's company, laughing, excited about the future.

We even found our bar – the Butterfly Bar, the one I'd seen in the advert. It's just across the way from where I'm sitting now, and it's perfect: overlooking the harbour and just a short distance from the beach. Harold and Brenda, the current owners, are sitting outside it now. He's wearing a Hawaiian shirt, stretched over his big belly like a drum, and has faded tattoos and a moustache. He waves over to me and I smile. He's drinking a cold beer at ten o'clock in the morning. It seems to be par for the course round here! Brenda is wearing a floral dress, skin as dark as my nan's piano. I wave back, whilst a hot rash of embarrassment runs up my chest and round my neck at the thought of what I've got to tell them.

When I saw the Butterfly Bar, I fell in love with it straight away. I knew it was the one. It has plenty of passing trade. There's room for a small band to play, and tables and chairs outside. And they're throwing everything in with the rental: glasses, optics, the lot! We'd just have to open up and hit the ground running. It's even got a small one-bedroom apartment upstairs. We were so excited, we shook on it there and then. Harold and Brenda seemed delighted too; said they wanted to hand it over to a young couple who reminded them of themselves, especially when they heard I was from Wales originally, like them. They thought we were perfect. We went out and celebrated, and plastered selfies of us drinking fizz all over Facebook. Life really was on the up. I was about to live my dream at last.

That night, there was a fiesta in the harbour to celebrate

Easter. There were firecrackers going off everywhere; music and drinking; a brass band and a procession of floats with bejewelled performers dancing on them. I'm not sure what half of them had to do with Easter, mind. After far too much sangria, Will saw me back to our holiday apartment; then, while I face-planted into my pillow, he went back to the precinct for a few more beers with a band we'd met in the Pink Flamingo nightclub. And then, well . . . I take another sip of my tea, which has now gone cold. I still feel sick at the thought of it. He came back to the apartment at some point. Packed his stuff, and left. Just like that. And then he texted me.

I pull my phone from my bag, check for any new messages and reread that last text.

I'm so sorry, Beti. I know I can't ask you to forgive me for what I've done. I think it would be better if we went our separate ways. I'm sorry.

I take another gulp of cold tea, but I don't taste it.

It was the bank that first alerted me to 'suspicious movements' on our joint account, and I realised he'd practically emptied it. The deposit money for the bar, the few thousand from my nan's inheritance, was gone.

I must have rung his number a hundred times. Each time it goes to voicemail. I've checked his Facebook status as many times too. But there's nothing. Like mine, it's stuck in time on the day we celebrated finding our bar and the start of our new life in the sun.

I asked around, of course. It was Craig who told me about Will's new travelling companions. A band, Itchy Feet, playing where they can, and a six-foot Swedish backing singer called Freya. According to Craig, Will got involved in a card game with a bunch of Scottish lads. There was too much sangria, and in one evening my nan's money was gone. He had to go to the cashpoint at least three times; I checked. I can still hear the whirring of the machine as I tried to withdraw money without success.

So that was it. Will picked up his guitar and his belongings, hitched a lift with the band in their battered camper van, and disappeared. And I've stayed here, waiting, making increasingly feeble excuses to Harold and Brenda about Will's whereabouts. I got this job in the meantime. I thought he'd be back by now. But he isn't and it's been nearly two weeks. I guess Freya just had something I didn't . . . Well, she has now. She has my fiancé.

So this is me, Beti Winter. Feeling foolish and sworn off Facebook for ever. My last status was 'Found my dream bar! Life just doesn't get any better.' I can't bear to put up 'Single and skint in Spain.' Uncle Paul would have a field day. He'd tease my dad mercilessly. Apparently it's 'banter'. Not to my dad it's not. He hates the way his brother makes me the butt of his jokes. But I have given him plenty of fodder. Not one of my weddings has come off, and now this, the bar in Spain that never was . . . Worst of all, I feel I've let my nan down. She trusted me with her china cow to make good use of it, and now it's gone. What I do know is that I have to tell Harold and Brenda I can't take over their bar, and I'm dreading it.

They're going to be disappointed, I know. They're planning to move back to the UK, to retire there. Their daughter's expecting another baby any time now, and they think it's time to be with the family. If there was any way I could make this work, I would. But as it is, I've been left high and dry, up shit creek without a paddle, and I have no idea how to get back to dry land without being an absolute laughing stock.

I stand up and toss the uneaten bacon bap in the nearby bin. It lands on top of the rubbish from the night before. The irony of it isn't lost on me. I look across at Harold and Brenda. I have to go and explain.

No more plans of owning my own bar in the Spanish sunshine for me. It's back to the real world. This silly dream is well and truly over.

Chapter Two

'Oh Beti, come over.' Brenda waves enthusiastically as I approach. The sun is warming up the paving stones of the precinct. The shops and cafés are open and there are plenty of people milling around, ordering coffees and pints. People are pulling out chairs and sitting at the chrome tables at the Butterfly Bar, enjoying the sun. Everyone is chatting, some are smoking, the white smoke curling up to meet the azure sky.

I slow down and stop when I realise quite how busy the bar is getting. Maybe now isn't such a good time to deliver my news after all.

'I'll come back later,' I call over, my throat still a little tight. 'After my shift.' I point back to the burger bar. I'll be done by two, after the lunchtime rush.

'No, it's fine. I've got a few people I want you to meet.' Brenda navigates her tiny hips around the tables as more chairs are pulled up and shuffled around to accommodate the group. All eyes turn to me. I swallow hard. My cheeks flush and my tired eyes sting. I can't turn away now.

'Hey!' An arm slips around my shoulders, making me jump; my heart leaps, and just for a moment, I catch my breath hopefully. Then I turn and see Craig standing there smiling his bright white smile, and my heart drops back to its regular sluggish beat, my face falling with it.

'Sorry, hen, didn't mean to scare you,' he says, smiling kindly. 'Or make you think . . . y'know. That it was yer man.'

I wave away his apology. Although just for a second, that was exactly what I thought.

'Looks like Brenda wants you to meet some of the locals.' Craig pulls me to him by way of support, his arm still round my shoulders. 'Lucky you! Shame she can't introduce me to someone. Preferably tall and tanned, like George Michael.' He gives a sad little sigh. 'He was my ideal man. He could have given me his heart any day,' and he starts singing 'Last Christmas', making me laugh and banishing my nerves. In only a short time, he's become such a good friend. He seems to know everyone around here, and everything that goes on, too, by the sounds of it. He gets to see it all from his vantage point behind his breakfast bar. That could have been me too, here in the Butterfly Bar, but it isn't going to happen now, and the quicker I tell Harold and Brenda, the better.

'Come on.' Craig gives me a squeeze, his silver and leather jewellery sparkling in the spring sunshine. 'Time to meet the welcoming committee.'

Brenda starts introducing people to me whilst trying to remember a big round of drinks. 'That's a G and T for you, Moira. Sun is over the yardarm, after all.'

'Just!' says Craig loudly, and they all laugh.

'Moira's a writer. She teaches creative writing and Spanish, and lives with Eric in an apartment on the front there.' She points from a man with a ponytail to a block of flats. 'A jug of sangria for Dan and Lynn – they run boating day cruises round the harbour.' She indicates a young woman in hat and sunglasses, with a scarf around her shoulders, and a man wearing a baggy sun-bleached T-shirt. They wave at me.

'And a cava for you, Maxine?' Brenda asks. 'Maxine runs the Pink Flamingo. She's worked here for years. A Cher lookalike, as you can see. She runs flamenco nights on Thursdays, Fridays and Saturdays.'

Craig takes over from Brenda, who is getting her drinks order mixed up. 'And that's Pedro and Alexis, who work in their family restaurant. One of the oldest families in the port.' He points to the two Spanish men, their hair smartly cut and slicked back, who raise their coffee cups to me and smile widely. 'And that's Jackie, she's a hairdresser from Tyneside . . . and Sue and Sandra, who have a cheese and honey stall at the market. . . . and Dick and Bev, who run a ready-meals business . . .'

'*Hola!*' comes a shout. A man with a big sack is heading for Pedro and Alexis's restaurant. He's a fisherman by the looks of it, straight from the boat. Pedro calls him over and looks in the sack. They nod, shake hands, then Pedro orders another round of coffees and a white wine for the fisherman.

'So that was a beer for Moira . . . no, a V and T. Or was it just a coffee? Oh, bugger it!' Brenda waves her pad and pen and laughs a chesty laugh. 'Everybody?' She tries to get their attention, ready to introduce me properly.

'Actually, Brenda, I need to talk to you,' I say quickly. I have to break the news before she tells everybody who I am . . . or who I was going to be. But I'm too late.

'This is Beti,' she announces. 'She and her fiancé, the gorgeous Will, are taking this place over. So I want you all to be kind to them and behave yourselves!' She hoots with laughter while various people say hello in English and Spanish and smile welcomingly. Harold looks misty-eyed and pats me on the shoulder proudly.

Oh God! It's like that film, *Sliding Doors*! If only my life could have been this. My sore eyes sting even more and my cheeks are positively on fire. I have to tell them now. I follow Brenda into the cool interior, across the burgundy tiled floor to the high bar.

'You can give me a hand with the drinks,' she tells me. 'Get you used to it! You'll be doing it all yourself soon.' She beams from behind the highly polished bar and shiny beer pumps.

'Actually, Brenda,' I say, 'I need to have a word.' I look at the busy crowd outside as I wonder how to begin. Every journey starts with the first step, as my nan used to say. I take a deep breath. 'It's probably not the right time, but you need to know . . .'

Brenda lets me talk until I'm done. When I've finished, she reaches for one of the light chrome chairs and plops herself into it, her hand over her mouth. The butterfly tattoo on her upper arm wobbles.

My mind is racing as I picture what might have been. I see myself winding up the metal shutters of a morning, pushing back the big glass doors and standing there with a *café con leche* in my hand as the world wakes up. I'd watch the late-night revellers going home, the Monday market being set up and the fishermen bringing in their hauls. I'd work out a simple menu to start with: toasted sandwiches, chicken wings, quiche maybe, the kind of things that I could cook in the tiny kitchen out the back. I'd string fairy lights and bunting around the doorways and the awning. There isn't anything that can't be made better with fairy lights; you can get all kinds these days – flowers, stars, and of course my favourites, chillis. I even brought my ones from the flat back home. They were the first thing I planned to put up when we moved in here. I also brought my wedding file, foolishly thinking that we were going to plan ours when the summer season was over. My chest tightens as the reality of this turn of events suddenly sinks in.

'You all right, love?' I hear Brenda say, but I can't see her. Everything is blurry. My chest hurts, and I know it's because my heart is finally catching up with the news now that I've said it out loud. Everything I wanted was within touching distance, and now it has disappeared overnight, quite literally.

'Get some water, Harold. And a cherry liqueur. Sit down, love. It's probably the shock. I know, I've had a few of those in my lifetime. Our daughter Mandy being one of them. Didn't think I could have children, see. Then . . . poof! These things always happen when you least expect it.'

'Here we are,' says Harold, putting two glasses in front of me. I have a drink of water, and then take a sip of the liqueur. It's sweet, creamy and cold, and tastes of cherries and anisette. It's weird but strangely delicious and seems to be having the right effect on my galloping heart rate.

'It comes from up in the hills where they grow the cherries,' Brenda tells me. 'Black-market stuff, that! One of the reps brings it for me. Says it's precious. Made from a special type of cherry that's left over when the picking is finished. They say those are the cherries they steal back from the birds. I get a bottle every year.'

I think about how many years these two have been out here, and wish with all my heart that Will and I could have taken over from them.

With the water and the cherry liqueur having done the trick, I say goodbye to Harold and Brenda, explaining that I've got to move out of our holiday apartment tomorrow and leave Spain. I can feel my shattered heart crumpling to dust.

'I'm so sorry it wasn't meant to be,' says Brenda. 'I was sure it was. What with you being a fellow Welsh girl. You're so like my daughter. Isn't she, Harold?'

'She is,' he agrees, watery-eyed again. 'Just like her.'

'A great girl, but a dreadful picker when it comes to blokes!' Brenda gives a little laugh.

Is that what I am, too, a dreadful picker? I suppose I must be. I've got it wrong three times now. Each time I thought I'd found 'the one', and each time my heart was broken.

Harold wraps me in a great big bear hug that reminds me of a hug from my dad, and Brenda gives me a bony squeeze.

'Good luck, love. Here, take the bottle with you. I've got another.' She pushes the bottle of cherry liqueur towards me. I go to protest, but she won't hear of it. Touched by her kindness, I take it.

It's all I can do to swallow down the lump in my throat and make my way back to work. Tomorrow I will have to return home and tell everyone what has happened. My stomach twists into a tight ball at the thought of Olivia and Uncle Paul's smug faces. I feel gutted at having to break the news to my mum and dad, who were so proud of me for following my dreams.

I try not to think about the Butterfly Bar and all the plans I had for it as I finish my shift at Buster's. Afterwards, I walk back to the apartment. The further I walk, the further away I am from my little dream.

I pull out my phone and check it again, as I have done every half-hour or so for the last two weeks. But still nothing. He's not replying to my text messages or my voicemails. I'm so frustrated. If I could have sent a carrier pigeon, I would have.

I text my mum to tell her I'm fine. I don't tell her that Will has left me, or that I've lost my money and my bar. I try and find a way to tell her that I'm going to be home tomorrow. I rewrite the text over and over, but I can't get it right, and instead I shove the phone back in my pocket. How on earth am I going to tell everyone? I have no idea . . . I'll work it out tomorrow, when I'm on my way home. I rub my tired eyes. I've hardly slept a wink since Will left.

Once inside our studio apartment, I shut the door firmly, flip the cork from the cherry brandy and take a large slug straight from the bottle, making myself cough. Outside the window, children are in the pool, families are sunbathing and groups of friends are meeting at the bar.

But I manage to drown them out as I allow the tears that have been building up all day to fall. Wave after wave of salty tears, never-ending or so it seems. I will never fall in love again, I vow, because if Will was the one, he's gone. And if he wasn't, then I just can't let myself believe that there is someone else out there for me.

My nan's words suddenly pop into my head: 'If it isn't a happy ending, it isn't the end!' I smile a watery smile. I wish I could believe that was true.

Chapter Three

The following morning, I bump and crash my way down the road in the bright cheery sunshine with my big case on wheels dragging behind me, like a reluctant child and a frazzled mother. I had to check out of the apartment by ten. My dark sunglasses cover my eyes, which are red and swollen from all the crying I did as I picked up the belongings Will didn't take with him when he did his night-time flit: a pair of his favourite socks, Batman ones that I bought him for Christmas for a bit of fun; a T-shirt, boxers, a pair of boots he insisted on bringing and a half-used tin of hair wax. Maybe he's using Freya's. Maybe he's given up waxing his spiky black hair and gone au naturel. Perhaps I should have just left it all behind, but somehow I couldn't bring myself to. It felt too final. If I had, though, I wouldn't be carrying my big wedding folder under my arm now, wondering how I'm going to fit it in my hand luggage. It's April the first, and I can safely say I'm feeling like a fool.

I'm making my way down the promenade towards the harbour, where the coach will pick me and all the other holidaymakers up to take us back to the airport. There are already people gathering at the stop wearing battered hats and bed hair. I recognise some of the faces from the flight out here, though they're all a little redder now. Everyone returning to their normal lives, apart from me, I hadn't expected to return at all. We'd booked the package holiday just to get us started whilst we were out here. It had worked out cheaper than to get the apartment and flights separately. We never intended to take the return flight home. I think about the empty seat that will be beside me, like doing the journey of shame. The woman who came out here with a fiancé and a plan for a shiny new life, returning home alone.

I reach into my bag to find my headphones, hoping to block out the happy holidaymakers with some Amy Winehouse. I find one earbud and put it in my right ear, then pull at the other; with it come the strings of my Buster's Burgers apron that I've hastily shoved in there, reminding me that I have to return it to them and tell them I can't work any more. The apron is followed by my name badge and hat, and a phone charger I hastily shoved in as I left the apartment. I'm still pulling at the cable, trying to untangle it, as I step down into the road, glancing right. Behind me, my case lurches and nearly topples over. I catch it and steady it, yanking it forward to the sound of a car horn blaring at me, making me leap out of my skin. *Look left!* I hear a voice scream in my head. *Not right!*

My heart thunders as a dusty truck comes to an abrupt halt to avoid running into me. My belongings spew from the top of my bag and tumble into the gutter, along with the folder I'm clutching. My heart is racing, like it's been injected with adrenaline. Furious with myself, I bend and scoop up my belongings, clutching them to my chest like a handful of spaghetti. The driver, a man with unruly black hair, has an angry vein standing proud in his temple, and his dark-skinned, weather-worn face is scowling as he swings the truck around me. He glares at me and accelerates forward in a cloud of dust, clearly in a rush.

My heart is still banging as I untangle the strings of my apron from my headphones and charger. Will's charger, I think; like Will, making a mess of things for me to deal with.

I finally find the other earbud and put it in my ear, then start off towards the bus stop and the gaggle of holidaymakers standing right in front of the burger bar. My case bounces along obediently behind me as I pull up beside the group. Now all I need to do is tell Victoria that I'm handing in my notice and not even working out my shift. I'm deep in thought when I hear my name being called.

'Beti! Beti! Yoohoo! Beti love!'

I look up to see Brenda and Harold outside the Butterfly Bar. Brenda is waving furiously at me and I raise a hand back, not really in the mood for big goodbyes. She waves even more manically, as if calling me over to them. I only have a few minutes until my shift starts, and I have to explain things to Victoria before I get on the bus. I drag my case with the folder on top over to the Butterfly Bar.

'Hey, you two.' I try and smile. 'Everything all right?' They obviously have news that they're bursting to tell me. My heart suddenly dips. Is it Will? Is he back . . . here? Do they know where he is?

'We've been thinking, haven't we, Harold?' Brenda looks at him like a bottle of pop about to fizz over.

'Yes, we've been thinking,' says Harold, but he doesn't get a chance to say any more.

'Like we said before, you really remind us of our daughter,' Brenda continues. 'She's had some bad luck over the years, hasn't she, Harold?'

Harold nods and sniffs.

'She's sorted now though, thankfully. We all need a break every now and again. You've had some bad luck, Beti. And if it was our Mandy, we'd want someone to give her a break too, wouldn't we, Harold?'

Harold goes to speak, but Brenda carries on.

'I see a lot of our Mandy in you. She's a great girl. Just had some bad luck with fellas along the way. And the mam in me can't stop wanting to help. I've been awake all night thinking about Mandy and you. Haven't I, Harold?'

This time, she doesn't even pause for breath.

'Like I say, if it were our Mandy, I'd want someone to help her . . . and I want to help you if I can.'

'And what with you coming from Wales, like us.' Harold finds his voice around the lump in his throat. 'We need to stick together. Help each other out when the going gets tough.'

'Oh Harold.' Brenda gives him a friendly dig in the ribs. 'This place means a lot to us. It's been our home,' she carries on. 'I want to pass it on to someone who will love it like we do. And out of all the couples we've met, we liked you and Will the most. I think you'll keep up what we've built here, not change it like that bloke from Newcastle who wanted to make it a football-themed bar. I want to know that there'll always be a bit of Harold and Brenda in the Butterfly Bar.' This time it's her voice that cracks. 'I can't think of anyone who would be better at running this place than you.'

I can't help nodding in agreement. I would be great at running this place. If I had any tears left, I could cry knowing they have such faith in me.

From the corner of my eye, I spot Victoria watching me and glancing pointedly at her watch. I have to get going.

'Even though your fiancé's done the dirty on you, we'd still like you to take over the bar.' Brenda beams at me.

'Well, yes, I'd love that, Brenda, but with Will gone and it being just me . . . well, I just don't have the money to buy the lease.'

Brenda holds up her hands to stop me, gold rings spinning round her long bony fingers. Victoria is now tapping the counter impatiently and glaring at me.

'We still have a few months until we need to be home. We thought . . . how about we give you until the end of June, three months from now, to raise the money. You'll need a month's deposit and the first month's rent. Then we can talk about you buying the lease after the summer,' she waves a hand dismissively, 'when you've had a chance to make some money from the season. What do you think? A month's deposit and a month's rent up front? Do you think you could do that in three months?'

'What, just me?'

'Why not? You could run this bar on your own. You don't need a man by your side to help you!' Brenda chides, and of course, she's right. This was always my dream, not Will's. Will might have come along for the ride, but he jumped off and abandoned me when it suited him. It's still my roller coaster.

'You're right, I don't!' An ember starts to glow in the ashes of my heart.

'Good.' Brenda nods and beams. 'You've got something about you. You remind me a bit of me when I was younger.' She gives me a gentle punch in the arm. 'You can do it. If you want it, that is?'

I look over at the burger bar and a now fuming Victoria and realise I need her job more than ever now.

'But I haven't got anywhere to stay.'

'Don't worry. Craig'll know of somewhere. He always does. I'll ask him.'

I look back at the Butterfly Bar. I'll do whatever it takes, I think. I realise I've been so busy putting my personal life before my professional one, I've forgotten that I have dreams . . . dreams that don't need a man or a wedding in them. This bar isn't just about me and Will; it's about me doing something I always said I was going to do, something I've always dreamed of. It's about proving to my family, Olivia and Uncle Paul in particular, that I can actually go through with a plan. About showing the world I've finally arrived; that I can be a success. I'll have something to stick up on bloody Facebook. Finally, come June, my status is going to read: 'Moving onwards and upwards!'

'So, what do you say?' asks Harold, his smile slipping, looking slightly worried.

'Yes!' I practically shout, a rush of adrenaline surging round my body, making me feel giddy. It's time I remembered who Beti Winter is! I need to show the world there's more to me than a thick wedding file. 'Yes please. And thank you. I won't let you down, I promise. I'll get the money. I'll do it.

Thank you again!' And I hug them both tightly.

I'm terrified and beyond excited all at the same time. I feel so grateful for my second chance. My nan trusted me to do something with the money from that china cow. To change my life. And I lost it. I can't let her down again. I have to earn it back and have something to show for it. The Butterfly Bar . . . my bar! Not Beti and Will's, or anybody else's for that matter – just Beti's. Will may have broken my heart, but I can't let him break me. I am going to do whatever it takes. I feel the fight rising from somewhere inside I didn't know existed, like a tiny glowing ember determined to grow and finally roar back into life. I am going to do this!

Chapter Four

I check and double-check the bank account to see if Will has done the decent thing and returned my money. But he hasn't. As I look at the screen of the cash machine, dread taking over, I think about Nan's china cow. It had been on her windowsill for years. Uncle Paul hated it, but Nan loved it. To be honest, it did have an odd look about it. It definitely had crossed eyes, whichever way you looked at it. Apparently it had been given to her by the family of an elderly lady she used to clean for. She ended up caring for the old lady and the family wanted to say thank you. Uncle Paul thought it was an outrage that they didn't give her a cash bonus. But Nan said she'd always loved the ugly old cow, and would wink at me.

When Nan died, she left me the cow by way of a thank-you for looking after her when she broke her hip. I'd just finally ended things with Tom, so it made sense. She needed someone there and I needed somewhere to live. I was happy to do it. I loved Nan, and we enjoyed each other's company. When I moved in with Will and was trying to find a home for the cow in his little flat, we had one of our few rows. He hated it – and secretly so did I, though I came to cherish it because it reminded me so much of Nan. And when

Dickinson's Real Deal arrived in town, I realised exactly what she had meant when she told me to use the cow to do something that would make me happy. It turned out it was worth a pretty penny. I put the money in a savings account, and was determined to make my wedding the best my money could buy.

Now I look at the practically empty bank account and withdraw the last of my cash to pay for the studio apartment Craig has set me up with. At least I've still got a job, despite Victoria's fury at my late arrival. I just need to find a way to get the deposit and rent money together for the bar. I still can't believe Will has done this to me. I'm so angry with him, but I'm not going to let that ruin things. This is the first day of the rest of my life. He doesn't love me. He's moved on. Now I have to learn to stop loving him back. I just wish I knew how.

I wait for the bus where Craig has told me to, and get on with my wayward case in tow. We chug through the developments of light-terracotta high-rise apartments and up a twisting mountain road. There are wild flowers starting to bloom along the roadside and up the craggy rock face, bright yellows, mauves and reds appearing amongst the greenery there. The countryside begins to roll as we head up into the hills, and the road matches it, bumping and winding. All around me there are silver-leafed olive trees, palm trees with their fronds swaying in the spring breeze, and tall dark-green conifers. As we approach the small whitewashed town Craig has described to me, I see terraced fields full of trees all in straight lines, with tightly shut buds on them.

The bus stops on the main road and the driver turns to me

and points up at the *pueblo blanco*. He tells me with a smile and a shrug that this is Colina de Flor. It's clear that he is wondering why I would want to stay in the tiny hillside town, away from the bustle of Lado del Puerto. I'm wondering it too. But I won't tell him it's all I can afford. I turn and look down at the busy port and the sparkling sea. It's not so far away, I tell myself. Just down the road, in fact.

'*Gracias*.' I thank the driver and drag my case off as the doors hiss shut and the bus pulls away.

Craig knew about the rental place because one of the hairdressers at Jackie's salon stayed there when she first arrived but couldn't stand the silence or the birds and moved into rented rooms over the Irish pub. It's small and very rural, he said, so it rarely gets rented out. But most importantly, it's cheap. And the bus goes straight into Lado del Puerto for my shifts at the burger bar. So it's all good, I try and convince myself as I start up the cobbled street towards the village square, dragging my case noisily behind me.

I walk between whitewashed walls with brightly coloured terracotta pots full of cheery red geraniums hanging from them. There are brown-and-blue-tiled steps leading up to houses, and tiled mosaics on some of the walls. I pass a small supermarket, then the street opens out into a square. There's a café with a green and white awning, under which metal tables and chairs are laid up for lunch, and a small souvenir shop with scarves hanging from the white wooden shutters. Down an alleyway to my right, a hanging sign points along a narrow cobbled street lined with whitewashed houses to what looks like a bakery.

There is a church, right there on the square, with large

wooden doors standing open. Inside I can see a huge painting on the back wall and wonderful lights hanging down over the empty pews. And in the middle of the square itself, in the circle of paving stones, are five trees just like those in the fields I saw on the way here. Beneath them are two benches, no doubt in the shade in the height of summer. The air is filled with the fresh, peppery smell from the velvety leaves of red geraniums. It smells earthy and dusty up here, not like the salty sea air of the harbour.

I look at the map Craig sketched for me. To the left of the church, the cobbled road becomes more of a track out of town. There is a restaurant marked with a cross; that's where I'm to meet the restaurant manager, Valentina, who'll show me the *finca* – the small country cottage – for rent.

According to Craig, it's just a short walk to the restaurant, but I'm panting, hot and dusty by the time I finally see the wide whitewashed gateposts. I stand for a moment and catch my breath. It's tucked away, but not out of the way. I look at the sign made from a tree trunk: *Cortijo Ana*. There is a long drive, lined with trees, and at the end of it a farmhouse with a wide terrace along the front with big stone archways and pillars. In front of that is a courtyard with what looks to be an outside grill under a terracotta roof. There is also a pergola covered in some sort of greenery, with chrome tables and chairs under it.

I set off down the dusty drive, my case bumping along behind me, my wedding file still under my arm. As I walk, I breathe in the fresh air, a promise of better things to come, I think. To my right, over a whitewashed wall and another track, is a well-swept yard surrounded by sheds and what look to be stables. Beyond that there's a paddock, with three . . . no, four beautiful horses in it, dozing in the sunshine and flicking their tails at the occasional fly. There is a big black one with a long mane, a bay with black mane and tail, and two greys. The bay looks much younger than the others.

The track continues round the side of the two-storey farmhouse, opening out on to a gentle slope full of trees behind the restaurant. As the field gets steeper, it's made up of neat, shallow steps, like the pages of a book.

'Hello? *Hola?*' I tentatively try out my Spanish, then, when there is no reply, poke my head through one of the doors leading off the tiled terrace. There is a small room there with a fireplace set into the wall and a set of whitewashed shelves; what appears to have been the old farmhouse kitchen. Beyond that is another room, larger, that looks like it's used as a storeroom. I go to the other door. Inside, it's dark and cool; in one corner I can see a bar, which looks new and sort of out of keeping. There are optics and a music system and a big TV screen on the wall. Beyond the bar, there is a big kitchen at the back of the house, with modern stainless-steel work surfaces and bright lighting.

'*Hola? Sí?*' A woman suddenly appears and walks towards me in high spiky heels. *Click, click, click* go her shoes on the dark tiled floor. She is small and slim, with dark waist-length hair. But despite being small in stature, there is something slightly intimidating about her. I take a step back on to the terrace, feeling like I'm trespassing.

'Um, *hola*. Craig sent me. I've come about the um . . . *finca* to rent. Are you Valentina?'

She says nothing at first; just looks me up and down, one

hand resting on her hip lazily, appraising me like she's buying a horse.

'*Sí*,' she says at last. 'I am Valentina. You want to rent the old *finca*, *sí*?'

I don't think there's an option to see it before I agree. I take a deep breath. '*Sí*,' I reply, then glance back towards the spacious kitchen. 'And I'm looking for work, too. I do lunchtimes down in the burger bar in the harbour, but I'm free in the evenings, if you need anyone.'

Valentina looks me up and down again, as if she thinks I'd be good for practically nothing. Eventually she says, 'We need a kitchen hand, someone to wash up, put out the bins, mop the floor at the end of the night. But if you don't think—'

'No! I'll do it!' I say quickly. '*Gracias.*' Anything is better than sitting at home alone night after night, and this way I'll be earning, too. I need every euro I can scrape together for the Butterfly Bar.

Valentina instructs me to wait. She goes away, coming back with a large key on a piece of string. She tells me the *finca* is in the top right-hand corner of the field behind the farmhouse, up the path, next to the old barn. Then, taking a pile of banknotes from me, she returns to whatever she was doing, not bothering to show me the way. But I don't care. I clutch the key tightly. It might not seem like much, but now I have somewhere to live, as well as another job, and I'm going to do everything I can to get my bar. No one back home need know there's been a change of plan. It's just been a bit . . . delayed. Oh, and I'm doing it on my own!

I can hear the birds chirping loudly to each other outside,

and I surprise myself by smiling for the first time since Will left and knocked my world off its axis.

Chapter Five

I swill the sheets around in the shower tray, chasing the dribble of water as it runs hot, then cold. I found some rather dried-out washing powder under the little sink, and now I'm rinsing the thoroughly washed bed sheets before wringing them out as hard as I can and carrying them outside to dry over the old wooden fence at the front of the little *finca* in the late-afternoon sunshine. The sheets flick-flack in the breeze and I have to chase one that flies off and attaches itself to the tree just in front of me. I hang it back over the fence and this time weigh it down with a couple of rocks I scavenge for.

Craig was right: this place is small and basic. Apparently, it was the original dwelling on the land before the farmhouse, stables and barns were built. It hasn't been lived in for a while, but for now it's a place of my own, and not the spare room at my parents' house. The building itself is made from stone – big ones, little ones, all different sizes. It has a terracotta roof in various shades of red and orange, and slightly listing shutters, painted cherry red, peeling at the edges. Outside there is a stone terrace, with a wobbly fence made up of two criss-crossed poles and one along the top where my sheets are hanging, faded but clean.

Down two steps there is a little patch of worn grass with a few big stones marking out the garden area, and beyond that, well, it's just trees. Row upon row of them, covered in tiny tight buds, the land dropping away like the layers of a flamenco dancer's skirt. My nan used to have one that went over the spare loo roll in the toilet – a Spanish doll with layers of ruffled skirt. Here in the *finca*, it's like sitting in a tree house, looking out over the treetops as they roll away beneath me. I can see the town square and the church tower, and in front of me, across the bushy green valley covered in more trees, another little white *pueblo blanco* nestled into the hillside.

Around the door there are some shrubs, overgrown and unruly: lavender and I'm not sure what else. There are birds chattering loudly, as if speaking Spanish at volume – because that, I have noticed, is how people are here in Spain, loud and excitable, just like the three blackbirds squabbling round the roots of that tree, flapping and dancing around each other in animated argument. And there are lots of little birds too: finches with gold fronts and red splashes on their heads, and even sparrows. But their sound is the only noise I hear. It is so peaceful. Just the birds and the wind in the trees. It is mesmerising.

But I can't stand here staring at the view. I have to get on. I have my first shift in the restaurant to get ready for.

Inside, I rinse out the bucket I've used to wash the worn terracotta-tiled floor, and wipe down the wooden draining board in the corner. At one end of the room, against the stone wall that joins the *finca* to the disused barn, which is three times the size of this building, is a big dark wooden bed, with solid headboard and foot. The mattress is thick and hand-stitched. There is a window looking out over the trees, and on the other wall a small bathroom with the dribbly shower. But when you wake up to a view like that, who cares! On the other side of the front door is the snug kitchen area: a wooden table and chairs, a bookshelf, and a sagging two-seater settee in front of a small woodburner. There are wooden beams across the ceiling and running through the walls, uneven, gnarled and knotted. It's about as rustic as it gets.

Having washed everything down, I unpack my case into the wardrobe that matches the bed, old, solid, deep-reddish-brown wood that smells slightly musty and feels like it has a lifetime of stories to tell. I leave the doors open ajar to air it. As I put Will's belongings in the back of the wardrobe along with my wedding file, I feel like I've stepped off the edge of the world. It's surreal. A tired leftover tear slides down my cheek, but I brush it away quickly with a big sniff, and push the belongings as far back in the wardrobe as I can.

Once I am ready, I step out on to the terrace, where the sun is slowly setting. As I turn to lock the door, I suddenly hear a hissing noise. Oh God! Don't tell me there are snakes up here! I freeze. It's right behind me! I whirl around quickly to see, not a snake, but a sprinkler on the ground at the base of the trees, dousing the roots. It coughs, splutters, stops and then starts up its constant hiss again. Feeling relieved, I find myself smiling. It's just the watering system. And then I realise: it's sprinkling my sheets! I run and gather them up in my arms like a toddler and carry them inside before they get soaked. Despite them only being out for a couple of hours, the warm sun and gentle breeze have done their job and they're practically dry. I bury my face in them and inhale their freshness. Then, feeling ready for anything, I put them on the bed and make my way down to the farmhouse.

Valentina shows me round the kitchen and the restaurant. As she checks the table settings with an exacting eye, she tells me that she divides her time between managing the restaurant in the evenings and her day job as an estate agent in Lado del Puerto. Her partner owns the restaurant, she explains, but is currently away on business, so she is in sole charge. My station at the sink at the back of the kitchen overlooks the field of trees. At the big cooker stands the chef, short and stout, an overall stretched over her wide bottom. She doesn't acknowledge me. She is scowling into a large pot she's stirring. I turn the taps on and start filling the sink with warm soapy water.

'*Hola!* I'm Frank. I am the waiter here.' A man in black trousers and waistcoat, brandishing a pad and pen, has arrived in the kitchen. 'The very best service all around!' he jokes. He is the spitting image of the chef, but about my age and smiling. I'm relieved to see a happy face, to be honest.

'*Hola!*' I smile back and go to hold out a hand to shake his, but it's covered in soapy bubbles so I wave instead, some of the bubbles breaking free and floating up to the ceiling.

'And this is my mother, Bonita. It means pretty one!' Frank beams at the chef, who tuts as he kisses her boisterously on the head, shrugging him off while squinting at a recipe book and muttering in Spanish. She's clearly not happy. Frank peers into the pot his mother is stirring with a large wooden spoon, then looks at her questioningly. She shrugs,

51

and he shrugs back and then goes out on to the terrace, where I can hear Valentina giving instructions. The mood in the kitchen drops again.

I stand over the big porcelain sink, ready to wash the dishes that come my way, nervous that I'm not going to meet Valentina's exacting standards. I watch her overseeing the food that Bonita is plating up. Despite there seemingly only being a trickle of customers, the atmosphere in the kitchen is tense, making me nervous.

'Sorry, *lo siento*,' I say as a pot slips from my soapy hand into the water with a splash. Valentina turns and glares at me sternly, hawk-like, and the chef rolls her eyes, making me drop a plate into the sink with a clatter.

I spend the evening waiting to be told that my services are no longer required and I'll have to find somewhere else to live to boot. No one speaks to me apart from Frank when he brings me the few plates from the handful of customers. His mother glares at them as they return, still with food on them, her face puckering up with disgust. And what's more, they're square plates, that won't fit in the dishwasher, I've discovered. So each one has to be washed by hand. When it looks like there will be no more customers, that's when the work really starts, as I collect up the pots and pans that Bonita has used and discarded all around the kitchen. I wash and scrub and clean like my life depends on it, until the ache in my back makes me forget about the ache in my heart.

'Frank!' I hiss to him at the end of service. 'What am I supposed to do with all this leftover food? I can't throw it away like Bonita told me to.' I stare at the big pan of soup and the plate of chicken.

He shrugs. 'People don't like it!' he whispers.

'They don't like your mother's cooking?'

'They used to. She has cooked here all her life. But Valentina, well, she wants different things. Things that will bring the tourists. Classy food.' He uses two fingers to make quote marks in the air. 'Not real Spanish food like my mama used to make. People came for miles for tapas made from whatever ingredients were in season. And her paella . . .' He looks dreamy for a moment, and I struggle to marry up the grumpy Bonita and her nondescript food with the expression on his face.

'Why doesn't she leave?'

'Jobs round here are hard to come by. And down at the harbour, that's a world away for people like my mama.' He smiles that infectious smile again. 'She has worked here since she was a young girl. She is trying to make the changes.'

'What about you, don't you want to go?'

He shakes his head. 'I love it here. You wait till the blossom on the trees comes. There is nowhere better. It's my home. We all want it to work here. This is our livelihood.'

We both look down at the dried-out meat.

'What was it?'

'Chicken tikka masala!' he says. 'Valentina thinks the tourists will come if we offer world foods. Mostly British with a modern twist.'

'What's the twist?'

'I have no idea!' Frank shakes his head, and I laugh.

'But what am I going to do with it all? I can't throw it away.'

'Take it,' he says, and nods. 'It will only go in the bin otherwise.'

I look at it and sniff. Well, a girl's got to eat, right? I put the leftovers in tin foil and wrap them up.

'Wait!' Frank goes to a shelf and pulls down a cake tin. He cuts a slice and wraps it in a napkin. 'To take away the taste,' he says. 'It's my mother's orange and almond cake. She makes it just for us, and sometimes lemon cake. When the cherries came out, she used to make cherry and almond cake too. Ahh! We loved that cake!' he says with a wistful smile.

I take the cake, checking over his shoulder that he won't be caught. 'Thank you, Frank.' I'm thanking him for so much more than just the cake. For making me feel welcome and for smiling. For helping me through the first day when there were times I felt so homesick I didn't think I could manage. For his jokes that kept me going.

'*Buenos noches*, Beti,' he beams back.

I call goodnight to Valentina and Bonita, who seem to be in heated discussion, looking at the bookings and deciding next day's menu by the looks of it. Frank grimaces and ushers me out of the back door, and I don't need telling twice.

As I step outside, I breathe in the fresh, scented air. Despite its invigorating effect, I am exhausted and pray that tonight, I will finally sleep.

I pick my way by the light of my phone to the path between the trees that leads through the field to the *finca*. I can hear the horses stamping an occasional foot to the floor, the odd snort and heavy breathing. I'm almost at the cottage when suddenly there's a rustling sound close by, making me jump and catch my breath. Then I smile and my heart rate slows to normal as a cat jumps down from a tree and starts winding its way around my legs in a figure of eight.

'Hello, puss.' I bend down and stroke her head, which seems to make her ecstatic. If only my touch had worked like that on Will! I manage to smile at my own joke.

I set off towards the *finca* again, and the little grey cat follows me, head and tail held high, seemingly glad of the company. As am I, I realise. At the cottage, I pull out the big key and unlock the door, and the cat wanders inside, where she prowls round as though to check that everything is in order. Once she's satisfied, she trots back out and hops up on to the ramshackle bench on the terrace, where she starts cleaning her paws and ears. I say 'she'. I have no idea really. But I get the feeling she's in charge and I'm just the lodger.

I smile and spoon some of the chicken tikka masala into a bowl, then pick out some choice bits of chicken and put them on a small plate. I carry the food outside and sit myself down on the bench. The cat sniffs her plate suspiciously, then looks up at me with an expression that tells me she'll accept the food, and that I can stay as long as I understand who's boss.

'Good,' I say. 'That's that sorted.'

I finish the food, despite its unusual taste, which might be the 'twist'. But the cake is delicious, and I savour each mouthful, as soft, fluffy and full of orange flavour as it looks. Then I gaze out over the trees falling away in the field below me. It's dark now, probably about ten o'clock. As if answering my question, the church bells ring out. The little town is dead, unlike the port, where everyone is only just going out at this time. I wonder where Will is, and if he's ever going to get in touch. I pull my phone from my back pocket and check it, as I seem to do every spare waking minute since he left. But there's nothing. I text Craig to tell him that I'm at the *finca* and everything is fine. He sends back a smiley emoticon and a glass of wine, with a kiss.

As I breathe in the night air, I spot a battered old kettle barbecue in the corner of the terrace. I pick it up and carry it down the wooden steps on to the patch of worn grass. Then I go inside to find a hoody and a box of matches. From the wardrobe I pull out my overstuffed wedding file. There isn't going to be any wedding now. Will has gone and I have to get used to that, starting with getting rid of this.

Out in the garden, I tear out the first two pages. Mood boards containing ideas for table settings and floral displays, with different themes and colour schemes. I give them one last look and then quickly scrunch them into balls. I toss them into the barbecue and strike a match, holding it high, then lower it into the barbecue.

Whooof! The paper goes up in dancing flames, turning to fluttering ashes, like grey moths flying off into the night. I open the folder and take out another page, and another. The flames keep dancing and the ashes lift on the gentle breeze over the tops of the trees.

I keep tearing out and scrunching until all the pages are gone. I watch the flames, mesmerised; all the plans I made going up in smoke, literally. As I stare into the orange glow, I tell myself that I will never again be stupid enough to believe that there is a happy-ever-after out there for me. It's over, well and truly over.

Chapter Six

'I'll have to bring home more leftovers,' I tell the cat the next morning, dishing out the last of the chicken as she winds her way around my legs, purring. I wonder if there will be leftovers again, or whether last night was just an unusually quiet one. At least the food – however questionable – helps me out now I have to watch the pennies. I put the saucer on the veranda, grab my cheery striped beach bag and pull the wooden door closed behind me. I wonder if the cat will be there to greet me after my lunchtime shift at the burger bar. I hope so, I find myself thinking, and smile at her as she greedily eats the chicken.

I look at the wonky barbecue, and the charred remnants of my wedding file. But I don't allow myself time to dwell on it. Today is a new day. The birds are singing all around me: blue tits, goldfinches and blackbirds. The air is so fresh and clean. The sky is blue over the mountains on the other side of the valley and the sun is starting to hit it, like it's throwing out handfuls of rays to cover a canvas. I can hear the horses stirring, and a cockerel in the distance is only just making its wake-up call. The buds on the trees look like they've fattened overnight with the dew. It's a clear, sunny morning but with a crisp chill in the air.

As I step down towards the path, I hear the hiss and jump back just in time. The sprinklers cough and splutter into life like my nan's old neighbour clearing his chest in the morning, living on forty fags a day in his terraced cottage. I jump sideways, working out how to pass without my feet getting a soaking.

I take the bus to the harbour and work the mid-morning and lunchtime shift at Buster's. Afterwards, I pop into the Butterfly Bar, where Brenda makes me a toasted sandwich and a coffee and tells me I need to keep my strength up. I don't tell her about the huge amount of leftovers I took home last night. She shows me the property app on her phone and the houses they're looking at back home. I use the Wi-Fi at the bar to catch up with friends and family, and can't stop myself from looking at Will's Facebook page. Where is he? What's he doing? Why did he leave?

'Urgh!' I catch my breath. There's a picture he's been tagged in. In a bar, in another Spanish town, drinking beer and playing guitar with the band by the looks of it. He's standing back to back with Freya, who's playing bass guitar, and he's smiling, laughing even. I study that familiar grin. I don't think I really believed he'd gone. I thought he'd come back and tell me it was all a silly mistake. But now, seeing this, I know it's real. I feel like my chest has been ripped open and he's reached in, grabbed my heart and stamped all over it. It hurts so much. How could he? My eyes burn with anger and desolation. How can he be smiling and enjoying himself, not giving me a second thought? How could he have moved on and started a whole new life when I'm still here, standing next to the empty black hole that he used to fill?

While I wait for my thundering heart and my shallow breathing to calm down and my stinging eyes to focus more clearly, I check my own timeline. There's a photo of someone I was at school with celebrating her fifth wedding anniversary; apparently it's 'wood', so her husband has taken her to a wooden cabin on stilts in some exotic beachside location. There are a few pictures of small children posing self-consciously in school uniforms and in oversized Easter bonnets with their proud parents – more people I was at school with. There's an album posted by my cousin Olivia of the Reykjavik hen party. There they are in bikinis in the Blue Lagoon, with the steam rising around them and the snow falling; standing by a huge gushing waterfall; posing in front of shooting geysers; astride snowmobiles. It's a long way from flipping burgers, I think to myself. She'd be laughing at me if she could see me now! There are also pictures of her and her boyfriend Gavin, who's made his fortune in car valeting. He and Olivia obviously went to matching teeth technicians.

Olivia's album has had 137 likes, including her dad, my uncle Paul. You couldn't find two people more different than Dad and his brother, and I've never understood why Uncle Paul, Auntie Rita and Olivia spend so much time in our tiny house, especially when they have a huge great modern place of their own. Uncle Paul seems to think he's really funny, teasing me and my dad and putting us down while continually bragging about his daughter. I just wish I could give Dad something to show off about. Uncle Paul will be boasting about Olivia's trip, recounting every detail – the snow, the hotel, the food – as if he were there himself.

My parents will listen, and Mum will ask all the right questions.

Uncle Paul has put up a post too, showing off his new golf driver. He's also commented on my post saying that I'm off to Spain to start a new life. 'Let's hope this one finally happens!' I don't know why he gets to me so much. I'm thirty-two, for God's sake! I think about my poor mum and dad, having to put up with him. Forever having to tell the family that my life has taken another downturn. Well, not this time.

It's with a shock that I realise my mum has taken to Facebook too. The world's gone mad! She's posted pictures of the cup of tea my dad brought her in bed and of my dad dozing in the garden, his pride and joy. It's only small, but he's always out there, weeding away. I smile and feel a pang of homesickness, then send her a quick message to tell her I'm fine and that my feet ache from working all day and night, which is true. Just not in my own bar . . . yet! I can't wait for the day when I can finally invite them out to see it.

Craig joins me and I shove my phone away with the same kind of force I'd like to use to snap Will's guitar neck.

'No word?' he asks after kissing me lightly on both cheeks. I shake my head. I love that we have become such good friends so quickly. It feels like I've known him for ever. And let's be honest, he knows more about my personal life than anyone back home. He tuts crossly. 'Sun and sangria . . . I've seen it happen so often,' like the seasoned expat that he is. But I haven't, I think. We weren't some passing affair; we were Beti and Will. We'd been together for five years. Everyone thought we were the forever couple.

Sunset over the Cherry Orchard

I drink the dregs of my coffee as Craig orders his first white wine with ice of the day. I think of the picture of Will on Facebook again. At least I know now for sure. He's moved on, just like I have to. But no one at home needs to know he's gone, not until I have the money for this place. And then when I am running a bar of my own, I will shout it from the rooftops for the whole world to hear.

Chapter Seven

I finish the sandwich and thank Harold and Brenda, who won't take any money, telling me to put it towards my rent fund. I kiss them goodbye on both cheeks, turn down Craig's offer of spending the afternoon at the beach bar down the road – 'to take your mind off things' – and run to the bus stop.

As the bus weaves out of Lado del Puerto and bends its way up the hillside, I gaze out at the scenery. More and more wild flowers seem to be appearing in amongst the cracks of the cream-coloured rocks on the roadside, and their floral perfume in the air is getting stronger. Up here, as we head towards Colina de Flor, the fields are full of the uniform lines of trees that I'm becoming accustomed to. Every spare bit of land is covered with them, as if lining the route into the town.

Getting off the bus, I walk up the narrow cobbled street, between the whitewashed houses with their cleanly swept tiled steps, brightly coloured mosaics and pots filled with fire-red geraniums. The town is quiet; there's no one around. The scarves from the souvenir shop flutter in the breeze, and the baker's sign swings to and fro. The café in the main square is all but empty, bar one table of walkers with rucksacks and sturdy boots and another of locals gathering to drink coffee and exchange family news, talking over each other insistently and incessantly, waving hands by way of explanation. They watch me as I pass, and I nod and raise a hand to them. They nod, wave and smile back.

At the farm, I turn up the dusty drive and walk through the line of trees. A squadron of sparrows flies through their branches, narrowly missing me. The buds on the trees look like marshmallows wrapped in green and pink tissue paper – like bridesmaid's headdresses, I think before quickly checking myself.

The restaurant is shuttered and silent. They don't open at lunchtimes. Valentina seems set on attracting the evening trade: high-end tourists who spend a lot. Unlike the bar on the square, she's not interested in serving an eight-euro all-inclusive three-course menu.

It's a shame. It's glorious out here. It may only be April, but the sky is a wonderful bright blue. The sun is warm on my face and I can feel its rays lifting my spirits. I walk up the path behind the restaurant towards my *finca*, and my spirits lift even further when the little grey cat comes out to meet me, meowing loudly.

I breathe in the fresh air and let it fill my lungs. Then I pull out my wages and count them. I find an old coffee jar in the cupboard, wash it out and put all my notes and coins in it. Once I've paid my rent and bus fares, there's not a lot left. I know I'm going to have to find a way to make some more money if I'm going to save.

I shut my eyes. My mind is too busy to let me have a nap before tonight's shift. I'd go for a coffee in the tavern in town but I don't want to waste my money. I decide to go for a walk instead. The little grey cat follows me, indignant that I've left the veranda. I stroll through the trees, running my hands over their thick trunks, picking at leaves, wondering about the sort of fruit they'll bear. I walk slowly along the terraces through the long tufts of grass and the stony shallow walls, taking in the amazing view of the port below and the glistening sea beyond. I head down towards the horses' enclosure, where a large black horse with a long wavy mane and tail snorts and shies away from me as I try to pat him over the fence. He trots to the other side of the paddock and stands in the shade of the trees.

I can't help but feel very alone. Am I mad thinking I can do this? Working for peanuts and trying to save for the bar? As I think, leaning on the fence, my elbow is knocked and I'm jolted out of my thoughts. I look up in surprise to see a grey horse there. She nudges my arm again. Right behind her is another horse, the bay. Could it be her foal, I wonder? I stroke her nose, and when it looks as if she likes it, I rub her forehead. The young horse stays back. As I stroke the grey's neck, I look at the buds on the trees all around us and decide to pick a few branches to brighten the cottage and cheer me up. The buds might even open up in water.

I pull a branch towards me and try to breathe in its fragrance but there is none. I snap it off, and another one next to it, then move on to the next tree and break off another one. These will really liven up the bare little room. I can see why people go for a spring wedding, I think, and check myself once again. No more thinking about weddings! I'm just about to take a fourth branch from a tree further down when a car door slams and there's a shout, making me startle and drop the branches.

A dusty truck has pulled up under the trees, a young man with a rucksack standing next to it. An angry-looking older man with wild dark hair, pushed back off his face but falling in all directions, is gesticulating and marching towards me. 'Hey! *Qué estás haciendo?* What the hell do you think you're doing?'

Oh God! That's all I need!

'You can't go around stealing branches. English, are you, eh? On holiday? Thought you'd take a souvenir?'

'*Lo siento,*' I say. And then, flustered, I revert to English. 'Sorry. Look, it was just a few branches . . . I didn't mean any harm, I just—'

'They might be just a few branches to you. But these blossoms will turn into cherries. This is a cherry farm. My cherry farm! If everyone stole the blossom, I would have no cherries when the harvest comes!' he continues, red-faced and furious.

'I'm sorry,' I say again, my shoulders slumping.

As I turn to go, I realise that there's something about him I recognise. Then it clicks. I look at the dirty truck parked on the drive. It's the one that nearly ran me down on the day I was due to leave! Suddenly all the fury I'm feeling about the position I'm in, left high and dry by Will, my money gone and my dreams smashed, comes bubbling up.

'Well I just hope your cherries aren't as sour as you!' I blurt out without even thinking. I wish instantly I hadn't.

We stare at each other, his dark eyes taking me in. He must be late thirties, even forty maybe. He has broad shoulders, but slim hips. His chin is dark with stubble and his thick eyebrows are drawn together in a scowl. The big, empty hole in my chest, where my heart used to be before Will ripped it out, is banging like a drum. I give him a final narrowing of my eyes and then turn to leave.

The young man with the rucksack – dark, slim, wearing jeans and a long-sleeved T-shirt, has walked round the back of the restaurant to an outside staircase there. He stops on the bottom step. His shoulders are slumped, but he lifts the corner of his mouth and gives me a nod, as if to tell me that whatever it was I said met with his approval. Somehow, just for a split second, we connect, and I give him a half-smile and a slight shrug. Let's be honest, this isn't the worst thing that's happened to me over the past couple of weeks. It's just the tin hat on possibly the most disastrous couple of weeks of my life.

There's a shout from the door at the top of the stairs over the restaurant.

'Antonio!'

It's Valentina. She is waving and calling to the man, and it dawns on me with a cold shock, as though I've stepped in the direct line of the sprinkler, that this must be her partner Which means that he's also my landlord, and my boss too. Brilliant. Just brilliant. I really know how to put my foot in it.

I drop my head, cheeks burning with embarrassment, and turn and trudge my way back to the *finca* through the plumes of fawn dust my feet are kicking up, feeling really alone and really, really foolish. The fact that I've just insulted my boss and landlord makes everything else seem fairly insignificant at the moment. He's bound to tell Valentina, and I could get the sack and lose my home. This is all because of bloody Will. I feel angry all over again. How could I have got it so wrong! Why do my instincts always let me down so badly?

Chapter Eight

Antonio stood and watched the woman, confused. Instead of heading out of the cherry orchard and back into the village square as he'd expected, she turned and started walking up the path through the orchard. Then the cold realisation hit him.

'Oh *mierda*!' Today couldn't get any worse. If it wasn't bad enough that he'd spent a night sleeping in his truck, in one of the dodgiest parts of Malaga, waiting for a boy he barely knew to show up, now this. She wasn't just a lost tourist, wandering in from the main square, assuming his farm was some kind of open parkland. Lots of them did, venturing away from the developments down on the coast and up into the mountain, wanting to discover the 'real' Spain, especially at this time of year when they'd heard about the annual natural phenomenon of the cherry blossom.

But he should have known. He looked at the trees, studying the branches. That time of year was probably still a week off. Outside of the ten days or so when the cherry blossom was out, hardly any tourists came here all. And that suited him just fine. He wasn't after the tourist trade. His restaurant here in the old farmhouse catered for local people; it always had done, despite Valentina's best intentions. It was the cherries that mattered here.

He glanced around with the sense of pride he always got looking at the trees on his cherry farm, the biggest in the village's cooperative. God, it was good to be home. He liked things the way they were. The restaurant ticked over, just. The cherry trees seemed to be doing fine at the moment. But anything could happen. He didn't want to take his eye off the ball – not like before. He needed to focus on the harvest. Unlike Valentina, he didn't want the restaurant to change, bring in more tourists. He didn't need any more headaches. And boy, did he have one! He looked at the woman walking up the path, the one he'd just caught breaking branches off his cherry trees. Not only was she by the looks of it renting the *finca*, the old cottage, but that must mean she was also the new employee Valentina had taken on. He shook his head and rubbed his temples.

'Antonio, Antonio!' Valentina was still leaning out over the concrete balustrade outside the apartment door, calling to him. He'd known bringing Miguel back here was going to cause problems. He knew he should've phoned Valentina, warned her. But it had been a spur-of-the-moment decision. It had been a tough couple of days.

His ex, Esmeralda, his son's mother, had been on the phone to him constantly, at the end of her tether. He barely ever heard from her other than when she wanted money. Not that he wasn't happy to pay for Miguel, of course. But this time it had been different. Miguel had been in trouble. In a fight. He was seventeen now. This wasn't just school-yard stuff any more. He was getting up to no good, on the street and with the authorities. He'd disappear with God knows who, and this fight and a night in the cells had brought it home to all of them.

'Something has to be done!' Esmeralda had wept when Miguel had finally arrived home from the police station with Antonio early that morning. Miguel had said nothing. Esmeralda's partner, Felipe, had snapped, lunging at the sullen and silent boy. Antonio had had enough. Miguel was coming home with him, he insisted. It had been a terrible scene. The gossips in the neighbouring flats would be talking about it for days to come. Felipe had thrown Miguel's clothes out of the door, followed by the rest of his belongings, and the boy was left picking them up from the street. Antonio couldn't watch the humiliation being dished out and helped his son to scoop up the clothes, hoping to save some of his dignity.

Antonio hadn't seen Miguel in years. He barely knew the boy. Miguel had never taken up his offer to come and stay at the farm. Esmeralda had always told him he didn't want to come and Antonio hadn't been able to leave his cherry trees or his horses. Years had slipped by. But at that moment when he was first faced with Miguel, it was like looking in a mirror, at a younger version of himself. He recognised the anger that was raging in the boy – he knew it all too well from when he'd been a young man himself, about to become a father. A rage he'd tried to hide away since then.

As he made his way over to his horses, standing by the fence to greet him, his fists clenched as he remembered the look on Felipe's face. The smirk as the man had finally rid himself of the last remaining piece of Antonio from their lives: his son. It had taken all Antonio's willpower not to punch him. But what good would it have done? He'd been there before. Done that. Felipe knew he was the stronger man. But it took more than one battle to win the war, and Antonio wasn't going to lose what he had because of this man.

Biting his tongue, he had lifted his head high and put an arm around his son's shoulder, leading him out of the narrow streets, past the women standing in groups, arms folded, gossiping. Neither of them looked back. But as they reached the end of the lane, Miguel shrugged off Antonio's arm from his shoulder, stepping away from him. Their moment of solidarity was over. It would take time. Antonio knew that. He also knew what Valentina's reaction was going to be.

He moved away from the horses puffing and blowing in the spring sunshine, took a deep breath and turned to the balcony, where Valentina's long dark hair, much like the beautiful mane of his favourite black stallion, was blowing in the light spring wind. Valentina was slim and very beautiful. Why then did he have no desire to whisk her off to bed right now and tell her everything would be OK? Instead he turned back to the horses. Maybe a ride would clear his head. He needed to reassure her, but he had to work out what was happening here. He suddenly had a son living with him. He had never been a parent before. What made him think he could do it now? What if the boy really was trouble? He'd acted on instinct when he'd told Esmeralda that Miguel was coming to live with him. Now he had to find a way to make it work.

He stroked the beautiful curved neck of his beloved horse, running his hands through the white streak in amongst the black. He had told Miguel to go on up to the apartment, make himself at home. He would be fine for a little while longer. They both needed some time to think; adjust. He strode over to the barn, pulled back the door, letting in the afternoon light, and picked up the light-tan leather saddle and bridle that hung there.

The horse stood patiently as he swiftly slung on the saddle, did up the girth and slid the bridle over its head. Taking up the reins, he swung himself up. He knew he should say something to the woman in the *finca*, apologise. He'd had a bad day. He shouldn't have taken it out on her. But she had damaged his cherry trees! He thought about her comment that she hoped his cherries weren't as sour as he was, and suddenly, without warning, for the first time in days, he found the corner of his mouth lift into a smile.

He took another look at the apartment. Valentina was still calling to him to get back and sort out his mess. He raised a hand and replied that he would be back soon. He would smooth things over with her later.

He made a clicking sound in the corner of his mouth and the horse set off, striding out up the pathway, eager to get going, up through the cherry orchard towards the *finca*. He wouldn't knock and apologise. He wasn't in the mood to speak to anyone. Instead he stopped and picked up the fallen branches, placing them on the doorstep on the small wooden veranda by way of apology. Then, as silently as he could, he remounted his horse, gave it a gentle kick on and rode away into the forest.

Chapter Nine

I step out on to the veranda to be greeted by the little grey cat, and almost trip over a pile of branches. I catch my breath. Is someone trying to tell me something? When I bend to pick them up, I realise it's the bunch I dropped earlier. But who would've left them here? Certainly not my unfriendly boss, that's for sure. I look around for signs of life, but there's no one there. I wonder if it was the young man I saw by the truck, and a tiny ember of happiness glowing in the pit of my stomach attempts to relight. It's such a kind thought; it would be a waste if they were thrown away now.

I wash out an old plastic water bottle and cut the top off it, then arrange three of the branches in it. I cut the fourth into shorter pieces and put them in a chipped mug, then set the mug on the little wooden coffee table on the veranda. I can't help but smile at how the branches brighten up the little *finca*, imagining them as centrepieces for the tables at a spring wedding . . . I stop and berate myself. No more wedding planning!

In the restaurant that evening, Valentina is conspicuous by her absence. Instead of watching our every move like last night, overseeing plates of food, table settings and my washing-up, she stays mostly in the apartment upstairs. And when she does appear, to bark out orders, she is far fiercer. I keep my head down and focus on my soap suds. Finally, at the end of service, she storms down the steps past the kitchen window, shiny dark hair swinging, overnight bag over her arm and her spiked heels piercing the ground as she marches out to her little red car. With a slam of the car door and a spinning of wheels that leaves the few diners on the terrace clutching their cutlery in terror, she speeds off in a cloud of orange dust. Silence falls over the restaurant and the diners look at each other with inquisitive stares and shrugs.

I make my excuses and go to the toilet, pressing the on button on the CD player as I pass it, just to try and soften the uncomfortable atmosphere. As gentle guitar music fills the air, the diners shake their heads, but start eating again. Frank looks at me and gives me a thumbs-up.

When I get back to my sink full of soapy bubbles, Frank and Bonita are carrying on with their work as if nothing out of the ordinary has happened, but the looks they give each other say that this turn of events is very much out of the ordinary. Who is the new arrival upstairs, and what is going on? I hear Frank asking his mother. Is it a full-time kitchen hand instead of the English girl? he adds, and winks at me, joking. But I wonder how close he might be to the truth. Is my time here over before it's even begun?

In the apartment over the restaurant, Antonio poured himself a large brandy with anise, a medicinal, restorative mix. Miguel was in the spare room, the door firmly shut. He wondered if he should knock, talk to the boy. But maybe he'd gone to bed. Frustratingly, the floral bedding was all Antonio had been able to find. He'd buy some more when he went to town. Something more suitable. Not that Miguel seemed to mind. But Antonio wanted to make him feel at home.

What did young people like? He didn't know anything about Miguel, his interests or hobbies. They'd barely spoken since he got here. The boy had just been plugged into that phone, headphones in, head down. He didn't eat either. Antonio had offered him the restaurant menu, said he could have whatever he wanted, but he'd just looked at it, bemused, and said he didn't want anything.

Antonio thought he'd get some food in tomorrow and use the little kitchen in the apartment. He usually just ate from the restaurant, but even he had trouble working out what Valentina's menu offered half the time. It was a long way from the old days when his grandmother was in charge. Maybe he could ask Bonita to cook Miguel something, like the dishes his grandmother used to make. Something traditional . . . not chicken tikka whatever it was! He just hoped Miguel would stay, not run off back to the city. Back to the gangs he'd got in trouble with. But he hadn't even unpacked, which left Antonio feeling on edge.

He took another sip of the drink and felt the burn in his throat as it went down. He let his eyes rove over the orchard. His trees were doing well. He hoped the blossom would be good this year. And in turn he hoped it would mean a good harvest. He knew where he was with his trees. Relationships of all kinds he appeared to be useless at. Valentina had stormed off in a fury at not being told of Miguel's imminent arrival, or the plans for him either. But that was because Antonio had no idea himself!

Movement caught his eye and he wondered if it was Valentina, back for another row. He didn't have the energy. He didn't want Miguel to hear another fight either. He'd had more than enough fuss around him for one day . . . a lifetime even. He looked closer and realised with guilty relief that it wasn't Valentina. It was the girl from the *finca*, the washer-upper. Well, hardly a girl, but younger than him. She was picking her way up the path by the tiny light of her torch. He remembered her comment to him again, and smiled. He liked that.

He still felt bad about chewing her ear off about the branches. By all accounts she was a good worker and a good tenant, having scrubbed the place from top to bottom. He really wasn't good at putting his thoughts into words. He hoped she realised he'd left the branches there as an apology. He wouldn't want her to move out and leave. Good workers and good tenants were hard to come by. Despite the efforts of the estate agent where Valentina worked, renting and selling apartments, the expats and the locals up here rarely mixed, each community keeping themselves to themselves. It was how it had always been. The real Spain, up here in Colina de Flor, was a long way from the apartments, bars and nightclubs on the front.

He sighed. He'd let Valentina down again. It was no wonder she'd driven back to her apartment down at the harbour. He hoped she'd be back tomorrow. He'd have to find a way to say he was sorry. How she put up with him he had no idea. She wanted so much more than he could give her.

* * *

Sunset over the Cherry Orchard

I leave the restaurant and walk up the path with my tin foil parcel of untouched leftovers for me and the cat, and a piece of lemon cake Frank wrapped in a napkin and handed to me without his mother seeing, with his usual cheeky wink. As I reach the *finca*, I look out over the old farmhouse. It really is beautiful, with its tiny rooms, full of original character. I can't understand why they're not used. People would love them, I'm sure. If I was doing a party . . .

I stop myself and look at the upstairs apartment, where two lights are on. I spot a figure and wonder if it's the young man I saw today. I wonder why he's here and why Valentina has left. He looked like someone who'd been through it, who'd lost their world. I have an inkling I might know how he's feeling, like your heart is a piñata at a children's party, brutally beaten to smithereens whilst others around you cheer and applaud, leaving you with the pieces to pick up.

Next morning, after feeding the cat and promising myself a cup of tea at Craig's breakfast bar, I head towards the path leading round the outside edge of the cherry orchard. As I pass the horses' enclosure, they stamp and neigh. I jump as I see Antonio standing beside the big black horse, its neck beautifully rounded, its mane long and wavy, like hair a young girl would die for.

I stop. He looks up. Neither of us says anything. Any words that might have formed, any apology, catch in my throat. At last, he nods firmly, just the once, and then steps into the stirrup and swings himself into the saddle. I find myself nodding back, and then quickly moving on to the opening between the whitewashed gateposts, past the restaurant and out on to the road.

In the square, the café is open for business. The scarves outside the souvenir shop flutter in the wind and people are coming out of the bakery with fresh warm loaves under their arms, stopping to exchange news with neighbours. They nod and greet me as I pass. Relief washes over me. It appears my job and my house are safe for now. Antonio would have said if he was going to sack me. It looks like my new boss has other, more pressing worries on his mind. I promise myself that from now on, I'm going to keep my head down and my thoughts to myself.

Chapter Ten

Finishing my shift at the burger bar, I pull off my apron and hat and step outside the back door just as a large drop of rain falls and hits me squarely on the head.

'Ah, bugger it!' I hear Brenda curse. 'Harold, it's raining!' She is standing outside the big glass patio doors, looking out on the precinct, just where I hope to be standing in a few months' time. As the rain gets heavier, Harold winds in the big awnings and I make a mental note to self: wind in awning in rain.

'It's April, Brenda. It does sometimes rain!' he shouts back at her. 'Otherwise nothing would grow!'

I run over and help move the chairs out of the rain, stacking them against the glass doors.

'You staying for a livener?' Harold waggles a bottle of rosé at me. I shake my head.

'Not before I work this evening. I'm already on thin ice there.'

'Problems, Beaut?' he asks, still holding up the chilled bottle of wine.

'Oh, nothing much. Just got off on the wrong foot with my boss, but y'know, I'll be fine. Keep my head down. Gotta go. The bus'll be here,' I say.

'Wait!' Brenda shouts. 'We've got Pilates here later if you fancy it. All the expat ladies are coming.'

'Can't. Working,' I call back and smile. Both of us know that the more hours I put in, the quicker we'll all get what we want. I wave, and then turn in the direction of the bus stop. Pilates! I'll have to plan a weekly events list. Maybe have a blackboard up and deliver flyers to the resorts. My mind is whirring with plans. Well, at least they're not wedding plans any more. They're ideas for *my* bar!

Holding my apron over my head against the rain, I make a quick detour into the souvenir shop, reappearing just as the bus pulls up. As we trundle out of the harbour, I take out my new 'start the rest of your life' notebook, with a dolphin diving through blue waters on the front cover, and a pack of pens. Ripping them open, I turn to the first crisp white page and run my hand over the smooth, cool sheet.

I write down 'Pilates', and then a few ideas of my own: 'Spanish for beginners', 'tapas and tunes night'. Will would have loved that, I think, and then try and push the thought out with a good shove. Maybe I could link up with one of the kayak companies down at the beach, offer a deal: kayaking followed by sangria at sunset. The ideas just keep coming, and for the first time in ages I start to feel good inside. At the back of the book I make a note of the hours I've worked, how much I've earned and, in a separate column, what I need to pay out on rent and bus fares. The figures make me dip. Even if I work every shift and spend no money on food whatsoever, it's going to be tight. But not impossible, I tell myself. I can do it. Maybe I'll see if there are some extra hours I can pick up at the burger bar.

I close the book and look out of the window, watching the rain slide down the glass, smiling at the sight of the now familiar cherry trees. I have a book and a plan, and that's all that matters.

By the time we reach the village, the rain has eased to a drizzle. I walk through the big trees in the middle of the square – which I now know are cherry trees too – under the wrought-iron black lanterns and around the drinking fountain tiled in brown, white and blue. I'm heading up the lane towards the restaurant when my phone rings. It's my mum. My heart fills up at the sound of her voice.

'Hi, Mum!'

'Hello, lovely, how's things? I've been looking for you on that Faceoff thing on the computer, but I can't see anything you've put up. Is everything all right?'

'It's great, Mum.' I can't help but laugh. My mum getting to grips with Facebook; who would have thought it!

'Sunny?'

'Of course! Well, mostly.' I look around at the big raindrops hanging from the blossom buds like fat, shiny crystals, and smile.

'Oh, smashing! I can see you now, sun on your face. Bet you're going a nice colour already. So much better than dreary Britain. Tell me what it's like where you are.'

'It's lovely, Mum.' I turn around, taking in the view. 'There are cherry trees all around me. And there's a little bakery and a gift shop. There's a supermarket and post office and even a school. And the restaurant here has a terrace area where people sit and eat. An outside grill,' not that it's used, 'and fairy lights everywhere,' I add, letting my imagination run away with me. Then I check myself. What am I doing? I'm describing Cortijo Ana instead of the Butterfly Bar and the port where I'm actually supposed to be living. I bite my bottom lip before I give myself away any more. I don't want Mum to worry.

'Oh, it sounds just lovely. I'm so proud of you for doing this.'

'Thank you, Mum,' and it catches in my throat.

'And how's Will?'

'Will?' My voice cracks and I feel my eyes prickle just at the mention of his name. Damn it! I was doing so well. I really thought I was pushing him to the back of my mind.

'Yes, you know, dear – Will, your fiancé!' and she lets out a little tinkle of laughter.

I swallow hard, trying to moisten my throat. 'He's fine,' I manage. And he probably is, I think. I can't tell her he's run out on me and taken Nan's money. Mum and Dad thought he was perfect. And he was! At least I thought he was . . . It will hurt them as much as it's hurting me. He was going to be their son-in-law, the son they never had, and who knows, maybe one day father to their grandchildren. Now that will never happen. It makes me even more determined to make it work out here, at least give them something to be proud of when I let them down about Will.

'He's got a gig, actually, with a band. He's away for a bit, playing . . . away.' I hate lying to my mum. By the time they come out for a visit in the summer, I'll have it all sorted. I'll explain about Will then, but not now. Not until I'm in my own bar.

'Well blow me! That is exciting. And you're OK, on your own?'

'Yes, fine, Mum. I'm doing just fine.' I walk towards the restaurant entrance; Frank and Bonita are on the terrace, having some sort of argument. The little grey cat comes trotting down the lane to greet me, meowing loudly as if telling me off for being away. She rubs her head on my ankles as I bend to stroke her.

'I'll leave you to it,' says Mum. 'You're probably very busy. Can't wait to see some pictures soon. Dad sends his love. We're very proud of you.'

'Send him my love too,' I say, and suddenly I feel a huge rush of homesickness for the pair of them. 'Bye, Mum, love you.'

'And you.' She blows a kiss and hangs up.

I stand and look at the restaurant, still imagining it covered in fairy lights, and some in the trees too. It could be magical, I think. And then I realise that something is different. The tables are missing from the courtyard, underneath the pergola, and there seems to be more furniture than usual crammed on to the terrace. Bonita is waving her bingo wings around, swishing her tea towel at tables and chairs. Frank is gesticulating back, talking quickly and loudly and trying to move tables into places they won't fit.

'*Hola,*' I say, stepping up on to the terrace. 'What's going on?'

'Valentina is not here and we have a birthday party. The baker's mother is eighty. It is a family party. As well as the town's baker, he is also the mayor of Colina de Flor. But now, with the rain, we have to move all the diners to eat on the terrace rather than under there.' Frank points to the bamboo-covered pergola, where little trickles of rainwater are leaking through. 'There is no sign of Antonio.' He shrugs. 'No doubt he'll be worrying about his cherries. It's all he ever worries about. That and his horses. If it rains, it can ruin the crop.'

'Oh no,' I say. 'I would have thought a little rain would be good for them.'

He shrugs and smiles. 'A little rain. But not lots. Too cold, or too much rain, and it will affect the amount of cherries. Too little water and it will reduce their size.'

'So are you a cherry farmer too?'

'I have a few trees. My family's.' He nods to Bonita. 'Everyone here has a few. But Antonio has the most trees in our town cooperative. Now is the most important time of year in caring for the cherry trees to ensure a good crop. We barely see Antonio at the restaurant as it is, but hardly ever in March and April, or June when the harvest comes.'

'And his visitor?' I ask, nodding towards the apartment.

'He hasn't come out of his room,' Bonita tells me.

Frank tries to move another table into an impossibly tight space.

'Here, let me help,' I say, pulling my bag over my head and dumping it on a chair. I try and help shift the tables this way and that, but it's a tight squeeze.

'And the patio heaters will need to come on here too,' Frank says, looking doubtful. Bonita throws her tea towel up in the air and waddles back off to the kitchen, her wide bottom swinging violently to and fro.

We finally fit all the tables on to the terrace amongst the

patio heaters, like a jigsaw puzzle, but there's no room to move between them.

'This is ridiculous!' I put my hands on my hips.

'It's the only way.' Frank shrugs.

'Why don't we just move some of them inside, into the house itself?'

He looks at me in disbelief, and then shakes his head.

'Valentina would never allow it. She thinks people come here for the outside, like the bars in the port: outside eating with heaters and cocktails.'

'But it's beautiful in here.' I glance into the small room with the old fireplace, then step in through the other door to the bar.

'And no one ever orders cocktails.' Frank follows me. 'The tourists don't come here. This is where the locals eat. They want jugs of wine, but Valentina makes them buy bottles from her supplier. There are so many producers round here who could provide the wine. Like they used to . . .' He tails off as Bonita appears to see what we're doing. I move back on to the terrace, looking at the tables.

'Here, help me move this.' I point to a small table. Frank frowns but does it anyway. Bonita puts her hand to her forehead and disappears back to the kitchen.

We carry the table into the little room. Beyond that, in the old storeroom, there are boxes of old terracotta jugs and brightly painted bowls – blues, whites and yellows. I pull them out and we move a table in there too.

I run down to the lane and pick some of the wild flowers from the roadside, then put a small bunch in a glass on each table. I arrange the terracotta jugs and bowls along the whitewashed shelves in the old kitchen, then move the stools no one uses out of the bar and put three tables in there at an angle.

I stand back and admire our work with pride. 'I can't believe Valentina hasn't thought of doing this.'

'She will never agree to it!' Frank shakes his head anxiously. Bonita is staying well clear and is busy banging around crossly in the kitchen; making sure there is a pile of washing-up for me to do when I get in there, no doubt.

'But it's lovely,' I say, puzzled. Outside is amazing, but these small whitewashed rooms are just incredible, so atmospheric.

'She thinks people want to eat outside, whatever the weather. She thinks the tourists want that. She doesn't want the locals. She thinks they don't spend enough money.'

'But at the moment they are the only ones spending any money,' I point out. He nods reluctantly.

I have a sudden idea. 'One last thing,' I say, and run all the way to my *finca*, returning out of breath holding the bunch of fairy lights I brought from home to put up in the bar when I finally move in. I arrange them in the old fireplace, along the shelves and around the door to the storeroom, and switch on the battery packs. They look amazing.

Bonita comes out, mutters some kind of prayer to the gods, then heads straight back to the kitchen.

'If Valentina turns up, blame me. Say I did it,' I tell Frank, not wanting to get him or Bonita into trouble. 'And if she doesn't turn up, no one will ever know. We'll put the tables back once the rain has passed. And this way you'll be able to serve everyone far more easily.'

He looks at me, unsure.

'Just give it a go. It's that or the tables squished on to the terrace.' I raise an eyebrow encouragingly.

Finally his face breaks into a smile.

'OK, washing-up girl, we'll try it. We can always put it back tomorrow.'

'Deal!' I return his warm smile and think about what Harold said earlier: 'It does sometimes rain, otherwise nothing would grow.' And something inside me feels like the rain might just help me grow a little bit too.

At the end of the evening I'm sweeping the floor, feeling not unlike Cinderella dreaming of going to the ball, only I'm dreaming that in just a couple of months' time I'll be in the Butterfly Bar, closing up and cashing up my till. The last of the baker's family are leaving, kissing each other and saying goodnight loudly. Everyone is in high spirits, shaking Frank's hand and thanking Bonita for cooking the specially requested menu: simple Spanish dishes, just as they like. Cool, refreshing gazpacho, tomatoey and garlicky, with a kick of chilli, served with fresh basil leaves and crusty *pan rustico*, made by Bonita in the outside bread oven. This was followed by big dishes of paella: dark yellow paprika- and saffron-infused rice, fat mussels in their shells and tasty squid, bright red peppers and chunky chopped tomatoes, wedges of sharp lemon scattered over the top along with juicy pink prawns. And afterwards, churros, soft fat doughnuts piped Spanish style, like plump sausages with grooves indented around the edges; perfect for soaking up the rich dark chocolate dipping sauce.

I smile as I watch them leave. I don't think there's going to be much in the way of leftovers tonight.

'All OK?' I ask Frank as he comes into the kitchen. I'm putting away the pans I've washed in the order Bonita likes them.

'Excellent,' he says, holding a bunch of notes. 'They left a good tip. Here, take this.' He hands me half of them.

I look at the notes. I'd like to refuse, tell him to keep them. But I can't. I need all the money I can get right now.

'It was your idea to move the tables inside. They loved it. Pedro – that's the baker – his nephew was sitting in the little room; they got engaged. The family were delighted. It must have been the romantic lighting.' He laughs. 'Imagine if we'd had to cancel because of the weather!'

He looks out. It's stopped raining now.

'Maybe you'll let me take you out some time to enjoy some romantic lighting of our own.'

'That's very kind of you, Frank, but . . . well, let's just say I'm getting over someone. I'm happier on my own from now on.'

He laughs and so do I, and Bonita, who's been listening to our exchange, seems to breathe a sigh of relief.

'I won't stop trying,' he says with a cheeky smile. 'The best way to mend a broken heart is to find new love. I can help.'

'You are a good friend, Frank. Thank you,' I say, laughing. If it hadn't been for his warm welcome, I might just have packed up and gone home after that first night here.

I look at the money in my hand. Nearly as much as I've earned all day. It'll go straight into my savings jar for the Butterfly Bar. I know now, absolutely, that this is what I want to do. I might never get to organise my own wedding, but running a bar will do me just fine. It feels like pieces of the broken person Will left behind are beginning to stick themselves back together.

'You go, I'll close up,' I tell Frank as he pushes his share of the tip into his wallet.

'If I can't tempt you out, I will try my luck at the casino down at the port,' he tells me. And with a spring in his step, he jogs across the wide terrace, following Bonita down the couple of steps and out on to the patio.

I pull the big black bag out of the bin under the sink, tie the top and carry it out through the back door.

'Oh, blow!' I realise I've forgotten to take out the scraps for the little cat. I know there was some chicken in there, and maybe some rice from yesterday's tagine . . . or at least I think that's what it was. I wish Bonita could choose to cook what she feels is right, like she did tonight. Local, fresh ingredients, prepared Spanish style. If her cakes are anything to go by, and tonight's birthday menu, she's a great home cook; just not this muddled stuff that Valentina has set her to. If she can't get it right, will Valentina look for someone else who can? No wonder Bonita's so grumpy. She's worried about her job.

I reach over into the big wheelie bin and undo the top of the bag. I can barely see in the dark. Oh God, I hope there're no rats lurking, waiting for their dinner. I pull out my phone and switch on the torch, then lean in to the bag and make a grab for a scrunched-up piece of tin foil. I smooth it out, then carefully pick out the pieces of chicken and scoop up some rice. I wrap it all in the foil and return to the kitchen to wash my hands. That done, I go back outside with another bag of rubbish.

'Aargh!' My heart leaps into my mouth. There's a big dark figure leaning against the bin. I'm frozen to the spot.

'*Pardona*. Sorry,' the figure says. 'I . . . didn't mean to scare you,' he adds in slightly stilted, rusty English.

'I . . .' I suddenly realise I'm in the middle of nowhere, on my own, with no idea how I'd get help if I needed it.

'I am Miguel,' he says, coming to stand in the light, and with a surge of relief I recognise him as the young man who arrived here yesterday with Antonio. 'Here, let me help you.' He takes the black bag from me. 'In here?' he asks, pointing to the big bin.

I nod. 'Yes. *Sí. Gracias.*'

'I am . . .' He turns to me, and then stops as if running out of words.

'You're staying here?' I try and help him finish his sentence. Up close, I can see he looks very much like Antonio. Big shoulders, though not quite as broad as Antonio's. A smaller nose, almost button-like. The same big dark eyes. His hair is shorter but just as unruly; it is scraped back off his face, but the odd strand attempts to escape as he runs his hand over the top of his head. He's young, in his late teens I'd say, judging by the teenagers I've served burgers to over the years.

He nods. 'I am Antonio's . . .' He seems to find the words new and unfamiliar. 'I am Antonio's son.' He shrugs, as if he's not really sure what that means.

'Well,' I smile, 'I'm Beti.' I put out a hand, then run it down my apron to dry it and put it out again. 'Looks like we're both new around here,' I say.

He looks at me and I feel some kind of solidarity between us. There is a sadness behind those eyes, and I get the feeling he senses the same thing in me too.

'Pleased to meet you, Beti,' he says, shaking my hand. For a moment neither of us knows what to say.

'I thought everyone had gone. I was just getting some air . . . trying to get signal,' he says, holding up his phone, 'but there isn't any down here. Works fine in the apartment.'

'Ah, you're in a dip down here. Up in the orchard is best,' I say. 'My *finca* gets it because I'm in the top corner.'

'When did you arrive here?' he asks.

'Just a few days ago,' I tell him.

'I came yesterday.'

I nod. 'I saw.'

'I take it you and Antonio don't get on.' He glances in the direction of the apartment.

'Truth is, I'd never met him before. I didn't know who he was at first.' I drop my voice.

'Well you certainly told him what you thought of him,' Miguel says, and suddenly laughs. I can't help but laugh too.

'I'm not sure it was the best first impression I could have made with my boss,' I say. 'I'd had a bad day. Now I'm not sure he likes me very much.'

'I'm not sure he likes me either,' Miguel says, though he's still smiling, 'and he definitely doesn't like my mother. He only seems to like his horses.'

'Well, we'd better stick together then. Um . . . you didn't leave some branches on my doorstep, did you?'

'No.' He shakes his head. 'Why?'

'Oh, no reason.' Perhaps it was Frank, I think. 'Nice to meet you, Miguel, *buenas noches.*'

'Nice to meet you too, Beti,' and he wanders off towards the path up the cherry orchard. I turn and return to the kitchen to finish up.

Upstairs, Antonio leaned against the concrete railing outside his apartment. Ah, the girl who had told him he was sour. A tiny sad smile pulled at the corner of his mouth. So his son thought he only liked horses, did he? He looked back down at his phone and the message from Miguel's mother. The boy was right about one thing: Antonio didn't have a lot of time for his ex. He might not have been much of a father over the years, but how could he let this situation carry on, allowing Miguel to grow up in a home where he wasn't wanted? He'd have to try and find a way to make it right. He'd start by ignoring Esmeralda's preposterous demands.

He pressed delete on his phone, firmly, then shoved it back into his pocket. He watched the light up in the cherry orchard where Miguel was searching for a signal, and another winding its way around the path up to the little *finca*. He would have to work harder to try and get to know both his new guests. He saw what she had done in the restaurant this evening. Saved the day, by all accounts. What was someone like her doing working as a washer-upper in his restaurant? She intrigued him. He must thank her. And, he resolved, he must get Valentina back. The restaurant needed her, and he needed to make it up to her for springing Miguel on her. He would have to make more of an effort all round if he was going to hang on to his son, his home and his business.

Chapter Eleven

I sit on the broken bench outside my *finca*, pull off my shoes and roll my aching feet around. The little grey cat joins me on the bench, trying to get my attention, rubbing against me one minute, and flicking her tail and walking away the next. I think she should have a name. Maybe Ana, after Cortijo Ana.

'*Hola*, Ana,' I say, and stroke her head. Then I close my eyes and breathe in deeply. The rain has stopped, and there's something in the air. It smells different. There's a perfume there.

I pull out my phone. As I expected, there is no word from Will. I slam the cover shut on it and hold it to my lips. It's time for the madness to stop. He's not coming back. We were so close; we nearly had it all. But like a game of snakes and ladders, I'm starting from go again.

I stand up and walk into the house. I put my phone in a drawer in the little kitchen area and slam it shut. I'm not being a slave to it any more. No more waiting for Will to get in touch. From now on, I'll check in on it once a week, to let Mum and Dad know I'm fine. That's eleven weeks, eleven weekly updates until I take over the Butterfly Bar and invite them out to see it.

I count up my earnings at the little wooden table and jot them down in my notebook. Then I put a few euros into my purse for bus fares and the rest in my jar, and screw the lid back on tightly. I've still got a long way to go, but at least I'm going in the right direction. I put the jar back on the shelf next to the cups and head for bed. It feels like I've finally thrown the dice again, moved off go and am making my way back up the board, hoping to land a big ladder soon!

The next morning I'm woken by the sun streaming in through the thin curtains of my little bedroom window. I climb out of the huge, high bed with effort. It's so comfortable; I haven't slept on a bed this comfy ever. Despite doing mental sums over and over in my head last night, fretting over how much I need to make, how many hours I need to work, I fell asleep as soon as my head hit the pillow.

I put the kettle on and open the front door to let the morning air in. For a moment the sun blinds me, but as my eyes adjust, I catch my breath, then rub them, just to make sure I'm seeing things right. It's like a snow scene, laid out in front of me all the way down the valley; a scene from a Christmas card. Except after a moment I realise it isn't snow at all. It's blossom. White cherry blossom. Overhead the sky is a clear cobalt blue. Just a few wisps of departing cloud. And all around me, everything is white. The branches reach out to neighbouring trees, creating canopies that I just want to run through. And the floral perfume – of red poppies, and white and yellow daisies, and the heady sensual scent of the jasmine that seems to have burst into life – it's amazing! As if Mother Nature has suddenly waved her wand, like a fairy godmother, and transformed everything around me. The sweet floral perfume is filling the air and my soul with it.

I dress quickly and walk through the orchard, enjoying every inch of the blossom and the bouquet from the vivid yellow broom plant growing up the hillsides. I suddenly feel properly alive and . . . well, happy. Happy to be here. Happy to have got this chance. I let the morning sun warm my face and drink in the heady perfume, lifting my spirits higher and higher. I think how much I would have loved to have told Nan about this, brought her here even. She loved flowers. Particularly daffodils. Her little back garden was full of them. Always enough for a vase on the kitchen table in springtime. She would have thought this was heaven. There are honey bees the size of bomber planes at work, flying from flower to flower, the noise like a swarm of drones. Over the pergola at the front of the restaurant the wisteria has burst into life, purple flowers opening up. And there are birds everywhere, singing, even shouting their love for each other and challenging rival suitors: goldfinches, blue tits, sparrows and blackbirds.

Eventually I return to the *finca*, where I feed Ana and grab my bag. It's time to get the bus to the harbour. I make my way down the path around the orchard, still enjoying the sight of the blossom, a spring in my step as I pass the horses in the paddock.

'*Buenos días,*' I say to the mare and her foal.

'*Buenos días,*' a deep voice replies, making me jump. Then I see Antonio, saddling up the big black stallion. I take a deep breath, keeping my distance from the beautiful but impatient animal. Antonio stands back and looks straight at me, making me feel as jumpy as the horse.

'The blossom is beautiful,' I manage to say, nodding towards it.

He pats the horse's hindquarters and then looks at the orchard.

'It is, yes, *magnífico*,' he says, taking time to look and enjoy it, as if reminding himself of its full glory. At least the black cloud that has been following him around seems to have lifted.

Our conversation starts and ends here. Not that I'm expecting any more. He clearly doesn't want to waste his breath on small talk with the washer-upper – not one who insulted him, at least! I nod to him and smile, then start to walk off in the direction of the road.

'It will only last about ten days,' Antonio calls after me, stopping me in my tracks. 'Make the most of it,' he adds, but without his previous gruffness. It strikes me that this may be his attempt at polite conversation.

'I will,' I say, as he puts a foot in the stirrup and swings himself up into the saddle.

'*Hola*, Beti.' I spin round and see Miguel coming out of one of the barns carrying piles of green netting, hood up despite the early-morning sunshine.

'*Hola*, Miguel!' I break into a smile and feel Antonio looking at us. My cheeks suddenly flush. He can't think I'm flirting! I'm practically old enough to be the boy's mother, for goodness' sake!

'Antonio has me sorting out and repairing netting.' Miguel rolls his eyes at the tediousness of the task, but looks pleased to feel useful.

'Work hard!' I smile warmly, feeling strangely glad that he's ventured out of his bedroom, and not just to get phone signal, then turn towards the bus stop with a definite spring in my step. Like the day itself, life is certainly looking brighter.

'What do you mean, you're letting me go?' I ask, horrified, having arrived at the burger bar after my bus journey into the port.

'Sorry,' says Victoria. 'End of the school holidays in the UK. I'm going back to do some job hunting. Got a couple of interviews lined up. It's just as a runner, but that's how they all start! Sorry, there just aren't enough customers at this time of year to keep us all on. It'll pick up again in July, when the summer holidays start. Dad should be back on his feet and running the place if you're still looking for work then.'

'But the cherry trees have only just come into blossom!' I protest, thinking about the farm back up the mountain.

She shrugs and shakes her head, looking around the precinct at the Irish pub, the nightclub, Craig's breakfast bar.

'No one here is here for the cherry blossom.' She smiles a little patronisingly at me, as if I know absolutely nothing about Spanish life and holidaymakers.

I hand over my hat, apron and name badge, and take my envelope of notes. Brenda is beckoning to me. I sigh and stuff the envelope in my big shoulder bag, then wander over to her. Craig is drinking white wine on ice. Brenda pours me a glass. I go to say no, but she waves away both my protests and my offer of money.

'You can buy me one when we come back and visit you,' she says cheerfully. Her smile drops. 'What's up? You look like you've lost ten euros and found a pound!'

I can't help but smile at how she has one foot in Spain and one back in the UK. But in fact that's exactly how I feel. I've lost my lunchtime job but I still have the warm sun on my face.

'Victoria's just laid me off. Says there isn't enough work for me until the summer holidays start.'

Brenda shakes her head sympathetically. 'We're the same. It goes very quiet in between holidays. I'd give you some shifts here if we had the customers, but it's dead. I mean, there's still the expats, and the themed evenings are quite good. The Pilates night, and the book club, oh, and film night on the big screen.' She points to the rolled-up projector on the far wall. 'Is there anything you could do? Start a class here in the evenings, maybe?'

I rack my brains trying to think of something, but draw a blank. All I've ever done is serve drinks and burgers. I went to some craft evening classes once, but that was to help with making wedding invites. I'm definitely not good enough to teach it. Not like Will; at least he had his guitar and could gig. I desperately need to get some extra income . . . I just have to work out how.

At that moment Valentina walks past the bar in high heels, slim jeans and a fitted shirt. Her hair is swinging and she's obviously on her way somewhere, tapping away on her phone as she goes. I have an idea.

'Valentina!' I call after her. She stops and looks around, at first not recognising me. I leave the bar and quickly walk over to her. 'Valentina!' This time she does recognise me, though she doesn't smile.

'It's you,' she says, looking down her nose at me.

'Hi! I was just thinking . . . about the restaurant. Well, I was wondering. I've got a bit of experience working in the food industry . . .' She looks at the burger bar behind me. 'And I was just wondering if you'd thought about opening at lunchtimes. I could help out, waitressing, washing up, whatever you needed. Maybe do a set menu like the tavern on the square.' I start to warm to my theme.

'Pah!' She stops me in my tracks. 'That restaurant will never work until he updates it. It needs a complete overhaul. Bring it kicking and screaming into the modern world, like these places.' She looks around at the brightly lit bars in the precinct, offering happy hours and deals on jugs of sangria. 'This is what the tourists want, not his grandmother's kitchen!' She looks as if she's chewing on a wasp.

I think about how glorious the farm looked this morning, and suddenly I feel a glimmer of hope. 'The blossom is out,' I say. 'It's beautiful. Why don't you come back and see it?'

She stares at me and I think she might be about to agree. Then, 'Is the boy still there?'

'Miguel?' I ask.

'Antonio's son. The one he just turned up with, with no discussion beforehand. The one I barely know anything about but who I will no doubt be expected to look after and love,' she adds with a grimace.

'Yes! He's doing great.' I think about him helping with the nets this morning, getting them ready to spread over the trees to keep the birds at bay. 'He's giving Antonio a hand in the cherry orchard actually. And he seems to be settling in.'

'Then I will not be coming back to see the blossom,' she

sneers. 'Whilst he is there, I will stay away. When he goes back to where he belongs, I will come back.'

'What? But Antonio . . . he just . . .'

'That man takes me for granted. How can he expect me to love another woman's child when I have none of my own yet? Not even a ring on my finger! And now he has someone new in his life, he will have even less time for me.'

I can't believe she's sulking because of Miguel's arrival. But what do I know? Maybe if I'd been a bit firmer about what I wanted in life with Will, instead of trying to get him to notice me with haircuts and underwear, I wouldn't be thirty-two, single and washing up for a living!

Valentina looks back down at her phone and walks away without another word. I'll have to try and find Antonio and see if *he* can give me any more work.

The amazing white blossom of the cherry trees hits me as soon as I step off the bus. They're everywhere: covering the side of the valley like a bride's veil, in small patches at the back of houses, in fields separated by low walls. Even here in the square, the trees are heavy with the snow-white blossom. I have never seen anything like it. I must take a picture and send it to Mum, I think, then remember my phone is in the drawer.

I walk up the lane and stop at the white gates to Cortijo Ana. There are trees on both sides of the drive, reaching out and creating an archway. It's just beautiful. Ana the cat appears, meowing crossly at me. I bend to stroke her head, then look at the tree-lined corridor again. I can't help myself. I take one step, then another, advancing down the scented floral aisle, imagining the person I love is at the end of it. But there's no one there. No one at all. Just the vibrant bougainvillea that has burst passionately into life around the archways of the veranda.

I open the door leading into the restaurant.

'*Hola!* Hello? Antonio?'

A gust of wind blows up and whispers through the leaves and blossom. Suddenly Ana shoots in through the door, her tail high, disappearing into the dark restaurant and the kitchen beyond.

'Damn it!' I say. Bonita will not be happy if she finds out I've brought a cat into the kitchen. 'Ana, here.' I purse my lips and make kissing sounds, trying to call her. Then it strikes me that she probably doesn't understand English, and I rack my brains to think of something more suitable in Spanish. '*Ven!*' I try, with no effect.

Suddenly she darts out from behind the broom and scoots through the bar into the small room we used the other night for the birthday party. The old terracotta jugs I put on the shelves are still there. Maybe I should take them down now the sun is out and move the tables back outside. It's a shame, I think; this room is lovely now. I'd love to eat here, with someone special looking at me over a candle and a rose. Not that I intend to have a romantic meal out with anyone again, I remind myself, and concentrate on the job in hand.

'Ana!' I make the kissing noise again, but she lifts her tail and runs into the next room, the old storeroom. I catch a glimpse of her disappearing through a cupboard door that has been left ajar.

'Got you!' I reach in and scoop her up, much to her chagrin.

Still holding her under one arm, I go to shut the cupboard door, but notice there are more terracotta plates and bowls in there, all just stacked up. Nothing like the square purple and white plates that are used in the restaurant and won't fit in the flipping dishwasher! I pick one up and study its deep terracotta glaze. There are candle holders in the cupboard too, with shapes cut out of them that would create beautiful shadows on these walls. Ana wriggles free from my grasp and I put her down, but this time she doesn't go anywhere; just snakes around my ankles. I'll let her out in a moment, I think, and bend down to look at the candle holders, taking one out and putting it on the table. Ana jumps up on to a chair and starts washing her paws.

'Table for one, madam?' I smile at her but she haughtily ignores me.

In the kitchen, I find a box of matches and a drawer full of candles. I light one and put it in the holder on the table. The shapes immediately throw light out on to the white walls. It looks amazing. I can't understand why all this stuff has been shoved away in here and replaced with a range of funky Swedish homeware.

Curiosity gets the better of me and I take another look in the cupboard. There are some pictures in here too, in frames. I pull them out. Old black-and-white photographs of a couple dancing flamenco, by the looks of it. He is dressed in trousers that come up above his waist, and a short jacket, a hat covering his face as it is turned into the crook of his partner's neck. She has dark hair, tied back, and is wearing a long black dress. One arm is around the man's neck, the other held in the air, her head high and proud. It's breathtaking. There is another picture here too. Similar but maybe not as old, like they were taken in the same place but years apart.

I go to prop them up on the shelf in between the jugs I've put there. This place could be amazing. I'm sure people would come up from the resorts if they thought they were getting something different, something authentic. My mind is whirring with possibilities. I think about all the classes in the port – there must be something I could do here to generate some income. I hold the picture against the wall with both hands and study it. What about . . . I've got it! I suddenly think with a huge grin.

'What do you think you're doing?'

My breath catches in my throat and I jump at the sight of Antonio's dark, angry expression. The picture falls to the ground with a crack, and Ana flits out of the room, leaving me to face Antonio on my own.

Chapter Twelve

We both look at the framed picture with the crack through the middle of the glass.

'Oh God! I'm so sorry.' I pick it up and inspect the damage. 'I'll get it repaired,' I tell him quickly, and wonder what kind of a dent that will make in my final wages from the burger bar.

'Just put it back,' he says. 'Both of them.' He scowls around the room, at the table where the candle is lit, but says nothing.

I put the pictures back in the cupboard, on the bottom shelf where I found them.

'I was just . . . I was looking for Ana,' I tell him.

'Ana?' He frowns deeply.

'Yes, I thought she was in here. Well, she was . . .'

'You were looking for my grandmother?' he asks in amazement.

'What?' I look back in similar shock. His grandmother? What, did he think I was trying to talk to ghosts? 'No, no,' I explain hastily. 'The cat that keeps me company at the *finca*. I called her Ana, after this place.'

Oh God, now he thinks I'm a mad cat woman . . . which quite possibly I am. Great! How is it every time I'm near this man, I end up making a complete idiot of myself?

'I didn't mean to interfere. I was just trying to think of some ways to generate some new customers, bring in tourists.'

He doesn't say anything, just looks around, so I keep going, taking my opportunity to try and prove that I could be useful here. I don't want to get in Valentina's way, but perhaps another eye on things might help.

'Look, I was thinking, this place is pretty quiet, especially with the school holidays back in the UK over. But it's so beautiful.' I nod to the blossom outside. 'And well, frankly, I could do with earning some more money right now.'

He raises an eyebrow.

'I was talking with one of the bar owners down at the port. The way she keeps going when the tourists thin out is by holding specialist nights for the expats. Book club, tapas cookery class, Spanish lessons . . .'

He shrugs. 'I'm sorry, I have a farm to run. I have many trees to see to and a watering system that seems to have a mind of its own. If you'll excuse me,' he holds up a roll of tape, 'there are hosepipes to mend. You'll have to speak to Valentina about your ideas.'

'But I thought, what with the cherry blossom being out, well, we could do something to bring people up here whilst it looks like this. You said it would only last about ten days and to make the most of it. What if Valentina isn't back by . . .' I change tack quickly, seeing his face darken again. 'I've thought of a way to make money. Might even help towards new hosepiping.' I nod and smile at the roll of tape in his hand.

There's now a hint of interest in his chocolate-brown eyes.

'Go on . . .' he says.

This could be it! A sudden surge of excitement rushes through me.

'Well, I was thinking, everyone should see the cherry blossom – it's gorgeous. We could move some of the tables off the terrace and put them into these little rooms, give people a taste of living in a real Spanish *cortijo*, of how things used to be.' I point to the table with the candle on it. 'We make it a more intimate feeling inside and create more space outside.'

'More space? Why would we need more space outside?'

I pause – not intentionally, but it seems to have the required effect. I can't believe they haven't thought of this before.

'Well?' he prompts me, waving a hand impatiently.

'We could hold flamenco classes on the terrace!' I announce. 'It was the picture that gave me the idea. The one I, er . . . dropped.' I get back into my stride. 'We find a teacher – I hear there's one in the port who runs classes at the gym. Or maybe you know someone a bit more local. We do an intensive week's course in the daytime whilst the blossom is out to pull them in, and then weekly sessions after that, say on a Monday. Even offer food, some traditional Spanish stuff like Bonita used to cook. It'll bring the expats up here, away from the port, and in turn the tourists too, exactly as Valentina wants. Wine and tapas and flamenco!'

He looks at me as if I'm talking a foreign language, which of course to him I am. Maybe I went too fast.

'Shall I explain it more slowly?'

He shakes his head. 'No.'

'So if you agree, I could go and hand out flyers,' I continue, my mind brimming with ideas and fingers itching to get to my notepad.

'I said no,' he says more forcefully, and slams the cupboard door shut. Then he turns to me and looks straight at me to make his point. 'No flamenco!'

'What?' I decide to push the matter. After all, this feels like my last chance to make some money. 'But it would be perfect! The restaurant is empty in the daytime, and you have that big covered terrace, with heating if needs be . . .'

With a huge resigned sigh he says, 'Flamenco has been banned in this town for many years. Our local priest ordered it, and that is the way it has to be.' He takes a final look around the little room and nods, as if closing my window of opportunity for good. Then he turns and leaves.

'Antonio, wait!' I run after him. He stops and turns back to me. 'Banned? Why?' I'm wondering if I've heard him right.

'It is how things are around here. That's all there is to it.'

He means it. Flamenco is banned. And by the sound of it, he's not wasting his breath explaining. But even so, I really need to find more work.

'OK, I get it. No flamenco. But would you have any other work for me at all, anything?'

He looks pointedly around at the empty tables and chairs, and at Miguel, who is sitting on the steps of the terrace with a large net on his lap, darning the gaping holes. 'I'm sorry. You can see how it is,' he says.

But to be honest, I can't. This place could be amazing with the right ideas.

'Valentina will be back soon, ask her. She runs the restaurant. Sorry.'

He obviously doesn't want to do anything that might step on Valentina's toes, and I understand that, I suppose. I watch as he shrugs and marches off to the sheds beside the horses' enclosure, where he stands over a large square piece of machinery and switches it on. It doesn't seem to want to jump into life, and coughs and splutters a few times before falling silent again. Antonio lets out a torrent of what I'm guessing are Spanish expletives. Miguel looks at me and raises his eyebrows.

'His pump is playing up,' he says with a hint of a smile as I pass him on my way up to the *finca*.

No flamenco then, I think, still wondering why on earth you would ban a dance. It's back to the drawing board for me and my money-making ideas, I guess. Looks like I've landed on a snake and slid back to square one again.

Chapter Thirteen

That evening as I walk to the restaurant, I take the time to breathe in deeply. The smell is amazing, filling the air and lifting my spirits, despite my worry about my current predicament. Contrary to what Victoria told me, it looks like there are people who have heard about the blossom and want to explore the mountains. They're different from the younger crowd down at the harbour and the beach: older holiday-makers, in walking gear, enjoying the trees in full bloom in the evening sun.

When I reach the farmhouse, Bonita is crashing about in the kitchen, complaining noisily about the dishes on the menu Valentina has set. It's all hands on deck by the looks of it.

'How can I help, Bonita?' I strip off my bag and hang it on the peg by the mop and bucket and broom.

She points to some potatoes. 'For French fries! What is wrong with *patatas bravas*? We are in Spain! You want French fries, go to France!' She tuts and shakes her head.

The restaurant is filling up. As I peel the potatoes, I look out on to the terrace and realise that it's just Frank, me and Bonita again tonight. I take a deep breath.

'Bonita, can you show me how you cut these for *patatas bravas*?'

She looks at me and frowns, then glances around nervously, puts a potato on the chopping board and cuts.

'*Patatas bravas*,' she announces, and steps back.

'*Patatas bravas* is it then!' I say, and start chopping. 'Blame me, I'm just the washer-upper. I don't know one end of a potato from another. I thought I was helping.'

She looks at me for a moment, and there is a tiny smile at the corner of her mouth as she goes back to the big pot of something indescribable and the printed-off recipe beside the stove.

Once I've cut up all the potatoes, Bonita tells me she's made a tomato sauce for them, just like she used to.

'Sounds lovely,' I say as she drains them ready for the oven. 'And maybe . . .' I take another bold step. There are people out there paying good money and expecting edible food. 'Maybe the chicken tikka could be something a little more . . . Spanish too, just for tonight. It looks like it's going to be busy. Might be easier . . .' I trail off, just as Frank calls me to help move the tables from the bar area back outside underneath the wisteria that has burst into life. As I leave the kitchen, Bonita is standing stock still, deep in thought.

A young couple are sitting in the little room where I put the candle and the terracotta pots. The fairy lights are on. Frank must have done it. He gives me a little wink. The two of them are leaning over the table towards each other like they're the only people in the world. I feel a little pang of envy, and try and remember when Will last looked at me like that. Did he ever? Or did I just imagine it?

I turn my attention back to the filling car park. Surely Valentina knows it's going to be like this when the blossom comes out and tourists venture out this way. But there's no sign of her little red car. And no sign of Antonio either.

I'm heading back into the restaurant behind Frank when I hear a shout from the direction of the sheds.

'Heeey!'

Followed by another.

'*Bravo!!*'

At the same time there is a sudden rush of water, like an unexpected shower of rain. But it's not. It's the sprinkler system for watering the cherry trees, suddenly erupting into life, making the diners turn and look.

As Antonio emerges proudly from the barn, he catches my eye, and for the first time since I've met him, he's smiling, actually smiling. He looks very different without his usual scowl. He goes to join Miguel, who is standing over the big metal box that is now chugging along noisily, like an unfit runner trying to make it to the finish line. Even Miguel looks pleased. I find myself smiling too, as father and son finally find common ground in getting the pump to work. But as Antonio raises his hand for a high five, Miguel suddenly looks embarrassed. Antonio drops his hand and the moment of united triumph ebbs away. Miguel turns away and wanders off up the path towards my cottage, checking his phone. Antonio watches him go, his face a picture of concern. Then he turns and looks at the sprinklers, hands on hips, the happy smile returning. And just for a moment, I can see what Valentina must have seen in him.

Back in the kitchen, I look at Bonita, who is beaming.

'Spanish chicken!' she announces, holding up a wooden spoon. I go over and taste the sauce. It's amazing!

'What's in it?' I ask, savouring the flavours as they run over my tongue.

'Chicken, paprika, oregano, chorizo, vegetables. Is simple but good, *sí?*'

'*Sí!*' I confirm. It's gorgeous. Soft, moist chicken; spicy red chorizo; deep orange paprika. My taste buds are tingling from their experience.

'I will save you some,' she says, and gives me a little wink. She actually winks! And I smile.

'Beti!' Frank calls me to help move a table from the bar area as another car pulls into the drive and a group of British pensioners get out and look around with wonder.

'Is it always busy at this time of the year?' I ask as the table catches my shin.

'Mostly. People like to see the cherry blossom. It is unusual. They have cherry blossom all over the Jerte valley, but here, in Colina de Flor, this is very special. A rare breed! It only grows here. That's why we have to look after it,' he tells me as he walks backwards with the table. 'You OK?' he adds kindly, and I nod that I'm fine.

We put the table back under the pergola. This time there is no rain leaking through, just the gentle pitter-patter of the sprinklers in the evening sun and the glow from the patio heaters on the outside diners. Frank has turned the CD player on, and the air fills with light Spanish guitar music. I look round the terrace. If only it was like this all the time: busy and buzzing. If only Antonio would let me organise the flamenco nights. I wonder again why flamenco is banned. It seems so odd, and how on earth is it policed? I can't imagine anything like that happening back home.

It would be like banning singing: impossible!

'Oh, how pretty!' exclaims a British woman in her early sixties. 'Is this table free?'

'Of course. I'll just get . . .' I look around for Frank, who is taking orders. 'I'll just lay it up for you,' I say, and run back into the restaurant to grab cutlery, glasses and napkins.

'Take a seat.' I pull out a chair. A rogue spray from the watering system catches me on the backs of the legs, and I move the table an inch or two away from it. 'The waiter will be with you in just a moment.'

'Thank you, dear. It's beautiful here. We were just passing, out walking, when we spotted this place. So tucked out of the way. What a find!'

I just hope the food lives up to the setting, I think to myself.

'Yes, thank you,' smiles her companion. 'It's our wedding anniversary. This is perfect.'

I smile. 'Congratulations,' I say, wondering how people manage to make it to milestone anniversaries when I've never even managed to get out of the starting blocks.

'Thirty years ago today. I knew he was the one.' The woman smiles and puts her hand over his. My heart aches momentarily, but I bat away my sad thoughts.

'I'll ask the waiter to get you some drinks,' I say. 'And can I recommend the chef's special, Spanish chicken and *patatas bravas*?'

'Thank you, dear. You've been most helpful. You've got a lovely place here.'

'Oh, this isn't . . .' but they are leaning into each other, enjoying each other's company, the music, the blossom and the scented night air.

* * *

The rest of the shift passes quickly, in a pile of pots and pans and those blooming square plates. The Spanish chicken and *patatas bravas* are a huge hit, and I see a hint of triumph on Bonita's face as she passes me the empty baking trays.

'*Gracias*,' she says as I take them from her, and she nods her head and smiles again.

'*Gracias*,' I smile back.

I'm carrying a black bin liner outside to the big green bin when the anniversary couple call me over and thank me for a lovely evening.

'I wish we'd done something like this when we were still young enough. You're very brave,' she tells me. 'I didn't have the nerve to risk everything on a new life overseas.'

'Oh, I'm not brave,' I say. I haven't even told my family I've lost all my money and that my fiancé has left me. A pang of guilt, followed by panic, hits me. At the rate I'm going, I'll never get a place of my own.

'Thank you again, dear. It was a wonderful evening.' She pulls her fleece jacket round her and I turn back towards the restaurant, cheered by their happiness. That's when I hear the voice.

'There you are!'

My warm, happy glow freezes over like Elsa's palace in *Frozen*, chilling me to the bone.

'My Find My Friends app says you're up in a field somewhere over there! I thought I'd never find you! I was beginning to wonder if this bar in Spain was made up!'

I turn slowly. There, holding out a phone in one hand, an oversized handbag over her arm and sunglasses pushed up on the top of her shiny chestnut head, is the last person on earth I want to see right now. And my heart sinks like it's been weighted with a stone and plunged into deep, dark, freezing-cold water.

Chapter Fourteen

What on earth is my cousin Olivia doing here! In Colina de Flor! I try and manoeuvre my tongue to form words whilst my brain is doing a crazy dance; questions and thoughts crashing into each other. Does she know Will's run out on me? Does she know he's taken Nan's money? Does she know I've blown everything . . . again?

'Wow! This place is actually . . . really . . .' She looks around in disbelief, clearly unable to bring herself to say that it's fabulous.

'It is, isn't it?' I nod several times, knowing I'm going to have to get back to the kitchen or Bonita, despite tonight's success, will be on the warpath. I can't afford to mess things up here; it's the only income I have right now.

'What is all this stuff?' She brushes the blossom with her hand.

'Cherry blossom. A rare variety that grows only here. It lasts about ten days, so you've caught it at just the right time.'

What am I talking about? 'Caught it at just the right time'?!

'Very knowledgeable,' she says with raised eyebrows. 'It looks . . . amazing.' She bleeps her key fob and an expensive-looking black car lights up. Clearly she isn't planning on leaving straight away, and my heart sinks.

'So, you remember Gav, don't you?' I look across to the car park, where Olivia's boyfriend from back home is walking towards us, phone glued to his ear.

'Yes, we've met,' I say. Oh God! This can't be happening. Why are they here? I had it all planned. I was keeping my head down until I got the key to the Butterfly Bar. Then another thought strikes me. What if it's bad news?

'Everything's all right, isn't it? I mean, at home? There's nothing wrong, is there?'

'No, no . . . Dad's still spending all his time at the golf club!' She hoots with laughter. 'Mum's busy with her charity work. Oh, and Reykjavik . . . amazing! Did you see our photos on Facebook? Great hen destination, but a bit done to death now, if you know what I mean . . .'

I zone out as Olivia rattles on. I need to know why she's here. Is it Will? Has something happened? Has she seen him? I swallow hard.

'So, this is where you've been hiding!' She looks around with an approving nod. 'I mean, a bit rustic and out of the way, but it's really not bad, for a bit of backward Spanish life.'

I can't decide whether to agree proudly or bristle defensively. Instead I clap my hands together, needing to get back to the kitchen. 'So. What brings you two here?'

'I've been trying to message you. You've gone dead on FB. What's up with you? But then I guess this is what's up. The pair of you must be working your butts off! Manual work must be exhausting,' she says, as if she has a high-powered office job. 'Where is Will? I must say, I'm stunned he agreed to this. I always thought you were punching above your weight there, but fair play, if he's gone along with living out here, you must have something I don't.'

I'm reading between the lines and digesting it all slowly. She thinks Will is here with me. That means she hasn't got news on his whereabouts.

'Can't wait to say hello.' She looks around, and I swear she runs her tongue over her top lip.

'He's . . . away. Got a gig. With a band!' I say quickly, without engaging my brain. *Just tell the truth*, a voice in my head shouts, but I silence it immediately. I'm not giving her the satisfaction of knowing I've blown it. I just need to buy some time . . .

'What? He's gone away, leaving you to run this place on your own?'

'Oh, this place isn't . . .' I stop myself. Do I own up now? Get it over and done with? Once she hears that Will has left me and taken Nan's china-cow money, I'll never hear the end of it. There is a moment of silence as she looks at me quizzically. I slowly roll my lips in on each other, and say nothing.

'God, the things you could do here. I mean, it's out of the way, but you could certainly tart it up.'

'Beti!' Frank calls to me and nods towards the kitchen. I raise a hand to say I'm coming.

'Are you here for long?' I ask Olivia as politely as I can.

'Just a weekend break. A bargain flight out of Cardiff to get a bit of sun. Isn't that right, Gav? I must admit, I thought the whole thing about you running a bar might have been a joke, another of your ideas that never came off.

So I said to Gav, let's surprise her! See if she's really pulled it off.'

Gav nods but says nothing.

Surprise me! She's certainly done that! But at least she's not staying long. They'll be gone very soon, and then I can return to getting my life back on track. With a bit of luck, and a few more nights with tips like we've had tonight, I'll have my own bar by June and then I'll invite them all out to see it.

'Beti!' comes the shout again. Frank is carrying armfuls of plates towards the kitchen, and I know the pile will getting higher and higher out there.

'Anyway, it's been lovely to see you both. Come and say hi again in the summer. Let me know!' I turn in the direction of the back door.

'Oh, we've time to eat, though. Couldn't go home and not report back, could we? I mean, I thought it was just going to be a bar. I have to say, I'm impressed, aren't you, Gav?'

Gav gives a silent shrug.

'You're staying to eat?' I repeat.

'Yes, that is what you do here, isn't it?'

'Yes, yes, of course!' I try and take control of the situation, which is rapidly running away from me. 'Um, I think we may be full.' I look around, desperate for an excuse for my unexpected and very much uninvited guests to leave.

'That one there.' Olivia points to the table the wedding anniversary couple have just vacated.

'Of course!' I say, more high-pitched than I expected, and quickly start to clear away the detritus of their meal.

'Oh, lovely!' Olivia claps her hands together. 'How romantic!'

They sit down and I practically run back to the kitchen, where the plates are indeed piled high, like the Leaning Tower of Pisa.

'We need more plates,' Bonita is chiding. 'We have run out!'

'I know, I know. I'm sorry!' I push up my sleeves, turn the taps on full blast and squirt in a big slug of washing-up liquid. Before I plunge the first plate into the scalding water, though, I have a brainwave.

'Wait!' I rush out into the restaurant, returning with a stack of terracotta plates from the cupboard.

'I'm not sure Valentina will be happy.' Bonita looks uncertain.

'Mama, Valentina isn't here; we are!' Frank joins in with my little act of mutiny. 'This is always our busiest week of the year. People we have never seen before come for the blossom.'

'And Antonio never helps! It's always the cherries first with him. Why can't the new boy help in here instead of out there?' Bonita nods towards the cherry orchard, branches touching each other like a snowy mountain range, and the sound of the gently falling water from the sprinkler system.

I wash the terracotta plates, then surge through the other plates stacked by the sink, head down, motoring on, like an Olympic swimmer heading towards the finish line. I'm just surfacing from the bubbles as Bonita serves up the last two portions of Spanish chicken and *patatas bravas*.

'For your friends.' She nods towards the crowded terrace, and the courtyard beyond.

'Oh, they're not my friends,' I say as I grab the plates. The last thing I want is for Frank to blow my cover.

'Wow! This place is busy!' Olivia says, looking round.

'Yup!' I nod, realising I'm soaked from the washing-up.

'You need more help,' she tells me. 'Get some more staff in the kitchen.'

I nod again.

'So, what are your plans for this place?'

'Well . . .' I try and think on my feet. 'Obviously it's all about al fresco dining,' I say, repeating Valentina's vision. 'That's what the tourists want.'

But my head is telling me that it should go back to being the farmhouse it once was. No fancy menus or square plates.

'I'm planning to cover all these trees in fairy lights,' I add, nodding to the line of trees leading to the white gates beyond the car park.

'Pull up a chair, Bet. Gav, pour her some wine. Hey! 'Scuse me!' Olivia shouts to Frank, and I cringe. 'Can we get another glass here?'

'Oh, I've really got to get back . . .'

'Surely you can have a bit of time off. You're the boss, aren't you? You can do what you like.'

'Yes, but . . .'

Frank comes over carrying a glass, and sets it in front of me. 'Bonita sent you this.' He puts down a piece of orange cake. 'To say thank you.'

I look at it and smile. Bonita has finally offered me her cake tin, and that feels very special indeed.

'Tell me more about your plans . . .' Olivia says.

I sit down slowly on the edge of my chair and glance at

the menu, overpriced and overcomplicated.

'We're looking at simplifying the menu,' I say. 'Maybe making a few changes to the seating area, make it more welcoming.' I gesture towards the terrace.

'Well it's certainly minimalist at the moment,' says Olivia.

'Focus on its strengths,' I continue, and as I glance around, I suddenly feel the colour drain from my face. Antonio is standing in amongst the trees on the drive, where he's obviously been fixing bits of piping in the watering system. He's watching me, one eyebrow raised in a mix of incredulity and possibly amusement. I freeze. He's the last person I want to see me in this position.

Chapter Fifteen

'Um, I really have to get back to the kitchen now . . . The, um, staff need . . . um . . .' He's still watching me, making my cheeks burn furiously. 'Supervising,' I finish painfully, trying to say it quickly and cover it with a cough.

'Well, I have to say, I never thought you'd do it, Bet. I never thought you'd get over the finish line. You may not have made it down to the altar after all those years of planning, but you've gone and got your own place in Spain. Respect.' Olivia nods, but I can tell she's finding it hard to get the words out. The bottle of wine she's sunk must be lubricating them somewhat.

Antonio's eyebrows rise even higher and my cheeks burn even more. And oh God! I think he's coming over.

'Beti? Could I . . .' He's going to ask me what the hell I'm playing at, sitting with guests and telling them I own the place . . . *his* place. I'm the washer-upper, for God's sake!

Olivia turns as Antonio approaches. 'Oh good. Could you get us another bottle, waiter?'

He stops in his tracks and his one raised eyebrow nearly reaches his hairline in utter astonishment.

'Quickly!' she insists, waving the bottle in his direction, and I think Antonio might explode with outrage.

'You were right that you have to supervise them,' Olivia tells me. 'You're having to hand-hold them. Your staff really do need to remember who's boss. And try and smile!' she tells Antonio.

I want the floor to just open up and swallow me. I'm going to have to come clean before Antonio blows a gasket and fires me on the spot.

'Look, Olivia, about that, the supervising thing . . .'

Suddenly there's a shout from Miguel. Antonio whips round away from Olivia, who's still waving her empty wine bottle in his direction, and then throws his hands in the air. There is a *phut, phut* and a splutter from the hoses running in between the cherry trees, and one of them suddenly starts spitting violently in Olivia's direction.

'Oh! Aargh!' She brandishes the bottle at the water spraying in her direction. But just as quickly as it started, it gives up and stops completely. The water pump, it would seem, has broken down again.

'*Mierde!*' shouts Antonio angrily, and marches off in the direction of Miguel and the pump.

'Well, really! You should get rid of *him*, for starters!' Olivia says, looking like she's been spat at by a passing orang-utan.

I have a sinking feeling it's going to be the other way around.

Finally, after some rather strange dishes of English trifle for dessert, Olivia stands slightly unsteadily and blows big wide air kisses as she gets ready to leave.

'I'm so pleased we found you! Thank God for Find My

Friends, eh?' She waggles her phone at me, beaming like a woman who's drunk the best part of two bottles of wine. 'And don't forget, don't take any nonsense. Get rid of that sour-faced waiter, or washer-upper, whoever he is. You need to take control. Like this, look.'

I turn to see Antonio walking down the path.

'Excuse me!' Olivia calls.

What? No! Antonio stops and looks behind him, then points at his own chest and says, 'Me?'

'Yes, you!'

The last of the diners sitting out on the terrace all turn and stare. Desperately, I start to gather up the dessert plates and glasses from the table. When I look up again, Antonio is marching towards Olivia.

'How can I help?' He pulls a tight smile through gritted teeth before his face falls back into its usual scowl. I can see why he doesn't get involved in the restaurant. People skills are clearly not his forte.

Olivia turns to me and grabs a stack of bowls from my hands. 'Here, take these!' she orders, and thrusts them at him, the spoons clattering against the sides. Then she dusts off her hands, gives me a look as though to say *that's how you do it*, and totters off on her high heels towards the expensive hire car.

Avoiding eye contact, I take the plates from Antonio's outstretched arms and make a run for the kitchen, where I hide in amongst the plates and pans and bowls of soapy water until I judge it safe to come out.

At last everyone seems to have gone, apart from Frank, who is still finishing up at the till.

'Here.' He puts a glass of red wine and a small bowl of olives down for me on the bar, and points to one of the stools. 'Have a seat.'

Reluctantly but gratefully, I attempt to sit on the high stool, which seems to have a life of its own, swinging round whenever I approach it. Finally I wrestle it into submission. I feel as if I've worked a twenty-hour shift. My back is aching and so are my feet.

Frank puts a small white plate down beside me with a piece of paper on it.

'What's this?' I look up at him and smile. He shrugs apologetically.

'Your friends' bill. They said as they were family that it was on the house.'

I'm so exhausted and fed up, I could weep. The few savings I have are gone, leaving me with nothing. Just like that, I'm back to square one. But at least Olivia has gone, and no one back home is any the wiser about the mess I've made of things. As I take a large swig of wine, I tell myself that it may have been ruddy hard work, but I've just about got away with it.

Chapter Sixteen

I slept like a log last night. I didn't think I would. I thought I'd lie there listening to the whooshing of the breeze in the blossom trees outside and worrying, but in actual fact my head hit the pillow and I was out like a light. I suppose that's the effect of being on your feet all day.

I make tea with the last of the tea bags I've brought with me, slip on my flip-flops, pull back the old wooden door and take in the fabulous white scene in front of me. The wind is chilly but the sky is blue and the sun is lighting up the valley slowly but surely. I grab my one jumper, slide it on and step out on to the veranda, where I sit at the little wooden table, surrounded by the smell of the jasmine and honeysuckle growing wild around my *finca*. There is only one thing missing: the sound of the sprinkler system giving the trees their early-morning drink.

Ana the cat meows and jumps up on the seat opposite me.

'Good morning,' I find myself smiling.

In the distance, down by the barns, I can see Antonio standing over the pump. The silence from the pipes weaving through the trees in front of me is all too telling. It's still not working.

I'd advise anyone to keep out of his way today, and that's exactly what I intend to do. I sip the tea and drink in the spectacle of the blossom trees once more, making the most of them. Today, I'm going to the harbour. I have a bar to finance. I need to find more work and I won't rest until I have some.

The pump chugged into life then expired again. 'Damn it!' Antonio muttered, clenching his fists and kicking the metal box. 'Miguel! Miguel!' he shouted up to the apartment.

He needed help. He needed to get this pump fixed, and quickly. If he couldn't water the cherry trees . . . It didn't bear thinking about. This was the most crucial time of the year, once the blossom was over and the fruit began to bud. If he didn't make the harvest – well, it wasn't an option. If he didn't produce his quota, he'd be letting the whole town down. He was the biggest farmer by far in the town's cooperative and they relied on him. He had to get these cherries ready for the buyer when he came. The supermarket would only take them if he could guarantee their full amount.

'Put down that phone and come and hold this,' he said as Miguel appeared, hood up and phone in hand.

'It's just a few photographs . . . I just . . . I sent some home. Wanted to see if they got them,' he finished. Antonio immediately felt bad. He'd been worried that Miguel was in contact with the gang he'd left behind. Now it seemed he was just sending pictures of the farm to his mother and her boyfriend. Where was the harm in that?

'Did she reply?' he asked. 'Your mum?'

Miguel shook his head and Antonio bristled, feeling for

the lad. Esmeralda had never been happy about becoming a mother. She hadn't wanted anything to interfere with her career. But to still be holding it against the boy . . . well, it was just cruel. Antonio had to keep him working. Take his mind off things. He could tell Miguel was still hurt by his mother chucking him out. He didn't want him running off, getting into more trouble. He knew what it felt like to be an angry young man; he had been an angry young man himself when his marriage broke down.

He thought about the text messages Esmeralda had sent him when Miguel had first arrived, demanding a divorce settlement. Ha! If he didn't get this pump fixed, he wouldn't even have a business for her to claim a piece of. It was a preposterous suggestion: a divorce and half his business! Never! Not after all he'd worked so hard for.

'Ouch!' He'd pushed down too violently on the spanner, wrapped around a rusty nut, and scraped his knuckles. Miguel looked up from his phone, shoved it away and ran over to help, distracted for the time being.

I grab my phone from the drawer on my way out. I close the door and bend down and stroke Ana, telling her I'll be back later. Then I smooth down my lightweight denim dress and make my way down the path through the orchard.

I'm rounding the last corner when there's a thundering from a pathway leading off into a field of trees.

'Aargh!' A stupid scream leaps out of my mouth and I jump backwards. The beautiful black stallion is cantering towards me, his legs high, his rounded neck gleaming with sweat under his long wavy mane, like an elegant ballet dancer. Fit, solid yet elegant all at the same time.

'Sorry, I didn't mean to scare you!' Antonio brings the animal to a halt and looks down at me from the saddle, running his hands over his unruly dark curls. He's not wearing a riding hat. The horse is dancing on the spot, like a jogger not wanting to stop, raring to keep going, shaking its head, traces of white foam in the corner of its mouth around the bit. Antonio talks to it in a low, measured voice, and the animal slowly starts to calm, finally standing still and dropping its head.

'He's beautiful,' I say. 'Can I stroke him?'

'Of course. His name is Suerte. His first owners named him Diablo, Devil, but I prefer Suerte. It means luck, chance, fate. It is also the word used for when the bullfighter attacks or makes a pass.'

I reach out and stroke the horse's hot neck. Suerte shakes his head, and flies flit around. I rub in between his eyes as Antonio sits relaxed in the saddle, dropping the reins so they hang loose like empty washing lines either side of the horse's neck. A sure sign that he trusts his horse not to bolt off, I think. I'm not sure he feels the same about Miguel yet, though.

I run my hand over Suerte's mane, jet black with a white streak two thirds of the way down.

'Why is this bit white?'

Antonio looks down. 'He was attacked, when he was a young colt, by a bull. He defended himself, but the bull left its mark.' He runs his hand over the white streak. 'I found him, brought him back here to my grandparents. The owner had left him for dead. Apparently he had been a difficult horse. Angry, strong-willed, wouldn't be broken. He found it hard to trust for a long time, but we learned a way to work together. Like two dancers finding each other's rhythm and finally realising how they fit together.'

I feel tears prickle my eyes and I have no idea why.

'What about the other horses?'

'They're not all mine, but they are all Andalucían horses, pure bred. They are beautiful creatures. A famous horse master once said, "An Andalucían horse is born with the knowledge of how to do it; it is us that have to learn how to ask." I take on horses that . . . well, that people are finding difficult; with behaviour issues, shall we say. I listen to the horses and work with them.'

'So that's what you do, as well as the cherry farm? Is that why Valentina runs the restaurant?'

'Yes, I'm much better with horses than I am with people.'

'You're a horse whisperer!'

He laughs, a full, rich sound, a glint in his eyes. 'Well, you can call me what you like. I just do what I do.'

His laughter peters out, and a slightly awkward silence falls.

'Um, Antonio, about yesterday. I really feel I should explain . . .'

He looks down at me from the horse's back. My mouth goes as dry as the dusty path under my feet, which is already staining the edges of my white canvas shoes a light orange. I try and put my thoughts in order and then look up at him again, expecting to see him waiting for my explanation. But he's not looking at me; he's looking up, at the sky.

'You see, the thing is . . . that was my cousin. She's

very . . . It goes back a long way. We don't really get along because, well—'

'Ssh! Ssh!' He silences me mid-sentence and, understanding him a little better now, I stand and listen. In the background I can hear a buzzing noise.

'Is it the water system working again?' I glance around at the hosepipe, like a black snake running between the trees, but it's lying dormant, still.

He looks at me and shakes his head. Even Suerte stands still as if listening. Then Antonio holds up one finger and a smile spreads from the corner of his mouth across his face.

'Bees,' he says. 'We need the bees to pollinate the trees. No bees, no cherries. It is good to hear them working.'

'Ah.' I nod, and now that he's said it, I recognise the sound. I turn around and watch the bees, like jumbo jets roaring around the skies, as they fill their pollen sacs and head back to their hives in the far corner of the cherry orchard.

'They only fly when the temperature is between twelve and fifteen degrees.' Antonio swings his leg over the hindquarters of the horse and lands on the ground in front of me with a thump. 'If the weather is warming up, we're all happy.' He twitches an eyebrow. Clearly the bees bring out the best in him. 'Last thing we want is any more rain. Rain is a cherry farmer's worst nightmare. Cracks the cherries, splits them. Ruined!' he says, and I realise it's the longest conversation we've had. He's obviously comfortable talking horses and cherries.

Suddenly he whistles and waves his arms and shouts, making both me and the horse jump.

'Birds,' he tells me. 'The cherry farmer's other nightmare. We must get the trees netted . . . Miguel!' he shouts.

'Um, look, Antonio, about yesterday . . .'

'Ah, yes. You were telling your friend your plans for your place.' He hooks the reins over Suerte's head and starts to lead the horse back to the paddock.

'About that . . . It was . . .' I search for an explanation as I fall into step beside him, not looking him in the eye. 'I was just joking,' I say, only it was far from a laughing matter. 'It's complicated. She's my cousin, my only cousin, but we don't really get along . . .'

'And you think I should have more fairy lights down the drive?'

I can't read his face. I can't tell if he's about to call me out for being so presumptuous, or laugh at me. I stop walking, and to my surprise he does too. He actually looks as if he wants to hear my reply.

'Yes, I do,' I say. 'I think there's loads you could do with this place. I mean, if you wanted me to, I could suggest some things. Help out a bit more. I've got some thoughts I could—'

'It's Valentina you'll have to talk to. She's in charge around here. I have enough to do with the horses, the cherry trees and a watering system that's given up on me. I don't get involved in the restaurant . . . or do the washing-up. Tell your friend!'

He raises an eyebrow and I think he may be smiling as he walks off, leading the horse with one hand, waving at a flock of starlings with the other. He calls for Miguel again, and the young man appears with a cup of coffee in one hand and his phone in the other.

'*Hola*, Beti!' he smiles.

'*Hola*, Miguel!'

Antonio looks at Miguel and then at me, and a look washes over his face, as if an idea is forming there. But I have my own thoughts crashing around my head. Antonio is right. I need to get in Valentina's good books. Get her onside and then come up with some other money-making ideas. And if she likes them, I could get her to give me more work. Let's hope she comes back soon. Obviously the flamenco is a no-no. I still don't know why it's banned, and I'm desperate to find out more, but I don't think Antonio and I are on good enough terms for me to pry. At least yesterday's embarrassing events seem to be forgotten. And with Olivia and Gav gone, I can put it all behind me.

I say goodbye to Antonio and Miguel and tell them I'm going to the harbour to look for a job. As I leave, Antonio has started fiddling with the pump again, whilst Miguel carries on working on the nets. I can't help but think he must be starting to feel like a prisoner in his own home. There's no one of his own age around here. I hope he doesn't get too bored. Bored teenagers are the ones that find themselves in the most trouble. What he needs is a purpose. I think about my own situation, and how if I can earn the money for the bar, I'll be able to show everyone back home that I've achieved something to be proud of. I hope Miguel finds his way in life too, and soon.

Chapter Seventeen

Down by the harbour it's perfect weather. Blue skies, not a cloud to be seen and gloriously warm. The market is set up around the precinct, selling produce of all sorts: cheese, fish, meat, honey and vegetables, olives and oranges. There are also artists selling their paintings alongside potters and soap-makers. All under cream awnings that look like pointed straw hats. There's a relaxed, laid-back feel to the market, to match the gentle sunshine; a heady mix of English and Spanish voices, setting up stalls and sharing laughter and chat. A lull before the crowds of holidaymakers return in the school holidays. I look at the wonderful variety of foods and decide to wander round after I've found myself some work. I wish I had a hobby that made something I could sell here at the market, but I really can't think of anything.

Now to the task at hand. I intend to start at the beginning of the line of shops and restaurants along the harbour and work my way around. I take a deep breath and set off with determination.

After a 'no, sorry' from the gift shop, the kayak hire shop, the waterside bar – where the owner, from Dover, asked if I would be prepared to do topless waitressing – I reach the Pink Flamingo nightclub, where Will and I spent our last night together before he went off to play poker and my life as I knew it came to an abrupt end.

There's no one on the front desk by the cloakroom. I push through a dusty, sun-bleached purple curtain. It's dark inside the club, and it takes my eyes a moment to adjust. There on stage is Maxine, the manager, pacing out what looks to be a dance routine, holding a bottle of water in one hand, miming to a Cher number.

'Hello?' I call. 'Excuse me?'

'Oh!' she says peering into the dark. 'It's you – Beti, isn't it?' She steps down from the stage. 'You caught me in the act, so to speak. I manage this place now, but I can't help keeping my hand in. You never know when you might have to fill in.'

'Sorry, I didn't mean to interrupt. I just wondered if you had any work going – cleaning, anything? Daytimes really, because I work in a restaurant in the evening.'

'Sorry, love, I'm all fine with staff, unless you've got some fabulous tribute act I could book you for. With those looks I'm thinking you could do a great Adele.'

'Thanks, but no.' I hold up my hand, thinking that that just about sums up my pear shape and mousy brown hair. I've always been a bit embarrassed about my less-than-slender figure, so unlike Olivia's. But I'll take it as a compliment – Adele is a legend after all.

Maxine takes a swig of water.

'You're great!' I tell her. 'Have you always been Cher?'

'Well, I started off wanting to be the next Barbra Streisand, but then who doesn't?'

'Not me,' I laugh.

'I ended up as a dance teacher in my local village hall. Thought, "Is this it?" I wanted a change of direction and moved out here. And yes, there was a man behind it! I was doing bar work, anything I could get – a bit like you – and then I realised there was money to be made as a Cher lookalike. Did it at karaoke one night and then developed the act. It's not quite what I thought I'd end up doing, but hey! Now, how are the plans going for taking over the Butterfly Bar?'

I let out a long, slow blow of air.

'Why the sad face?' Maxine asks.

'Let's just say things aren't going how I'd hoped they would – and yes, there's a man behind it!'

We both laugh.

'Come on,' Maxine says. 'I'm meeting Craig for a drink. Looks like you could do with one too.'

'Oh no, really, I should get on. I need to find some work and check my emails. Though my phone's dead at the moment.'

'Plug it in at Brenda and Harold's. They won't mind. We could always work up that Adele tribute act!'

'I'm not sure,' I say slowly. 'I don't know if I'm ready to see everyone until I've got my money situation sorted.'

'Well, you know what they say, fake it until you make it. Never let the audience know you're bricking it!' Sensing I need a little more persuading, she puts her arm around me and directs me out of the club and in the direction of the Butterfly Bar.

Craig is already there when we arrive.

'What's it to be?' Harold asks cheerfully. 'Wine, sangria, cherry brandies?'

I smile and kiss him lightly on the cheek. I'm glad I came. I plug my phone in just inside the glass patio doors and wait for it to come back to life. It hasn't been charged since I threw it in the drawer a couple of days ago. Despite promising myself I wouldn't get it out for at least a week, I thought it might be useful if any jobs came up and I needed to give out my number.

'Just coffee for me, I have to work tonight,' I say, wondering if tonight will be as busy as it was yesterday.

Brenda joins us and shows us some new photos of their three grandsons. Then Craig and Maxine toss around ideas for my tribute act, which is never going to happen. I hate getting up on stage. I hated it at school, when we had to do singing, dancing and poetry competitions for the annual eisteddfod. I was quite good at Welsh folk dancing, actually, but I hated every second of being stared at. But Olivia sang and everybody made a fuss of that, of course.

Finally there is enough juice in my phone for it to blink back to life. There seem to be a number of Facebook messages for me, so I click on the app and scroll through them. The colour drains from my face and my heart seems to stop momentarily.

Olivia has posted an album of photographs of Cortijo Ana showing the busy terrace and all the cherry blossom around it. It's titled 'My cousin's restaurant', and underneath she has added: 'Very proud of my cousin finally living the dream!'

Oh God! Everyone's going to think I own this place! I have to get her to take it down. I can't let this get any more out of hand. Even my mum has commented: 'Me and Dad are so proud of you, Beti!'

Oh no! Tears prick my eyes. How could I have let this happen? Why didn't I think before going along with Olivia's silly assumption? Of course it wasn't going to go away as soon as she left. She may be out of my world here, but she must have gone straight back home and told everyone! Holy moly, the album has already been liked seventeen times! How do I get this to stop?

As I'm trying to work out what exactly to say to Olivia, a message pops up on Facebook Messenger. I check and then double-check. My eyes blur and then refocus. It's Will.

'You all right, Beti?' says Craig.

'You've gone very pale,' says Maxine. 'Don't tell me, it's the man behind the mess you're in!'

Olivia's photo album blurs into the background as Will's message practically glows at me. I'm holding my breath and I wonder if he's holding his, waiting for me to reply. I feel hot and bothered.

Hi, I finally type.

Just seen Olivia's pictures. Your place looks fab. Always knew you'd do it. I really am sorry for everything. I hope you can forgive me some day.

I'm trying to work out what to say, how to tell him I want to kill him, how to tell him he's ruined everything, when the little green light beside his name goes out and he's gone.

How dare he just pop up like that, say sorry and then leave . . . again? I'm furious! He took my money and my dreams, and now he thinks it's OK to drop by and say hi as though we're old mates.

Then I spot another message Olivia has posted.

'Looks like I've found the perfect venue for my thirtieth

birthday! Who's up for a party at my cousin's place in Spain?'

Oh no. No, no, no, no, nooooooo! This can't be happening. There is no way she can have her birthday party at Cortijo Ana! My mouth has gone dry and my head is aching as I reread the post. There are thirty-two likes, and my name is tagged under a photo of me and Olivia outside the restaurant. I am almost hyperventilating.

Silently Brenda puts a large brandy glass in front of me, with an umbrella and a hunk of orange balanced on the rim, which slowly slides off and on to the table. I flick off the umbrella and down the cherry brandy in one go, feeling the burn. Somehow, I have to put a stop to this.

Chapter Eighteen

Hi, Olivia! I type on Messenger, my heart still pounding.

Hey, Bet. How's sunny Spain? she types back immediately with a smiley face. She's never usually this friendly to me. Suddenly, after thirty years as reluctant cousins, our relationship has completely changed, now that she thinks I can give her what she wants.

Getting hotter! I type, trying to work out how I'm going to tell her the truth.

What do you think of the photos? Should get you loads of publicity. She adds another smiley face.

Great, I reply. And they were – well, of the restaurant and Olivia. I had my eyes shut in mine, and I certainly wasn't smiling. My finger hovers over the keys. *About your idea for a party . . .* I type.

Yes!! Brilliant, isn't it? And of course, you've organised enough engagement parties, so you'd be able to sort the whole thing out, a real Spanish-themed bash. You could do one of your mood boards and send it over.

I'm really sorry, no, that's not going to be possible, I type, adding a sad face.

What? Why not?! I can hear her voice as she types. Like the princess that she is, Olivia doesn't ever expect to hear the word 'no'.

It's just too busy, I tell her, even though I know that by next week, when the cherry blossom has gone, it will be back to just a few locals every night.

Well book it in now! June, the second weekend! she demands.

June, I think: just when my time here will be coming to an end. If I haven't found the deposit and first month's rent on this place, well, that's when I'll be going home. June, the cherry harvest. Like the cherry trees being stripped of their fruit, I'll be back to having nothing, starting from scratch again.

I'm sorry, it's just not possible.

But Gav's paying for everything as my birthday present: hire of the venue and the cost of food, drink and entertainment. It could be a really good earner for you!

I'm sure, but . . . I start to write.

Here's the budget! She sends over a figure before I've had a chance to finish.

My eyes almost pop out of my head. How can people spend that kind of money on a party? That can't be right.

I'm not a party organiser, I don't have the experience to lay on an event for that many people, I try again.

Yes you do! You've organised three engagement parties and planned three weddings. And they've all been like military operations. Surely you can organise a birthday party! Especially when it's your own venue!

It hits me, hard. That is what I've spent my adult life doing. Whilst others have had careers, homes and families, I've been planning weddings that never happened, chasing my happy-ever-after that never came.

Purleeeeese! Olivia is begging now. *It would really knock the socks off some of the other thirtieths. Some people are doing nightclubs or skydiving, but a party in a place that my family owns in southern Spain would be perfect.*

So that's it. A place her family owns! She wants people to think she has a piece of prime real estate in Spain. Something else to brag about. My hackles start to rise. Then I reread the figure she's sent over. It is so hard to turn down – this could change everything.

Gav will send a deposit, she persists.

It's exactly what I need, extra income to pay for the Butterfly Bar. It's what Antonio needs too: actual customers when the blossom has gone and the locals have tired of Valentina's world-food menu. My brain is turning over slowly. I couldn't really do this, could I? It would solve everything if I could just pull it off. One big party and this place would be mine. My eyes are drinking in the Butterfly Bar and the friendly locals as if it's the first time I've ever seen it and I'm falling in love with it again. It's perfect. It's the one! I think of Will. Am I really going to let him ruin everything?

OK, I type. *I'll check the diary.*

Woo-hoo! This is going to be the best thirtieth party any of them has seen! I win! It's so retro! Rustic Spain! Make sure it's the best party you've ever put on, Bet! My whole reputation is riding on this!

I think of Olivia and her wealthy circle of friends, all competing for the best parties and weddings. I think of my mum and dad, how proud they will be when I've got something to show for my life. I think of Uncle Paul's face. *Everything* rides on this! I put my phone down on the table and look around.

'I think I'll have another cherry brandy,' I say, and for the first time in weeks I finally have something to smile about. Life is about to get back on track.

'To new beginnings,' says Brenda, and Maxine clinks her glass with mine. Now all I have to do is convince Antonio.

Chapter Nineteen

'No, no way. Sorry, but no,' he says firmly.

Maybe he hasn't heard me right. He wouldn't be saying no if he understood what I was telling him.

'She wants a party, here at Cortijo Ana. A big one, for her thirtieth birthday. A themed event, pulling out all the stops. A party that everyone will remember. She's even sent me the budget. Her boyfriend's paying for it as a present. He'll give us a deposit up front and the rest in June, at the party. It could be a real money-spinner for this place, and if you got more events like it . . . well. It could really turn things around. And I've got . . .' my mouth goes dry, 'a fair bit of experience in planning events.'

A gust of wind blows ups, and blossom swirls around us like confetti. Miguel is in the cherry orchard, mending more of the nets.

'No, no big parties.' Antonio is using the hose to fill the water trough in the horses' paddock.

'But why not?' I follow him as the water reaches the top of the trough and he goes to turn off the tap.

'Birthday parties here are family gatherings, a meal together, maybe cake. They are not big themed parties. There's a place for that down at the harbour. Try the Pink

Flamingo. Or even the beach bar. I believe they have topless waitresses.'

'No, you don't understand. It's this place she wants. It has . . . rustic charm!' I smile. 'It's different from the places down at the harbour.'

'I do understand.' He winds up the hosepipe and hangs it over the tap, then straightens up and looks at me. 'Balloons and castanets, piñatas and pints. She thinks she is having a Spanish party, but that is not the real Spain at all!'

He walks into the barn and comes out carrying a bridle and a long leading rein, then heads back to the paddock. I follow him and stand in front of the gate. I can't let him say no, I just can't.

'But Valentina wants the tourists. She wants the young professionals with money. That's exactly what these people are.'

'Excuse me, please,' he says, and I step aside. He puts the bridle on his shoulder, then, instead of going through the gate, climbs the fence, swinging his long legs over it, and sets off purposefully across the dusty paddock towards the group of horses standing under the tree, swishing at early-morning flies with their tails. I call after him.

'Can't you ask Valentina? See if she thinks it's a good idea?'

He is talking quietly to the horses, stroking their necks. The young colt dances around, sidestepping him. But finally he settles, and Antonio slides the bridle over his head with very little objection. Then he starts to walk back towards me.

'Valentina is still catching up with her work in the harbour. Meetings and stuff,' he tells me, even though I haven't asked about her whereabouts. 'She has an apartment there. We are both happy keeping our lives separate.' He nods to indicate that he's given enough away as he leads the young horse out of the gate.

'So you'll ask her about the party?' I say hopefully.

Suddenly the colt explodes in youthful exuberance, leaping and dipping and kicking out. Antonio holds on to the young horse, following him and letting him blow himself out before leading him into a smaller paddock. Then he turns and looks at me.

'And what do you get out of this party? Why so insistent?' he frowns, putting me on the spot. I look back to see that Miguel has his headphones on and is oblivious to our conversation.

'It . . . it's my cousin. It's *her* birthday,' I say with a sigh that I didn't mean to come out.

'The one who was here the other evening?'

'Yes.' My shoulders drop at the memory, but I get the feeling Antonio is almost enjoying it.

'The one who wanted me to wash up?' he carries on.

'Yes, yes . . . just a misunderstanding.' I try and move things along.

Antonio turns to the horse and urges him forward into a walk with a clicking noise in the corner of his mouth. The horse suddenly dips and jumps and kicks again, leaping this way and that. Antonio follows the animal, giving it its head, and slowly pulls it back towards him, soothing, talking in gentle tones but never letting go of the rein, no matter how many times the animal dips and rears, until miraculously it starts to walk along the worn track. As it strides out, at first it tosses its head and pulls on the rein. Antonio speaks calmly, settling it again, and the horse slowly starts to respond, finally dropping his head and forming a beautiful curve like the black stallion.

I watch in wonder, and glance over to see if Miguel is watching too. But he isn't. He's hunched over the nets, hood up, checking his phone with one hand. The horse now seems to be going steadily through its paces on the track, making the transition from walking to trotting and back again, its mane flowing with each rhythmic step. And then suddenly Antonio turns his attention back to me.

'Like I say, what's in it for you?' he asks not taking his eyes off the colt. I'm still in awe of him working his magic with the young horse.

'Er . . .' I try and refocus on my own dilemma. 'Well, more hours basically. If I'm organising and planning the party, I can make up my money now that I'm not needed at the burger bar down at the harbour.'

'Whoa,' he tells the horse, and it obediently and surprisingly comes to a standstill. Antonio takes his eyes off it for a moment and looks over at me. I hold my breath. Is he going to agree? A ripple of excitement runs up and down my spine, making me shiver. Then he lifts his chin, clicks in the corner of his mouth and the horse sets off again with a dip of the head.

'I'm sorry. It's not possible.' Antonio's focus is back on the horse.

'What?'

'It's June. Nothing can happen in June. It's the cherry harvest.' He nods towards the trees. 'This is what is important around here. These trees and the harvest. The restaurant will close. I need all the hands I can get. If I don't focus on my harvest, I could lose everything. I can't have any distractions.' His face darkens, and something tells me I really shouldn't ask any more. 'However . . .'

'Yes?' I feel a skip of hopefulness in my dipping spirits.

'If you want more work . . . What with the sprinkler system broken, I have to do everything by hand. So if you need extra hours, I will pay you to water the trees for me. That is the water bowser.' He nods towards the orchard, where a big rusting orange barrel on wheels is sitting.

I sigh. '*Gracias*,' I say.

'*De nada*.' He nods in reply.

Extra hours *is* what I need. I just hadn't expected it to be that. What on earth am I going to tell Olivia? Right now she thinks I'm organising her birthday party. And how on earth does a water bowser work?

Antonio felt the tug on the lunging rein, him at one end, the colt at the other, the two of them working together. He glanced across at Beti, who had walked over to talk to Miguel. The boy was still sitting on the ground working on the nets, but he had pulled out his headphones and was showing her what he was doing. She seemed to be able to talk to Miguel far more easily than he could. In fact, she seemed to be able to turn her hand to pretty much anything. He'd seen how she'd saved the day at Pedro's mother's eightieth.

He looked at her again. He would have liked to agree to the party, as a way of thanking her and making sure she stayed on. She was certainly a good worker. But he couldn't have any distractions during the harvest. He'd taken his eye off the ball once before and nearly lost the lot. It must never happen again. The farm had to come first. He had to make sure that nothing threatened it. Not the birds – he looked up at the electricity wire where they were gathering – not a themed party at the restaurant, and certainly not Miguel's mother. He'd had another message from her, and a letter as well, from a solicitor, repeating in formal language that she wanted a divorce and half of everything. Of course! Now that she'd seen the photographs Miguel had sent her, she suddenly thought she was on to a big payout!

He finished by working the colt the other way around the circle and then led him back to his mother, who fussed and nuzzled him on his return. The young horse was coming on a treat. It would be a shame to sell him. He had something special about him; Antonio could feel it.

He looked over to where Miguel and Beti were standing together, looking at the water bowser, laughing and joking about it. He shook his head. Horses he could understand; his son, on the other hand, was a completely different challenge. Other than that fleeting moment when they'd got the pump to work, he couldn't connect with him at all. He had no idea what he was thinking. Did Miguel want to be here? Did he want to go home? Or was he planning to make a new life for himself somewhere completely different? Antonio needed to find a way of getting to know him.

He turned and walked back to the pump in the middle of the courtyard. If he couldn't get the cherries watered, he wouldn't have a harvest to pick or a farm to fight for. He flicked out his foot in frustration, and the pump shuddered, chugged into life for a hopeful moment and then fell silent again. Thank God he had extra help in Miguel and Beti. He watched as the two of them turned on the hose and attempted to spray each other. She was intriguing. Totally eccentric! There was that evening with her cousin for starters, and he'd heard her talking to the cat as well. Who was she really? And what was she doing living here on her own, watering cherry trees and washing up? He knew nothing about her, but she might just be the answer to his prayers. If she could handle a water bowser like she could Bonita in the kitchen, and if she could keep Miguel from getting into any more trouble, she might just turn out to be a godsend.

Chapter Twenty

'How often have we got to do this?' Miguel huffs as he pulls the trailer whilst I walk behind sprinkling the roots of the trees.

'Well, Antonio said they need to be watered every couple of days, what with the heat here. There are four fields. How many trees?'

'Three hundred and fifty,' Miguel sighs.

'So, if we do this field now and the next one this evening before the restaurant opens, and then the other two tomorrow, we should be about right. And then we have to finish netting the trees once all the blossom has gone.' I think back to the branches I picked on my first day here. Every branch will bear fruit for the harvest. I can't believe I didn't think about it at the time.

The wheels on the trailer squeak as they turn. There is a gentle hiss as I spray the roots, trying to remember Antonio's instructions about how long to keep the water on each tree before moving on to the next one. '*Un, dos, tres . . .*' I mouth. Above me, the birds are chattering on the wire, as if passing on the locations of the best cherry-picking locations this season.

'So how are you settling in?' I ask as Miguel moves the

bowser on to the next tree and I follow. Ana the cat has come to join us, darting up and down the tree trunks. 'How are you finding life here in Colina de Flor?'

'It's boring. There's nothing to do here!'

'Well, I wouldn't say nothing exactly.' I look at all the trees we're going to have to water by hand. Still, I'm very grateful for the wages.

'There's no one, nobody!' He stops pulling the trailer and holds his arms out. 'Just birds! Hello, birds!' He waves up at them, making me laugh. 'And horses! Hello, horses!' He glances apprehensively towards the paddock. 'And I'm definitely not getting near one of them,' he says.

'But Antonio is amazing with them,' I say, still impressed.

'I clearly don't have my father's genes. I wouldn't know one end of a horse from the other.'

'You didn't do much riding growing up then?' I point the hosepipe and start to spray. *Un, dos, tres* . . . I count silently in my head.

'You could say that. Where I grew up, there weren't horses and fields. Just gangs from different apartment blocks or families. I didn't even know places like this existed! Even though my dad was here all along . . .' He trails off, as if he's said too much.

'Is that why you came here, to see what it was like?'

He sighs deeply, as if from the depths of his soul. Perhaps, I think, depths that such a young man shouldn't really have.

'My mother is one of life's "free spirits".' He crooks his fingers in inverted commas to demonstrate. 'She hated living where we did. But she had family there, sisters and their husbands and children. My cousins.' He rolls his eyes. I know how he feels about cousins, but I don't interrupt him. He clearly isn't used to talking about this. 'Neither she nor her "boyfriend"' – more inverted commas – 'ever really worked. They are flamenco dancers. They take part in the odd show, but nothing regular. They lived in the apartment with my aunt. I slept on the settee and went to school. They said they were living there so I could get an education, and they never let me forget it. But actually it was because they had no money and nowhere to go. Apparently my mother's career was on hold because of me. She said she could have been a huge name had she not had to take time out to bring up a child. They said it was my fault they were stuck there and not on the road, touring, dancing. I was an annoyance to them. They couldn't wait for me to leave. And neither could I. But where would I go?' He shrugs, seeming almost oblivious to me now, reliving his story.

'It was noisy, crowded where we lived . . . and a bit dangerous. But it was all I knew, it was my home. And I could handle myself,' he adds quickly. 'It was just this one day . . . I was late. I took a short cut. Met the wrong people down a side street, two rival gangs: one my cousin and his lot, and another family from a different apartment block. There was a fight. They thought I was there for my cousin. Like I say, I can handle myself. It wasn't the first time I'd had to fight his battles for him.'

I can see the fire behind his eyes, a deep passion that probably comes from self-preservation. He can protect himself because he's had to, and not just from street gangs but from the bullies at home as well, by the sound of it.

'My aunt wanted me to leave. My mother had warned that

if there was any more trouble, she'd send me to go and live with my dad. And here I am!' He holds out his arms, then drops them to his sides. 'We've never even really met properly.'

My heart twists. I can see the pain burning like fire in his eyes; I can practically feel the hurt, like he's touched a raw nerve.

'Do you have family?' he asks.

'Um, yes.' I nod reluctantly, but he clearly wants to know more, having told me all about himself. 'Well, not children.' It catches in my throat. 'But my mum and dad,' and I feel a sudden rush of love for them, realising that this is something this young man clearly hasn't felt. 'I have an uncle and aunt, and a cousin too. My uncle, he . . . well, he always makes me feel bad about myself, puts me down.' I rush out the words, feeling they might resonate with Miguel. 'We all grew up near each other. My dad and his brother worked at the same place, the same factory, but my uncle always wanted to do better than my dad: a better house, better car. He got promoted and liked to look down on my dad because of it. His daughter, my cousin, was always doing better than me, or so he told us. I tried to keep up with her, but we couldn't afford all the things she had. I didn't think it bothered me. But clearly it did. I spent years trying to prove to the world that I could have something lovely of my own, by planning a wedding – well, three, actually . . .'

'Three?'

'I was engaged to my last fiancé Will for nearly five years. And I had two engagements before that, if you can believe it!' I find myself nearly laughing as I realise how ridiculous it sounds, saying it out loud. Five years!!

'But why? Why is your uncle so down on your dad?'

I stop and look around at the cherry trees we've watered and the ones we've still got to do. Well, I might as well tell him; we've got a lot of time to fill.

'I suppose it was because of my mum really. When they were all much younger, Uncle Paul was hoping to ask her out. He took my dad along to the local dance for moral support. But when my mum and dad met . . . well, they just knew they were meant to be together. And that was that. I don't think Uncle Paul ever got over it. He's been punishing them ever since.'

'And they're still married?'

'They are!' I smile at the thought of my mum at home, my dad in the garden. They just fit together. Oh, that's not to say they don't argue – they do! They're not perfect. But they're meant to be together.

'And Uncle Paul?'

'He married Rita.' I give a little laugh. 'They met shortly after Dad and Mum announced their engagement, and got married just before them. A big showy do in a hotel. My mum and dad were just having a small get-together in the back room of the local pub.'

'Are they still together, Uncle Paul and Rita?'

I laugh again. 'Yes, they're still together. Rita has her own hair salon, but her staff can't stand her. She likes her gin bottle more than she likes Paul. But she also likes her house on the big estate and her daughter getting the best Daddy can afford!'

'You're lucky that you have parents who love you.' Miguel has a wistful look in his eyes. 'I mean, my mum resented me because I stopped her travelling, stopped her career. And her boyfriend? He hates me because of who my father is.'

'Who your father is? Antonio?'

'Uh huh.' He nods. 'He hates Antonio.' The words seem to hang in the air.

As we reach the end of the row, the sun is starting to heat up, and with it the swapping of our parents' stories slowly comes to a natural end. I go to the front of the bowser and help heave it up the hill to the next terrace, where I can see bits of the watering system's piping that have perished in the sun.

'And what about now?' Miguel asks as I start to water the first tree in the row. 'Where is your fiancé now?'

I'm jolted by the question, as if all my insides are trying to work out how they fit together. 'Let's just say . . . I'm trying to get over him. He . . . Will left me. Three days after we'd arrived here to start our new life together.'

'He left you?'

I nod, wondering if I trust myself to say any more. I take a deep breath. 'And took my savings. It was my wedding fund, but we'd decided to use it to rent a bar. It kind of finished before it started, my new life,' and I'm suddenly spilling the contents of my heart like a genie being released from its bottle.

'So that's how you ended up in Spain. But you're still here, at Cortijo Ana.'

'Yes, I'm still here. I haven't told my family about Will yet. I'm going to rent the bar on my own. Show everyone I can do what I set out to do. And I am never getting engaged or making plans to get married again!'

'Ha! Never say never,' Miguel laughs. 'And where is your bar, the one you're going to rent?'

'Down at the harbour. You should go down there, see if you can make some friends. I'll take you down if you like. Show you around. I could show you the bar.' A little surge of pride rises up in me.

He breaks into a wide smile. 'I'd like that. Thank you.' He nods. 'Who knows, I may find a whole new gang.'

'Miguel!' I warn, sounding like my mum.

'Just joking.' He waves a hand. 'I'm not sorry to be away from where I came from. I . . .' He pauses and looks around. 'I just don't know where I'm going, that's the problem.'

'Nor do any of us really,' I say. 'You can only hope it's in the right direction.' I realise that I have spent so many years trying to plan my life, but you never know what's around the corner. I flick the spray of water at him.

'Hey!'

'Shall we go to the harbour then?' I ask as we pull the empty, now much lighter water bowser back to the old stone barns. 'I could ask Bonita if I can get any shopping for her while I'm there. Perhaps she could do another special dish if it's going to be busy again. That way you can go and explore without me chaperoning you.'

'Sounds like a plan. Wouldn't want you cramping my style,' he replies. I flick the hose in his direction again and a last bit of water arcs out of it. He laughs.

'Better check with your . . . with Antonio,' I tell him. 'There'll be a bus soon.'

Having cleared it with Antonio, we travel in companionable silence to the harbour, lost in our own thoughts.

Sunset over the Cherry Orchard

After introducing Miguel to Harold, Brenda, Craig and Maxine, I arrange to meet him back at the Butterfly Bar, wondering if this is what it would be like to have a younger brother. As I sit back in the warm spring sunshine outside the bar with Craig and Maxine and catch up on the tales of the crazy holidaymakers, I can't help but smile. This place is starting to feel a lot like home.

Chapter Twenty-one

It's been ten days since we started watering the cherry trees by hand. It's now the middle of April and I have been at Cortijo Ana for just over two weeks, though it feels like so much longer. I've started going down to the harbour regularly with Miguel and shopping for Bonita, who is now cooking one traditional rustic Spanish dish every night. They have been selling out as visitors come to see the blossom before it disappears. And more locals have come to try them too, calling out from the souvenir shop or the bakery and even the taverna to ask what Bonita's daily special is.

Harold and Brenda introduced me to the fisherman who comes to the bar. I've also met some other producers in the market, cheese makers and local veg suppliers. My bargaining skills from organising all those weddings have come in handy on a number of occasions. So far Bonita has cooked *pollo al ajillo*, garlic chicken; *pisto*, a rich ratatouille bursting with onions, garlic, tomatoes, courgettes and peppers slow fried in olive oil, served with fried eggs and *pan rustico*; big fluffy Spanish omelettes with green salad; and *paella* like I've never tasted before, with rabbit, saffron, runner beans and fat, sweet prawns. Word has been spreading, locals alternating between the taverna and Cortijo Ana in the evenings.

I've seen Valentina again in the market, and she asked what I was doing.

'Just getting a few bits for the kitchen.' I tried to smile, but it was met with frostiness. Then she asked after 'the boy', and once again I told her he was doing just fine and settling in well. She lifted her head, and walked off on her high spiky heels. Still feeling taken for granted by the looks of it, and making sure Antonio knows it.

'Miguel! Miguel,' I call. It's evening, time to water the trees, but he's nowhere to be seen . . . again! He's done this a couple of times in the last week. Vanishing when it's watering time. I stand over the bowser, filling it from the tap by the horses' paddock. There is a gust of wind and the white blossom swirls around me, making me feel like I'm in a snow globe, then flutters to the ground. It's started: the blossom snow, when the petals fall from the trees. I stand in the gently swirling blossom and let myself enjoy the moment, as if I was a child again, feeling the fluttering of snowflakes on my skin and face.

'Have you found him?' Antonio's deep voice makes me jump.

'Er, no, he's just nipped to the bathroom, I think.' I find myself covering for Miguel.

'He . . . I just . . .' He trails off, then starts again. 'He's been off down the harbour a lot this week. He doesn't know the place or his way around. I just . . .'

I realise that Antonio is worried about him.

'He's fine. He's just been finding his feet. Exploring the place,' I try to reassure him. And he has. He goes off for a couple of hours while I join the others at the Butterfly Bar or shop in the market for Bonita. And then we meet up and travel back on the bus together.

'He's unhappy. I think he hates it here,' Antonio says bluntly, taking me by surprise. 'But from what I saw, I'm pretty sure he hates where he came from too. I saw it in his eyes. He doesn't know where he belongs right now. He barely speaks to me. The last thing I want is for him to run away. But it has been over two weeks now and he hasn't even unpacked his bag properly yet. I'm worried he'll just go. And, well, I'll have let him down . . . again.' He doesn't seem to realise that he's talking out loud. 'I haven't seen him all afternoon. He wasn't there before siesta and he's still not back.' I can see he doesn't believe that Miguel has gone to the bathroom. 'He doesn't stay with you when you go to the harbour; you let him go off on his own?'

'Of course. He's not a child, Antonio. He's making friends . . .' I trail off. Antonio's eyebrows lower and his face darkens. I can see how concerned he is. Suddenly I start to feel worried too. What if Miguel has decided to leave, move on somewhere to get away from here? What if he wasn't joking about finding a new gang to hook up with? What if, while I've been shopping and having coffee at the Butterfly Bar, he's been making plans to flee? He might be out there now, on his own. What if something happens to him? My heart starts racing. This is my fault! I was the one who suggested going to the harbour! Oh God!

'I'll check the square,' Antonio says. 'See if he's waiting for a bus.'

'I'll go to the top field. He might be looking for signal

on his phone.' I point up the slope towards my *finca*.

'Miguel!' I call, and break into a run up the zigzag path.

I'm halfway up when I stop suddenly, listen and look around. I'm sure I can hear something. A sort of banging noise; a thumping or beating.

'Miguel?' I call again more urgently, looking this way and that. I head in the direction of my *finca*, the blossom flying in front of my face as I run. Then I turn and look back down the orchard, taking in the full vista of the valley below. I'm bound to spot him from here. I scan the fields of white cherry trees as they fall away from the *finca* towards the restaurant on the right, the barns and paddock on the left and the town square beyond that. I can see Antonio, out on the road heading for the square. I hear the thumping noise again. But where's it coming from? There's nothing up here! My heart starts racing. What if he's in another fight, getting beaten up?

'MIGUEL?' I shout as loudly as I can, with my hands around my mouth, panic rising in me, fingers of fear wrapping themselves around my throat. The thumping sound has stopped. Now it's just the birds twittering their excitement and the wind in the branches of the cherry trees.

'Hey, Beti!'

I spin round to the top corner of the cherry orchard. Relief floods over me as I see Miguel running towards me from the direction of the old barn adjoining my little *finca*.

'Miguel? Are you OK?'

'Yes, of course. Why? What is it? I heard you shouting.'

'Your dad . . . Antonio was worried about you. We couldn't find you. He thought you might have left. I was worried too!' I manage to return his smile. He doesn't look like he's been beaten up. A bit out of breath, maybe, but happy enough. In fact, happier than I've seen him in a long time. 'You keep vanishing into thin air. Where do you disappear off to?'

'Tell him I snuck out for a cigarette.' He breaks into a laugh.

'Did you?' I feel like his older sister again.

'No, no.' He shakes his head and laughs some more.

'Have you been meeting someone?'

'No, of course not! I don't know anyone! I was just getting a signal on my phone.' He waggles it at me. But he can get a signal in the apartment. And I can't help but wonder who he's phoning, if he's cut off all links with his friends and family. I have a feeling that he's hiding something.

'Come on, Beti, let's water some cherry trees,' he says, slinging his arm lazily around my shoulders and guiding me quickly back down the hill towards the restaurant.

And I have to admit, I'm relieved.

'And find your . . .' I trail off. He still looks uncomfortable at the word dad. 'Go and find Antonio,' I correct myself, 'and tell him you're OK.'

'OK, as long as you don't make me call him Dad!' he grins cheekily. I smile with relief. He's all right, I reassure myself. He hasn't got into anything dodgy. I allow my shoulders to relax, letting the sun work its magic on my face, drinking in the beauty and tranquillity of this spot.

Suddenly there's a bang behind me, making me jump. I turn round. The barn door next to my *finca* is swinging open. I narrow my eyes and peer up the hill, but there's no one there. Or was there? Did I catch something, a shadow disappearing into the trees? Or is my imagination running away with me, with all this talk of trouble?

'Just the wind,' Miguel tells me, and smiles widely. 'I'll go and shut it.' He turns and jogs away back up the path.

But as I look into the dark shadows of the woods beyond the *finca*, I can't help but feel there's more to this than just the wind.

Chapter Twenty-two

We walk back down the hill, both in thoughtful contemplation, towards the restaurant and the waiting bowser. My arms ache just thinking about the work they're going to do. What do I tell Antonio? Should I let him know I have a sneaking suspicion something's going on in the barn, or should I say nothing? After all, Miguel is fine.

'You can pull this time if you like, and I'll spray!' Miguel tries to make light of the work we're about to do. We round the corner by the horses' paddock and see Antonio standing in the middle of the empty car park.

'Hey! Antonio! It's OK, I've found him!' I call over to him. 'He was just skiving off!' I add in a lower voice, so that only Miguel can hear me. He nudges me jokingly, knocking me slightly off balance, like a playful pup.

Antonio looks up at us as we near the barns, and an expression of relief spreads across his face. At the same time, a small red car pulls into the car park at speed, spraying dust, making him step back and wave a hand in front of his face.

The car door opens and Valentina slides out, then steps forward, reaching up and wrapping her arms around Antonio's neck and kissing him full on the lips.

I feel Miguel's shoulders sag, as do mine. I have a feeling

things are going to be a bit different around here from now on. Miguel goes quiet, as if he's retreated back into his shell, and he slips his hood up, despite the warm sunshine.

Antonio is holding Valentina by the upper arms, clearly making his apologies. She looks suitably placated and smiles at him, pushing her body up against his and talking in low tones, looking sultry. Obviously the air has been cleared and promises have been made. Then they both turn to look at us, Valentina's arm possessively around Antonio, stroking the back of his neck. Antonio looks relieved. Valentina looks ready for battle, clearly seeing Miguel as a rival for Antonio's affections.

'She hates me being here,' Miguel says in a low voice. I reach out and rub his arm, not knowing what else to do. 'I'll get the bowser up to the top field,' he says, obviously deciding to postpone the meeting, and I'm not sure I blame him. The Miguel I have got to know over the last two weeks seems to have disappeared, like the blossom falling from the trees.

I take a deep breath and pull down the hem of my long T-shirt so it nearly touches the edge of my denim shorts. Valentina nods at me, then turns to Antonio, telling him she's going to the restaurant. She lifts her head, shakes out her hair, then marches on her high heels over the rough ground to the terrace, her large handbag hooked over her arm.

'I rang her,' Antonio tells me. 'Asked her to come. I told her I'd taken her for granted, not telling her I was bringing Miguel to live here – but then I didn't even know myself. I have agreed to make it up to her.' I detect a reluctance in him, but he's doing what he feels he needs to do to keep things together. 'Miguel needs a friend,' he continues. 'I've seen how you get on with him. Maybe he will respond better to a woman, someone younger than me.'

'And Valentina?' I dare to ask.

He looks over at her as she strides towards the restaurant.

'Valentina needs commitment from me. A plan for our future. She needs to be listened to,' he says thoughtfully. 'I'm just not sure how I can give her that . . .' He trails off, deep in thought.

I turn towards the restaurant, bracing myself to explain to Valentina about the rearranged tables and Bonita's specials.

'Oh, and Beti.' Antonio stops me in my tracks. For a brief moment I wonder if he's going to tell me that Miguel will be taking over the washing-up and I'm no longer needed. 'Thank you for finding him,' he says, taking me by surprise. 'I'm sure I was worrying about nothing.' And there and then, I decide to say nothing about the barn door. 'I'm sure things will be easier now that Valentina has agreed to come back and help out,' he adds, and even though I don't agree, I try and smile anyway.

I slip in through the back door of the kitchen, by the sink. Bonita is standing by the stove, simmering like the contents of the big pot she's stirring.

Valentina is looking in the fridge, shaking her head, pulling out ingredients. 'No, no, no!' she says. 'No specials! We must stick to the menu!'

Bonita puts down her big wooden spoon and comes to get a large metal frying pan from beside the sink. She looks as if she might use it as a weapon if provoked any more.

'She says no to the specials,' she growls to me out of the corner of her mouth.

'But your specials are selling really well!' I whisper.

She shrugs, her neck disappearing into her shoulders, making her look like a human ball.

Valentina slams the fridge door shut and stalks into the bar.

'She wants to keep the menu how it was,' Bonita tells me. 'We are a modern world-food restaurant that the discerning tourists will want to visit, apparently.'

'But they're coming for the blossom and your home-cooked food!'

Suddenly there is a shout from inside the *cortijo*; more like a shriek really, as if a mouse has run out, or worse.

I hurry through the bar and then round to the rooms on the other side.

'Who has done this?' Valentina is looking at the storeroom and the old kitchen I decorated for the dinner.

'That was me.' I try to sound apologetic, but at the same time I'm feeling quite proud. 'It was raining, you see, so we thought . . . I thought . . .'

Valentina's face darkens and I feel like I've come face to face with a raging, barely contained bull. She starts pulling at the fairy lights that I draped around the fireplace and the shelves.

'No, no, no! No fairy lights! And definitely no old pots!' She sweeps up all the jugs I arranged along the whitewashed shelf and with her arms full of them marches to the cupboard and drops them in with a clatter. I think about arguing that the customers loved the decor, but decide against it. I still need to work here. It's not my place. I'm just the washer-upper.

'No fairy lights, no terracotta pots and no rustic specials! We stick to the menu.' She picks one up and waves it at me.

'But . . .' I suddenly feel a rush of loyalty towards Bonita, and for Antonio, who is trying to run his farm and his horses and could clearly do with the money if the ancient water system is anything to go by. 'People round here don't want this sort of food. It's too . . . confused,' I finish before I can stop myself.

'It's classy, that's what it is!' She stalks out to the terrace, where Antonio is waiting, one arm folded across his chest, the other hand pulling at his little goatee beard. 'We are becoming known for being a boutique restaurant. Not some rural rustic *finca*! Isn't that right, Antonio?' She looks to him for backup, but he shrugs and holds out a hand, as if to say he neither knows nor really cares and has other worries on his mind. He looks over at the redundant pump.

'Have the trees been watered?' he asks, unable to stop himself making his priorities totally clear. I get the impression the restaurant is more of an irritation in Antonio's life than a business he cares about.

'Just about to,' I tell him, seizing the moment.

This could work for all of us. It could be just what Valentina wants to hear. If she doesn't like it, if she decides my time is up, so be it. I have no other option. This is my final chance at pulling this party off. The party that is the ticket to a place of my own.

'Look, Valentina,' I say. 'I have a friend . . .' I can't bear to admit that Olivia is actually my cousin.

'A friend?' She raises a highly plucked eyebrow.

'She wants to book a big party for her thirtieth. She'd be bringing lots of people over from the UK. They'd want a meal, a bar, maybe some entertainment and dancing later.'

'For a birthday party?' She looks bemused. 'Sounds more like a wedding.'

'The thing is, she wants it here, at Cortijo Ana. She has a big budget. And if she's happy, she will have a lot of friends, wealthy ones, who might want to have similar events in the future.'

Valentina says nothing, but is thoughtful for a moment.

'How many guests?' she snaps eventually, lifting her chin in my direction and putting a long painted nail under it.

'Probably fifty, maybe more.'

'And they want a big party. Classy?' she checks.

'Oh yes, classy, definitely.' I nod a lot, and think I may be getting somewhere.

'When?' she says, looking at her phone.

'June. It could make a good profit for the restaurant if you planned caref—'

'I will look at the diary,' she announces, and turns to go.

'No. Not June. No way. It's the harvest!' Antonio cuts in.

Valentina waves her hands in the air. 'Why must you always make things hard? You said you wanted me back. You promised, gave me your word – a show of your commitment, you said – that I could continue to run the restaurant with no interference.'

'*Sí*.' He nods slowly, apologetically.

'Well then, leave me to run the restaurant. This has

nothing to do with you or the farm!' She throws a dismissive arm towards the barns and paddock.

'But I will need pickers,' Antonio tries to reason.

'Then get pickers. But not my waiting staff. There must be others.'

He sighs deeply, realising that he's losing ground.

'Then . . .' Valentina holds up a hand, red-painted nails like talons, and silences us. How does she do that? How can she make everyone look at her like that? If I did that, no one would even notice. 'I will look at the diary and get back to you. A big budget, you say . . .'

'Yes.' I nod.

'Then perhaps it will be good for this place.' She gives a tight smile, then nods and turns away, her dark shiny hair swinging, her pert rounded bottom bobbing up and down in her tight jeans, and her pointed high heels making a rapping sound on the tiled floor.

'Um . . . there's just one more thing, Valentina . . .' I call after her. She stops and turns back slowly. I glance at Antonio for support, but he's holding his hand over his mouth, almost as if he's hiding a grimace.

I turn away from him. He thinks I can't do this. Well I can, and I will.

'The thing is, Valentina, about the party . . .' She narrows her eyes, giving me her full attention. 'The thing is,' I repeat, 'it has to be me.'

'Sorry?' She cocks her head to one side with another tight smile, like a praying mantis enticing its prey.

'It has to be me organising the party and, well, hosting it.'

For a moment she doesn't say anything. The words hang in the air.

'You would be organising the party?' she says, as though unable to comprehend what I'm saying.

'Yes,' I confirm. 'Because she's my . . . friend.' I swallow.

The air practically crackles with disdain. 'You are the washer-upper? No?'

'I am,' I confirm, and swallow again.

'Absolutely not!' she says.

'But—'

'The subject is closed. I run this restaurant. Your job is to wash up, and I'd appreciate it if you'd stick to that. If not, there are plenty of others who will.'

She stomps down the steps and round the back to the apartment, instructing Antonio to bring her bag up from the car.

I turn to him and he holds his palms upwards and tilts his head, a sympathetic smile at the corners of his mouth.

'She means well. She's just . . . she is still cross because I didn't tell her about Miguel. She is feeling like her nose has been pushed out of joint. She'll calm down.' He folds his hands over his wide chest.

'I don't know why you put up with it!' I mutter furiously.

'It is her that puts up with me,' he tells me evenly. 'I am not known for my commitment – or should that be success? – when it comes to relationships. I like things the way they are. Why change? Why spoil what we have? I thought things were fine. But Valentina, she wants more.' He looks over to the sheds, changing the subject quickly. 'Now, I have a pump to try and mend, and hosing to replace.' He starts down the steps from the terrace, then turns back. 'I'm sorry about your party.' And then he jogs over to the barns.

It's over. It's not going to happen. I don't have any other ideas to get the money together. I've tried everything. My throat tightens and I blink back hot, angry tears. I'll have to break the news to Olivia. And then . . . well I guess I'll have to tell Harold and Brenda and start planning to go home. I can't believe it. I feel like I've fallen just before the finish line, and it hurts like hell. It's like all the air has been punched out of me. I thought I could fight back, make something from the ashes of disaster, but I couldn't.

Shoulders slumped, I start to walk back towards the *finca*, thinking about how much I've loved being here. Miguel is watering the trees on his own. He looks up at me. I hope he'll be OK, I think, feeling sad that I won't be around to see him flourish. He just needs to find his path and hopefully he won't get knocked off it like I have.

As I flick away cross tears of frustration, I hear a vehicle pulling into the car park. I glance around. It's the post van. The postman leans out and hands Antonio a bundle of letters – mostly bills, if the expression on Antonio's face is anything to go by. He shuffles through them, then shoves them in his pocket. All except one. He stops and looks at it again, then glances up and waves the letter at me.

I frown, puzzled. Who on earth would be writing to me here at Cortijo Ana?

Chapter Twenty-three

'For me?' I point at my chest, checking with Antonio. He looks at the letter again, and nods.

I walk down the hill towards him. Could it be Will? Has he returned the money? Antonio holds the letter out to me with a shrug. I recognise the writing straight away and my spirits plummet. It's not Will. Why would it be? We're over. He's gone. I have to get used to it.

I open the envelope and pull out a letter on headed paper. Something falls out of it and flutters to the floor, dancing around in the breeze. Antonio and I both chase it around a bit, nearly bumping heads. Eventually he traps it with his foot, picks it up without looking at it and hands it to me. I glance at the headed paper, but I know what it is. It's from Gav's company. A handwritten note from Olivia. The deposit for her party, it says. Then with a huge flourish, her signature and lots of kisses.

I show it to Antonio. He raises an eyebrow, clearly surprised that my letter should contain anything that might involve him.

'It's a cheque,' I tell him. 'The deposit for the party my cousin wants to hold here. Look at it.'

He takes it from me and his eyebrows shoot up.

'This is just the deposit?' he asks, surprised.

I nod. 'These people spend a lot of money on these things – birthday parties, hen parties, weddings. They want the world to see how well they've done in life. Show it off.'

'How much money they've made, you mean. Doing well and showing people how much money you can spend on a party are not always the same thing.'

'The rest of the fee would have followed when they flew out in June,' I say with a resigned sigh, and point to the figure in Olivia's note.

'It's a lot of money,' he says slowly.

'Yes,' I reply, my frustration clearly showing. I look down at the rusting, ancient pump. 'It would pay for a new one of those, for starters.' Antonio pulls down the corners of his mouth and nods in resigned agreement. 'Just think, a whole new watering system. You wouldn't have to rely on Miguel and me to water the trees. And what about next season, if we're not here? You'll definitely need a new system then.'

Antonio is silent, chewing his bottom lip. Briefly I wonder where I will be this time next year. If I can get enough money together, if I can work extra hours in the orchard, washing up in the restaurant and setting up this party, I could make the money I need. This time next year, I could be in the Butterfly Bar.

'You need a new watering system. I need the work. We both get what we want from this,' I say persuasively.

Still Antonio says nothing. I hold my breath. Hoping.

'Can't she have her party another time of year, not June?'

'No, her birthday is in June.' I point out the obvious as patiently as I can.

He falls silent, pondering again, and I think it's best to say nothing.

'Why can't Valentina organise this?' He looks at me with his dark brown eyes, the colour of the beautiful bay horse in the paddock behind him.

'Because,' I sigh, 'because it's my name on the cheque. They think . . . they think I own this place, remember?' I add quietly.

He nods, and I know what he must be thinking. He's laughing at me. A blush spreads up my neck and into my cheeks.

'Oh yes. I remember now. And that perhaps . . . I am the washer-upper?' He looks serious, but there's a twinkle in his eye. Miguel has that same twinkle when he's joking.

'Yes.' I hang my head, my embarrassment growing by the second. 'Look, I'm sorry. I know I should have said something, but my cousin . . . well, she's always looked down at me. I came out here to run a bar with my fiancé, but it hasn't quite turned out like that. And I'm not ready to own up to it yet.'

'And she thought this place was yours? You didn't tell her the truth?'

I let out a deep sigh. 'It's a long story. My cousin and I, we have history. She's always got what she wanted in life, while I seem to be constantly pedalling up blind alleys. Everything she touches just turns to gold, whereas for me, nothing ever quite comes off.'

'And your fiancé?' He leans against the fence, one foot on the lower rung. I stare across at the terrace and wrap my arms around myself.

'He left me. As soon as we got here. Took the money my

grandmother left me. It wasn't much, but it was enough to put down the deposit and rent on a bar. I thought a new life in the sun was just what we needed. A fresh start. I thought that one day soon I'd be getting married – who knows, in a place like this.' I look around as a gust of wind blows more of the cherry blossom off and it swirls around me.

'So, no wedding,' he says in his direct way.

'No, no wedding. Just years of planning.' I sigh again. 'I shouldn't get engaged. As soon as I start to make plans, it all goes wrong. I was engaged before, you see, but it didn't work out.' I give a hollow laugh. 'My instincts always seem to let me down. I haven't even told my parents that he's left me. I thought that if I could earn enough, take on the bar on my own, maybe,' I swallow hard, 'maybe he'd come back.'

The realisation hits me hard and shatters the protective casing I've been building up around my heart over the past couple of weeks. I didn't even appreciate that I wanted him back until now. I take a deep breath, allowing the fact to sink in, before carrying on.

'But even if he didn't come back, I would have achieved something. I would have my bar to show for it. I wanted to feel my nan would have been proud of me, that I hadn't wasted the money and opportunity she'd given me.'

I shut my eyes to stop them stinging. Who am I kidding? I can't go through life pretending I've finally made something of myself. It's never going to happen. I'm going to have to go home and confess. I open my eyes, then put my hand out to take the cheque back and stuff it in the envelope.

'We all have history. It makes us who we are,' Antonio says finally, and I can't help thinking there are hidden depths in those dark eyes that I know he's not going to share with me. 'As we get older, we learn to listen with our hearts,' he places his hand on his, and looks over at Miguel, then back at me, 'and not with our heads.'

But my heart is too busy noisily breaking in half to make any sense of what he's said.

'Look, I should leave,' I say. 'It was a moment of madness, this party thing. My stupid pride getting me into trouble again. But,' I take a second and breathe, 'I have loved being here, seeing the blossom, meeting the market traders in the harbour, watching you work with the horses and getting to know Miguel. He's a really great kid.'

'You seem to have got to know him a lot better than me. He's still angry with me for leaving him in the first place. I never wanted to be without him, but I don't know how to tell him. I thought having Valentina back might help, that she might be able to make friends with him too. But maybe,' he pauses, choosing his words carefully, 'maybe Valentina is more of a . . . businesswoman.' We both can't help but give a laugh, releasing all the tension in the air.

'Look, organise your party,' he says, handing me back the cheque.

'Sorry?'

'Go ahead. Organise your party.'

'But . . . but what about Valentina?'

'I'll square things with Valentina,' he says. I have no idea how he'll manage that, but I don't ask. 'Just . . . just stay out of her way.'

'OK, no problem,' I tell him, still shocked by his change of heart. My plan, my new life, has suddenly been shoved back on track. 'I should be able to cover the costs from the deposit, and then that way the final cheque will be profit,' I gabble. My head is suddenly popping with ideas and I have a spring in my step. I'll get a new notebook! I may not want to organise another wedding as long as I live, but this . . . well, this is a birthday party, and planning parties is what I know how to do best.

'Keep a note of your hours and I'll pay you for that and for the watering,' Antonio says. 'Oh, and Beti?'

'Yes?' I hope he hasn't suddenly changed his mind.

'No flamenco!'

'OK, no flamenco.' I smile and nod. I don't want to ruin this. He's agreed and that's all that matters.

'And do me a favour in return,' he adds a little more seriously. 'Keep an eye on Miguel for me.'

'Of course,' I reply firmly.

'I hope this party gives you everything you want.'

I suddenly feel a little prickle in my eyes, not of sadness, but of hope.

'I hope so too,' I say gratefully.

'Now go and help Miguel with the watering, and I'll break the news to Valentina.'

'What news?' I turn to see Valentina standing out on the terrace, like Elsa the ice queen surveying her land, and I swear Antonio gives me the tiniest of winks. But I'm not waiting to find out how she reacts, so I turn and run to join Miguel at the bowser.

'My turn to pull!' I shout, stuffing the envelope into my back pocket just as I hear Valentina erupting like firecrackers on fiesta night.

* * *

Later, as Miguel and I return the bowser to the barn, I hear soft murmurings from the open apartment window. It sounds as though Antonio and Valentina have moved the discussion and their fireworks upstairs and found a way to finally agree on the matter. Clearly this is a relationship that works well for both of them in that area. If only I could say the same about Will and me. I can't remember the last time we resolved our differences in that way; in fact, I can't remember the last time Will looked at me as if he really wanted me at all.

As the sun sets over Cortijo Ana, I arrive to wash up in the kitchen. The CD player is silent and the music channel on the big TV in the bar is on instead. There are just a few customers, looking at their square plates with suspicion, querying and inspecting each other's food.

I fill the sink with hot water and bubbles and turn to take a small pile of plates from Valentina. But she holds on to them tightly and raises a pencilled eyebrow at me.

'You may have got your party to organise,' she hisses, 'but don't imagine you can get your claws into anything or anyone else around here!'

Oh God! She thinks I'm after Antonio. She couldn't be further from the truth. There is nothing about him that I find attractive. He's moody and loud, and his hair is as unruly and unpredictable as he is. I go for smaller men, not big bears like him. I mean, look at Will: slight, funny, charming, stylish, popular. Antonio looks as if he could clear a room with that scowl. I wouldn't go near him if she paid me!

'Oh no, I really wouldn't . . .' I start, but she's not

listening. 'Don't go getting your feet under the table. When the cherry harvest is over and your party is done, so will you be. And don't imagine anyone here is going to help you organise it. They work for me!' She releases the plates and they catapult into the soapy water, soaking me and letting me know exactly where I stand: on my own, again.

Chapter Twenty-four

'Miguel! Hurry up or we'll miss the bus!'

Honestly! I've no idea where he's been disappearing to over the past ten days, since Antonio agreed to the party. As April has slipped into the start of May, the sun has turned up its brightness a notch, and we've been watering like mad. We've been so busy, I've only made it to the harbour a couple of times. But the last time we went down there, we nearly missed the bus back. Miguel turned up, out of breath, laughing and apologising, just as the driver was closing the doors. And now he's disappeared up to his room to get showered and changed and we're in danger of missing it again! I'm the sort of person who likes to be there in plenty of time, not leave it until the last minute. This boy is doing nothing for my stress levels.

'Miguel! Hurry! I want to get to the shops before they close for lunch.' I need to go to the bank and see that the cheque has cleared, and then buy a new notebook. I want to sit in the Butterfly Bar and jot down the ideas I've been scribbling down on an order pad I borrowed from Frank. But what I really want to do is find out what's going on with Miguel, like I promised Antonio. Where does he go? Who is he meeting? I've become genuinely fond of him; he really is a great lad, funny and helpful. It would be awful if he was to get in with the wrong crowd again.

'Hello, love!' Brenda comes out to greet me as I pull my new notebook from its paper bag, along with a pen with a light-blue gem on the top. She puts a steaming cup of frothy coffee down in front of me. 'How's it all going? You look like you mean business.' She nods to the open notebook and the blank page.

'I do, Brenda, I do!' I look around at the little bar. 'I have plans.' I can't help but beam.

'You look very pleased with yourself, I must say.'

'Well, I think I might have got things sorted.' I finally feel confident that it's going to go ahead. For the first few days I was certain something else was going to go wrong, but now the cheque is in the bank, I feel I can talk about it. 'I've found more work. I'm doing an event, putting on a party for my cousin. She wants it to be the best thirtieth her friends have seen. With the extra hours I'm going to have to do up at the restaurant, it should give me the money I need to take over from you in June!' My cheeks hurt I'm grinning so widely.

'Oh! That is fabulous news! Isn't it, Harold? That's brilliant news! Let's have a sangria to celebrate. Harold? Pour us a couple of sangrias!'

Harold nods. 'Righto, Beaut!' Smiling, he picks up a large glass and pulls down the handle on the shiny pump. Without turning it off, he fills a second glass and adds a slice of orange with a cocktail stick.

'Cheers! Here's to happy endings!' Brenda raises her glass, and the Spanish sunshine shines through, lighting it up like a jewel. 'That's brilliant news, Beti love. We can book to see those flats now. He'll be so excited.' She nods in Harold's direction. 'He'll be Skyping back home already.'

'How's your daughter?' I ask.

'Getting bigger by the day!' She laughs. 'It could be any time.'

I get a little pang of envy on behalf of my parents, who would have made wonderful grandparents.

'We can't wait to be more involved with all the grandchildren on a day-to-day basis. They grow so much when we don't see them.' Brenda looks around, misty-eyed, and I can't tell if it's because she's missing her family, or because she's going to miss this place. 'Everything changes,' she says with a smile and a sigh, and turns to go back into the bar.

I look around and barely let myself think it. It is actually going to happen. I'm going to be taking over the Butterfly Bar! I can't help but smile happily again.

'Hey, Carlos!' Brenda waves at the fisherman coming in from his boat, his daily catch in a sack over his shoulder. 'Do you want something to take back to the restaurant today, love?' she asks me.

'I have sardines . . . or prawns.' Carlos pulls one out of the sack and holds it up. I put my hand up and shake my head, laughing.

'No, but thank you. Not today,' I tell him. 'Valentina's back at the restaurant,' I say to Brenda. 'She's put a stop to the daily specials.'

'Oh, that's a shame.' Brenda grimaces.

'But it has given me an idea for the party.' I make a note to google seafood tapas. I'll need to prepare lots of dishes in advance. I look around the market. There's a British couple selling ready-made British meals in foil takeaway dishes. I wonder if they could do tapas but with a traditional British twist. Mini Yorkshire puds with a slice of beef, tiny fish and chips in a cone, that kind of thing. Or even retro ones like vol-au-vents, cheese and pineapple on sticks and mini prawn cocktails. I'm sure it's the sort of touch Olivia and her friends would like. Maybe I could introduce similar food when I take over the Butterfly Bar. I write down the idea and make a plan to talk to the couple in the market, and to Olivia. I've started my list and suddenly it feels like life is back on track.

'Thank you, Carlos,' says Brenda. '*Hasta luego.*'

'Not if I see you first, baby!' he jokes back in a thick Spanish accent, and we all laugh. Clearly a well-rehearsed line. It is wonderful how these two communities have embraced each other and are living harmoniously together down here at the harbour. Shame the same can't be said for Cortijo Ana. Despite Valentina trying to attract the tourists, they never seem to visit twice. Who wants foam dots on square plates when you could be eating fresh seafood straight from the sea or Bonita's special Spanish chicken?

I wonder if Harold and Brenda will miss all this when they go home. But with a new baby to enjoy, who can blame them? I think with a tiny pang in the pit of my stomach. I would have loved a family: me, Will and our children sitting round a table with their grandparents eating paella. I'd get Bonita's recipe from her, but it's not like I'm going to have anyone to cook for now.

I look out towards the harbour, where the boats are

bobbing about the jetty and a group of elderly men and women are taking a swim.

I carry on making my list, wondering if we can do a grown-ups' piñata. If only I could ask the flamenco teacher from the Pink Flamingo to come and do a class. That would have been perfect, but I have to keep to my word. No flamenco. I sigh. What else could we have instead? Maybe I could speak to Maxine about doing her Cher act. It could be great fun, very retro, though I wonder if it's classy enough for Olivia. And karaoke! Everyone thinks they're the next Robbie Williams after a few drinks. I make a note to find out where I can hire a machine.

I look around at the precinct. Maybe I could organise for them to have a kayaking trip at sunset and cava on the beach before the party starts. But that would involve a minibus. Scrap that idea. I could offer it as an option for the following day instead. Oh, and I must find out about drink suppliers and make sure I have enough glasses. I'll ask Frank. My head is buzzing with plans and ideas. The only trouble is Valentina. How am I going to make any of this happen with her not letting me have any help? The rest of the organisation I can handle no problem, but I'm going to have to find waiting staff from somewhere. By way of distraction, I start sketching table layouts and napkin-folding ideas.

'Another?' Brenda points to my empty sangria glass. I hardly noticed it slipping down, I was so busy scribbling notes.

'A coffee this time, please, Brenda.' I don't think Valentina will be too impressed if I turn up to work half cut. I think she'd find any excuse to sack me right now. I jot down 'sangria' on my notepad and make a note to get the recipe from Harold. Oh, and we'll need jugs. Maybe I could use the jugs from the cupboard in Cortijo Ana. Let's hope Valentina won't notice.

I glance at my phone, checking the time. Miguel should be here by now. I look around.

'Hey!'

It's Craig, swinging his man bag beside him. He kisses me on both cheeks.

'How's things?' he asks. Before I can tell him all about the party, he says, 'I've just seen that young friend of yours, the good-looking lad, heading up towards the club in the old town.'

'A club? In the daytime? What sort of a place is it?'

He shrugs. 'It's not somewhere the expats or tourists go really. It's a locals' place. Not heard much about it.' He shakes his head and orders a white wine with ice.

Something about this doesn't feel right. What on earth is Miguel doing in a club? I imagined he'd be going for coffee somewhere, or hanging round the beach, making friends over at the bar there. But a back-street club? All my fears rush into my head at once.

'Was he on his own?'

'Yes. Didn't see me. He was too busy texting.'

'This place, this club . . .' I pick up my notepad and quickly stuff it in my bag. 'What's it called?'

'Los Picadores, I think.'

'I'll be back!' I call, leaving Brenda holding a hot cup of coffee that right now, I really need. I don't know if it's the sangria or the thought of losing Miguel to some den of drunks and drug dealers, but I'm feeling a little light-headed.

I follow Craig's directions and head up the narrow road leading towards the old town. It's not somewhere I've been before, and nor have many tourists by the looks of it. It's just a stone's throw from the harbour, and yet so different. Dark, narrow streets, with shadowy doorways. Walls stained green from poor guttering, and washing hanging out of tiny balconies that will barely see the sun, which is blotted out by the huge apartment blocks all around. There are overfull plastic bins and all the shutters seem to be closed. No wonder not many tourists visit here! They could do with brightening the place up: a few flowers, some white paint. I think of lovely Colina de Flor and the blossom in full bloom. So full of light and life! My spirits really lift when I picture it, as if . . . well, as if it's my happy place right now.

I finally reach a fork in the narrow road. In front of me is a big wooden door that looks like it's been there since the beginning of time, and a worn painted sign of a man on horseback in traditional Spanish bullfighting outfit, with two words underneath: *Los Picadores.*

I stand and look at the door, which is firmly shut. I feel suddenly nervous. What do I do? Knock and see if they'll let me in? Panicking, I wonder if I should just go to the bus stop and wait for Miguel; give him a chance to explain. Just then, a man arrives carrying a large black case. He pushes the door open and slides in. For a moment I can hear voices, calling and shouting, stamping. My heart leaps and starts thundering. And then the door slams shut again.

I look around. There doesn't seem to be anyone around on these quiet streets. There's no way I can leave. What if

Miguel's getting into trouble again? I imagine Antonio's set and angry face, but then also remember the look on it when he asked me to keep an eye on the boy. I must find out what's going on. I have to try and keep Miguel safe. Safe: that was how I felt with Will. But it turned out I was anything but. He left me on my own, in a new country. That's not what you do to people you care about! I suddenly realise that I'm not upset any more about what he did; I'm angry. You don't leave people you care about. You just don't!

I step towards the door. There is nothing here to tell you this is a bar or a club. No posters or signs. What is this place? As I put my hand on the rough, dark-stained door, I can feel it vibrating. The walls are thick and solid, but there is something going on in there that is making it shake.

Slowly, copying the man I just saw, I turn the metal ring handle, push open the door and slide in, wondering what on earth I'm going to find behind it.

Chapter Twenty-five

The noise hits me straight away. Loud shouts and stamping of feet, making me jump and my nerves jangle. It takes a while for my eyes to adjust to the dark smoke-filled room. Clearly the smoking ban hasn't ventured this far. It's cool in here, and smells musty. There are people standing around, leaning against the old stone walls and pillars. Pairs of women share seats, leaning forward, arms on their knees. There doesn't seem to be a single red- or pale-skinned tourist in sight. No straw hats or patterned shorts and flip-flops. These women have long hair, flowing free or piled up on top of their heads, some with flower clips at the side. They are wearing off-the-shoulder tops, full skirts or trousers with triangular scarves tied across their tummies. There are even children sitting cross-legged under tables and on the floor. Whilst the rest of the country is taking its siesta, this place obviously comes to life.

At the back of the room is a woman standing with her arms poised. The audience is silenced. Then a guitarist begins to play and she starts to sing, a long, slow lament that comes right from the heart. I'm mesmerised. I slide into the shadows along the wall, and tuck myself away so I'm not noticed. She stamps her feet, and the women surrounding her clap in rhythm. '*Olé!*' they shout, making me jump.

Another guitarist joins in, and the woman's feet begin to move, stamping and clicking on the worn stone floor. The music and dance build and build and seem to whisk me along with them. In what seems like no time at all, I have felt this woman's worry, her pain, her grief, her anger and finally her determination to carry on. The song builds to a heady climax, and I feel practically moved to tears.

When it's over, I feel a strange sense of release, elation and exhaustion. The people round me clap, and call, '*Bravo!*' and '*Olé!*' They start moving around, talking animatedly. The guitarist, an old man, stands and stretches. From my hiding place in the shadows, I scan the room for Miguel. At last I spot him, talking earnestly with a small dark-haired girl. He takes her hand and gently tugs at it. She shakes her head. The old guitarist walks over to them, and the three of them look to be conferring in hushed tones. I don't know what's going on, but I promised Antonio I wouldn't let Miguel get into any trouble. I step forward.

'Miguel?' I call. 'Miguel!'

There is a sudden hush, and Miguel turns and stares at me. I feel like I've announced to the whole club that there's a tourist in the mix. Miguel looks as though he's been caught red-handed. But red-handed at what? My heart is in my mouth, and in the space where it used to be, there's a furious banging, like the heels of the woman dancing on the stone floor.

The girl standing with Miguel dips and turns and is suddenly gone, lost in the crowd.

Miguel puts his hand on the old man's shoulder, bidding

him farewell like there is unfinished business to settle. Then he turns and runs to me, ushering me out of the big dark door into the bright sunlight and back to the real world outside.

'What is that place?' I ask as soon as we're outside. 'Is it some kind of flamenco club? Why don't tourists go there? What were you doing there?' The questions rush out, one after the other.

'Nothing!' he laughs. 'Just making friends, like you told me to.'

He slings his arm around my shoulders in his lazy way and ushers me back through the narrow streets towards the bus stop.

'Who was that girl? And the old man?' I persist.

'What girl?' he says innocently. And I know in my gut that he's hiding something from me.

'I promised Antonio,' I tell him.

'Promised him what? That you'd spy on me?' His cheerfulness suddenly disappears and the sullenness he arrived with descends again.

'No,' I say gently, keen not to push him. I don't want him to pull the shutters down completely. 'That I'd look out for you. Make sure you were safe.'

'I am safe. Don't worry, Beti.' He smiles, and the good-natured Miguel I have come to know and care about is back. 'Now come on, we have evening watering to do!' he says.

I don't know what's going on, but he's up to something, I can feel it. And I have to find out what, because by the looks of it, Miguel's lips are sealed. I'll have to stay out of Antonio's way whilst I do, though. I can't tell him about today, not until I've got something more than a head full of worries. I gulp, hoping it won't come to that.

Chapter Twenty-six

The next morning, I'm up early. It's clear and fresh and promises to be another sunny day. The birds are noisily courting one another, dancing to and fro, and I'm reminded of the dancer I saw yesterday, mesmerising me with her story and her movement. Ana the cat walks across the small terrace of my *finca*, tail high, demanding my attention, again like yesterday's dancer. I reach down to stroke her but she trots away; then, when I stand, she comes back and twists around my legs. I dress, feed her and make my way to the bottom of the hill, where Miguel has promised to meet me on time.

'Miguel? Miguel?' I call up to the little balcony at the back of the farmhouse, but there's no reply. He is nowhere to be seen, again!

'Everything OK?' Antonio's head and shoulders appear over the stone balustrade. I curse to myself; I thought he'd be out with the horses.

'Um, yes, fine,' I smile. 'Just looking for Miguel.' I try and sound casual.

'How was yesterday?'

'Um, good . . .' I swallow, nod and find myself chewing my top lip. What else can I say?

'Sure?' he pushes.

'Yes, we had a good time down at the Butterfly Bar. We met up with Craig; he runs a breakfast bar down there. Saw a few of the other locals. It was great.' I find myself lying and hating myself for it. But I can't tell him about finding Miguel in the club, not until I have something more concrete.

'He wasn't drinking, was he? He's only seventeen.'

'No, no, not drinking.' I hold my hand over my eyes in the early-morning sun and start to turn away.

'He seemed in good spirits when he got home. Did he meet some friends?'

'I . . . er, I'm not sure,' I say.

'You were with him, weren't you? You didn't let him go off on his own?'

'Yes . . . no . . . I mean, we had a lovely time. We drank coffee. He said he was interested in getting a job, maybe at one of the cafés or bars, or possibly the water-sports place.' *No he didn't!* shouts a voice in my head. *Stop talking before you make even more of a mess of things!*

Antonio lifts his eyebrows and nods approvingly. 'Good, good,' he says. 'But there is plenty of work for him here in the orchard for the time being.' He indicates the corner of the orchard. 'He has gone to start on the trees over on the far side.'

'Oh yes, of course. He must be waiting for me up there,' I say without thinking. I have no idea why I'm covering for him. But if he is getting into some sort of trouble, Antonio might blame me and pull the plug on the party.

I run to the yard to see if the bowser is still there. It is. Which means that Miguel hasn't gone to start on the watering. Where on earth is he?

I pull the bowser out of the yard. It groans and creaks,

and I know how it feels. I'm annoyed about Miguel's disappearance, but a little worried too. Has he gone back to the club in the old town? Who was that girl, and the older man who joined them? What has he been getting himself into? The questions keep running round my head as I struggle up the zigzag path pulling the heavy bowser, my upper arms aching and the blood whooshing in my ears.

I'm nearly up to the top field when I stop to catch my breath. As I thought, no sign of Miguel. I'll have to try and find him as soon as I'm done here. As I turn and look out over the cherry orchard, the blossom all nearly fallen, I'm startled by a noise. I whirl round and catch sight of a slight figure, dark-haired, running from the barn.

'Hey!' I shout, and drop the handle of the bowser. It rolls back slightly but doesn't go anywhere. 'HEY!' I shout again, louder.

I break into a run, chasing after.

'Come back!' I call as the slight figure disappears over the wall and into the woods. I try to follow, but find myself hooked in brambles. By the time I've freed myself, the figure has disappeared. They're either hiding or are long gone.

I'm out of breath as I make my way back to the barn. I'm not even sure if the figure was a girl or a boy, but there was something vaguely familiar about them . . . I look down at the scratches on my arms and legs where I got caught in the brambles. I rub them, but it's not the scratches I'm thinking about. Something is nagging at me – I just can't put my finger on what.

I turn and see Antonio riding the stallion through the cherry orchard.

'Antonio!' I wave at him with both arms. 'Quick!' I point towards the woods. 'There was someone in the barn; they've gone that way!'

He turns the horse and canters up the path in the direction I'm pointing. Suerte clears the wall with ease, Antonio leaning forward to duck beneath the low leafy branches, and disappears into the trees. I wait, holding my breath, until I see them returning, the horse taking big relaxed strides, the reins loose and low. Antonio is shaking his head.

'Whoever it is, they've gone.' He jumps down and leads Suerte through a small opening in the wall, then comes to join me. Catching sight of the scratches on my arms, he takes hold of my hand and inspects them. 'Are you OK? Are you hurt?'

My heart starts clacking like a pair of castanets. It must be the shock.

'Here, you need something on those. Let's get them cleaned up.'

He takes my arm and guides me to my *finca*. I find the key in my pocket, but I'm feeling shaky. This place has been my little safe haven since Will left, where I can hide away from the world and no one will bother me; where I can be alone with my thoughts, thinking about Will, about what might have been. Now . . . well now I'm not so sure I'm alone at all.

'Sit down on the veranda and I'll make you some coffee. Then I'll check the barn.'

'Oh, it's OK. I can do that,' I say, not wanting him to see the cheap coffee I've bought, or my empty cupboards. But it's too late: he's in the kitchen, banging the cupboard doors.

'There's nothing here!' he shouts. 'I'll get some from the restaurant.'

'No, really,' I try and insist.

'It's the least I can do when you're chasing intruders from my property,' he says, firmly but kindly, and my insides seem to jolt again.

'Hey! Beti!' I turn to see Miguel walking towards us. 'You OK?'

I manage a smile. 'Yes, fine. I . . . There was someone in the barn. They ran off into the woods. I have no idea what they were after.' I'm desperate to ask him where he's been, but I can't, not with Antonio here. I'm not going to worry Antonio before I get to the bottom of this. He has enough on his plate already.

'Someone in the barn?' Miguel raises his eyebrows in surprise, but something about the way he says it makes me stop and look at him. Does he know what's going on here? Has he got something to do with it? Is something being hidden in there?

'You fetch coffee,' Antonio tells him. 'And something to eat,' he adds. 'I'll go and check the barn.'

'Of course,' says Miguel, and he runs off in the direction of the restaurant. I watch him go with narrowed eyes.

Antonio is back quickly. 'It's all as it should be,' he says. 'Nothing to worry about. Maybe just kids messing around.' He looks at me again. 'And you're sure you're OK?'

'I'm fine, really. Thank you.' I nod towards his horse, tethered to the rickety old fence. 'Where did you learn to ride like that?'

He strokes Suerte's soft nose. 'I have always ridden, when

I used to come here to visit my grandparents. This was their farm. My grandfather was putting me up on horses before I could walk. My mother and father travelled a lot, so I used to stay here for long periods of time, even went to school here. Then when I was a young man, I started to travel too. But when my grandparents grew old, I came back to the farm. My grandfather wanted to hand over the cherry orchard to me, to pass it on to someone who would care for it and carry it on. The restaurant used to be Grandmother's; just their front room and porch really. She would cook her home-made dishes, and almond and cherry cake when the season came. Bonita came to work here as a young woman; she learned everything from my grandmother, all the old recipes. I worked on the cherry farm and my grandfather taught me how to understand the horses, how to listen with my heart and not my head. I hope I can pass that on some day,' he adds quietly as we watch Miguel walk up the grassy path carrying a tray loaded with mugs and a plate.

'She sent cake . . . lots of cake!' Miguel's face breaks into an excited smile, and Antonio smiles back, seeing a glimpse of the boy he never knew.

The plate contains three huge slices of cake, which we all tuck into as we sit, deep in our own thoughts, looking out over the cherry orchard. The *finca* feels like my safe place again.

'I'll leave you to it,' says Antonio when he has finished. He starts to lead Suerte back down the path.

'We'd better get on with the watering,' I tell Miguel.

'Let Miguel pull the bowser!' Antonio calls back good-naturedly. And then, more seriously, 'And call me if you're worried at all, any time.'

My stomach does a little skip by way of thank-you. Clearly I'm still recovering from spotting the stranger in the barn, and my painful attempt at scaling the wall.

'Right, let's get to work,' Miguel says. 'Or I can do it on my own if you're hurt,' he offers.

'No, I'm fine,' I say. I sit and look at him, giving him an opportunity to tell me what's going on, but he says nothing; just checks his phone.

'Do you know anything about who might have been in the barn?' I ask eventually.

'Me? No.' He shakes his head.

But something tells me otherwise.

By the time we've finished watering, the sun is starting to warm up the ground. Like every day now, we'll do more come sunset, before I start work in the restaurant. But now that the blossom is nearly gone, the visitors seem to have disappeared too. No one comes to see branches with leaves and buds on them. Only the bird visitors seem to have increased in numbers.

'We need to get these nets on the trees,' I hear Antonio call to Miguel from the paddock where he is working with the bay colt again.

'Are you going down to the harbour, Beti?' Miguel walks over to where I'm standing watching Antonio. He leans on the fence beside me and watches too.

'No, not today.'

Antonio is talking calmly to the horse, never raising his voice, clearly able to communicate with animals much better than humans. I look at Miguel, who at least has his hood down.

'I'm going to check out the barn. See if I can find any clue as to who's been in there. Perhaps you'd like to come with me?' I suggest, and push myself away from the fence.

As I start to walk up the field, Miguel falls into step beside me. I can sense Antonio taking his eyes off the horse and watching us go. I turn and give him a little wave of the hand, to reassure him that Miguel is coming with me. He nods his head slowly in return, and my stomach does that little skip again, making me smile. I feel I'm finally doing something worthwhile. If Miguel is with me, he's not disappearing and getting into trouble, and maybe I can find out a little more about what's going on with him.

'So where were you this morning?' I'm slightly out of breath as we walk side by side up the grassy path. I find myself having to almost run to keep up with his long strides.

'Overslept!' he quips quickly and gives me a killer smile.

'Funny. Antonio said you left the apartment early and were looking for me to start watering.' I try and speak as non-combatively as I can. I don't want him to close up on me again.

'He must have been mistaken. I was in bed until I heard you shouting for him.'

We fall into silence. I have no idea how to get anything else from him. It's not like I'm his mother. He's probably thinking, What's it got to do with you? And he'd be right! But I made a promise to Antonio that I'd look out for him, and I'm going to stick to it.

When we reach the barn, I try and look in through the dusty cobweb-covered window, but it's too dark to see anything. I feel a little nervous, which makes me cross. But maybe Antonio's right; maybe it was just kids messing around. We move around to the door and I reach out tentatively for the handle. I don't know why I should feel nervous; it's not like I'm going to find an armed gang in there.

'Do you want me to do it?' Miguel asks. I shake my head.

'I need to see for myself,' I say.

Miguel steps back, and I take hold of the handle and slowly turn it. A shaft of light cuts through the darkness as I open the door and peer in. In it the dust moves this way and that, and I'm reminded of the dancer I saw in the club, telling her story, baring her soul. What do we do in the UK when times get tough? We certainly don't dance, or sing. Maybe we do everything we can to ignore it. Bury our heads in the sand. Hide our feelings away and tell the world we're doing great – with posts on Facebook about holidays, weddings, children – instead of sharing how we really feel and not caring what others think. I swallow hard. People in Spain tell each other what they think all the time. I think of the group that gathers in the taverna on the square, swapping news, talking loudly and consistently over each other. Back home, we just put up more pictures on social media.

I slowly push the door wider, scanning the huge space, checking the lurking shadows – and there are plenty of them. The place is piled high with chairs, round tables and boxes of picture frames and terracotta pots. I pull out my phone and switch on the torch. It's just a barn. Nothing exciting to see. I turn to Miguel, but he's gone.

Chapter Twenty-seven

A few days later, I'm heading up to the *finca* in the early evening to get my newly washed sheets in off the fence. I love the smell of the sheets when they've been dried out here. I want to get them on the bed before I start my shift at the restaurant. I've been in the harbour all afternoon, talking to the couple from Folkestone who make ready meals about my ideas for Spanish tapas with a British twist, and they're well up for it. So that's something sorted on my list. Tick, I think, satisfied.

After I've done my bed, I need to find Miguel to help me water the trees. He didn't come to the harbour with me and I have no idea where he is. I can see that more trees have been covered with nets; I passed Antonio doing that this morning, and he raised his hand to greet me, almost as if we're becoming friends.

I'm striding up the final sharp incline, towards where my sheets are flapping on the wooden railings in the warm sunshine, when suddenly I hear it again: the thumping sound from the other evening. This time I'm not hanging about. I run towards the barn as quickly and quietly as I can, my heart thudding to match the sounds coming from inside. But as I get closer, I realise that I have no idea what to do next.

Do I just burst in, or should I run back and get Antonio, like he told me to? But by then whoever is inside will have run off. I have to deal with this now, on my own, I tell myself.

I stop beside the window and flatten my back against the cold wall, then take a deep breath and peer in. At first, like last time, I can't see anything. It's dark in there, but there is a shaft of light coming in from the window at the far end, where the shutters have been opened. As my eyes adjust, I can make out piles of chairs, tables and stacks of cardboard boxes. The light is shining right at the yellowing walls, and I realise they're completely covered in some sort of paintings or posters, aged, weather-worn and cracked. And there, in front of the fireplace, I can now make out two figures: one short, one tall, standing facing each other.

I recognise the taller one straight away. It's Miguel. I don't know whether to be relieved or terrified. Who is he squaring up to? Then, as the light suddenly streams in, I catch my breath in recognition. That's who I saw running away the other day. It's a girl! The girl Miguel was with at the club that day. But they don't look happy to see each other. They're standing with chests out, shoulders back, as if challenging each other. Is she from the gang he left behind; is she a messenger? I need to find out.

I move towards the door, which is slightly ajar, and crouch down, peering through the crack, barely letting myself breathe. I can see them, just. But they're not arguing as I thought. As I watch, they begin to clap, not taking their eyes off one another. Then their feet join in, kicking upwards behind them and stamping with their heels. Clap, clap, stamp, stamp. They begin to move their arms, lifting them with elbows high and fingers turning, curling in their little fingers as their arms rise. Stamp, stamp, stamp, stamp; she grabs at her skirt and whips her head away from him coquettishly, then turns back to him, her eyes on his, lifting her chest as if in encouragement, and the two dance slowly and sensually around each other.

If I thought the woman at the club touched me, this is unbelievable. Totally mesmerising. No music, just the clap of their hands and the stamp of their feet, heel to toe, toe to heel. I can't take my eyes off them. I might not know anything about it, but I'm pretty sure this is flamenco.

Suddenly a blast of wind makes the door bang shut and open again. The pair drop their arms. The spell is broken. They spin round to look at me as though they've been caught red-handed, and freeze. And I do too, though I'm not sure why. Is it because I've discovered them hiding out, or because I feel I've watched something so intimate . . . not just a dance, but an outpouring and sharing of emotion without words?

The girl suddenly grabs her bag from on top of a pile of old sacks, and goes to run out of the door.

'Whoa! Not so fast this time!' I step in front of her, blocking her way. 'You're the girl I saw in that club with Miguel, aren't you?'

She spins round to Miguel, wide-eyed.

'It's OK, Sophia, Beti is a friend. We can trust her,' Miguel says in English for my benefit, and then smiles at me. 'Can't we?'

I'm not sure what he's talking about, but I don't move; just look between the pair of them.

'Well first of all, I think you'd better tell me what's going on here.'

We sit down in the barn, me on one of the old chairs that Miguel puts out for me in the shaft of dancing dust, Miguel on an old wooden fruit box and Sophia on a rung of an old cherry-picking ladder leaning against the yellowing poster covered wall.

'Flamenco has been banned in this town for years,' Miguel tells me. 'It was Sophia who told me all about it when we met. I was wandering around the back streets near the club and she asked me if I was waiting to go in. I thought,' he shrugs, 'why not? I have grown up around flamenco all my life. Often I was the kid sitting under the table in smoky clubs, up late, and then sleeping on piles of coats at the parties after shows. I was always in the way.'

My heart twists thinking about him as a little boy, feeling like an uninvited hindrance.

'But I did learn flamenco. And once I met Sophia, we have been dancing together every day since. Pedro, the guitarist, says we have great potential, that we need to start to perform in public, at flamenco gatherings, competitions, to get our name known.'

'But it's hard, because no one here must know Miguel is dancing.' Sophia speaks with a strong Spanish accent. 'It would cause a lot of trouble, and for me and my family too if they knew I was encouraging him.'

'But why is it banned here?' I finally get to ask what's been niggling away at me.

'I am from the next-door village, where flamenco is not

banned.' She carries on without answering my question. 'We are free to dance there. Miguel has been coming to visit me. But when he can't make it because he has to be here to water the trees, I have been coming here to practise. And then of course there is the club, where we go to dance with Pedro, where they hold the *peña*.'

'The what?' I ask.

'It is not like the flamenco shows that are put on for the tourists, like in the Pink Flamingo; a few girls dancing in floral dresses. It is where the real dancers go to share their love of flamenco. The aficionados of the art.'

'And that's where I saw you. Were you going to dance?'

Miguel laughs. 'I thought we might, until you turned up!'

I smile, with huge relief. He isn't getting into trouble again then; no gangs or violence. It's flamenco! But I get a pang of guilt thinking about how Antonio feels about it.

'Well, they missed out on something quite special. You two are amazing!'

They smile at each other shyly and I can't help but beam back.

'And what is this place?' I look around.

'It was once a *peña* club too. People would come for miles, so my father tells me. Word would get around and they would turn up to see their favourite dancers.'

'But not any more?' I look at the posters on the walls and realise they're advertising *peña* nights.

'Like Miguel says, flamenco is banned in this village. My father told me there was a fight one year. The priest banned the dance because it brought too much trouble at a time when the cherry harvest needed to be brought in. No one here dances any more. No one even mentions flamenco,' Sophia reveals.

'A priest banned it? After a fight?' I say, shocked. I understand now why Antonio was so against me suggesting it; it sounds like it has a troubled history around here.

As I look more closely at the barn, it dawns on me that it could be the perfect space for Olivia's party. I honestly have no idea where I would start, but it's full of possibilities. I'm feeling a little apprehensive, but excitement is starting to bubble up inside me, followed by a great big wave of anticipation. I've got a party to plan, and whatever my feelings for Olivia, I'm going to give it my very best shot.

'So, you will keep our secret?' Miguel asks earnestly.

My mind is still whirring away, thinking about the party. It's a huge job, I realise, maybe even impossible.

'I tell you what, I'll keep your secret if you promise to help me clear out this place and plan my cousin's party here. Agreed?'

Their smiles are infectious.

'Agreed!'

And suddenly my impossible task looks like it might just be doable. The three of us gaze at each other, the excitement palpable.

Nothing can stop this happening now.

209

Chapter Twenty-eight

'You want to hold the party in the old barn next to the *finca*?' Antonio asks.

'Yes, it's perfect, and well out of Valentina's way,' I explain.

He rolls his head from side to side thoughtfully. 'That place hasn't been used in years,' he says. It's clear that he can see the advantages of me keeping the party away from Valentina and the restaurant, but he's still reluctant to agree.

'Miguel has offered to help me.' I nudge Miguel, who nods enthusiastically.

'Yes, no problem.' He smiles widely.

'OK, OK. It's a deal. But Beti . . .' Antonio stops me in my tracks as he slides the bridle off the sweating horse he has been exercising.

'I know, I know . . . No flamenco!' I hold up my hands and feel myself blushing guiltily.

'Now let's get to work putting on the rest of the nets. Very soon the drop will come – that is the time when many of the new buds will fall and we will know exactly what kind of a harvest we will be having this year. Let's pray for a good one!'

As we all nod in agreement, I feel that Antonio and

Miguel are finally on the same page, dancing to the same tune. If not quite in harmony yet, they're moving closer.

I can't wait to tell Brenda and Harold my new plan . . . It's going to be brilliant, and I know they'll be excited for me. I can't help but feel in celebratory mood. Plan Butterfly Bar is firmly back on track!

Antonio has returned the colt to its paddock and Miguel and I have started walking up to the barn when we all stop and turn at the sound of an old car belching its way into the car park. Miguel stands and stares. Then he says, 'Oh no.'

The handbrake is yanked on with a crunch and the car doors slowly open. Antonio straightens up and stands very tall. Valentina comes out on to the veranda to see what's going on, her heels making a clicking sound. No one moves as a Cuban-heeled boot appears out of the driver's door. It is followed by a man dressed in a tight-fitting black shirt and thigh-clinging jeans with a big ornate black belt. He slides out and looks around, nodding appreciatively.

From the passenger door emerges a woman with long dark flowing hair, wearing a sleeveless T-shirt and tight-fitting jeans with high-heeled shoes, a scarf around her shoulders with long tassels hanging over her upper arms and elbows. She stands with her chin held high, looking around slowly, like a meerkat taking in its surroundings. No one moves; no one speaks. We stand watching as the wind whips up the tassels on her scarf.

It's as if tumbleweed has rolled into town, signalling that trouble is close behind. The man grabs the heavy belt around his slim hips and pulls it up with both hands. Then the couple approach the veranda, where Antonio joins Valentina, his good mood completely evaporated.

'Who is that?' I whisper to Miguel.

'That,' he says with a huge sigh, 'is my mother, and her partner, Felipe. What on earth could they want?'

We look at each other in dismay, knowing there is only one reason for her to be here: to take Miguel home.

Chapter Twenty-nine

Miguel and I come to stand with Antonio and Valentina on the terrace.

'Are you going to send me back?' Miguel whispers to Antonio.

Antonio spins round, and for a moment the two of them stare at each other.

'Do you want to go back?' He nods towards Miguel's mother and her partner, who are still taking in their surroundings.

Miguel looks like a young boy, scared. He gives a tiny shake of his head.

'Then absolutely not!' Antonio says with force, and I see Valentina's lips purse.

Antonio puts his arm around Miguel's shoulders and draws him to stand beside him. I see Miguel relax a little. Valentina, on the other hand, tenses some more.

'Esmeralda, what brings you here, away from the city?' asks Antonio.

'I've come to see my son, of course.' She smiles at Miguel but it doesn't reach her eyes. She doesn't move forward to hug him, like I'd expect a mother to do.

I see Antonio's fingers tighten on Miguel's shoulder, and

my stomach twists into a knot. I may only have known this little family for a short time, but somehow, they matter. I step forward to stand beside Antonio.

'So . . . this is your girlfriend, Valentina?' Esmeralda nods to me and looks me up and down, making me feel about as small as a mouse.

'No . . .' Antonio begins, but Esmeralda isn't listening.

'*I* am Valentina!' Valentina declares, and Esmeralda gives her the same assessment, though this time a little less disapproving.

'It's a long time since I've been here.' She struts around the patio and then looks up at the farmhouse. 'I see nothing much has changed.' She glances over towards Antonio's barns, where a huge pile of logs is waiting to be chopped. There is a bridle hanging on the gate. 'Still mad about his horses, I see,' she says, addressing no one in particular.

I wish I had the nerve to say yes, he's amazing with horses. That I've seen how he is with the stallion that was left for dead, how gentle he is with the mare and firm but fair with the young colt. And how desperate he is to find a way to connect with the son he's only just met. But I say nothing. I feel like a schoolgirl in front of a bully, waiting to be dealt my punishment.

'Glad to see you've got rid of all the old farm stuff. At least it looks as if it's trying to join the twenty-first century.' She looks me up and down again. 'Who are you? Staff?'

I don't respond. I'm too angry to speak, fury bubbling up in the pit of my stomach. I have no idea why I feel so defensive of Antonio, but I do. How dare this woman talk to him like this? Miguel's shoulders have dropped, along with his head. Just like when he first arrived here. Gone is the laughing boy that I have got to know. He's back to being that closed-in teenager, shunning the outside world.

I know Antonio has sensed it too.

'What do you want, Esmeralda?' Like a prisoner waiting for their sentence, we all want this over and done with.

'I told you, I came to see my son. He sent me pictures.'

'Which you never responded to!' Antonio's nostrils flare.

'I wanted to see for myself what kind of a life you were making for him here.' She lifts her chin. 'Not much of one by the looks of it. But still . . . as long as he's not in trouble.'

'He's not coming back with you.' Antonio cuts across her in a raised voice, barely containing the fire that is obviously burning inside him. He may not know Miguel that well yet, but it's clear he feels passionately about him. Miguel snaps his head up and looks at him, for the first time with a glint of admiration in his eyes, and unexpected tears spring into mine.

But instead of arguing with him, Esmeralda throws her head back and laughs. Then she stops just as suddenly.

'Oh, I think he's served his punishment now. He won't cause me any more trouble.'

Punishment? She threw him out, called Antonio, knowing he'd take him in, as punishment? She didn't send him here to spend time with Antonio, but to teach Miguel a lesson? Shock reverberates through the air. I have never heard anything more hurtful!

Antonio's knuckles whiten as he grips on to Miguel's shoulder. But Miguel's head isn't drooping any more. He's holding it high, just like Antonio, their profiles mirroring each other as I glance sideways at them.

'You've seen he's well,' Antonio says. 'You can leave. There's nothing else here for you.'

I'm so infuriated and enraged, my heart is pounding like it's trying to punch its way out of my chest. Let's hope they do just that. Leave! Leave us all to get on with the lives we've started to build here. And suddenly it strikes me that I *am* building a life; a life without Will. This is just me here; just Beti. Not Will's fiancée; not the girl with three failed engagements under her belt.

I wish Esmeralda would go, but more than that, I wish she would hug Miguel, tell him how much she loves him. Tell him how proud she is of him. But she doesn't. Instead she says to Antonio, 'I am still your wife. And I have needs. With Miguel old enough to leave school, we are free to travel. We want to go on the road again with flamenco, follow in the footsteps of our forefathers and be free spirits.'

'Fine, send us a postcard,' Antonio says dismissively and turns his back on her.

'Like I say, Antonio,' Esmeralda's voice is slow and controlled, 'I am still your wife and I need to collect what is mine.'

Antonio turns back slowly. Does she mean Miguel? Surely he won't let that happen?

'You know what I want, Antonio . . . And since you have ignored all my messages, I have come to get it myself.'

Antonio says nothing.

'You need me to spell it out?' There is a smile at the corner of her mouth, teasing, victorious, and the bubble of fury is rising in my stomach again. 'I want what I am owed. Half of this place!' She looks around. 'If you can't buy me out, you'll need to sell and give me what is mine.'

Miguel and I both gasp. Valentina lets out a squeal of outrage.

'Never!' Antonio practically growls.

'I am still your wife.' Esmeralda raises her chin further.

'Only in name. This place belonged to my grandparents, and their parents before that. I will never sell up! You are owed nothing.'

'I mean it. I want what is mine,' she replies.

And suddenly I see a passion in Antonio that I thought was lying dormant but seems now to have roared into life.

Chapter Thirty

'How dare you!' Antonio marches with slow, measured determination towards the pair, dust flying up from under his boots. Felipe instinctively takes two tiny steps back before steadying himself and jabbing out his chest, but Esmeralda doesn't move an inch. She lifts her chin to Antonio's enraged face and stares straight at him. There is a taunting smile playing round her lips, as if she is enjoying his reaction. He is looking down at her, his chin lifted too. His nostrils are flaring.

Miguel goes to follow, but I put a hand on his arm and hold him back.

'Stay here,' I say, feeling that if he gets involved it could turn really unpleasant.

'I am your wife and I want what is mine. Half of this place,' Esmeralda repeats.

'What, now that my generous monthly payments for Miguel's keep have stopped, you're looking for another way to make money?'

'What? You told me he never paid a penny towards my upkeep.' Miguel looks at his mother, surprise written all over his face.

'Pah!' Antonio practically spits. 'I suppose she told you I

never tried to contact you either, never wrote or sent gifts on your birthday.'

'She did.' Miguel looks incredulous.

Antonio looks over his shoulder at his son.

'I sent letters every year, with your birthday and Christmas gifts,' he says slowly and quietly. 'And invited you to come and stay, every year. But I was told you didn't want to know.'

Then he turns back to Esmeralda, his face thunderous. Just for a moment, she looks uncomfortable.

'I didn't want to confuse the boy. His life was with me and Felipe.' She finds her footing again and lifts her chin in defiance.

'I told you. There is nothing for you here. You are entitled to nothing. This place was in my family before I met and married you.' Antonio rolls his eyes up before fixing his stare back on Esmeralda. His chest is rising and falling with every quick and angry breath he draws in and pushes out.

She turns away from him, and slowly and steadily starts to walk a large circle around him, her heel hitting the ground first with each deliberate step, before rolling her foot forward, her elbows lifted, her hands on her hips, her gaze taking in the farmhouse and the veranda.

'A place like this must be worth a lot of money, with the tourists all wanting to come to Spain.' She waves a hand in the direction of the coast and the resorts that have sprung up all the way along it. 'So either you buy me out or put this place on the market. It would be snapped up in no time.'

'Never!' Antonio spits.

'We've spoken to the lawyer. You've had the letters.' Felipe speaks for the first time, tucking his thumbs into his belt.

Esmeralda stops pacing and turns to Antonio. 'I have brought up your child. We have given the boy a home for the last seventeen years!'

I grip Miguel's shoulder, worried that this might spill over into a fight, my heart racing. Antonio clenches his fists.

'Huh, some home!' he says. 'A home with no love, no warmth. A settee for the boy to sleep on in your sister's crowded apartment.'

'It is more than you have done!'

'You wouldn't let me near him!' Antonio's fury is suddenly unleashed. 'You kept me away, no matter how hard I tried to be a father! You have admitted you even hid the letters I sent!'

She lets out a sneering laugh. 'What kind of a father would you have been?'

'One who works hard and could have given him a life and a home! A home full of love.'

'One who has forgotten where he came from, forgotten his roots, his passion!'

'If anyone has forgotten, it's you!' Antonio explodes.

'Me?' She looks him up and down.

'You were nobody when I met you. I taught you all you know.'

'You taught me? Ha!'

'You knew nothing about . . .' He stops himself.

'Say it!' she taunts. 'You have forgotten who you are; you cannot even say the word.'

'Flamenco,' he says evenly. 'You knew nothing about flamenco before you met me.'

'I wish I had never met you. People shunning us for your

radical moves, for not sticking to the traditions. You were an embarrassment. You made a show of me!'

'I *made* you. I made you the dancer that you became. People would come for miles to see us dance.'

'And I would still be that dancer if I hadn't had to bring up a child for the past seventeen years!'

I can't believe what I'm hearing. I feel like I'm intruding, as if I shouldn't be here, in the middle of this family feud. But I'm rooted to the spot. I can feel Miguel's whole body shrinking back, like he's been hit right in his solar plexus.

'Yes, people came, but only because they had heard of your radical ways, your way of dancing. And look at you now. As soon as we married, as soon as the baby was coming, you wanted to turn your back on it all. Settle down. Be like other people. You forgot who you really were.'

'No!' he shouts, making me jump. 'I shut the door on that part of my life the day . . . the day you told me you were leaving me, with my unborn child, with him!' He points at Felipe.

Esmeralda looks between the two men. 'Felipe is a much better partner than you. It is not called the fire dance for no reason. He still has the fire in his belly. Whereas you . . .' she turns up her nose, 'you would rather be watering cherry trees.' She flicks out a dismissive wrist.

'I have a good life here. I could have given my son a loving home if you'd let me. I am still trying to.' He looks back briefly at Miguel.

'I thought he didn't want me,' Miguel says quietly, and I squeeze him to me. 'I thought that's why he never came.'

'If it had not been for him, I would have had a life of my

own!' Esmeralda exclaims. 'I am a dancer with a name, someone people want to see.'

'No!' Antonio shouts again, then drops his voice. 'You were a dancer who people wanted to see because of *me*.' It is as if he is finally saying what has been locked away for so long. 'It was *my* dancing they came to see. I taught you all you know,' he says finally and evenly. 'It could have been anyone.'

She shakes her head. 'If I was such a beginner, such a nobody . . .' She is walking again, deliberate steps, heel to toe, holding one hand on her hip, the other in the air, her little finger curling first, the other fingers following. 'If I was such a beginner . . .' she repeats, 'if it could have been anybody . . .' Antonio follows her with his eyes as she walks, as we all do, as she commands our attention.

'Enough of this.' Antonio raises a hand, as if breaking the spell she is trying to weave. 'I have work to do. You've seen the boy is safe and well. Now go! On your way.'

'Not until I get what I have come here for. We plan to travel. Set up a flamenco troupe and go on the road, back to our real roots.' She looks around dismissively at the farm. 'Miguel will join us.'

'Never! Miguel has no interest in flamenco.'

I can't help but look at Miguel as his cheeks go slightly pink and his jaw twitches.

'It is you who owes me, Esmeralda, not the other way round. For the years of fatherhood you stole from me. For the dancer I made you.'

'I never wanted him. He ruined my life!'

Miguel slumps into me, his head dropping forward.

I wrap my arm around his waist and stand as strong as I can, feeling his heartbreak.

'All those years I have had to bring him up and put a roof over his head. It is time he repaid me, by dancing with the troupe.'

'Leave! Now!' Antonio is furious.

'If you think you made me . . . do it again!' she says with a wicked glint in her eyes.

'What?'

'Do it again. Teach someone else to dance like you taught me.' She smiles at Felipe, who is frowning, confused.

'Pah!' Antonio dismisses her.

Esmeralda flashes a smile at a dumbfounded Felipe, and then looks straight at me and points.

'Teach her!' she says with a flick of her chin. 'Teach her to flamenco like you taught me. One dance. A dance-off between the two couples.' She holds her head up triumphantly, like a winner on the Olympic podium claiming her prize, whilst the rest of us freeze, stuck in a surreal moment. 'Winner takes all, the farm and the restaurant. Then we'll never have to see each other again.'

Chapter Thirty-one

'Never!' Antonio roars, breaking the spell.

'It's a good offer.' Esmeralda glances at her partner, who now has a smile spreading across his face.

'What? No!' Valentina shrieks. 'That's ridiculous! Antonio! Do something!' She turns on him crossly.

Esmeralda smiles wickedly again. 'If you win, you get to keep your farm and home. If not,' she shrugs, 'we sell it and you will never see us – or Miguel – again.'

Antonio turns to look at Miguel.

'No, don't, Pap—' Miguel stops himself before the word is fully formed.

'Papa?' scoffs Esmeralda. 'He's never been a father to you! It's Felipe who's been that!'

'Look, I'm the one who has caused all this trouble. I can just leave with them . . .' Miguel trails off.

'I won't hear of it.' Antonio bangs his fist into the palm of his hand. 'This is your home, for as long as you want it to be, and I'm not going to be forced into selling it. You have had enough years of uncertainty.'

'We have been living in cramped apartments when we should have been free to travel. This is payback for all those wasted years. If you hadn't forgotten who you were, a dancer—'

Antonio interrupts her. 'If you hadn't decided to leave me that night, here at the *peña flamenca* when my grandparents offered me the farm and I agreed to stop travelling, to settle down to make a home for you and our baby. And what did you do? You left me, for *him*.'

'For someone who was a dancer through and through,' she says with a smirk in the corner of her red-painted mouth.

'He's half the dancer I was,' Antonio says, as if stating a fact.

'At least he still wanted a life, not . . . this!' She throws out an arm.

'But you had a child. Life on the road was no life for him. Neither was years of sleeping in someone else's living room!'

'It would have been fine if he had stayed out of trouble. We couldn't get anywhere of our own because trouble kept following us around. No one would rent to us!'

'You should have brought him here, to me, sooner.'

'And lose out on your maintenance payments?'

I can feel Antonio's pain as well as Miguel's. Both of them victims in all of this.

'That money was meant for Miguel, to provide a home . . .' Antonio is seething.

'It was payment for me to bring up the child. But now that you have stopped it, I need money. Call it compensation for the years of my career I have lost. So . . . it's a good offer. Once dance, to take place here. One month from now.'

'That's June. That's the harvest.' Antonio shakes his head.

That's Olivia's party, I think.

Valentina's head is flicking between Esmeralda and Antonio like a cat watching a ping-pong ball, back and forth.

'To fit around the cherry harvest,' Esmeralda concedes graciously. 'No longer than six weeks from now. We win, we take the lot and sell up. You win, we will part and you will never see us again. We need to be on the road for the summer season of tourists.'

They both turn and look at me. I glance down at my shorts and baggy T-shirt, dusty from watering the trees. I am just the restaurant washer-upper. No wonder they're laughing at me.

Antonio looks away from me with what appears to be resignation in his eyes. He could never teach me, he knows it. I have never felt so utterly useless and worthless.

'My answer is still no,' he says firmly.

'Then you will be forced to sell by the courts. My lawyer will be in touch.'

'Wait! I'll do it! I'll dance,' Valentina proclaims, furious, pale and visibly shaken at the prospect of losing her restaurant.

'No.' Esmeralda smiles. 'It has to be her.' She flicks a hand towards me and I feel humiliated all over again.

Valentina glares at me, then stomps off into the *cortijo*, her heels clacking as loudly as bullets being fired from a gun. We hear her marching up the stairs, and then the door slamming in the apartment. I look back at Antonio.

I wish I could help him. I wish I could stop him and Miguel losing their home. I can see Olivia's face in my mind. The years I spent feeling like I couldn't live up to her, like I had achieved nothing. And then when I thought I was going to succeed at something at last, by coming out here, I had the rug pulled out from under me and hit the ground face first, smashing my dreams and my pride. I have even let my nan down. She left me that china cow because she had faith I would make something of my life. What would she say if she could see me now? I know exactly what she'd say. She'd never go down without a fight.

How can Esmeralda treat Miguel like this, her own son? He is funny, kind and brilliant. I think of Uncle Paul putting me and my family down, rubbing my face in my failures . . . How dare people treat others like that! And as for Antonio, he may not be dad of the year at the moment, but it sounds like he tried to fight for his family. And he needs to fight now! I don't care if they think I'm frumpy and lumpy. I don't care.

An anger is bubbling up in me that I have never known before. Anger and injustice brimming over from inside. Fury at Will, at Miguel's mother, at always being the laughing stock who can't pull anything off. My nan believed in me then and she would have believed in me now. You can't go down without a fight, otherwise I wouldn't be here washing up, watering cherry trees to get my dream bar, would I? And I wouldn't be doing what I'm about to do. No matter how much of a fool I will probably make of myself, I have to try.

'I'll do it!' I suddenly say loudly, and everyone freezes. I look round at each of their stunned faces.

'This is ridiculous,' Antonio finally says.

'Ridiculous maybe,' I say, realising I'm shaking with anger 'But if you don't agree, you will have to sell up and give half to her anyway. This way, at least you get to try and keep what is yours . . . yours and Miguel's.'

'So, it is a deal! *Olé!*' Esmeralda throws a triumphant hand up in the air.

'*Bravo!*' She and Felipe both cheer and laugh, making me feel sick.

'No, no deal!' Antonio shouts and waves his hands in protest.

'Yes, deal!' I stand with my hands on my hips, my heart banging so loudly it can't hear my head saying, *You fool! This is ridiculous. Back out now!*

Antonio looks straight at me and I can't read his face.

'Do it!' Miguel finally says. 'Please . . .'

'One dance. If you win, we divorce and you keep everything. You lose . . .' Esmeralda shrugs tantalisingly.

Antonio looks at Miguel as if he's being thrown a lifeline for all the years that he's missed out on. Guilt and pain are written all over his face. Then, as if there was any doubt as to whether or not he wants to be a real parent, like a wounded lion cornered, defending his pride, his pack, he erupts like an volcano.

'A deal!' he roars to the sky. 'OK, a deal!' His head is shaking, fury and anger coursing through every vein. I too feel a rush of something – adrenaline, injustice, who knows, but it sets every nerve ending alight and fans the raging flames in my belly even higher.

Chapter Thirty-two

We are still standing on the veranda. The battered old car has left in a plume of sand-coloured dust. What have I done?

Antonio marches into the *cortijo*. Miguel and I stare at each other. I see the fear in his eyes and I know that I must look like a rabbit caught in headlights.

'This is madness. You have no idea what you have let yourself in for . . . It is impossible.' Antonio comes stalking out of the front door, holding a large glass in his hand. He throws the dark drink down his throat. I stay silent. 'You know nothing of this world. Nothing of flamenco. Only someone who has been studying it for years can pull this off,' he continues.

I sit down at a table. I feel like someone has thrown a bucket of water over me and the flames that were raging there only minutes ago are now spitting and hissing. Miguel goes inside and returns with a glass of brandy, and I take it with shaking hand. He hands another one to Antonio, who drinks it down like the first.

'This is not her farm. It was my family's. Now I am likely to lose everything because of—'

'Me,' I say flatly. I have made everything worse. It seems to be my unique skill in life. I try to grab on to life's opportunities and seize the day, and end up choking the life out of them.

'I'll go and do the trees,' Miguel says, with a look that seems to say he thinks this is all his fault.

'I'll come with you,' I say, putting down the brandy.

'No, stay. I'll do it. It's the least I can do.' He puts a hand on my shoulder. 'And thank you, Beti.'

'What for? All I seem to have done is make things worse.'

'For trying. For standing up to her,' Miguel says, and suddenly all the emotion of the morning catches in my throat and tears sting my eyes. I gaze up at the ceiling of the tiled veranda, until my eyes stop filling up.

Miguel puts his hand out and touches his father's shoulder. Antonio places his hand on top of Miguel's and they stand motionless like that for a moment. Then Antonio steps forward clumsily, accidentally knocking over a chair, which lands with a crash on the floor, and throws his arms around Miguel, pulling him into a huge bear hug. For a moment Miguel is stunned, and then, as if giving in to years of feeling rejected, he wraps his arms around his father and hugs him back. Tears once again fill my eyes and blur my vision.

Finally both father and son pat each other on the back and slowly release each other. No words necessary. Everything that needed to be said was in that hug. For Antonio, all the guilt about not being there for Miguel, the pain of knowing that his son had to grow up in a loveless home, and the promise that although he might not be able to offer him the world on a plate, he was trying. And for Miguel, the years of feeling pushed out and unwanted, finally letting down his guard and allowing Antonio the chance to be trusted.

'I'll do the watering now,' Miguel says hoarsely and steps quickly off the veranda, heading back towards the abandoned bowser.

'And more nets!' Antonio shouts after him, as if trying to bring some normality to the situation. Only his wavering voice says that this is far from normal. 'Keep those thieving opportunists from taking what is ours!' He points to the starlings on the wire, but I know he's not talking about the birds.

Miguel raises a hand in acknowledgement.

Antonio crosses his arms across his chest, hunches in on himself and begins to pace up and down the veranda. At that moment, Ana the cat weaves her way towards us, clearly thinking it's safe to come out now the shouting has died down. She rubs her head comfortingly against my legs. I feel grateful for her in that moment.

'Look, Antonio,' I say, 'I'm sorry, but I couldn't just—'

'You have no idea what you've let yourself in for, what you've let *me* in for!' He releases his arms and throws them up in the air, then crosses them again even tighter and resumes his pacing. His eyebrows are practically knitted together. 'Now I just have to work out how to get us out of it.'

'Get us out of it? But we can't—'

'This cannot happen! Flamenco is banned here! My whole livelihood is at stake. Not just my home, but the cherry orchard and the horses. Where will they go if I have to leave?' He looks in the direction of the paddock, and I can see the worry in his eyes.

'But we could keep it secret. No one need know. Just us,' I try and convince him. 'If we win, we'll save your farm.'

'But we cannot win. It's impossible! You have never danced flamenco in your life. You know nothing about what flamenco means, where it comes from.'

'I know it comes from Andalucía, where we are now.'

'Not like that!' He throws his arms out. 'Yes, it comes from Andalucía. Actually, it more likely originated in India, before the gypsies moved around and ended up here. But I'm not talking about that. I'm talking about *where* it comes from!' He throws his arms up again, as if they have a life of their own and refuse to be restrained.

It's my turn to frown. I have no idea what he's talking about, but I do know that despite the day starting to warm up, I am feeling very cold. Have I really just lost this man his home and his livelihood? Why didn't I keep my mouth shut? He's right, what do I know about flamenco? I may have done a bit of dancing in school, but that was nearly twenty years ago! I recall Maxine's comment that I'd make a good Adele lookalike, and realise that with my pear shape and ample thighs, I'm not even built like a dancer. 'Chunky', Uncle Paul used to call me when I was a teenager. I think that's how I'll always see myself.

'All I'm saying is, I'm a good learner. I've learned how to water cherry trees. I can learn how to dance flamenco.'

'But like I say, you know nothing about where flamenco comes from. I don't mean its origins; I mean about in here.' He bangs his fist to his chest. 'It is about the pain, the suffering, the heartbreak, the feeling of exclusion that my people have felt. Of being shunned and pushed out. An outsider . . . It is about passion, in here.' He bangs his chest again.

Something not unlike the volcano I watched erupt earlier in Antonio bubbles in the pit of my stomach, and it's getting hotter. Just like before when I thought about Will and what he had done to me. The humiliation, the heartbreak, the feeling that everyone else is getting a life for themselves and I'm still here, a washer-upper with not a pot to piddle in of my own.

'Do you . . .' I hear a really deep voice, full to the brim with emotion and hurt, and realise it's mine. 'Do you not think that I don't know what it is to have my heart broken, to be left without anything, not even my dignity? For years I have tried to prove to my family that I can achieve something worthwhile. I've watched my parents' faces as I've failed over and over again, and all the time I knew they must be wishing I could finally give them something to be proud of.'

'Phuff!' he says dismissively, fanning the flames of fury in my belly. I stand up, my chair falling back as my hands start to fly around. Clearly the door that I have kept firmly shut on my emotions seems to have been ripped off its hinges.

'You know nothing about me. Do you think I would be here, a thirty-two-year-old woman with nothing to my name except a rucksack, a folder of dreams and a coffee jar for storing every spare penny that I can earn, if I didn't know about heartbreak? Do you think that when I cry myself to sleep every night I don't know what it's like to feel that everything I knew and trusted has been stolen from me?'

I grip the back of a chair.

'Do you think that if I didn't know what it felt like to be

an outsider I would be lying to my cousin about owning a restaurant that is clearly way out of my league and my wildest dreams? Or getting up early to water cherry trees and all the time planning to lay on the best party I can for a woman who has made my life a misery since I was a child? Since the day she stole the boy I thought I loved and was going to marry, just because she could.

'I was always the kid that tried to fit in. Who tried to be like everyone else but never managed to pull it off. The kid who always ended up the laughing stock. And my poor parents, who have supported me in every madcap attempt I have made to create a life for myself, to show the world I could be like everyone else, have had to stand by and watch as one by one every attempt failed. Don't tell me I don't know about suffering and heartbreak . . . because I do!'

The low voice returns and I bang the chair down on the veranda, hot, angry tears welling up. I glare at him, my eyes flashing, my heart racing like I have never known it race before, as if it has had a shot of adrenaline right into its very core.

'I may not be like Esmerelda, or like Valentina with her style and elegance. But I would have given it my best shot. I would have tried to help save your farm . . . your home and Miguel's. Because I know what it feels like to have your hopes and dreams snatched from you.'

We stand there facing each across the veranda, with just the sound of the birds on the wire and the gentle hiss of Miguel watering the trees in the field. My chest is still slowly rising and falling. Antonio says nothing, one hand across his chest, the other on his chin.

Then finally he says, 'I'm going to see to the horses. Check on the trees . . .' and he turns on his heel and leaves me standing all alone on the veranda.

Not content with losing everything of my own, now I have even managed to lose Miguel his new home and Antonio his farm, not to mention my hopes of making a new life for myself. Finally, the hot, angry tears start to fall.

Chapter Thirty-three

Antonio leaned forward, rising up out of the saddle, urging Suerte to go faster, putting as much distance as he could between himself and his problems. He lowered his head over the horse's long neck, its mane flowing out as they galloped along the track through the green corridor of fruit-laden trees across the top ridge of his land.

What was it with that woman? How did she keep doing this to him? Getting him to agree to things he'd had no intention of doing? It was utter madness to even consider this!

Suerte's hooves thundered rhythmically under him on the worn grassy path. Antonio pushed the horse on and it responded eagerly; it was as though the gathering speed would help him to clear his head of the fug. The harder he rode through his trees laden with buds and full of hard-working bees, the clearer everything became. One thing was for sure, he told himself: the woman understood passion. And that was all you really needed to be able to perform flamenco. You needed to have lived and to have passion.

And with that he slowed the horse, easing him back to a steady canter, along with his confused thoughts, sitting back in the saddle, taking control of the pace once more.

* * * .

With Suerte in his paddock taking a long drink from the water trough, Antonio returned to the restaurant. He was hot and sweaty, running his fingers through his damp hair. Beti and Miguel had finished watering and were sitting on the terrace, clearly waiting to speak to him.

He strode over towards the steps, not missing a beat. If he faltered he would lose his nerve, he knew that. He was putting all his trust in this woman. But something told him she was worth it. She stood as he approached, looking apologetic, and he hoped she wasn't going to change her mind. But he couldn't be distracted. He marched up the steps and stopped in front of her, his heels marking his arrival.

'We start practising tomorrow. After watering. Here. Ten a.m. Don't be late. Oh, and no one – no one,' he emphasised, 'must know a thing about this, or you will put my business, my reputation and my livelihood in jeopardy. Not that you haven't done that already,' he added under his breath. 'Flamenco is still forbidden in this town and no one must find out about this. Understand?'

She nodded, just once.

He turned to walk away, and then turned back,

'And wear shoes with a heel,' he instructed, before marching up to the apartment, where he stood under the shower for a very long time wondering what on earth he'd let himself in for.

Chapter Thirty-four

What on earth have I let myself in for? I think, trying to read Antonio's face and wondering if he's feeling the same.

I'm terrified, panicked but excited all at the same time. I can't believe that he trusts me enough. He wants me to learn flamenco, and everything he owns now depends on me. I can't let him down. I can't let Miguel down. He's just a boy who's starting to actually have a childhood.

'Now all he has to do is tell Valentina!' Miguel laughs with relief and excitement.

'Tell Valentina what?'

We both freeze. Miguel glances at me and Valentina stares at us both.

'Tell Valentina what?' she repeats slowly, and I wonder where she's been all this time. She's wearing sunglasses, maybe to hide her swollen red eyes. But her tongue is no less sharp. 'This seems to have become a habit with you around, making plans without my knowing!'

She comes to stand in front of us, as though we are pupils summoned to the head teacher's office to explain our naughty behaviour. 'So let me get this straight,' she says. 'You . . . not me,' she points at me with a manicured red fingernail, and I feel like I've been Tasered, 'you are going to dance flamenco with my boyfriend.'

'To win the bet,' Miguel says. 'You heard what was said.'

This is the most excited I've seen Miguel since he's been here. I just wish it wasn't me holding his expectations in my hands. And it's the most he and Valentina have spoken since he arrived.

'To win my restaurant,' she says.

'Antonio's restaurant and farm,' Miguel corrects firmly, and I don't know if it's brave or stupid of him to correct her. Valentina has a poise about her, like Antonio's wife, and I just know it's something I don't possess. If I did, she wouldn't be looking at me quite so incredulously right now.

'Look, I know it's not ideal . . .' I begin. What am I saying? I don't have a chance!

'Why did that woman not choose me to dance with him?' she suddenly asks. 'I have some flamenco.'

'Because they wanted someone who didn't have a hope in hell.' Miguel is still grinning, then he looks at me and realises what he's said. 'Sorry, Beti, I didn't mean . . .'

'No, you're right. Who am I kidding? Of course I can't dance flamenco.' My spirits plummet through the floor. 'This is madness. It will never work. How did I ever think I could help him hang on to his farm and get his divorce?'

'Wait! Did you say get his divorce? Did I miss that bit?'

'Yes, the winner gets the farm and restaurant. If Antonio loses, he loses it all. If he wins, my mother will walk away, give him a divorce and take nothing,' Miguel informs her like he's laying down the rules of a boxing match, which in a way this might as well be. I'm going to be knocked out before I've even left my corner.

'He will be free, then,' Valentina says, sounding as though she's thinking out loud. 'Free to marry again. To marry me!' Her eyes widen with hope and desire.

'I'm sorry I couldn't help it happen.' I shrug.

'You are going nowhere. We have a dance-off to prepare for. You will practise, hard! I will help you. I insist.' She points her terrifying talon at me.

And I'm not sure which is the more frightening thought: losing the dance-off or having Valentina help me!

That night as I lie in my big bed, arms outstretched like a starfish, listening to the soft breeze in the trees and the gentle rattling of the window shutters, I replay everything that has happened over and over in my head. Esmeralda and Felipe turning up out of the blue. The argument. The fury and the pain. Will and I never fought like that. In fact, we never really argued at all. We laughed at the same things, shared in-jokes. We were the perfect couple, everyone said. We didn't fall out, just drifted apart. There was no row, nothing that came from the heart; just a text and a mumbled apology, like our time together had never been. Not like the marks and scars left over from Antonio and Esmeralda's relationship.

Maybe I had a lucky escape. Will left before we could get married or have children. While Antonio and Esmeralda will always be part of each other's history in the story of their lives, mine and Will's chapter seems to have just been rubbed out, like all the life stories I planned before that. Maybe I have been so busy trying to plan my life that I have forgotten how to actually live it, I think before falling into a deep, exhausted sleep.

Chapter Thirty-five

'The thing about flamenco is that originally it was just about the voice, a cry, and a rhythm beaten on the floor with a stick. Nowadays flamenco is made up of four elements: the voice, *cante*; the dance, *baile*; the guitar, the *toque*; and the hand-clapping, foot-stomping and shouts of encouragement, the *jaleo*. Some call this the hell-raising. But it is not just any sort of hand-clapping. The *palmas* is an art. The *palmeros* sets the rhythm and the pattern to the song, like percussion. It works with the *zapateado*, the footwork. The stamping. And then you have the final ingredient – the *duende*.' He pauses and looks at my frozen, terrified face as I try to take it all in, *palmas*, *cante* and *zapateado* flying round my head. 'But the *duende* we can leave for another day.'

I can hear the birds on the wires chatting to each other, sounding like they're laughing at me, waiting for me to fail.

'Flamenco is at the heart of Andalucía. It began in India.' He starts his history lesson, but I'm having trouble concentrating, the words jumbling up and over each other I'm so nervous. 'When the gypsies arrived in Andalucía from India in 1425, they brought their music with them, but they were persecuted and forced up into the mountains along with the Moors and the Jews. It is here their music and dances blended to make flamenco. In the eighteenth century, attitudes changed and bands of gypsies arrived in small towns bringing their music. Some called it seductive and mysterious. Their songs told the stories of suffering and were often sung at private gatherings of gypsies.

'As time went on, people became more and more interested. Performers began to be hired for entertainment, and flamenco clubs sprang up. But many gypsies refused to perform, thinking flamenco should be spontaneous. Non-gypsies started to perform and troupes were set up. Traditional flamenco struggled. But in the fifties, it started to come back. There were festivals in small towns where people could go to perform, not as entertainers, just for the enjoyment of their art. There are many who think that flamenco should remain pure. Others believe that it was born from a melting pot, and that flamenco fusion, the new way, is the way to keep it alive.'

He fixes me with his stare, obviously feeling it important to tell me all this before we start. But I am becoming more and more nervous about what flamenco is going to entail. I look around. All the tables have been pushed to the edges of the veranda, just like I imagined when I first suggested flamenco here, not knowing anything about the fact that it was banned.

Antonio walks over to a small table in the corner of the veranda by the door into the bar. On it is an old grey record player, its electricity cable snaking in through the door. As he walks, his heels make a sound with every step, as if making each one count. I notice he's wearing different boots from his usual worn brown leather pair. These ones are black suede with a very definite heel and, if I'm not mistaken, metal studs on the bottom. He switches on the record player, lifts the arm and gently places it on the black disc. It crackles and hisses, and then a single, heart-wrenching, gravelly voice floats out: 'Aiy, aiey.'

It hits me right in the solar plexus, an emotional punch taking my breath away. It is someone singing about their life, their hurt, their heartbreak, and my own heart twists. There is sorrow, but excitement too, pulling my emotions this way and that. I don't understand the words he's singing, but I can feel the pain in them.

Neither of us moves. Antonio stands next to the record player, one arm across his chest, the other hand pulling gently and rhythmically at the little goatee beard below his lip, his unruly hair pushed back off his face. I am transfixed. I've heard Spanish music before, but never anything like this. I feel as if my insides have shifted and this music has reached right into my soul. It knows how I feel; it feels my pain. My eyes are filled with unshed tears when finally the song finishes.

'This is the music of flamenco,' Antonio says evenly. 'Of my people. My father and mother and my grandparents before that.'

'So you were all flamenco dancers?' I state more than ask.

He nods. 'My grandparents moved around a lot, until they had a family and then settled here. They were well known throughout Andalucía, my grandmother mostly, Ana. When they stopped travelling, the dancers came here to see her, in the barn by the *finca*. They would come for miles, for the *peña*. Not shows for the tourists. More informal affairs, for the people who loved the art. A small poster would go up and word would get out. People who wanted to see my grandmother perform, other dancers. The club would be bursting at the seams. She was a very talented woman, but she liked to push the boundaries too. Not sticking to true traditional forms, mixing it up a bit. She had quite a reputation!'

'And your parents?'

'My father was a dancer too. He came here for the *peña* and met my mother. She left with him. They travelled around. But I stayed here more and more. I was happy here. That's why I wanted this for Miguel.' He looks out from the veranda, clearly remembering the place when it was his family home.

'And which are you? Traditionalist or part of flamenco fusion? Were you as renowned as your grandmother?' I ask, fascinated.

He doesn't respond, but I'm sure I see a twinkle in his eye before the door that has been eased open on his past is slammed tightly shut again.

'Now! I have chosen a dance for you to learn. The *sevillana*. It is danced at family occasions. It is a type of folk dance. Some argue it is not true flamenco. But it is danced by many flamenco dancers today. It is a good choice for our purposes, I think. It has a story, in three parts. We'll start with the first and hope to make it to the last. Let's begin with some basic warm-ups.'

All of a sudden, my mouth is dry. I'm terrified.

'Stand with your weight on the balls of your feet. Your knees slightly bent so that when you stamp, they take the impact rather than your back.' He stamps his foot on the terracotta-tiled floor and my heart leaps. I never expected it to be so loud!

Valentina arrives clutching a cup of coffee and stands in the dark-wood doorway, scrutiny written all over her face.

'Keep your elbows high at all times. Lift them.' Antonio nudges them higher with his own and I feel like I'm about to do the birdy song.

'There are two types of clap in flamenco: the soft one like this, with air cupped into it; or like this.' He claps loudly.

'Keep the elbows high,' he repeats as they droop. I try to lift them again, but my God, this is going to hurt. As if the watering alone wasn't making me ache. I bet you don't see many flamenco dancers with bingo wings! 'And when you stamp, kick back and up, towards your bottom. Up and back, as high as you can.' He stamps again. 'Now you!'

I lift my foot and stamp. It lands with a soft thud. Slowly, his eyes move from my face and down to my feet. I look around, feeling like the class idiot already.

'What are those?' he asks slowly, pointing.

'Um . . . well, you said to wear shoes with a heel. This was all I had.' And it's true. I've lived in espadrilles since I've been here. These wedge flip-flops are the closest thing I've got to a heel.

'Here, take mine.' Valentina makes me jump. She whips off her high heels. 'We're roughly the same size,' she says.

I put them on. They're too tight, of course, but I buckle them loosely. We might be roughly the same size, but we are totally different shapes. Valentina leans back against the door frame in bare, tanned and beautifully manicured feet.

Nothing is going to stand in the way of her getting Antonio's divorce signed and sealed, it seems. Certainly not me. With her eyes fixed firmly on me, I try the stamp again.

'OK . . .' says Antonio with a deep breath, and I think he may be realising that this is going to be an even harder task than he originally thought. His patience is already looking as if it's wearing thin from the way he's rolling his bottom lip in and chewing it. 'Now, lift your elbows. You need to learn to count.'

'Well, at least that's something I *can* do!' I try and lighten the mood, but neither of them laughs. Valentina is positively glowering.

'Flamenco is all about the rhythm. So,' he starts to clap, '*doce, un, dos* . . .' Twelve, one, two . . .

I try to repeat the rhythm, staring at his hands. They are big, strong and marked, hands that work with horses and cherry trees. So unlike Will's I think, which are soft and smooth. Will has never done any outside work. His fingers are long and slender and often moisturised.

'And again,' Antonio orders, and starts the rhythm once more.

Clap, clap, clap and . . . bugger it! I try again.

'And never,' he says without stopping clapping, 'never join in clapping if you don't know the pattern of the song. The rhythm comes first, then the dance and song. Like in life, we have to listen to the rhythm to be able to work with it. You have to go with what it dictates.' He is staring right into my eyes and I can feel a fire starting to burn in the pit of my stomach. It sends my head spinning and my hands clapping like I'm catching flies. Bugger it! Messed it up again. I focus back on his hands, count all over again, trying to burn it into my brain. I have to get this.

'Oh, and Beti, one last thing . . .'

'Yes?' I look up slowly from his hands, terrified in case that fire starts blazing and I lose coordination again.

'You have to stand like this.' He lifts his chin and his chest and his elbows. 'You have to say to the world: come and have a look!' He waves a hand at his chest. 'Look but don't touch! Look at me! Be proud!' His eyes are on me and my insides feel like they've been microwaved again. My limbs turn to porridge, my elbows droop and my knees sag. I've only been doing this for a few minutes and I'm a mess already. 'You have to lose this Britishness. Don't be apologetic. You have to learn to be proud of who you are.'

I have a sinking feeling I am never going to be the person he needs me to be . . . or the person I'd like to be, for that matter.

Chapter Thirty-six

'One and two . . .' I count over and over, spraying the roots of each tree in rhythm, beating it out with the hose in my hand, the sun getting hotter and hotter on the back of my neck. My arms ache from practising holding up my elbows, but Miguel keeps me smiling, and when I get lost, he joins in with the counting, putting me back on track, encouraging me to repeat and repeat the *palmas*, the hand-clapping of the dance, as he pulls the bowser through the trees, which are now full of what look like tiny cherries.

Every morning and every evening I count my way through the watering, and then Antonio begins to add 'the feet', as he calls them, the footwork and steps of the dance.

'The first part of this dance is like two strangers meeting. The second verse is getting to know each other, sussing each other out. And the third verse . . . the third verse is when they are passionate and close. You will learn the basics, the *palmas*, and then we will add our own interpretation of the moves. We will only move on a verse when you are truly ready.'

Valentina is there again, watching me like a hawk, leaning against the door frame every morning after watering. Miguel has seized the opportunity to disappear, off to meet Sophia no doubt. But I know that by the time I've finished my morning class, he and Sophia will be waiting for me in the barn, ready to help clean it.

A week into my new regime and I'm aching from head to toe. I'm not sure I can do this again, I think, as I lift my legs painfully up the steps, through the pillars and archway on the left of the veranda.

Antonio is there, waiting for me. The tables are pushed back. Valentina is there too, in her usual place, with a black coffee in her hand. The smell mixes with the perfume of the wisteria and the fresh scent of wet grass where we've watered the trees, the water droplets scattered around the roots like handfuls of crystals.

'Here.' Antonio holds out a box to me as I walk across the cool tiled floor. 'Take it,' he orders, waving the box at me.

I reach out and take it cautiously. What on earth could it be? Please God, not castanets!

'It won't bite.' He rolls his eyes. I came to realise very early on that Antonio doesn't suffer fools gladly.

Intrigued, Valentina leans away from the door frame and strains to see. I take the box and open the lid. Inside there is white tissue paper, and nestled in it, a pair of bright red shoes with white polka dots.

'Flamenco shoes,' he tells me. 'Well, you can't learn to do flamenco without shoes.' He shrugs.

They are beautiful. I reach into the box and pull one out. Valentina comes over and peers at them, frowning. I hold the shoe up, looking at the leather, the heel shaped like a woman's waist, and the four eyes to lace it up.

'They're lovely. Thank you,' I say, feeling strangely choked. I know Antonio hasn't got money to throw around, otherwise he'd be buying a new watering system rather than relying on Olivia's party for the funds. I'm touched.

'And expensive,' Valentina harrumphs.

I blush and look at Antonio. 'I can pay for them,' I offer quickly, knowing I really can't afford to.

'No,' he says flatly, and stares at Valentina. 'They are a gift. After all, it is you helping me out here.'

Valentina sniffs and nods in agreement. 'Let's hope they help you learn the dance quicker and look less like a duck laying an egg!' she says, grabbing up her keys and heading for her car. 'See you tonight. Work hard!' she adds, more of a command than a cheery goodbye.

'Ignore Valentina, she's just . . .'

'Anxious,' I finish for him.

'Yes, anxious. Now, let's try these steps again. Put on the shoes.'

I sit down and do what he says, loving the feel of sliding them on to my feet. They're a perfect fit. I stand up, suddenly feeling taller, my head held higher. As I walk around, there is a swing to my hips. I feel . . . well, feminine and yet confident.

'Thank you,' I say again, feeling like Dorothy in *The Wizard of Oz* in her ruby slippers.

'And now, the steps . . .' Antonio claps his hands as I step up to stand beside him. '*Un, dos* . . .' He starts the count again and I follow his lead, this time with more determination than ever before. Stamp with the right, then left and a heel touch . . . or was it right with the heel touch and a stamp?

'And again, one, two, three, *un, dos, tres* . . .' He repeats and claps and repeats and claps. And I keep going until I'm getting it right. I am hot. The back of my hair is damp, my mouth dry, but I won't stop.

'Look up, look up,' he shouts. 'Not down at your feet. They will still be there when we're finished.'

I don't tell him it's *his* feet I'm looking at.

And *bang*, I stamp right down on the toe of my left foot.

'Ow! Ow, ow, ow.' My shoes may be beautiful, but the metal heel cap hurts like hell when you stamp on your own foot.

'That was one way of getting a break!' Antonio actually smiles. Even he is out of breath, I notice. 'Beginner's luck I'm afraid. Here, have a drink.'

He hands me a bottle of water from the table. I put my hands on my hips and try and catch my breath. Even my eyeballs are sweating. I open the water and drink greedily. The sun is hot now. Everywhere looks so green and lush as I look out on the grass around the cherry trees and the bright red poppies scattered along the edge by the stone wall.

I pull out my hair band, scrape back my hair and retie it. 'Blow!' I say as the band snaps and I'm left holding my hair back with one hand.

Antonio reaches into his top pocket and pulls out a piece of baling twine. I take it, thank him and tie my hair back off my hot neck.

And I'm ready to start again. '*Un, dos, tres* . . .' My limbs cry out in pain but I'm determined not to be beaten.

There under the shade of the veranda we keep going until lunchtime.

'We cannot practise during the siesta,' Antonio says. 'We will be heard. Someone will hear the music or the clapping, whilst the town sleeps. The siesta is like a religion here.' He gives me a relaxed smile – clearly the flamenco workout has eased some of his worries and tension.

In the afternoon, I carry a broom, mop and bucket up to meet Miguel and Sophia at the barn, where with Antonio safely out of the way they have been practising most of the morning. We get to work emptying and cleaning out the dormant and dusty space. I open up the big double doors and gaze down the valley of cherry trees. Antonio is back in the paddock, working with the colt, only this time he is actually riding it. He works the horse on the circle, first with just the saddle on, then with him lying across it. The young horse spooks and jumps to begin with, but then settles into a confident walk. Before long, as I bring out piles of chairs and boxes so we can start to really clean the place, Antonio is sitting upright on the colt's back, trotting round the circle, his long curly hair bouncing with every stride. I can see he is talking to the horse, encouraging it, working as hard as it is, working with it.

By the time I come back outside again after sweeping down the whole room, coughing in the dust, he has returned the colt to the big paddock. The mare is fussing over the young horse as usual and he is responding. Suerte has gone, though, and I'm guessing that Antonio has skipped siesta to go out riding and check the cherry trees.

We carry on working, cleaning the windows, the barn starting to look brighter. Miguel makes me practise my counting and my steps as we go.

'Everything OK?' Antonio makes me jump as I take a bucket of water outside to throw on the grass.

'Antonio!' I say louder than necessary for Sophia's benefit. 'I wasn't expecting to see you here.'

He is riding the grey mare now, the colt on a leading rein beside her. The colt is like an athlete ready to race again, despite still being damp with sweat around his chest and belly. The boisterous animal flicks up its tail and head and takes a tiny leap, like a teenager getting bored as the grown-ups talk. I glance into the barn. Sophia has tucked herself away behind a pile of chairs.

'Yes, everything is fine,' I say, though every limb in my body is aching.

'And your cousin, she's happy with her party plan?'

'Very. She keeps messaging me. I've said I'll send pictures when the barn's ready. But I've given her colour schemes, menu ideas, that kind of thing. I'm keeping it rural and rustic but with a British flavour. Spanish setting, tapas on arrival. Then there'll be a hog roast; the catering couple have put me in touch with a friend of theirs. Also a tribute act and karaoke. I'd like to get a band to play if I can. Jugs of sangria and Spanish wine with the meal. Am I OK to borrow those terracotta jugs in the cupboard in the restaurant?'

'Help yourself,' he smiles. 'Valentina will be happy to see the back of them.'

The colt is snorting and shifting around, tossing its head up and down impatiently.

'Are you sure you don't ride? I could do with some extra hands here.' Antonio waves the leading rein at me.

I hold up my hand and shake my head. 'Learning to dance

is one thing, but learning to ride as well? I think that might be a step too far!' I laugh, and he smiles and nods back.

'She's a good horse,' he says, patting the mare's neck. 'Kind-natured. I call her Mamá. She is a great mum.'

I step forward and rub her nose. 'I can see,' I say, giggling. 'He's a handful!'

'His real mother died when he was born. The owners brought him to me to find a foster mare. She was a good mother to her own foal, but it died. She is very patient with this boy.'

'She didn't give birth to him?' I'm surprised. She is so protective of him and he follows her everywhere, despite his bravado.

'You don't have to give birth to be a good mother . . .' He trails off, and I know he's thinking about Esmeralda and the way she's treated Miguel.

He looks around at the trees. From this vantage point, he can see the whole of his land.

'Another couple of weeks and it will be . . . how do you say?' He frowns, searching for the words. 'The big drop! The buds that haven't pollinated will fall, letting the tree put all its energy into ripening the ones left behind. You see the green buds; they will turn to straw colour. Then they will drop. This is when we find out whether we will have a good crop or a poor one . . . whether the cherries have been well watered and cared for.' He raises a teasing eyebrow.

'I have heard of some parts for the watering system in a town nearby. I will go over and see if I can get them this evening. Try and keep it going until I can afford a new system.'

'Well, this party should help with that.' I nod at the barn, aware that poor Sophia is still crouching behind the chairs.

He smiles but looks unconvinced. I know he can't think about what the future holds right now. I just hope he still has a farm and trees to water this time next year . . . and that, now, is all up to me. I swallow hard, feeling the weight of his worries on my shoulders.

Miguel, standing in the shadow of the barn, leaning on the broom handle, snatches a smile at Sophia. Antonio looks at him and Miguel quickly drops it.

'Behave yourself, eh?' Antonio says as light-heartedly as he can.

'Don't worry,' I say. 'I'm keeping an eye on him and working him hard!' I turn to look at Miguel. When I turn back, Antonio nods, and I get the feeling he's saying thank you.

Once Antonio has gone, riding off at a fast trot, the colt following, Miguel gives Sophia the all-clear, and she emerges from behind the stack of chairs.

'Why don't you meet Antonio?' I suggest. 'Let Miguel introduce you as his friend. It's not as if he knows . . .' I hesitate, 'what you're up to.'

Sophia shakes her head. 'He knows I'm from the other village. He might suspect I'm leading Miguel astray.' She smiles, and her pretty heart-shaped face lights up. 'It's better this way,' she tells me.

I shrug and get back to cleaning, running the routine for the first verse of the dance over and over in my head.

Once we've cleared some floor space, with lots of laughs and banter, we sit down to take a breather. We hand round

255

bottles of water and slices of almond cake that Bonita has provided us with. Then the two of them stand up in front of the fireplace and prepare to dance. They encourage me to clap along with them, but I don't think I will ever be able to dance like these two. They are mesmerising together, really beautiful. Tears prick my eyes. I must be tired, I think. I try and focus on the rhythm I am clapping out.

'No, no, Beti, like this.' Miguel corrects me, just like Antonio, as I clap along and miss a beat. I pick up the rhythm again and watch them dance. Something in their chemistry brings me to tears once more, and I have no idea why. Is it because of the love I've lost? Or the love I had hoped to find? Or is it the frustration I feel at not being able to do this? I want to get it right so badly. I can't bear the idea of letting Antonio down like I feel I have let everyone else down before. My big toe throbs to let me know I still have a very long way to go. But at the same time an unfamiliar sense of joy grows in me as I watch these two young people together, and Miguel starting to love life for all the right reasons. I am so proud of the young man he has become.

Chapter Thirty-seven

Practise, practise, practise. Antonio's mantra goes round and round my head. For the next two weeks solid, that's what I do. It is now the third week of May, a fortnight since Antonio bought me my flamenco shoes. I practise in the cherry orchard with Miguel looking on. I count my stamps as I wash up in the evenings under Valentina's careful eye. I practise every day with Antonio, clapping, trying to add the footwork and the turns.

'Pick a spot on the wall and look at it, then turn your body and let your head be the last thing to turn, like this . . .' He turns his body and flicks his head round. I turn my body and stumble over. We have been working on the second verse of the song for some days, over and over.

'You need to feel flamenco,' Antonio tells me. 'This verse is an important progression in the song. This is when the couple are sussing each other out. The emotions are building slowly. You must feel it!'

'I'm trying!' I practically cry with frustration as I once again stamp the ball of my foot, trying to perfect the move.

I sit down on a seat that has been pushed back against the wall of the veranda outside the *cortijo* to make space for us to dance. Valentina has reluctantly left for work in the harbour, though she seems to be spending more time here than she used to. She still barely acknowledges Miguel's existence. They give each other a wide berth. And actually, I think he's had a lucky escape. All her attention seems to be on me right now, checking my day's progress when she arrives back in the evening to open up the restaurant to the trickle of customers – adventurous tourists and the occasional loyal local – when all talk of flamenco must stop. She has stopped looking over Bonita's shoulder, and the cook has started to introduce a few little touches of her own again. *Patatas bravas* for one. Instead Valentina focuses exclusively on me, in the corner of the kitchen by the sink, beating out the steps and counting as I wash up.

'Take some time off,' Antonio tells me the next morning as I practically fall over my own feet with exhaustion and burst into frustrated tears. 'Go down to the harbour. See your friends. We can try again later. You are working hard.' He pulls off his boots and swaps them for his worn working pair. I think he's as frustrated as me but realises that just going over the same ground isn't going to help.

I stand up and brush at the tears, taking several deep breaths. He's right, a trip down to the harbour is what I need. I haven't been in what seems like ages. I'll take my phone and catch up on some emails, update Olivia and reassure my mum and dad that I'm still alive. A lump catches in my throat. Actually, it would be really good to talk to my mum right now.

I slip off the red shoes that seem to transport me into being the sort of woman I want to be whenever I wear them. I wrap them in the tissue paper they came in and put them into my bag. I certainly wouldn't be able to do any of the steps I have learned so far without these shoes. Antonio stands up, looking hot, his face tight with tension. He nods and heads over to the stables, where the horses whicker in greeting as they see him approaching. He will feel better for doing something he can actually see results with, I think. I pull on my espadrilles and call for Miguel, but he isn't joining me on my trip to the harbour. Antonio has jobs for him to do this morning. With an *adios*, I head for the bus stop.

I am determined to forget all about flamenco for a few hours. On the bus I get out my notebook to concentrate on Olivia's party. I can hear music playing, leaking from the headphones of the young woman in front of me . . . flamenco music. It would be good to have some live music at the party. I try and focus. Maybe someone playing when the guests arrive, or later, after Maxine's act. My mind flips to the guitarist I saw in the club, the music, the soulful singing, Miguel and Sophia dancing. No! No flamenco! I tell myself off. I'll ask Maxine if she knows of a magician instead. He could walk around the guests doing some tricks as they arrive for the drinks reception, and I'll make up a playlist of songs on my phone.

I hear the music change on the young woman's headphones. My feet start to beat out the rhythm I am starting to know so well, and as I begin counting in my head, I envisage Sophia and Miguel in flamenco outfits, perhaps serving drinks to the accompaniment of Spanish guitar. No! I tell myself again firmly. We'll have a disco and karaoke and a good old British dance around our handbags!

I slam my notebook shut and look out of the window. I

stare at the trees, trying to distract myself. They're now all heavy with buds, awaiting the drop. As I think about watering the trees on the farm, the music from the headphones washes over me and I start counting the rhythm of the *sevillana* again, but this time I don't fight it.

'We haven't seen you for ages,' Brenda says as she guides me into her favourite seat, from where she watches the world go by. 'We've been getting worried, haven't we, Harold?' Harold nods from behind the bar. 'You must be working your socks off.'

'You could say that.' I sit, happy to be in the shade. It's market day and all the stalls are set up. I wave to the young couple who are doing the tapas for me at the party. And to Maxine, who is changing the poster outside the club to advertise 'Ladies' night, strippers and free shots'. It's getting busier in the harbour now that summer is just around the corner. Craig is serving cups of tea and bacon rolls, but he waves over and I wave back, feeling cheered by seeing familiar faces.

'You look . . . well, glowing. Look at your tan already, and I love your hair tied up like that.'

'Thank you,' I say. I have wound my hair into a tight bun to keep it off my neck whilst I'm practising.

'Makes you look very Spanish,' Brenda tells me. She picks up a fake flower from the vase on the table and slides it into the side of my hair. 'There!' she announces, and I don't protest, but smile and leave it there. I admire my reflection in the glass of the patio doors as she gets up to fetch me a drink. 'Sure you don't want a cherry brandy or a sangria?'

I shake my head. 'Coffee's fine. Thank you.' I put my

hand up and touch the little flower again. It makes me smile as I pull out my notebook and put it on the table.

'What have you been up to then?' Brenda rejoins me.

'Working,' I smile. 'Getting my rent money together,' and I nod towards the little bar behind me. 'Antonio's watering system has broken down. Lots of the hose has rotted and the pump has packed up. So I've been watering the trees by hand. Lots of them.' I show her my rough red hands.

'Oh my word.' She inspects them closely. 'You're a braver woman than me.'

'I've also been organising Olivia's birthday party, the one I told you about. I'm holding it in Antonio's barn. I've been clearing that out and getting it ready. And then of course there's the washing-up in the restaurant in the evening. There aren't many customers at the moment, but still, it needs doing. Gives me time to practise my . . .'

I stop myself, realising what I'm about to say. No one must know about the dance-off! 'Spanish,' I finish, and Brenda doesn't seem to notice my hesitation.

'My goodness, you have been busy. Watering cherry trees? Who knew?' She smiles, pulling out a vape machine from her pocket and lifting it to her lips with one conker-brown arm. She inhales and blows the smoke in the other direction to me. 'I'm giving up the fags.' She inhales again, and the air fills with a sickly-sweet strawberry smell. 'Not good around the grandkiddies,' she tells me.

'Actually, I'm glad you've come in today. I wanted to see you. Ask a favour, so to speak. But it may not be possible now you've got so much on.'

'Well, you know what they say,' I reply, actually feeling

delighted that I might be able to help with something and can start to repay some of the kindness this pair have shown me. 'If you want something doing . . .'

'Ask a busy woman!' Brenda finishes, disappearing in a cloud of vaporised smoke.

Harold is behind the bar, quietly cleaning the pumps, listening to Tom Jones singing about the green, green grass of home and, if I'm not mistaken, getting a little watery-eyed.

'Is Harold OK?' I ask Brenda.

'Yes, well, no . . . This is his favourite. He's a bit homesick, see.'

'Homesick?' I say, surprised.

'It's this time of year. He misses the seasons changing back home. Here it just gets warmer and then really hot. Don't get me wrong, he loves it here, but he just gets a bit mournful at certain times. And what with Brexit and all that . . . Well, I think he really wants to get back now. It's like he thinks we don't belong here any more. He misses the mountains and the countryside.'

I look at the concrete buildings all around me and think about the hills and fields only a short drive away at Antonio's farm. It's a completely different world from life down here in the harbour.

'Oh, poor Harold!'

'So that's the thing, dear, I thought we'd take a trip home, see our daughter. The baby won't be long coming and we could see the other grandchildren too. Catch up on what they're up to. Just for a week. And we could go and have a look at the flats we've seen on PrimeLocation and Rightmove.

Put down a deposit on somewhere to rent for the time being, near the grandkids. Get things in place for the move back.'

'Well, that sounds like a great idea,' I say, sipping the thick layer of froth on my coffee. 'Once you've put down a deposit, it'll all seem very real.' I feel a skip of excitement for them. 'So are you going to close up for a bit?' I suddenly realise I'll miss them not being here on my trips to the harbour. They've become like a second family to me.

'No, well not if I can help it. It won't do you any good if we close up and you lose regular customers who go elsewhere.'

'No.' I realise she's right. Once I take over the bar, I'll need the regulars to keep my money coming in.

'That's why I was wondering if you could come and run the place whilst we're away. Just for a week. Get a feel for the place. Then anything you don't understand we can help you out with when we get back.'

'Oh that would be great.' I could almost be touching my future. It would be real. 'But I can't let Antonio down with the trees.' I chew my bottom lip. And of course there's the practising, and the party planning, and the barn to sort out. It would be impossible. There's no way I can get away really. 'Let me think about it. I'll get back to you,' I say, wishing there was something – anything – I could do to make it happen.

When I get back to the farm later in the afternoon, after swapping emails with my mum, reassuring her that I'm happy and working hard, Antonio and Miguel are standing in the yard outside the barns. Antonio is practically jubilant. I've never seen him like it. Maybe Esmeralda has called off the bet. Then I realise that they're gazing at the pump as it chugs noisily away, looking for all the world like proud parents.

'It's working!' I say as I walk up the drive to join them, and I can't help smiling too.

'*Sí!*' Antonio spreads his arms, as if thanking God, and beams at me. 'I swapped some winter wood for these parts. Everyone wants cherry to burn. It smells so good. He was happy to do the exchange.' I notice the wood pile is practically all gone, and hope he's left enough for himself. 'The parts are a bit old, but they've done the job for now,' he adds.

'So does that mean no more watering?'

'For you and Miguel? *Sí*, no more watering! For Miguel it means helping take down some old trees and chopping more firewood!' He laughs and slaps Miguel affectionately on the back, and Miguel rolls his eyes and smiles, recoiling playfully from the slap as if in pain. It's lovely to see these two starting to get along, and I feel warm and fuzzy at this rare show of warmth between them.

'Now.' Antonio slaps his hands together and turns his attention away from the water pump and on to me. 'We practise, *sí*? You are feeling better?'

I nod, but my arms and legs cry out in pain at just the thought of it.

'Let's get the pump to the orchard first, and then we will start.'

We carry the pump to its place behind the restaurant and Antonio shows Miguel how to connect it. Then we switch it on and wait with bated breath for the water to work its way through the snaking pipes and start to drizzle from the watering holes.

'Yay!' we all cheer when it does. I know I'm going to lose paid work, but I'm so grateful not to be watering this evening. I think I can hear my shoulder muscles cheering too.

'OK, we will practise now,' Antonio says when he is confident the watering system is working.

Miguel makes his excuses and I know he's nipping off to meet with Sophia. Antonio doesn't ask, too caught up in the excitement of the resuscitated water pump. He lifts his head, shuts his eyes and breathes in deeply, obviously feeling rejuvenated just by being here in his cherry orchard. I can see that his face has relaxed, his shoulders have dropped, the twitch has gone from his jawline. A far cry from when I left him this morning. He lifts his chest and rolls his shoulders, then opens his eyes again.

'Sometimes you need to feel something rather than see it. Like you with flamenco. You are so keen to learn the moves, commit them to your memory. You count the right beat, but you cannot feel it yet. Watch me.' He bends and takes off his boots and socks, and then stands in the long grass and starts to beat with his heels, lifting his elbows. 'A man never twists his fingers like the woman; he keeps them straight. Although these days I believe things are changing. A sign of our times! Everything is changing.'

He claps and then begins to sing, his eyes shut, a song from deep within, his voice deep and husky, and I am rooted to the spot, watching him in utter amazement. I sense something in his song and his dance, a longing and love that I had no idea existed within him.

'Now you try,' he says when he has finished. And before I know it, I have slipped off my shoes. The long grass in between the cherry trees tickles my toes, and my soles feel the soft, newly watered dampness beneath them. A fresh smell rises up with every stamp of the heel. I want to feel a little of what Antonio did. I want to feel alive.

'Now, we count and clap. Close your eyes, feel the earth beneath your feet.' He claps and sings again, and I shut my eyes and begin the steps of the *sevillana*. At first I'm counting, my lips barely moving, but as I listen to his singing, I feel the urge to dance. He is standing behind me, curved around me so that we are like the layers of an onion. I can feel his breath on my neck as we beat out the steps and he claps and sings. I step and step, feeling the solid earth beneath the soles of my feet, drawing up the moisture, its earthy energy, as if feeling the rhythm that keeps the world turning. We dance around each other. I hold the front of my baggy T-shirt as if it were my skirt ruched around my belly, and feel the breeze on my skin travelling up and over my breasts, making them tighten and tingle.

'You need to feel the dance, let yourself go. Forget about holding back,' he says, and he reaches for my hair and pulls at the end of the baling twine holding it back, letting it fly free in the wind. 'Everything has a natural rhythm; you just have to learn to feel it.'

I open my eyes and see his face, up close, feel his breath on mine, his chest lifting up and down with mine as we dance faster, clap harder, stamp harder until I think I can't dance any more. It is as though every bit of heartbreak and betrayal I felt when Will left me is pouring from me in an emotional release. Every bit of hurt, anger and grief. And then there's the worry over what other people think of me; my shame, disappointment, failure. Every taunt and put-down I have ever endured fires my moves, charging me up. I lift my chest higher, my chin and face, drawing me towards Antonio until we are practically touching. And in that moment, with my nerve endings standing to attention, I want more than anything for him to reach down and put his lips on mine, press his body against me.

I feel more alive than ever before. Exhilarated and strangely free from everything that has weighed me down. I want to live in this moment for ever. I feel my hips move towards his and look straight into his chocolate-brown eyes, as if we are locked there and cannot move apart. Our lips are drawing closer together. It's like a magnetic force and I can't stop it happening. I feel as though I'm waiting for an explosion in my head, in my stomach, like the fireworks going off on New Year's Eve. I'm waiting to be blinded by their brilliant colours, deafened by their explosions. My head feels like it's about to burst with excitement. And then suddenly . . .

'Ow!' Something hits me in the face and I reel away from him, coming to my senses like someone's poured a bucket of cold water over me. What was I about to do? I feel like someone has just turned a pressure release valve. The blood begins to flow around my body again, shaking me to my senses. 'Ow!' It happens again. I look around, expecting to see Valentina glaring at me and throwing stones. OMG! What about Valentina? What was I thinking? This is her partner!

Antonio has the same look on his face, mirroring what I'm feeling, as if to say, 'Whoa! What was that about?' Then he looks around and suddenly his expression changes and he breaks into a huge grin.

'The big drop!' His eyes are alive with excitement. 'It has started! Now we will see what kind of a harvest we are in for!'

It wasn't Valentina throwing stones at all; it was a cherry bud. Thank God! She didn't see what nearly happened. I feel my cheeks flush with shame and reel backwards, bumping into a tree and leaning against it. The grass is still damp under my feet, but this time, instead of filling me with new life, it's bringing me back to earth. I look around for signs that anyone might have been watching us. As I do, I see Valentina's little red car pulling into the car park. My heart is thundering – *bang, bang!* – like a round of firecrackers going off.

I try and calm my breathing, snatching a look at Antonio. I have no idea what happened there. But I know it can absolutely never, ever happen again! I feel like my heart just hijacked my head and my body, like I was invaded by this feeling of passion and lust for life. It was the flamenco making me feel this way! A feeling that I should very much keep shut away, I realise. Hastily I pull on my shoes, vowing never to take them off and dance barefoot in a cherry orchard again. The earth and its flipping rhythm indeed! What was I thinking? Getting carried away like that. He must think I'm such a fool.

Chapter Thirty-eight

This couldn't be happening. Not now. The timing was all wrong. The woman was all wrong! It wasn't as though they even really liked each other. That was why he should never have let flamenco back into his life. It only ever ended in trouble. Antonio fumed at himself, feeling hot and bothered and angry that he had let himself give in to the feelings that had been growing by the day.

She wouldn't even be here after this ridiculous party for her cousin. She'd be gone and he'd be left with . . . probably nothing if Esmeralda had her way. His farm, his restaurant, his horses – his son, who he had only just started to get to know: it would all be gone. He needed to think of a way of finding a home for the horses. That was what he needed to focus on. He must forget any feelings of falling in love. Love was for fools! It certainly made fools.

Whatever had just happened there, he couldn't let it happen again. He couldn't fall in love with this British woman! But my God, he mused, she certainly had the heart for this. The energy and instinct. The chemistry was undeniable. If only she'd let herself go more. She had the *duende*, he could feel it. She felt the soul of the song, and so did he. But it could go no further than this dance. Just this one dance.

He was with Valentina. He wasn't free to fall in love, he thought, guilt pushing down on his chest like a heavy weight.

Still, she was certainly ready for the third and final part of the *sevillana*. The bit where the couple finally fell in love, where the passion lay. He bit his lip hard. He must not let that happen. They just needed to win the competition. Maybe, just maybe she had what it took. Dare he let himself think it, that they could save his home and livelihood? And then maybe Miguel wouldn't leave after all.

Chapter Thirty-nine

'Wait! I have something for you,' Antonio says, pointing at me but walking off up the cherry orchard. 'Something I think will help you.' All around him little buds are dropping from the trees. Even the birds seem to have stopped dancing around each other to see what is happening to the cherries.

'Help me?' Help me to do what? I think desperately, my cheeks burning with embarrassment. Something to help gag me so I don't try and kiss him again, probably!

'Up here. Come.' He beckons me up the orchard.

My heart is still racing for all it's worth, like one of his horses galloping through the canopy of cherry trees. But I follow him in the direction of the top field and my *finca*. What's he going to do, demand I get in a cold shower to cool down? He marches on, moving as if his feet are on fire, and I'm practically running to keep up with him. Suerte sees him from the paddock below, recognises him and whinnies, and I can't help but be amazed at the relationship he has with his animals.

I can hear the watering system hissing, gently watering the trees, feeding the cherries left hanging on. Helping them thrive and become the best they can be. Once again I'm glad it's not me having to do the watering tonight. With that taken care of, I decide that now might be a good time to tell him about Harold and Brenda. 'Actually, Antonio . . . friends of mine in the port are going away for a week. They want me to look after their bar, the one I'm trying to take over. I know it's not great timing, but if I promise to keep practising . . . You could come to me. I mean, now that the watering system is up and running. And it would give me a chance to finalise arrangements with suppliers for the party—'

'Ssh!' He stops suddenly and I practically run into him. I jump back. I can hear the beat of my own heart, still banging after the dance. I feel like all my nerve endings are standing on end, electrically charged.

'Sorry, it's just . . . I'm suppose I'm excited. It's such a great chance to get my hands on the bar before I take over—'

'Ssh!' he says again, more forcefully. God, how can this man be singing songs that nearly bring me to tears one minute and infuriate me with his abruptness the next? He really doesn't need to be so rude.

'Look, I realise the timing's not great . . .' I start, and then I hear it too. I stop, and all the fire in my belly fizzles out. My body turns to ice, like someone has turned on the deep freeze.

Antonio starts marching towards the barn, not bothering with the path. Leaping over and climbing up the small stone terraces where the trees sit in lines.

'No, wait . . . Antonio,' I call to try and stop him, but the clapping and stamping is clear to hear as its rhythmic sound rides on the wind, blowing down the orchard to meet us. It is unmistakable.

He turns back to me from the terrace above as I attempt to follow him, stones tumbling from beneath my feet as I scrabble along behind. His eyes are flashing, but he doesn't waste any time asking me what I know. He turns back to the barn and marches even faster towards it, if that were possible. Through the damp soft grass, ducking and pushing the branches of his beloved trees out of the way as he goes. The smell of the newly watered earth, combined with the May sunshine working its magic, is like a heady cocktail, filling my nostrils as I follow him as quickly as I can, trying to find the words I'm going to need and put them in the right order in my head.

As we reach the barn, the sound is all too clear: the clapping, the stamping and even the sound of a guitar. Antonio gives me one final glare before reaching out to the barn door and throwing it open.

Miguel and Sophia freeze, their arms poised in the air, wrapped around each other but not touching, their faces lifted high but now turned towards Antonio. In the corner of the room is a guitarist, the one I saw with Miguel and Sophia at the club. He stops playing but he doesn't have the same look about him as the two young people: a look of being caught out. They stand, poised and wide-eyed, and no one moves or speaks as we all take in the barn, looking more and more like the rustic, rural Spanish flamenco club that it used to be. Antonio is staring at it all as if he has come face to face with his past, like it's come back to haunt him. He looks at Miguel and Sophia and then slowly round at me.

'You knew about this,' he says in a low, gravelly voice. Miguel drops his arms, as does Sophia, who looks terrified.

Only the guitarist doesn't move or seem unduly concerned. He sits on his low chair, his guitar resting on his knee and across his body.

'I . . .' I'm speechless for a moment, and then suddenly a fireball swells inside me. I'm absolutely furious. What on earth was I doing behaving like that in the orchard with him? He's the last person I'd ever want to lose my inhibitions with!

'No, now wait! It's not Beti's fault.' Miguel steps forward, putting out a hand.

'This cannot happen!' Antonio suddenly raises his voice. The peace that once reigned over this corner of Spanish countryside is shattered, the chattering song of birds silenced. I, on the other hand, finally find the words and can't stay quiet.

'What do you mean, it cannot happen? That's ridiculous! They're just dancing, for goodness' sake. It's not like they're injecting drugs into their eyeballs up here! You should be pleased. And anyway, *you're* doing it, dancing in secret.'

'That's different. I am only doing it to save my farm, our home. Of course I am not pleased. If any of this gets out, the locals will shun me, my business will close.' He holds his face in his hands.

'They're just two young people having fun, that's all. They're not doing any harm. You should be pleased that Miguel and Sophia have become friends, that he's found a hobby.'

'A hobby?' Antonio pulls his hands from his face and stares at me. 'Flamenco is not a hobby!' He's gone red in the face and there is a prominent vein running down his neck that is now pulsating. Miguel puts his arm protectively around Sophia's shoulders and pulls her to him, whilst taking the tiniest of steps back.

'We do not let the young people dance flamenco. You have to have experienced life to understand it; its pain. Miguel is too immature to learn flamenco.'

'Oh, you think I don't know about pain,' Miguel says quietly, and turns away. When he turns back, his voice rises with every word. 'You know nothing! You weren't even there when I was growing up!' He swipes at a chair in anger and it crashes to the floor. Sophia jumps back.

'Miguel, don't.' I shake my head, trying to quieten him. He is stock still, shaking. Sophia looks unsure of what to do. I nod to her, and she runs to him and throws her arms around him, hugging him hard.

The guitarist stands up. Antonio glares at him.

'I cannot believe it of you, Pedro, allowing them to do this! Here! Of all places!'

'I have been around flamenco all my life, and I have known you all your life, Antonio. I know passion and pain when I see it.' He looks straight at Antonio. 'I also know talent.' He glances at Miguel.

'No! He cannot dance flamenco. It ruined my life. I will not let it ruin his too! I forbid it. I forbid you from seeing each other.' Antonio gestures to the two of them and then turns away, his head down.

Sophia looks at him, tears rolling down her cheeks. She takes her arms from around Miguel, who is holding his face in his hands, and runs straight past us, out of the barn door and over the fields towards the whitewashed village nestled into the hill on the other side of the valley.

Antonio, breathing more slowly now, his head still low, speaks.

'I'm sorry, Miguel. But I must forbid it. For all our sakes. I cannot take any more risks than we are already. Flamenco is still banned around here.'

Miguel takes his hands from his face and straightens up, facing away from Antonio, in the direction in which Sophia has run. He drops his shoulders and lifts his head, but doesn't look at Antonio.

'We will lose everything if we let flamenco back into our lives. I knew this dance-off was a stupid idea! You know nothing about flamenco, or the way things work around here,' he throws at me.

I am furious for Miguel and for Sophia. The anger, the injustice of it all rages away inside me. I may not be a mother myself, or ever likely to have a family of my own, but the fire in my belly is roaring and won't be ignored.

'And you clearly know nothing about being a parent!' I shout, raising my voice like I've never done before. It's out before I can stop to think. My cheeks flushing and my eyes flashing. I look at Antonio and I know he's wounded. That was a dreadful thing to say. It's nothing to do with me. I'm not this boy's mother. I'm just passing through here. 'I'm sorry. I didn't mean that. It's none of my business. I'm truly sorry,' I gabble.

'That friend of yours,' Antonio says slowly, 'who wants you to look after their bar. I think it would be best if you went now. Don't you? Miguel can cover your washing-up shifts. It will keep him out of trouble.'

I don't need telling twice. I run to the *finca* to gather some clothes and say goodbye to Ana the cat, hiding my hot, angry tears in her fur.

'And you're sure you remember the alarm code? And don't forget, if the fridge door gets stuck, talk to it in Spanish. It responds better.'

'No worries.' I smile and wave as Harold tries to edge the car forward while Brenda has the window wound down, still double- and triple-checking everything. 'Now go! Have fun! I'll be fine. Enjoy your family and being at home.'

Eventually they leave, and I turn back into the bar and stand and drink it all in. Cortijo Ana seems a very long way away. A world away from this place. The Butterfly Bar is probably only the size of my mum and dad's front room, but it's all mine! Well, for this week anyway, and then in three weeks from now, after Olivia's party, it will be mine properly.

I hold my money jar in both hands and look at it. It's fairly full now, and any extra tips will help. Nearly there. I put it down beside the till, then start setting out the chairs around the outside tables and doing a little adjusting, just to make the space work a bit better so that there's more room to move around. I'm sure Brenda won't mind. I can always put it back before they return.

Then I run through everything behind the bar – the coffee machine, the lager and sangria pumps, the spirit optics – and I'm ready for business.

'Ah, my first customer!' I say as Craig walks in and looks at me in surprise, kissing me good morning as I fill him in about Brenda and Harold going home.

'So you're here. How does it feel?'

'Fantastic!' I say. 'Now, don't tell me. White wine, lots of ice!'

'That's my girl. It's like you own the place already.' He pulls his zip-up wallet from his man bag. 'Have one yourself,' he says, and I smile.

'Thanks, I'll stick to coffee.'

As the coffee machine gurgles into life, I take down a large glass for Craig's wine. And all the time I'm serving the drinks, I find myself counting in my head, counting the beat of the *sevillana* . . . *Un, dos, tres* . . .

When everyone has finally left for the evening, off out for dinner, home to their apartments, or on to clubs for the younger customers, I stack the chairs, pull down the shutters and lock the doors. Then I pour myself a large glass of wine and make my way upstairs to the little apartment. It's full to bursting with ornaments, but the front window looks out to sea, a stunning view I'll never tire of soaking in. My thoughts turn back to Cortijo Ana, wondering how Miguel is, and Sophia too. Is Valentina even more furious now I'm not there, now the divorce isn't imminent? Is she taking her frustration out on Miguel?

I get a pang of guilt thinking about leaving Miguel, and then another as I think about the near kiss in the cherry orchard. Valentina may not be my friend, but she certainly doesn't deserve me trying to make a move on her boyfriend. I know exactly how that feels, after Olivia did the dirty on me with Tom. I think about Antonio, with the weight of the world on his shoulders, about to lose the farm and his horses. I think about Ana the cat and wonder if she's cross that I'm not there. And then, despite being exhausted and wanting nothing more than to collapse into bed, I hold my head high, open my chest and begin to practise. I can't help myself. I have no idea if I'm ever going to dance this dance now, but I can't resist the urge, needing the release and the energy it brings me.

The next few days slip into a simple routine, much like my days at the farm did, and once again I'm grateful for it. It stops me thinking about everything that happened. I get up, sort out the bar and open up; and then in the evening, when the early drinkers have gone off for dinner, I check and double-check suppliers for the party and reply to Olivia's stream of emails asking about the photographer and the colour of the napkins. Being here in the harbour, I can speak to everyone face to face. Everything is in place.

After that, I practise. I have worked out that the floor in the bar is particularly good for stamping on, and the physical and mental effort required for the dance stops me lying awake at night, turning things over in my mind, wondering what's going to happen at the end of this week. Am I going to go back to the farm? Is the dance-off still on? Will I ever see any of them again?

That evening, just as I'm thinking about closing up for the evening, the lager barrel runs out. I'll have to change it. There's no point in leaving it until the morning, when I've got customers waiting. I go to the cellar and try and remember how to do it. It's hard and heavy work and I'm exhausted, but I think I've managed to swap over the pumps. I grab a crate of tonic waters and carry them back up to the bar, putting them down near the shelves. Looks like my muscles have improved. Must be from watering the trees, I think. Or was it the flamenco? I push it out of my mind and go to the pump to pull the beer through as Harold showed me. It spits and splutters and soaks me in the process.

'Aargh!' I am shattered, and now I'm dripping in lager. This is all I need. Maybe I could give myself the night off practising flamenco. Just have a shower after I close up and flop in front of the telly. Give myself a break.

But as I go to take the chairs in from outside, a loud, slightly scruffy group, all ripped jeans, faded T-shirts and leather jackets, is walking towards the bar. They're about my age, maybe younger. I can't close up now, I think, with my business head on. I want Brenda and Harold to realise I can run this place on my own, no problem. And that means them coming back to see a healthy, full till.

I wash my hands and arms, tie my hair up with a twist into a pleat, which I can do now that it's longer, and try and ignore the lager stain down my front. It's hot this evening; close. The days and nights are really starting to warm up, and my skin is glistening from my exertions.

The group pull out chairs around a table, laughing and joking loudly. I sneak a glance. There's a woman with them I recognise. Tall, blonde, in frayed denim shorts. I pull out a tray ready for their order and fill a bowl with peanuts. How do I know that woman? Long tanned legs with ankle braids . . . who is it? Maybe I'll figure it out when I take their order. I hold my head high, lift my chin and roll my shoulders back as I walk to where the blonde woman is sitting, but she's not in a chair; she's sitting on someone's lap. He's tall, wearing faded jeans with holes in, and is turned away talking to his neighbour, almost obscured by the blonde girl's hair.

'What can I get you?' I ask.

In that instant, two things happen. One, I recognise the blonde woman. And two, the man whose knee she is perched on turns around, and my whole world swoops and dips. Alarm bells go off in my head, telling me this is not a drill. This is it! The real deal! The moment I've been hoping, wishing, praying for all these weeks.

'Beti?' he says in surprise. 'I thought you were . . . somewhere else.'

'Hello, Will,' I say through what feels like a mouth full of sawdust.

Chapter Forty

He stands up quickly, almost upending the blonde woman from his knee, much to her chagrin.

'I thought you'd gone . . .' He looks around. Clearly he wasn't expecting to see me here, in the bar we were due to take over together. 'Wow, so . . . you, er, you did it?' he babbles, sounding shocked. 'I didn't think you'd . . . y'know, go ahead. On your own, like . . .' He peters out.

I don't reply. I'm too busy taking in the fact that Will is standing here, right in front of me. He looks just the same, if a bit more tanned. Although momentarily thrown, he is still fun-loving, easy-going, charming Will, wearing a worn Rolling Stones T-shirt and braided bracelets, even more attractive out of his stuffy work suits. The man I imagined I would one day be married to, even planning a family with, running this place together. Changing barrels, clearing tables, cashing up the till and enjoying a nightcap looking out to sea after a hard day. Not standing here like total strangers whilst his new girlfriend fumes quietly nearby.

We stare at each other in awkward silence, as do the rest of the group.

'This is Freya,' he says eventually, trying to make it sound like the most natural thing in the world, but also with a look of such discomfort, as if someone has filled his pants with cold custard. Good, I think to myself. But I have no idea what to do now. Do I run into the bar, slam down the shutters and tell the group we're closed, or do I just stand here feeling like a fool? Antonio's voice suddenly fills my head – 'Be proud!' – and the counting starts in the background. I hear him roaring the words at me over the sound of his clapping hands, and I lift my head just a little. It's not like *I've* done anything wrong.

'Hi.' Freya holds out a hand and smiles with a smugness that makes me lift my chin higher still, despite my knees wobbling like Brenda's bingo wings. A few weeks ago, I realise, I would probably have run off and collapsed into a blubbering heap. But now I seem to be standing taller, firmer, feeling like I'm somewhere I belong. I say nothing. I roll back my shoulders as surreptitiously as I can and open up my chest, then steady myself by putting a hand on my hip, and suddenly, I'm feeling it. I'm feeling proud. Despite a tiny voice in my head telling me to get over myself; that I look ridiculous, Antonio's voice is louder.

'This is the band.' Will waves a hand awkwardly around the group. 'The band I've been . . .' He trails off and pulls his jeans up at the back, as though trying to get rid of the cold custard. 'I thought you'd gone somewhere else . . . a restaurant. I saw the pictures Olivia put online. Looks great! Thought you'd gone there after . . .'

'After you emptied my bank account and ran off with someone else?' I look at Freya, who seems to have her own serving of cold custard to contend with. I can't believe I actually said that! I have no idea where it came from, but it feels good.

'Wait! I can explain . . .' He starts towards me, as if wanting to move me out of earshot of his friends.

'Let me get your drinks first.' I take control again, giving myself breathing space. My heart is banging and my knees are still wobbling, but on the outside I'm acting as cool as anything. 'Be proud!' Antonio's voice keeps saying in my head, and this time I can hear the approval in it.

I move round the group taking drink orders and writing them down. I can't rely on remembering them what with the car crash that is going on in my head, 'Will is back!' clattering around and clashing against Antonio's bark.

I'm grateful that my legs actually work as I walk back inside, leaving the band members to lean towards each other and whisper. Will follows me and stands on the other side of the bar. My heart is banging so loudly in my chest I think he must be able to hear it. It's all so odd. That's not where I imagined he would be, standing on one side of the counter, with me on the other. I pick up a glass and start to pour lager from the pump.

'God, Beti, if I'd known you were here, we wouldn't have come. I mean, look . . . Oh Christ.' He rakes his hand through his dark hair, giving him the bed head I remember. 'I just feel so . . . I really wouldn't have rubbed your nose in it if I'd known you were here. I never meant for any of this to happen. I feel such a prat.'

I let myself breathe. At least he feels bad.

'You look, erm, well, really good,' he says. 'But then you don't need to hear that from me.' He rakes his hair again, one hand in his back pocket, and looks around uncomfortably.

Will is here and he says I'm looking good. He noticed me. My traitorous heart does a little skip but I say nothing. I can't. My tongue is tied in knots.

'So . . .' he begins tentatively, 'are you here with anyone?'

I was supposed to be here with you! I want to scream. You stole my money and my dreams! Instead I say, 'No, just me.' I don't owe him any explanation, after all.

He nods, a bit too hard. My hands shake and the froth on the beer bubbles up and overflows down the side of the glass. But he doesn't seem to notice. He's too busy looking around the bar, clearly gathering his thoughts.

'Look, Beti.' He turns back to me. 'I'm sorry. I really am. I totally messed up, I know. I just . . . I just panicked. I'd stuffed up, I'd let you down. You're the last person who deserves to be treated like that. I'm ashamed to admit it, but I got cold feet – about everything. I took the money, lost it and ran. I know we always talked about settling down and starting a new life together, but when it came down to it, I freaked out. God! I never even made an honest woman of you. I was such a fool. I had everything and I let it slip through my fingers . . .'

He looks at me, those familiar eyes, that familiar face. My Will. But my words have left me. How can I tell him that even after all he's done, I want more than anything for things to go back to how they were?

'I will get the money back to you, Beti. I will try my hardest. Look . . .' He pulls his wallet from his back pocket and takes out thirty euros, holding the notes out to me. I look at them. Thirty euros! The cheek. I don't take it. I can't.

I have one hand on the pump and the other holding a glass.

He puts the money on the bar. 'That's just a start. I've got work. I'll be able to pay you back, in time.'

'Work? Here?' The words slip out as a squeak.

'In the club, with the band. Now the season is about to start up. We saw the owner this afternoon.'

My brain is still slowly processing the fact that Will is here. Will is here and my world is slowing tilting back to where it's meant to be. But now it's shaken violently again when I realise that this isn't just about the money. He's here with somebody else. He's not here for me.

'And Freya?' I finally manage to say.

'Freya, yeah . . . we just sort of got together . . . once you and I had finished . . .'

'After you'd texted me, you mean?' I feel the fire in my belly again, beginning to roar into life, the flames reaching higher and higher, like something inside me has been unlocked.

'I should have called you . . . waited. Told you what I'd done. I just panicked and ran . . . Look, Beti, if I could turn back the clock . . . I'm an idiot!'

'Yes, you are,' I can't help but say, and I look at his bed-head hair and his apologetic blue eyes and just for a moment our gazes lock, like a compass resetting to the home position.

'Everything OK?' Freya saunters into the bar, her slinky hips swaying from side to side, making Will spin away from me. Outside, the band members have returned to their noisy, boisterous banter as they greet a passing group of locals they've obviously met before. Everything and everyone in

Spain is noisy, I've discovered. It's how they say *I hate you*, *I love you*, *I'm happy*, *I'm sad*. They say it loud and clear and don't keep it bottled up.

'Thought you'd got lost.' Freya smiles and wraps herself around Will, who looks as uncomfortable as I feel.

'No, just helping with the drinks. Here, let me.' He goes to step around the bar and take the tray.

'No thank you,' I say firmly, putting the boundaries back in place. 'I'm fine. Just fine on my own.' And I thought I was. I was fine on my own, here in the Butterfly Bar . . . until you turned up again!

'You seem right at home here,' Will says with a smile of admiration and regret as Freya goes back out to join the group.

'I am,' I reply, and realise I mean it.

I carry the tray outside, pass round the drinks and leave the bill on the table. Then I return to the bar, pick up the money that Will has left on the counter and stick it in my money jar. It's looking really quite healthy now.

I watch the group outside the patio doors. Freya is holding Will's hand tightly, and it makes me feel a bit light-headed. That's my fiancé's hand, the hand that has been mine for five years. But we're like strangers now. Will looks as if he's listening to the group and laughing at the right moments, but then suddenly he glances straight through the open patio doors at me, our eyes once again resetting to the home position. I catch my breath, and my treacherous heart does a double skip. Damn it! I'm not over him at all. I think I might still love him.

* * *

They don't stay for a second drink. As they stand up to leave, I go out to collect the glasses. Freya turns and flicks her head for Will, who seems to linger as they start to move off.

'I'll catch you up,' he tells her, his Bristolian accent suddenly strong. Freya wanders off reluctantly to join the group, laughing and trying just a little too hard to look as if all is well in her world. Slowly they move towards the Pink Flamingo's open doors.

'Beti, I am so sorry,' Will says quickly, and he grabs my hand, taking me by surprise.

'For what?' I hear the bold voice coming out of me again and barely recognise it. 'For stealing my money, for cheating on me, for sabotaging my dreams?' The last bit catches in my throat and I find myself lifting my chin a little higher again. I've discovered that that way, the tears don't fall.

'For everything.' His face softens. 'If I could do anything to make up for it, I would.'

I look at his familiar face, the face I woke up to every day for five years. I have dreamed of it so often in the eight, nearly nine weeks since he's been gone. He may be an idiot, but he was my idiot! Maybe that's why I held on to his stuff from the apartment: the Batman socks and the hair wax and all the other things that are still in the bottom of my wardrobe in the *finca*. Because I couldn't quite let go.

With a squeeze of my hand, he bids me goodnight and turns to lollop over to join the others, glancing over his shoulder as he goes with a look of a kicked puppy. I suddenly want to run after him and tell him it's fine. We can work it out. I have a plan. But as he reaches the group, Freya wraps her arm around him territorially and flashes me a look that puts me in my place.

I carry the empty glasses inside, then take a cloth out and wipe down the table. The band are gathered outside the club, still jostling and joking with each other. Freya's arm is hooked through Will's. I stand and look. He has his head down, not joining in. I wonder . . . I wonder if he meant it. If he wants to go back to what we had. For everything to be as we planned. Could it be . . . is there a chance he would want to rub out this part of our story, look back on it one day as a blip and live the life we imagined together, here in the Butterfly Bar?

I wash the glasses, replaying his words, still trying to read between the lines. Was there anything there that said he missed me? He said he'd do anything to turn back the clock. But what am I thinking of? He's with Freya now. He's made his bed and he's lying in it, for God's sake. My hackles start rising. He abandoned me, emptied my bank account of my savings, and now he rocks up here with the woman he got straight into bed with the night he left. What am I thinking? There's no way I should want him back.

I plunge the glasses into the soapy water. It's too hot, but I don't care; it distracts me from the pain in my heart right now. Will being here has brought it all back. I thought I was fine. I thought I was over him. But what if I'm not; what if he really is the one after all? I pour cold water over my hand and it stings. The shock makes me shake. My shoulders sag, my head droops over the sink in the little kitchen and I let out the tears I didn't even know I had left in me.

Suddenly I hear a noise, and my heart lurches. I sniff back the tears and run my hand under my nose. Someone has come into the bar. There's only one person who pops into my mind, and he's been there, going round and round, for the last hour. What if it's Will? What if he's got things he still needs to say? Or what if he's come back to tell me he and Freya are the real deal? Perhaps he wants to show me photographs of the new home he's planning to buy with her, for the kids they'll have and the dog I always wanted. Or could he . . . could he possibly be coming back to tell me he's made a mistake and he realises I'm the one?

My heart thunders and bounces around inside my chest, not knowing which direction it's supposed to be turning. I grab a tea towel and wrap it around my hand, then run the other hand under my nose again. I can't let him see me like this.

'We're closed, sorry,' I call, hoping he'll go away and come back when I'm less of a mess; hoping he won't realise it's all because of him.

But there's no reply.

'I really can't talk now, Will. Come back again tomorrow,' I say, moving closer to the doorway to the bar.

'I didn't come for a drink,' says a gravelly voice, and my heart seems to stop.

It's not Will at all.

Chapter Forty-one

'Antonio?' I say, suddenly not caring how much of a mess I look. I step out from the kitchen, feeling awkward. The shame of our near kiss burns at my cheeks, and my anger when we rowed about Miguel is as fresh as if we're still in the middle of it. He looks just as uncomfortable as I feel. We stand and stare at each other across the bar, my banging heart still feeling furious. Why is he here? Suddenly a thought strikes me and all my fury drains away.

'Antonio? What is it? Is it Miguel?' I scan his face quickly for clues.

'Miguel is fine,' he says with a nod, reassuring me, and my panic subsides. But then he frowns, concerned. 'Unlike you, by the looks of it.' He puts the case he's carrying down by the table. 'I came to apologise. You were right. I'm not much of a parent. I'm sorry I shouted at you. I am here to ask you to come back.'

My heart flick-flacks just like it did when Will turned up.

'Actually, it was Miguel who told me to come,' and I can hear the smile back in his voice. Good old Miguel, he has more sense than any of us. 'I have apologised to him and been to see Sophia's family. But I still have to insist: no flamenco on my land. I can't risk losing him to it. Not when

I've only just found him again. I just want to protect him. But I got it wrong.'

Two men apologising to me in one day, I think, and sniff again. I try and smile back, but end up wincing.

'What is it, what's happened?' He moves towards me, round the bar, and I don't stop him like I did with Will.

'Nothing, nothing, just scalded my hand,' I say, holding the tea towel around it.

He takes hold of my hand, and at first I resist, but he looks at me firmly and I stop protesting. He takes the tea towel from around it and studies it closely, just like I've seen him studying the water pump, searching for answers.

'How was the big drop? All finished?' I ask, trying to distract myself from his intense gaze and the fact that my insides seem to be melting and I have no idea why. Must be Will's arrival still having an effect on me.

'*Muy bien*,' he looks up, not letting go of my hand. 'Very good,' he translates. 'We are going to have a good harvest, really good. There may even be enough to make some more cherry brandy this year.'

'Great!' I say, suddenly realising that I won't be there to see it. I'll be here, I tell myself firmly, in the Butterfly Bar. 'You'll have to bring me some.'

He looks at me, and then glances around the bar, but says nothing more on the subject. Instead he turns his attention back to my hand.

'It's fine. Here, more cold water,' he says, leading me to the sink and turning on the tap, holding my hand under the stream. 'So, now are you going to tell me what's really upsetting you?'

He lets go of my hand and goes to the bar, where he locates the brandy bottle – the good one under the counter – and pours two large measures of the amber liquid into large balloon-shaped glasses. I finish up at the sink and then follow him to the table in front of the patio doors looking out on to the precinct. He takes down two chairs from the stacked pile and holds his hand out for me to sit.

I do as he instructs, though I have no idea why. I have no idea why I do half the things that Antonio tells me to do. Why didn't I stop him from coming behind the bar like I did with Will? This is my space, no one else's. But I do sit down, my hand still red but not stinging any more.

'Here, drink.' He slides a glass across the shiny tabletop towards me.

I pick it up and hold it up to the light. Just beyond, I can see Will and Freya about to step through the club doors. Suddenly Will turns and looks back at me, and my cheeks burn. I take a big swig of the brandy to cover my blushes, and cough. Antonio doesn't miss it, following my gaze over to where Will is now disappearing into the doorway, one hand in the small of Freya's back, like he used to do to me.

'So?' Antonio picks up his glass. 'Who is Will?'

I take another sip of my brandy, smaller this time, and find the words I'm looking for.

'He was my fiancé . . . the reason I moved out here. The reason I ended up working in your restaurant. He's why I can't admit to my family that I've lost everything. That I've messed everything up.' I take another sip of brandy and snatch a look over at where Will was standing.

'He's back,' Antonio says economically.

I nod.

'And not alone, by the looks of it.'

This time I don't even nod.

'And do you want him back?' he asks, and suddenly tears leap into my eyes again and my disloyal heart starts to pick up its pace.

'It's too late.' I shake my head, trying to get rid of the last of the best-laid plans that were lying dormant in there.

'Is he sorry?' Antonio asks. I swallow and nod again.

'But like I said, it's too late.'

'But would you want him back if you could have him, even after everything?'

The silence hangs between us.

'I want . . .' I finally croak, and my heart beats even faster. 'Yes. Even after everything. I think I still . . .' I trail off and then start again. 'I want him to notice me. To look at me like he used to. I want my world back. Will, me, this place. I want to show everyone I can be like all the others, getting life sorted.'

'Then I can help you,' Antonio says, lifting the case off the floor and moving the glasses to put it on the table.

'How?' I recognise the case: battered leather with mottled bronze clasps that he pops open with effort. It was in the barn when I was clearing it out.

'You have proved yourself to be an excellent flamenco student,' he says.

Really? I think, surprised.

He smiles. 'You have shown your passion on more than one occasion. You have shown you have the *duende*, the day you left, back there in the orchard.'

I remember it only too well and sink into the chair with embarrassment.

'You have the heart and the passion for this. It is time you learned the final part of the song.'

'Are you sure? You really want me to try still?'

'We cannot go down without a fight. You will learn this dance, and in return,' he looks back in the direction of the open club door, 'I will show you how to get your boyfriend back. Deal?'

I look at him. Could I really go back to where I left off with Will? The man I have loved for five years. The man who, granted, made a total mess of things, but realises what an idiot he's been.

'Deal?' he asks again, staring straight at me.

I nod slowly. 'Deal,' I agree and a smile spreads across my face.

Then he says, 'The date has been set for the dance-off.'

'What?'

'Now that the big drop has happened, we know roughly when we'll harvest. The second week of June. In just over two weeks. The dance-off can happen the weekend before. Then it will be out of the way and I can focus on the harvest the following week.'

'But that's next weekend! The same weekend as the party!'

'There's nothing we can do to change it.' He shakes his head. 'Esmeralda and Felipe already think I am trying to stall. I need it to be over. I need to be able to concentrate and judge when to pick. I cannot let the dance-off or the party interfere with the harvest. Nothing must disrupt it. Not like last time . . .'

'Last time?' I frown. 'What happened last time?'

He ignores the question. 'It has to be that weekend,' he says firmly, shaking his head.

I suddenly feel totally unprepared for all of this.

'Don't worry. We will keep the dance-off and the party far apart. Like I say, no one must know about the flamenco. We will do it when no one else is around and they are all distracted in the barn. No one from the village will suspect anything; they will think it's just noise from the party. It will be the perfect cover for it.'

My jaw opens and closes, but no words come out.

'I brought you a present,' he says, pushing open the lid of the suitcase. 'It's what I was going to the barn to look for . . . when I found Miguel . . .' He trails off and flips the old leather lid of the case back. It flops on to the table, and slowly he unfurls the pile of black fabric within.

I catch my breath. I recognise it straight away. 'The dress!' is all I can say.

He pulls it out carefully, the big ruffles, trimmed with a tiny line of red, unfolding as he holds it up. It is the dress in the photograph. The photograph I dropped and cracked when I was clearing out the storeroom.

'It was my grandmother's. My grandparents, as I told you, were well-known flamenco dancers. My grandmother, well, she was a bit of a maverick. She would push the boundaries, upset the traditionalists, excite the pioneers. I learned my dancing from her. She was a strong, proud woman. Sometimes even terrifying!' He smiles, seemingly enjoying unlocking these memories. 'Flamenco was in her blood. She couldn't give it up. So they set up the *peña*, the flamenco club in the barn, and people came from all over to see them perform. I grew up with it; it was food for the soul. I grew up with her maverick ways too. I travelled for a while when I was a young man with Esmeralda, but when Miguel came along I wanted to settle, give him the upbringing I'd had. But Esmeralda decided she wanted to stay true to tradition. She wanted to travel and be with a more conventional dancer.'

'Felipe.'

He gives a single sharp nod and throws the rest of his brandy down his throat.

'That night at the *peña*, in the barn, she told me she was pregnant, but leaving with Felipe. There was a fight between me and Felipe. She left and I . . . well, I went off the rails. The harvest nearly didn't happen. My grandparents couldn't do it on their own; I was worse than useless, and we nearly lost the contract. The villagers had to pitch in. I let everyone down that year. It was then that the club was closed down and flamenco was banned in the village. So you see, the ban is because of me. It is why no one must know what's going on. I rely on local trade, and if they think I have brought trouble back to their door, they will shun me and I'll have to close down and sell up anyway. The horses will all have to be rehomed. The odds are against me at the moment.'

We both take a moment. He's the first to speak, quietly, and it makes my skin tingle.

'But you have it in you to dance this dance. I know you can. We have just the final verse to learn, the most heartfelt one. It won't be easy, but you can do it. This is when you learn to be a flamenco woman with pride in her heart and passion in her belly. You will learn to hold yourself with confidence at all times, to invite your audience to look at you. We will teach your man Will that he can look but not touch, no matter how much he desires you, until you permit it. He will be begging you to take him back, praying for your forgiveness and determined never to stray again.'

My skin is now on fire. I am zinging with anticipation. My eyes are wide and my breathing shallow, making my chest rise and fall.

'Become a flamenco woman,' Antonio continues, and every word makes me come alive a little more. 'You have already shown you have it in you. Remember how you felt in the cherry orchard and how you stood up for Miguel? That is passion. Feel it. Use it.'

'But you told me I knew nothing about flamenco and your ways,' I say as quietly as him, like the calm before the storm, feeling like I'm just about to go on the ride of my life. Sick, terrified and excited beyond anything I have ever known.

'I was wrong. I'm sorry. We may not be from the same tree, but we come from the same root, you and me. We have loved and lost. Use it when you express yourself. Let him come to you, but do not let him touch. As in the dance, give a look to invite him to you, and then snatch it away. Until you know he wants you more than life itself. You will help me safeguard my home and I will help you get your heart's desire. It's a deal. You want him back? I will show you how.'

I look at his softened face and then at the dress.

'I know my grandmother would think you are a worthy person to wear this.' He holds it out to me and I take it, a lump in my throat.

'It's beautiful,' I say, my voice tight with emotion.

'Put it on,' a smile spreads across his face, 'and let's see how it makes you feel.'

A shiver runs up and down my spine.

Chapter Forty-two

I come down from the upstairs apartment as carefully as I can, lifting the folds of fabric to my stomach and placing my feet deliberately in the red and white shoes that Antonio bought me. I've brushed my hair and retied it into a pleat.

In the bar, the shutters are down and the chairs and tables pushed back to the wall. Antonio has lit small tea lights from a shelf behind the bar and placed them along the polished counter and on the tables, giving the whole place a soft orange glow. This is how it should look, I think, and my stomach does a quick *stamp, stamp*, like it's started practising the dance without me.

Antonio turns when he hears me and I swear he catches his breath.

'You look beautiful,' he says finally, holding out a hand for me to join him in the middle of the bar area.

I feel like a butterfly: light, beautiful, yet with wings that could take me anywhere.

'Thank you. And for this.' I hold up the front of the dress and look around.

He smiles another rare but very attractive smile. 'You deserve it. You are a beautiful woman,' he says, and my stomach starts up its dance again.

'Now, let's get to work!' He gives a single, firm nod, and with a CD playing, we begin putting the final verse of the song in place. There in the soft candlelight he shows me the steps.

'This third verse is more extravagant. After the first verse of meeting, the second of sussing each other out, now it gets passionate. This is where we use the foot stamps and your fire.' We dance in the candlelight, looking into each other's eyes, moving around one another as though it's the most natural thing in the world.

Suddenly there's a banging on the patio doors, making me leap out of my skin, shattering the moment. Is it Will? Valentina? Esmeralda? Have the villagers heard about our plan to dance?

'What's going on in there?' I hear the familiar voice and I feel like I've been caught throwing a party while my parents are away.

'What's that banging, Harold?' says a second familiar voice, making me smile.

'Beti? You all right, love? Don't worry, we're coming in!' The shutter door rattles as the key goes in and the shutter starts to wind up. There on the other side of the patio doors are Harold and Brenda.

'Bloody hell!' says Brenda, looking around at the candlelit bar. She takes in my dress, and then catches sight of Antonio.

'You're a day early,' I laugh. I'm just so relieved it isn't an angry Valentina thinking we're up to no good – which we aren't, I tell myself firmly. We're just practising.

'Harold had had enough,' says Brenda, bustling through the door with her big beach bag. 'Said the beer was rubbish, as was the weather, and we're worn out being babysitters twenty-four seven. I mean, I love the kiddies and my daughter, but God, it's hard work! We've come home for a rest. What's going on here?' She looks around at the candles again with a beady eye.

'Um, well, we're practising. For a surprise for my cousin's birthday party. No one must know.' I hate myself for lying, but I can't think how else to keep this secret. 'This is Antonio, from the cherry farm where I live and work.' Antonio nods to Brenda and then Harold.

'Pleased to meet you, love. My lips are sealed.' Brenda gives a big wink. 'Now, who's for a cherry brandy?' and she slides behind the bar, looking like she's happy to be back where she belongs.

'Ah, from my village.' Antonio nods at the bottle.

'Really? It's lovely.' Brenda hugs the bottle to her.

'I hope there will be more this year.' Antonio looks wistful, and I know that he's hoping he'll still have a farm to grow the cherries on. He looks at Brenda and Harold. 'Nice to meet you both. I have heard a lot about you.' Then he turns to me. 'Valentina will be waiting,' he says, dropping his voice. '*Buenas noches*, Beti,' and it's like the cherry orchard all over again, when I let passion get the better of me. A few stray fireworks, like bangers from a fiesta, go off in my belly.

'*Buenas noches*,' I say quietly, and shut the door behind him.

'He seems nice,' says Brenda, sipping her cherry brandy.

'Nice isn't how you'd describe Antonio,' I tell her, tidying up our glasses.

'How *would* you describe him?' she asks as Harold comes in lugging two big suitcases.

'Fiery, passionate, caring, would walk over hot coals for the people and animals he loves.'

'Just like you, Harold.' Brenda laughs and then looks at my dress again. 'Cracking frock, love, though it could do with a bit of gussying up. I could do it if you like? A few fake flowers, some tassels . . .'

'Actually, Brenda,' I smile, 'I think I like it just the way it is. No frills. A bit like me.'

'All right, love,' says Brenda, looking at her watch. 'It's late. You'd better stay here tonight. You won't get a bus at this time . . .'

After a good old catch-up, I fall asleep on the sofa in the apartment, not counting steps this time, but feeling like I'm dancing free. Only I'm not dancing with Will like I've dreamed of in the past; this time I'm with Antonio, and I'm dancing on air.

Outside, on the side street next to the precinct, beneath the orange glow of the street lamp, Antonio leaned his back against his truck. This way, he thought, I can help her get her fiancé back, and then she won't fall in love with me. She mustn't ever know how he'd started to feel about her, and neither must Valentina. He must concentrate on Valentina. He had never been the man she wanted him to be. This would just confirm to her that he had been running away from commitment for years. But even if he wasn't with Valentina, he had nothing for Beti. This time in ten days, he might have lost everything – his home and his livelihood.

He took a big breath and suddenly had a strong urge to be back on the farm, drinking in the night air under the big sky, not surrounded by concrete towers blocking out the sky and the smells from the hills behind. He climbed into his truck and drove away from the harbour, trying not to replay their dance over and over in his head.

Chapter Forty-three

'Bye, love! Thanks for everything!' Brenda waves me off with a hug and a kiss as I leave the bar with my backpack the next morning. I look around, but Will is nowhere to be seen, and I wonder where he is. We wouldn't have met yesterday if it hadn't been for the row at the farm and Harold feeling homesick. It seems like fate has brought us back together again, and now Antonio has a plan for me to win back everything I ever wanted.

I turn and look at the bar as the bus pulls up. I can see the Facebook status now – me and Will standing in front of the Butterfly Bar, smiling, thumbs up: 'Made it!' I won't have to tell my family about yet another failure after all.

I drink in the familiar route up from the harbour. When the bus pulls up in the village, the driver wishes me his usual cheery '*Adios!*' and I step out on to the narrow whitewashed street.

The woman from the souvenir shop is putting out the board draped with scarves. She smiles and waves at me in recognition, and I raise a hand back. I call a greeting to the taverna owner, who is setting out tables and chairs in the square, then stroll up the lane beside the church and in through the white stone gatepost. As I make my way through the line of cherry trees, I breathe in deeply. It feels good to be back, I realise. As if I'm coming home.

Ana the cat comes trotting down the path, meowing loudly and noisily, as if telling me off for being away. She weaves around my legs, entreating me, and then darts away as I try and stroke her. She is like a flamenco dancer, appearing aloof but knowing her own beauty, dipping her head, inviting me in and then snatching herself away before I can touch her. Finally, she lets me rub her head, and when I do, she purrs happily, shedding her cold indifference and letting me know she forgives me.

As I walk up past the restaurant, I hear raised voices. I stick my head in to say hello to Frank, who kisses me with unexpected gusto on both cheeks. Even Bonita looks pleased to see me back, smiling before she starts complaining loudly about Miguel's lack of washing-up skills. I'm surprised to see them there in the daytime, and Frank tells me with a grimace that Bonita is working on Valentina's new recipes.

'They are impossible!' Bonita cries. '*No entiendo!* I don't understand them!' Her face starts to crumple and she mops it with a tea towel.

'Valentina has told her to learn how to make these things, "toad in a hole" and "beef in a wellington", or lose her job,' Frank tells me, shrugging and shaking his head.

'What? But that's terrible! Can I help?' I put my rucksack down on the floor behind the back door.

'Can you cook these things? You are British,' says Bonita, suddenly brightening up.

I shake my head. 'Sadly, cooking has never been my strong point. I can do burgers on a grill, to a timer, and that's it.'

Bonita's shoulders slump again and the tears begin to slide down her face.

'Years I have worked here. Practically all my life. I worked for Antonio's grandparents cooking proper rustic meals, like my mother taught me, but now . . . This is impossible.'

'Look, don't be upset. I think I might be able to help. I met a British couple in the market. I'm going to use them for Olivia's party. They're both chefs. They do private dinner parties for the holiday villas, but they also sell tapas at the market and home-cooked ready meals for holidaymakers. I'm sure they'd be happy to help. I could get them to supply frozen portions, and you can send it out on plates as if it's your own. No one need know. Especially not Valentina. And I'd get us a good price for a bigger order. I'm sure we could make it work. Tell you what. In return, you could make them some of your almond and cherry cake!'

She brightens up, dabbing her face. 'It may not be what the customers want here, but it is what Valentina wants, and it could save my job,' she says gratefully. '*Gracias*, Beti.'

I smile, grab my rucksack and pull out my phone, making the call as I walk towards the zigzag path that leads to my *finca*. As I do, I hear a commotion from the horses' enclosure. I turn back.

'Miguel? Is that you? Are you OK?'

'Hey, Beti! You're back! Yes, fine,' he calls, sounding slightly strained.

A moment later, he appears from round the corner, bouncing around in the saddle of the grey mare, Mamá.

'Whoa!' he says, pulling on the reins like washing lines, so he has to lean right back, nearly tumbling off the horse's hindquarters. I grab hold of the rein, while Miguel rights himself in the saddle and shortens the reins.

'Hey! Great to have you back!' he beams, still looking very unsteady.

'It's great to *be* back,' I say, and I realise I mean it. I've missed them all. 'What are you doing up there? I didn't think you could ride.' I'm still holding the horse and patting its beautiful rounded neck under its long wavy mane.

'Antonio needs help with the horses. So that's what I'm doing.' He waves a hand at the mare and nearly topples out of the saddle again.

'Really? I thought you were terrified of them.'

'Some things are worth getting over your fear for,' he beams, and winks.

'Miguel, I'm so sorry about what happened in the barn. I wasn't thinking when Antonio started heading up there. It was my fault. I was . . . distracted.' I can't think of any other way of explaining what happened between me and Antonio. 'I'm sorry you and Sophia won't be seeing each other any more. I thought you were the most amazing dancers I've ever seen. Not that I've seen a lot, but you were . . . well, just beautiful together.'

'No worries, Beti. It was bound to happen sooner or later.' He suddenly looks downcast.

'What's up?' I ask, looking up at Miguel. He sighs, deeply.

'There is a competition, a few miles away. In a town where flamenco is allowed!' he says with sarcasm. 'Pedro, the guitarist, he thinks we should enter. We could begin to make a name for ourselves, and maybe even the start of a career. But we can't go.' He shrugs again and the corners of his mouth turn down. 'Antonio would never allow it.'

I think for a moment. 'I could cover for you,' I suggest. 'Say you've got a headache. That you've gone to bed early.'

He shakes his head. 'We would need to stay overnight. It's a long way and there are no buses late at night.'

'You could be back here early in the morning,' I say. 'It would be fine.' There I go again, weaving a web of untruths! But it would be worth it, surely. It could change everything for him. 'And Pedro thinks you have a chance?'

'He says we have a real chance, not just at this competition but as dancers known throughout Spain. He thinks we could go all the way,' Miguel says sadly.

A thrill of excitement goes through me like a shooting star.

'Then you must go!' I tell him.

Again he shakes his head. 'It's impossible. We would need clothes, shoes and money for buses and hostel. I have none, and I can't ask Antonio. Not with how things are. He has enough to worry about, with the horses to feed, the cherry harvest, and your dance-off too . . .'

'You have to find a way to keep going. You and Sophia are so good. I'm sure you'll find a way of getting your dream if you keep at it,' I say, wishing I could help.

'And like I say,' he says deliberately and slowly, waggling the reins, 'some things are worth getting over your fear for.' He raises his eyebrows at me as if willing me to understand what he's saying.

Slowly the euro starts to drop. 'Oh . . . and would you be going far on the horse?' I ask.

'Hmm,' he says. 'Maybe just to the next village.'

'To the next village where Sophia lives?' I break into a smile, and Miguel suddenly looks around seriously, clearly worried that Antonio might hear. 'Well, have fun and stay safe,' I say. 'I mean it, be careful!' I let go of the horse's rein, and Miguel sets off unsteadily down the long drive.

'*Adios!*' I call after him, and he raises a hand but quickly returns it to the reins to try and stay in some sort of control.

I smile. I'm happy for him. Despite understanding why Antonio is so against flamenco, I'm glad that Miguel and Sophia are still dancing. This is a wonderful opportunity for him. A possibility of a whole new life, away from gangs and away from his mother. This could be his chance to find his own way, instead of trying to do what others think he should do. He's risking everything to meet Sophia, to follow what's in his heart. Something I should have learned to do a long time ago, instead of always looking for other people's approval.

'Wait!' I shout before I've really thought this through. I run down the drive, my rucksack wobbling on my back, warm almond cake from Bonita in a tin-foil parcel in my hand. I pass Miguel the cake, put my rucksack on the floor and open it, pulling out my money jar and thrusting it up at him. 'Take this.'

'What? I can't take that!' He looks as if I'm a pirate handing him the black spot.

'You can. You have to. This is your chance to go and make something of your life. Take the money. Buy your shoes and clothes and use whatever you need for fares, hotels and food. Make sure you eat!' I add.

He looks at the money jar. 'But this is for your bar, your

dream. The one you came here for,' he says quietly.

'And it still will be. Once the party happens, Antonio will be able to pay me for my hours and I'll be fine. Harold and Brenda will understand that I can't pay until then. With the hours I've put in, I'm going to have more than enough. Take the money. Take it!' I insist. It feels good to be able to help Miguel with his dream and know I'll still be able to have mine.

He reaches out a hand and takes the money jar while the horse stands patiently still.

'Go and do it! Grab your dreams and don't let go! I should have done this years ago. But at least I'm here now, not still sitting at home thinking "Is this it?" and "What if I'd gone?" You can't live life with "what ifs"; you have to follow your heart!' I tell him, feeling hot and suddenly a little teary.

'No one has ever done anything like this for me before,' Miguel says, then he suddenly leans forward to hug me and I have to practically catch him before he falls off the horse altogether. Once he is safely back in the saddle, he puts the jar in his bag, slung across his body. 'Thank you, Beti. I will never forget this. I will pay you back somehow.'

'Just go! You'll be amazing,' I tell him. 'And bring me the change!' I call after him, remembering my mum sending me off to the shops. I never did give her the change, and she never asked either. I wave him off down the lane, and then turn and text the chefs from the market for Bonita, feeling a huge swell of pride in my chest.

As I reach the final little slope up to the *finca*, enjoying the sun on my neck and shoulders, I look up. My heart lurches and then starts to thunder loudly. Antonio is waiting by the barn.

'*Buenos días*, Beti.'

I blush. I'm not sure if it's because of what I've just told Miguel to do, or what I'm doing for Bonita. Or that I remember how I felt dancing with Antonio last night and the dreams that followed.

'*Buenos días*, Antonio.' I press send on my final text and shove my phone in my bag, next to my big, full notebook.

'Are you ready to pick up where we left off last night?'

I bite my lip nervously, still thinking about my dreams. He looks at me with his dark brown eyes, as if trying to read my thoughts.

'Ready to get your man back?' he asks, and the dreams evaporate like the early-morning mist that weaves its way through the trees in the cherry orchard before the sun comes up; in its place, something more tangible. Will. Beti and Will. The perfect couple, back together, as it used to be. More than anything, though, I realise I want to learn this dance for Antonio and Miguel, for their home and their future. I'm terrified of doing it, but then I remember Miguel making his secret plans to see Sophia. Some things are worth getting over your fear for, I think.

'I am,' I reply.

'Let's get to work then.' He opens up the door to the big space waiting to be filled with music and dance again. Pedro the guitarist is there waiting, sitting by the fireplace, just like when he played for Sophia and Miguel.

'Hey, Pedro.' I smile warmly at the man who has given

Miguel his purpose in life. Antonio must have been to the harbour and asked him to come.

'*Hola*, Beti.' He smiles broadly back from under his big white moustache. I can see the gaps where teeth once were. His rosy cheeks are covered in white stubble that matches his thick wavy hair. His arm is slung over his guitar, which rests on his thick thigh clad in faded jeans. 'I have heard a lot about you, Beti,' he says, and plucks a few notes with a flourish and a twinkle in his eye. I am terrified but excited all at the same time.

I slide my feet into my shoes, loving the feeling they give me. They make me stand tall. They make me feel that I can do this.

Chapter Forty-four

The next morning, as if sensing my return, the watering system splutters, spits and dies for good, judging by Antonio's fury as he stands over the pump, shouting, before finally kicking it and throwing up his hands.

'Looks like it's back to watering the trees by hand,' he tells me, coming to find me on the terrace of my *finca*. 'But the harvest shouldn't be too far away now. Maybe two weeks at the most.' Just after the dance-off in eight days' time. 'The longer the cherries can stay on the trees, the better.' He looks up at the sky, as he seems to be doing constantly now, checking the clouds and the weather.

For the next few days, I stamp and count my way through the orchard, waving the hose in the direction of the trees as I mark through the dance. Miguel, when he's not pulling the bowser, claps and occasionally shouts, '*Olé!*' when he thinks I've done well. It's all hands on deck. Antonio is in the orchard too, checking the nets stay intact, making repairs, helping with watering.

'At least once this party is over,' I tell him, tipping my head to the barn, 'you'll have enough for a new watering system.' I remind myself to check the bar prices for drinkers who want something other than the sangria and wine on offer. The bar alone could be a big money-spinner. 'Olivia and Gav will be here the day after tomorrow. Then you'll get the cheque.'

'If there's anything left after I've paid the party planner's wages,' he grumps, but I know he's teasing. He has far more important things on his mind, like whether or not he will still have a farm and restaurant this time next week. And that is down to me, I know it.

I practise, practise, practise until my arms ache and my feet throb, whilst double- and triple-checking the drinks supplier, the caterers and the entertainers, and dealing with the numerous emails from Olivia about who likes what food and who doesn't get on with who.

I take deliveries of the frozen meals from the British chefs without anyone seeing, much to Bonita's relief. The meals are tasty and exactly what they should be, even if the local customers don't quite appreciate shepherd's pie and sausage and mash. With everything safely stored in the big freezer and knowing that Bonita's job is safe, I practise all over again, my red shoes never leaving my feet, giving me the courage and the confidence I need.

With the party and the dance-off just a couple of days away, Antonio is preoccupied with the trees and the weather, riding out, checking each tree and its fruit for ripeness. Miguel, on the other hand, is getting ready for his big competition with Sophia.

'Wish me luck,' he says as he sneaks down the stone steps from the apartment, ducking out of view of Antonio, who is in the orchard, pulling down the branches and inspecting the fruit.

'Oh, come here.' I pull him to me and wrap him in a great big hug. 'Now, do your best and have fun!' I tell him, feeling surprisingly choked. When I release him, he's smiling.

'Thank you, Beti, for everything.' He gives me a peck on the cheek and I hug him all over again. 'We will pay you back. I promise.'

'You've got everything? Shoes, jacket, address of the B and B, bus tickets for you both?'

'Yes, yes.' He laughs, then tries to contain it so he doesn't attract Antonio's attention. 'I have everything. I'm meeting Sophia at the harbour. We catch the bus from there.' His face drops with concern. 'What will you tell Antonio?'

'Leave Antonio to me. You just go!' I give him a gentle push in the direction of the drive, and he doesn't need telling twice. With his rucksack on his back, he jogs off, turning to give me a little wave and then making a run for it to the square. Once he has disappeared, I return to the orchard and Antonio.

'Was that Miguel I heard?' he says, studying the branches.

'Erm, yes. He's . . .' For a moment I have no idea what I'm going to say. 'He's got a bad headache. A migraine, I think.' I start to warm to my story. Despite feeling bad about lying to Antonio, I'm feeling excited for Miguel. 'I've told him to take some painkillers and go to bed. Get an early night. He's been working hard, here in the orchard and with the horses,' I finish.

Antonio looks at me with his chocolate-brown eyes and nods in agreement. 'Although I'm not sure he's got the hang of horsemanship quite yet!' he says, and breaks into a lazy smile, the corners of his eyes crinkling. I suddenly feel excited all over again and laugh with him at the thought of Miguel trying to hone his riding skills on the kind, faithful mare.

'I'll look in on him later,' Antonio says. It is almost a throwaway comment, but my dancing heart suddenly lurches and stumbles.

'No need,' I say quickly. 'He says he's just going to go to sleep. He'll see you in the morning. I'm going to finish the evening watering.'

'I'll give you a hand. You're right. No point in disturbing him. The sleep will do him good.' Then he looks at me and says, 'Thank you, Beti, for everything.' And I blush, knowing I'm deceiving him. I feel tears well up in my eyes. I'm going to miss this place, these people. And much as I hate to admit it, that includes Antonio.

'Here.' He reaches into the tree, its boughs heavy with fruit, and picks a cherry and holds it out to me. It is shiny and bright red and looks like a heart. 'Try it,' he urges. 'This is the fruit of our labour. Literally!' He smiles again. 'It was why I shouted at you on that first day, when you picked the branches.'

'I'm sorry about that.' My cheeks colour.

'You weren't to know.' He shrugs. 'I was sorry too. That's why I brought the branches and left them for you. They were already broken. I thought you might as well have them.'

'The branches on my doorstep? That was you?' My eyes widen.

'Yes, of course. Who else could it have been?' He looks bemused.

I throw my head back and laugh. I never thought it was him. But then there's a lot about Antonio I never realised.

Like how someone so big in stature can be so graceful on the dance floor. He is always there for me, making sure I don't fall, and if I do, that he's ready to catch me. Now that's what a partnership should be about, I realise. Being there for each other in case you stumble and need saving. Utter trust. Valentina, I think with a sigh, is a very lucky woman to have this man by her side. Is that how I feel about Will? I suddenly wonder. But before I can think about it any more, Antonio breaks into my thoughts.

'Come on, try it!' he instructs as firmly as if he's teaching me flamenco, holding out the cherry to me. 'They are ready.'

I take it from him and bring it to my lips. I bite, and its juices are released on to my tongue. It's like an explosion of flavour in my mouth. It's firm on the outside, and soft as anything inside. And sweet! So sweet! I take a bite from the other side and shut my eyes. It is so full of fruity flavour, reaching into every corner of my mouth. That's what a cherry should taste like. I've never eaten anything like this. It isn't like the cherries I'm used to. This is on a whole different level. I feel as if my taste buds have come to life . . . a bit like the rest of me feels.

'That's why these cherries are so extraordinary,' he says, and I slowly open my eyes to find him staring at me. 'Sometimes we think we have tasted the perfect cherry, until we find one that really is special. That's when we know for sure that the others were just poor imitations.' He keeps his eyes on mine, and for a moment I wonder if he's still talking about cherries. 'It doesn't look different from the others; it's not any bigger, or better, or more colourful. It's what's on the inside that counts, and you know it as soon as you taste it.

Like falling in love.' He's still looking at me, and every part of me wants to fall against his broad chest and stay there for ever. But I don't. I swallow, still savouring the flavour in my mouth. Even though the cherry has gone, its taste is imprinted in my memory and will forever remind me of how I felt here. Special.

Was that how I felt when I fell in love with Will? Or were we perfect from the outside only? 'You know it as soon as you taste it.' I hear Antonio's voice in my head.

I fleetingly think of Miguel getting on the bus with Sophia, and send up a silent prayer of love and luck to them both. What they have is special, like the cherry, I can feel it.

'I should get up to the barn, check everything is in place,' I say, wanting more than anything to stay in the cherry orchard with Antonio, remembering his hot breath close to my lips the day we danced here, but knowing that's a taste I will never get to try again.

'I'll catch you up,' he says, and heads down to the farmhouse.

I push open the doors, and take a moment to look around the barn. It is perfect, even if I say so myself. Everything is ready. It has been cleared, then cleaned and scrubbed to within an inch of its life. The tables are set around in a club style, and there is room in the middle for the acts. I have tapas and sangria for when the guests arrive, and have booked Sophia and her friends as waitresses. I haven't told Antonio that, but he won't be anywhere near the party so he won't know. It's not like he'll want to come along and join in with the fun!

The shelves are cleaned and lined with glasses. The jugs are ready for the sangria. The hog roast is booked. I look down at my list on the table by the door. Tick, tick, tick. I feel a huge surge of pride looking at what I have achieved. I realise I'm actually quite good at this. All those years of planning engagement parties and weddings has paid off! I can organise events! I smile to myself.

And while Olivia and her guests are listening to Maxine doing her Cher act, and enjoying the disco afterwards, we will be in the restaurant for the dance-off. Just Antonio and me, and Esmeralda and Felipe. Oh, and Pedro, who will be playing his guitar, plus a couple of flamenco aficionados who will act as judges. Pedro has organised for them to come and they understand it is to remain a complete secret.

'Hey.' Antonio arrives at the barn slightly out of breath. 'You've done a fabulous job here.' He stands and looks around as if drinking it all in. 'It's just like it used to be. Here.' He holds something out to me. I look down. It's the picture. The one I broke.

'I had it mended,' he says. 'I think it should go back where it belongs.' And he points to the wall above the fireplace.

'You do it,' I say.

A slow smile spreads across his face. He nods, just once, as I have come to learn is his way, and turns towards the fireplace, his footsteps ringing out, walking where his grandparents walked before him. He lifts the picture to the empty hook there, straightens it and steps back.

'Where it used to hang,' he says, turning to me. 'Where it should be. Thank you,' he adds.

He looks around the barn one more time, then takes a

deep breath, as if this place is where he left his heart and his hopes and dreams. Then he looks back at me.

'Pedro will come tomorrow for a final practice. A dress rehearsal. We can do it here.'

It's my turn to nod and smile. I realise it would mean a lot to him to dance in this room once more, on this floor. 'Now, get in touch with Will and tell him you want to meet with him. Invite him to your party. He needs to see you at your best,' Antonio says, and suddenly I'm a bag of nerves.

I pull out my phone and type the message, inviting him and the band to Olivia's party on Saturday. This is it . . . this is where I finally get to go to the ball! I just hope my Prince Charming will come. Fingers shaking as I set the wheels in motion to win Will back and begin the rest of my life, I press send.

Chapter Forty-five

The following morning, I'm dreaming about Miguel and Sophia dancing, and then it's not them, it's me, and I'm as natural and elegant as they are. I'm in the cherry orchard and Antonio is there with me: *stamp, stamp. Stamp, stamp.* I can feel his hot breath on my neck, his strong body next to mine as we circle each other. The flavour of the cherry is still with me. The feel and taste of it on my lips, sweet and floral on my tongue, its juices reaching into the corners of my mouth. A feeling of something special.

I come round and open my eyes, but the stamping is still there. *Stamp, stamp. Stamp, stamp.* But it's not stamping, I realise with a jolt. It's someone banging on my front door.

I pull on my short towelling dressing gown and run to the door. What on earth could have happened that someone's come to find me all the way up here? I pull the door open wide.

It's Miguel, and Sophia. I pull them in and hug them to me, home safe and sound and tumbling into the *finca* together, out of Antonio's sight. They tell me all about the competition, the other performers – and their win! We hug each other tightly and Miguel hands me an envelope.

'It's the winnings. It's not much, I'm afraid.'

'Keep it.' I push it back towards him. 'Enjoy it. Pay me back when you have more. I'll be fine. Gav and Olivia are coming today, and I'll be paid. I'm even going to open a Spanish bank account!'

We are beaming at each other, standing here in my little kitchen, our arms wrapped around each other. I'm so happy for them. I have a feeling things are about to change for all of us.

'You are ready,' Antonio tells me as we stand in the orchard together later that morning. Sophia has slipped off home to her whitewashed village, and Miguel and I have been watering the cherry trees while Antonio attended to the horses. 'Valentina has asked to join us for our rehearsal. She wants to see how hard we've been working. I'm sorry. She is very . . . determined for my divorce to happen. Do you mind?'

Suddenly I'm shaking with nerves again. Give me a party to organise for nearly fifty guests and I'm fine. In fact, quite good at it! But this dance-off . . . I'm terrified.

'No, that's OK,' I lie.

Pedro the guitarist arrives, in a very battered old Fiat. He gets out of the car, pulling his guitar case behind him.

'*Buenos días.*' He nods and smiles from under his bushy moustache. 'Ready for Saturday?'

'Ready as I'll ever be!' I say, not feeling it. '*Café?*'

'*Café, sí!*' He accepts the offer and adds, 'And a little bit of Bonita's almond cake if possible?'

'I'll check the cake tin.' I smile and run to the restaurant.

I deliver the cake and coffee to Pedro, now in the barn, warming up on the guitar and then disappear to my *finca* to get changed. I will miss my little home here, I think with a pang. After this weekend, I'll be moving to the apartment above the Butterfly Bar. I look into the mirror in the bathroom and put my hair up. Then I add a red silk flower I bought in the market that matches my red shoes. I take a deep breath. I'm as ready as I'll ever be. I bend down to stroke Ana on the terrace, willing her to bring me luck, then look out over the cherry trees waiting to be harvested and breathe in deeply, drawing in big lungfuls of fresh air.

Valentina is already in the barn when I arrive, and I swear she catches her breath when she sees me walk in, but quickly shakes it off.

'I see you are the same shape and size as Antonio's grandmother,' she says, looking me up and down. 'Obviously it would have been too big for me.' But her words don't touch me. Nothing seems to when I'm dressed for flamenco. I feel just wonderful. And with my red shoes on, I'm ready for this.

'You look beautiful,' Antonio says from the doorway, and Valentina snaps her head round and glares at him, nostrils flaring.

'Yes, well, if you dance as well as his grandmother supposedly did,' she says with a slight sniff, looking around the barn like she has a bad smell under her nose, 'we will win this stupid bet and we can finally be married. I could transform this place. Change its fortunes.' Antonio doesn't respond. There is a strange, uncomfortable silence hanging in the air. Pedro looks at me and raises an eyebrow. Antonio stares at the floor while Valentina prowls around the barn, her hands on her hips, inspecting every bit of the space. I can't read his face, but I can sense he's not happy. Eventually she shrugs.

'Not bad. I will get it painted when this is over and you've gone.'

'What? You can't paint these walls!' Without realising I'm doing it, I fling my arm out in the direction of the posters advertising events here at the club, the yellowing, aged walls that feel to me so warm and full of life.

'I will get it painted,' she repeats. 'Bright, modern colours. Maybe even use the place for our wedding.'

Antonio's fists curl and clench into tight balls.

'We are here to dance, not to discuss paint schemes,' he says. He is like a bubbling pot on the stove, about to simmer over.

Miguel arrives, still grinning, and takes a seat in the cool shadows of the barn at one of the tables. He runs his forearm over his hot brow and sips from a water bottle he's brought with him.

'Ready?' Antonio asks me quietly. I nod that I am, and we take our positions. I'm shaking, and I'm not sure if it's anger at Valentina's disregard for Antonio's grandparents' legacy, or fear at the idea of performing in front of an audience, albeit a small one.

'Don't be scared,' Antonio whispers, and I glance down at my red shoes.

Pedro starts to play and sing, and I look back up into Antonio's eyes, feeling like I'm about to either fly or fall flat on my face. As we begin the dance, I am counting out the rhythm in my head. Antonio's eyes barely leave mine, or mine his. I can hear the singing and the guitar, clapping from Miguel and my own heart beating, but then a chair scrapes and I am aware of Valentina walking around us, scrutinising, mercurial and moody. I stumble.

'Keep going.' Antonio catches me and urges me on. 'Feel the music. Let it into your soul.'

But all I can feel is Valentina watching me, judging me. Her eyes boring into me. I try and count louder, focusing harder on my footwork. *Un, dos, tres . . . un, dos, tres . . .* But it's no good. This time I crash into Antonio as I turn the wrong way, hitting him in the face with the back of my hand.

'Pah!' she says loudly, tossing her head, and I stop.

Antonio lowers his hand from his cheek. 'Listen to me, Beti. Look at me.' He takes hold of my hands and gets me to look into his eyes. I'm beginning to panic. I don't think I can do this. 'Listen to me and trust me,' he says firmly, letting go of my wrists. He claps his hands and counts, '*Un, dos, tres. Un, dos, tres,*' evenly and firmly, reminding me of the set rhythm. 'OK?' he asks me with a smile, his eyes not leaving mine.

I can see every line of his face. The redness where my hand landed. The stray curl springing up and down across his forehead. The hope and encouragement in his dark eyes. It is a look I will remember forever. No one has ever looked at me like that before. Making me feel I'm the only person for miles around. Making me feel ten feet tall. As though if I were to fall, he would be there to catch me.

'It is useless!' Valentina shouts, throwing up her hands.

'I think it would be best if you left, Valentina,' Antonio says evenly, without taking his eyes off me.

'Fine. Get the girl to practise harder. You will lose everything! I'll come back when she can actually do it.'

Frustrated tears sting the rims of my eyes. But before I can say anything, Antonio suddenly turns sharply and walks over to her.

'Enough!' he shouts, making me jump. Then he lowers his voice, clawing some control back. 'Beti has worked hard,' he says evenly. 'She will be fine. She understands where all this comes from.' He gestures around at the poster-covered walls.

'Pah!' Valentina says again, not in the least bit reprimanded. 'She is living in the past. This whole place needs to be modernised. The restaurant and the barn.'

'No,' he interrupts her. 'I think it is *we* who are living in the past. You and me,' he adds quietly.

She turns to look at him sharply. 'Look at me, Antonio,' she commands. He cocks his head, and she nods slowly, as if a realisation is slowly washing over her. 'You never look at me the way you looked at her just now.' She points a red fingernail at me, and my cheeks burn.

'I'm sorry, Valentina,' he says. 'I think it would be better if you were to leave.'

'I'm going. I'll be in the restaurant.' She turns, yanking open the barn door.

'No, I mean I think it would better if you were to leave for good. Things have changed, Valentina. I'm sorry. I want . . . different things.'

'But what about the business?' She looks incredulous, like a storm is on the horizon.

'Since this all started . . .' Antonio begins.

'Since you started dancing flamenco . . . with her!' Valentina points, and I shrink away, feeling I've done something wrong. But all I really did was learn to dance. I just wanted to do my best for Antonio and Miguel.

'Yes, since I started dancing again.'

'You've changed. I thought you were finally going to get over your fear of commitment and marry me.' Her nostrils flare as she glares at him.

'I want different things now, Valentina. Dancing again has made me realise that. I feel alive, in here.' He bangs his chest with his fist. 'You wanted to manage our relationship like you managed the restaurant. It was all based on practicalities. It made sense at the time, but now . . . well, I don't think we're the same people any more. This place,' he looks around, 'this is who I am, and I'm not sure that's the person you want me to be.' He looks at her, his hand on his heart. Mine is pounding loudly in my ears.

'But the restaurant? I am needed there. I run the restaurant!' she says, rattled.

'Bonita will cope. She always has; she will again. It is nearly the harvest anyway. Everyone will be picking soon. I think it would be best if you went.'

She glares at him and none of us move. Then, with a high-pitched yell of frustration, she stomps out of the barn and in the direction of the apartment.

'I'll go after her, check she's OK,' Miguel says.

'I'll go too, see if there's any more cake.' Pedro follows Miguel down the zigzag path. There is silence, except for the banging of my heart; then Antonio turns back to me and lifts his head slowly.

'We have work to do here,' he says quietly. His expression is a mixture of sadness and relief, as if he has finally put down a heavy weight he has been carrying around. 'I have my livelihood to save, my family's home.' He gestures towards the fields.

'Don't you want to go after her?' I ask quietly, my heart still banging and my hands trembling.

He shakes his head. 'Valentina and I have been coasting for years. Maybe there was a reason I didn't push for a divorce before now. Maybe in my heart I knew things weren't right. But it is only now that I have realised it is time for it to end. Seeing this place, like this, I know I can't hide from the past any more.' He looks around at the posters on the walls, as if being transported back in time. 'I would sit here, under the table, when I was a boy, watching the dancers. No one knew I was there. It feels like yesterday. I can't keep on ignoring who I was, or who I am. Valentina wants me to be someone I am not. She wants this place to be something it is not. This place is the fabric of where I'm from. I am woven into it. Valentina would have modernised it, stripped it of its heart. Covered over the past.' He puts his hand out and places it on the yellowing wall. 'It is time to listen to what is in my heart. It is time to take the path I have shunned for so many years.'

'But what if Valentina says something about the dance-off?'

'We must just keep going now. We have to stand up and fight for what we want. You, for your fiancé. And me . . . well,' he swallows, 'for everything I have right here.' For a moment he holds my stare, and I wonder if he means more than the farm, Miguel and the horses. But as soon as the thought arrives, it disappears again. 'Whether we win or lose, at least I won't have been responsible for burying my grandparents' legacy. You have made sure of that here. Now, let's try this *sevillana* again.'

My heart is still thundering as he stands in front of me. I smell his freshly showered body, lemon and pine mingling with the heat of the June day.

'This time, listen. Listen to what is inside you, not what's going on around you.' He takes my hand and holds it to my chest, where my heart is beating so hard it feels like it may actually burst out from there. 'Listen to the rhythm. Listen to what is in here. When you do, you'll know you've got it right. You must listen to your heart and it won't let you down. Trust me.'

I look at him, and slowly he takes his hand away. Then he starts to clap, his eyes on mine, reminding me that he won't let me fall. I lift my chin, open out my chest and listen to the beat of my heart, loud and clear, because I trust him. I absolutely trust him with my life, like he is trusting me with his.

Chapter Forty-six

As the dance ends, we stamp the final beat and stand breathless and elated, holding the pose, not wanting the moment to end.

'You were amazing!' His face is lit up. 'You see! Just do it like that and you will definitely win the judges' hearts.' He beams, standing close to me, just like in the orchard. And for a mad moment, I wonder whether this time he is going to kiss me, and what I'd do if he did. But as the sound of blood rushing in my ears subsides, I hear a kerfuffle outside the door. It sounds like a woman's high-pitched voice, and Miguel's.

'No, sorry, you can't go in there,' Miguel is saying firmly.

Antonio and I drop our arms and stare at the door, rooted to the spot. Is it Valentina, or maybe one of Sophia's family, unhappy about her relationship with Miguel? There is a scuffling of feet, and suddenly the door flies open.

'I'm sorry,' Miguel says to Antonio. 'I tried to stop her, but she said it was important.'

'Bet? Are you in here?'

I recognise the voice straight away. 'Olivia? You're early. I thought you were going to phone from your apartment.'

'Oh, that's all I need. The bossy cousin!' Antonio says

under his breath, putting his hands on his hips.

'Ssh! It's her party that's paying for your new pump!' I nudge him with my elbow, then turn to Olivia. 'Still, as you can see, we're all sorted. Everything's organised.' I hold my hands out for her to see what I've done with the place.

'About that . . .' She looks around the barn and catches her breath, taking everything in. The menus on the tables, the fairy lights strung from the rafters, even the birthday bunting around the bar. 'It's beautiful!' she gasps. Then she looks back at me, her eyes wide. 'And so are you. Bloody hell. I never knew you could scrub up like that.'

'I'm just trying on this . . . costume. For tomorrow. To meet your guests. Everything's just about ready. Caterers booked, musicians, waitresses,' I say, slipping into more comfortable territory. 'Let me just get changed and I can show you around if you like.' I catch up the ruffles of my dress, showing off my red shoes.

'It's just . . . fabulous,' she says quietly. 'Everything I hoped it would be,' and her voice cracks.

'Hey,' I say, and smile, all my worries and tension seeping out of me. It's going to be OK. She likes it. Thank God! I've done it! I've pulled it off! Put that in your pipe and smoke it, Uncle Paul, I think with a big smile growing across my face.

I hand Olivia a tissue from the box I've placed on a table by the door, in case of emotional speeches or sweaty foreheads when the dancing sets in. 'Is Gav with you?' I ask. I wonder if he's still parking the car, or writing out the final cheque that's paying for all of this. I'm waiting for her to dab her teary eyes and tell me he's on his way when she suddenly breaks down into uncontrollable sobs and falls on to my shoulder. Instinctively I wrap my arms around her, then look at Antonio, wondering what on earth's going on. He shrugs, as bewildered as me.

'So let me get this straight . . .'

We're sitting on the broken bench on the veranda of my little *finca*. I've slipped out of my dress and shoes and put my espadrilles, cut-off jeans and T-shirt back on. Antonio has brought cherry brandy from the restaurant and handed us each a glass.

'You and Gav . . .' I repeat slowly. 'You've split up? And the party,' the words catch in my throat, 'is off?'

'God, I can't believe it! It's so selfish of him! And everything here is ready.' She swallows, as if finding the next bit hard to say. 'I'm sorry, Bet. You've gone to all this work. The truth is, I saw your new life and . . . well, I suppose I was jealous. Envious of what you've made for yourself here. I thought the party would make me feel that I could have a bit of your life too. I suppose that's why Nan left you the china cow. She knew you'd do something with it.'

I suddenly feel a little pang of guilt over my white lie. 'Oh, Olivia . . . it's me that should be owning up. This place isn't—'

Antonio puts a hand on my shoulder, silencing me. 'Beti has brought the farm back to life. She has made it what it is today.' He looks over at the barn. 'She is the heart and soul of this place.'

Olivia's mouth drops open, and for once, she's silenced, looking up at the tall figure of Antonio silhouetted by the sun.

'I don't think anyone's ever said anything like that about me,' she says eventually; and then realising that she's spoken out loud, she clamps her mouth shut and readjusts her skirt and her uptight shoulders.

I don't say any more, just find myself glowing in his praise and enjoying the sensation of his warm hand on my shoulder giving me strength.

'Mum and Dad are expecting a party, with guests.' Olivia gets back to important matters. 'They've told everyone on Facebook. I don't know what to do.'

'Your mum and dad are coming?'

'Yes.' She nods matter-of-factly. 'And yours.'

'What? Oh God . . .'

'Oh, sorry, it was supposed to be a surprise,' she says, not sounding very apologetic, just sorry for herself.

'Well it's certainly that.' Not only are they going to realise I don't own a bar in Spain; they're also going to discover that Will has left me, and that by the end of the weekend, I may not even have anywhere to live!

'Okaaaayyy.' I try and gather my thoughts, work out what needs to happen next, before even thinking about the bigger implications of what on earth I'm going to say to Harold and Brenda, who have been so good and kind to me, waiting for me to get my deposit together so they can start their new life back home. And then there's Antonio, who has just lost the biggest money-maker of the season. If I can't even pull off a party, what hope do I have of winning a dance competition that will save his home, his livelihood and his livestock? I've let him down. There is no extra income coming in. No new watering system.

'Excuse me, I have horses to see to,' Antonio says tightly, putting down the bottle of cherry brandy on the table and turning to leave. I want to put my arms around him and tell him that just because I've let him down now, it doesn't mean I'll blow our chances for the dance-off. But can I really promise him that? My insides churn like a washing machine as I watch him jog down the pathway. I feel the excitement I have come to experience every time I'm near him these days as we dance the *sevillana*, and at the same time a deep sadness that after Saturday, it will all be over. I will never feel the same again as I do when I'm dancing with him. Miguel is still leaning against the terrace, looking out over the cherry orchard, biting his bottom lip, deep in thought.

I run my hands up and down my thighs. 'Well, I'm going to have to cancel the performers and the caterers. We can't pay them. We'll lose the deposits I've put down obviously. But I need to give them as much notice as I can.'

'Owwwww!' Olivia suddenly wails like a teenager having a tantrum, and blows her nose noisily again. 'I thought he was going to propose. Here in the cherry orchard. With everyone watching. It was going to be perfect! Top proposal ever! What on earth is everyone going to be saying about me?'

'Tell them . . . just tell them there's been a change of plan and the party isn't going ahead. If they're real friends, they'll understand.'

'They really won't. Most of them were Gav's friends anyway – well, employees. They're still coming over. He's booked a party down at a beach bar for them. A staff party, tax deductible. Apparently they have topless barmaids.'

'Has he now.' I find myself bristling. What I had planned was going to be far classier. I realise with a pang how much I have loved organising this party, despite the fact that I didn't want to do it to start with. I'd jump at the chance to do it again. Maybe I'll go into events planning. I'm going to have to think of something, after all, given that I won't be able to take over the Butterfly Bar now. I'm gutted, exhausted, battle weary.

'When exactly did all this happen, Olivia?' I sigh.

'Just before we left for the airport. He changed his flight to travel with friends. I didn't know what to do, so I just got on the plane and came anyway. I'm going to be a laughing stock.'

Not as much as I'll be on Saturday if I dance as badly as I did in front of Valentina, I think. It won't only be the watering system that I lose. It will be this place. Miguel and Antonio's home. I know he's down there now, with the horses, working out what's going to happen to them if we don't win. Where will they go? Will he be able to keep the mare and colt together? My heart twists. I may have lost the Butterfly Bar, but he has so much more to lose. He has people and animals who rely on him for their home and security.

'I haven't even got anywhere to stay,' Olivia sniffs. 'Gav's in the apartment. I got a taxi here. My case is down in the car park.'

I sigh heavily again. 'Go and get your stuff. Grab a shower. It won't be what you're used to, but it'll freshen you up. I'll ask Harold and Brenda if they know of a B and B for a few nights, until you can get your flight back home.'

She stands up and goes to make her way down the steps to the zigzag path. 'Will it have Wi-Fi?' she asks, and I roll my eyes.

'Perhaps staying off social media for a bit would be the best thing you can do,' I say, wondering why I ever found Olivia intimidating.

Once she has gone, Miguel and I turn to look at each other. He knows exactly what I'm thinking.

'I'm so sorry, Beti. Your deposit money . . . I spent it and now you have nothing!' He puts his hand into his pocket and pulls out the envelope with his winnings in it. 'Here, take this. I insist!' he says with tears in his eyes. 'What are you going to do? You need to pay for your bar on Saturday.'

'Keep it, Miguel. It's not enough to help me out. It's fine. I'd need a miracle to get me out of this one.' I think about Harold and Brenda. All their hopes and dreams resting on me. I feel sick thinking about the people I'm letting down.

Miguel looks out over the cherry orchard again, leaning against the hand-made railings. Neither of us speaks, lost in our own thoughts. Finally he turns to me.

'I do have an idea . . .' and his eyes sparkle, looking just like his father's did when we ended our dance, when anything seemed possible; and my insides do a little clap and an '*Olé!*', making me shiver with excitement.

'We can't!'

'We can!' His eyes widen as the idea grows. 'It's the only answer. Pedro will help get the word out, and once he does, I'm sure everyone will want to come.'

'But it's against the law!'

'It's not against the law. It was just banned, by an old priest who isn't even alive any more.' Miguel stands up and waves his arms in the direction of the sleepy square. 'A bit like this town!'

He's right. In my heart, I know he's right. I look at him. He is so much older than his seventeen years, and yet still a boy too, albeit one who has thrived since being here.

'Will people really want to come?' I ask him.

'Look!' he says, leading me back into the barn. 'Look at these posters on the walls. My father was a well-known flamenco dancer. People came to see him from all over the country. They will come if they hear he is dancing again. Pedro has told me of his reputation, his career. He was greatly admired. He was known as the Horse Whisperer, El Susurrador de Caballo. Or just Horse.'

'The horse whisperer. That's what I called him when I first saw him working with the colt.'

'He is known for his work with horses as much as his dancing. Look!' Miguel points at the posters, and I see Antonio's faded face, under a wide-brimmed hat. I'd recognise that determined chin and knitted brow anywhere.

'We will tell everyone it is the return of the Horse Whisperer, and they will pay!'

Even I am feeling excited about the return of the Horse Whisperer. And really, what choice do we have?

'So let me get this right, you're suggesting we sell tickets, make it a proper . . . what's the word?'

'*Peña*,' he tells me. 'Just like they used to hold here. Not for tourists, but for the real lovers of flamenco. We bring the barn back to life. Sell tickets on the door.'

I look around. It would be wonderful to see this place being used.

'What? Put up posters in the harbour and spread the word?' I'm beginning to think this might actually be a good idea. It's growing like the swell of music and footsteps as a dance gathers pace.

'Yes! And this.' He waves his phone. 'We put it on social media.'

'But what about Antonio? He will go mad!'

'He won't know. Not until it's too late.' If we tell him, he'll say no. But it's that or lose the lot! You lose your bar. We lose our home.'

'And Harold and Brenda's dream of moving home will be over. They'll be practically packed!'

'This way the dance-off can go ahead. No one in the town will know it isn't a party for tourists. Your cousin's party. Antonio can still try and save the farm and you can still try and get the bar. It has to be worth trying!'

'And I'll have to dance in front of everyone? The crowd that turns up?' I say, beginning to shake as the nerves rush in.

He nods slowly but says nothing. And with my fear growing by the second, I nod too. I have to try.

Olivia joins us with her huge pink case bouncing off the tufts of grass. She's hot and sweaty and out of breath.

'I can't get hold of Mum or Dad,' she says, holding up her phone with her spare hand. 'I don't know what to tell them. I've never been dumped before. And they were so looking forward to showing off to their friends!'

'Well, just wait a bit. You may yet have a party that will

get everyone talking,' I tell her, and glance at Miguel, who is busy on Facebook.

'God! Really?' says Olivia, and she throws her arms around me. 'Oh I knew I could rely on you, Bet. You're a star! I knew you wouldn't let me down. Thank you for doing this for me.'

'Oh, I'm not doing it for you, Olivia,' I say evenly. 'I'm doing it for me . . . and the people I've come to care about.'

She looks at me blankly, but I'm pretty sure we understand each other. If only she knew . . . I might be making the biggest mistake of my life. If I fail now, everyone will see my mistakes. This has to go according to plan or I will have let everyone down. Nothing can stop it happening, and I'm absolutely terrified.

Chapter Forty-seven

'What? No! It can't be! Not this weekend!'

Antonio is pushing his phone into the top pocket of his checked shirt, open over a white T-shirt. He's standing by the horses' paddock. Miguel and I are escorting Olivia and her case down to the square to get the bus to the harbour. He has put up a hand to stop us and deliver the news.

'It has to be. The harvest has to be brought forward. It must happen now. Next weekend will be too late. It's how these things are. There is heavy rain forecast. I must get the cherries in or they will be ruined. I need pickers. Everyone out to the orchard. I mean everyone.' He looks at Olivia firmly. This time Olivia is well aware of who's in charge.

'But the p . . . p . . . party?' I stop myself saying *peña*.

'What party? There is no party now there is no money to pay for it,' Antonio barks, and I hear Olivia squeak. 'And the dance-off will have to be cancelled.'

I can't believe what I'm hearing. People are expecting a *peña*. Word has gone out. They are expecting the Horse Whisperer to dance again!

'No!' I reply. 'You can't do that! That will mean they think you couldn't do it, that you've given up. You'll lose the bet! You'll lose this place!'

'I cannot risk losing the harvest. I cannot let this town down again. Maybe this place would be better in someone else's hands. Someone who can pay for a watering system. Someone who can take care of the land and all its history better than me,' he says, beaten.

'No, Antonio! You love this place! No one could love it like you do,' I find myself blurting out, wanting to reassure him. He turns to look at me but says nothing. 'How long does the harvest usually take?' I ask.

'About a week,' he replies flatly.

'And how long have we got to do it in?'

'Two days,' he says, as deadpan as before. 'The rain is due Saturday evening.'

'Can any of the locals help?' I ask helpfully.

He shakes his head. 'They have their own harvest to bring in. We are all in the same boat.' He goes to the barn, bringing out a stack of crates and plonking them on the ground before looking up at the sunless sky.

I take a huge breath. 'If I can get you pickers, if we can get the harvest in, the dance-off can still happen, yes?'

He narrows his eyes at me. 'If you think you can get me pickers and we can get the harvest in, then yes, we will still dance.' He glances at Olivia, who, unusually, says nothing.

'Miguel, tell people to come, to help pick the cherry harvest on Saturday.' I nod meaningfully to him and his phone. 'Here, let me see.' I take the phone from him and type in the words 'cherry harvest festival' at the top of his post, then hand it back.

Antonio frowns deeply.

'Don't worry, Papa. Social media is a wonderful thing.

We'll get you pickers.' Miguel grins at me and starts tapping on his phone. Antonio is looking at him, amazed that he has finally called him Papa.

I feel like I can sense the storm about to come. I'm hot, my head feels heavy, giving me a headache. I just want this to be over. I don't even know if anyone is going to come. All we can do is spread the word far and wide in the flamenco world. 'The Horse Whisperer is dancing again. Come and be part of the cherry harvest and see him dance again.' It might all be for nothing. Perhaps no one will come and there won't be any money anyway. And if Antonio finds out what I've done, or any of the locals get wind of it, there will be hell to pay.

'Well then, let's get picking.' I clap my hands together to try and quell my nerves.

For the rest of the day, Miguel, Olivia, Bonita, Frank, Antonio and I work the rows of cherry trees in the orchards. We operate in pairs: one up the tree on a ladder, the other picking the lower cherries. Hardly anyone talks. Only the birds on the wires chatter, as if watching chefs at work preparing a long-awaited meal. The clouds begin to build. We're all watching the sky every few minutes. Valentina is nowhere to be seen, other than a glimpse of her car in the car park. I'm guessing she's been for her belongings and gone again. In the distance there is the sound of other family farms all doing the same as us, picking to save the cherry harvest.

We work until we can no longer see the cherries on the trees. Aching and weary, we stack the crates of fruit, and then Bonita feeds us the most amazing *tortilla española*,

Spanish omelette. We sit out on the terrace. It is pitch black all around us. Bonita cuts the vast yellow omelette and serves each of us a big triangle, and we help ourselves to a bowl of salad, crunchy leaves drizzled in glorious green olive oil. I take a mouthful of the fluffy eggs. I'm almost too exhausted to chew, but it slowly melts on my tongue. The onions are sweet like caramel, and the potatoes tender. It's all lifted by the glorious taste of parsley that Bonita will have picked from outside the back door. There are pools of herby oil and butter on my plate that I mop up with a handful of *pan rustico*, crusty on the outside and soft as a pillow on the inside.

Having eaten everything on my plate, I sit back feeling thoroughly satisfied. I glance across at Bonita.

'I don't know how you did all this as well as helping with the harvest.'

She beams. 'There is always time to cook for the ones we love,' she says with a satisfied smile, looking round the table.

Restored by the wonderful food, we all begin to find the power of conversation again, talking about the picking, and the bits of our body that ache. Even Olivia seems like a different person. Everyone is chatting away, except Antonio, who sits in contemplative silence, the weight of the world on his shoulders.

Later, we close up the *cortijo*. Antonio offers Olivia a spare bed in the apartment, and I feel a strange pang, wondering if she is going to attempt to move in where Valentina has left. None of my business, I tell myself. Ridiculous to worry. I'm overtired and my emotions are playing havoc with me.

I heave my weary body up to my *finca* by the light of my phone, little bats darting in front of me as though guiding me home. In bed, I try and focus on Will's face, wondering if he's going to come to the dance-off. But my thoughts, despite my best efforts, keep turning back to Antonio and his worried expression. I wish I could reassure him that every-thing will be fine, but I can't. I have no idea if any pickers will turn up, or if I can win this bet for him.

I sit bolt upright in bed. It's Saturday. It's today! It's dark outside and I wonder if I've actually slept at all – it feels like my head hit the pillow just five minutes ago. But no, I check my phone and see it's time to get up. Today is the day. We must get the harvest in in order to compete in the dance-off. The clock is against us. I wonder whether to lay out my dress and shoes, but don't want to tempt fate. We have a huge amount of cherry trees to get through. I have no idea how we'll do it before the rain comes if we don't get help.

As dawn comes, we all gather on the terrace outside the *cortijo*, drinking strong coffee and eating bread with butter and home-made cherry jam that Bonita has brought in a basket from home. There's a strong wind blowing, hissing through the trees. I feel too nervous to eat, but Bonita insists, and the taste of the jam – thick, sweet and full of fruit – is out of this world. Even Olivia is up – well, upright. She looks totally out of her comfort zone. Antonio apparently insisted there was no time for things like showers and make-up; there was work to be done. Olivia, it seems, has done as she was told. She's standing here looking like Patsy in *Absolutely Fabulous*, with her hair on end and yesterday's make-up still smudged into the corners of her eyes. What would her picture look like on Facebook now? I wonder with gentle amusement.

'To work!' Antonio orders as the light starts to creep over the hills on the far side of the valley. 'The rain is due at sunset. We have to get the harvest in!'

I swallow hard. Miguel and I swap glances, hoping that the word he's put out is going to work. I scan the car park. But as it stands, it's just us and a whole bunch of cherries to get in. The wind whips around my ears and I pull my hoody up. Everyone is silent. Even Olivia senses the urgency of the situation. Antonio marches to the barn, where the horses have already been fed and watered. He pulls out the crates and starts handing out the wooden ladders. We turn to the orchard, my heart in my boots. It's just us. We'll never get all the cherries in before sunset tonight, before the rain is due.

Heavy-hearted, we set up the ladders and the crates. The wind is rolling through the trees, rubbing up against our faces, teasing and taunting us. The light on the horizon is growing all the time. The horses, sensing something in the air, are galloping at speed around the paddock, their tails flying high, the colt dancing and bucking more than the rest.

As the dawn rolls in, so does a battered old red car into the car park. The doors squeak open on their rusty hinges and three young people step out. The one on the passenger side pulls the seat forward, allowing a young woman to get out from the back. She hands him a guitar. The driver looks around and smiles. They're all dressed in colourful clothes, soft billowing shirts for the men and a full layered skirt for the young woman. They shiver at the wind and pull on jackets and jumpers from the boot.

'Who's that?' Antonio frowns.

They've come. People are coming! Miguel and I look at each other, and if we could, we'd jump for joy. Maybe we will be able to get the harvest in, have the dance-off and save the farm after all.

A second car pulls in behind the first, and my heart gives another leap of joy.

'Beti? Who are these people?' says Antonio.

'Pickers!' I announce.

'What?'

'Pickers. You need pickers, and these people have come to help pick!'

'You have got me pickers?' He looks astounded. He glances over at the young people again, then back at me, and as his face breaks into a wide smile, my heart starts stamping out its familiar beat, the rhythm of the *sevillana*, the beat of the courting couple. Stop it! I tell myself. Think of Will. Tonight, if Antonio is right, I will be back with my fiancé!

'*Gracias*,' he says, and turns towards the cherry orchard.

'And Antonio . . . if people have come to pick, we can still dance tonight?'

He looks at me and gives a single nod. 'If the cherries are in, we will dance.' He walks off up the orchard to organise more crates, and I smile watching him go.

Miguel jogs over to greet the pickers.

'Is that him? Is that the Horse Whisperer?' I hear them ask. Miguel looks round at Antonio, and I can see his chest filling with pride.

'Yes, that's him.'

'And is it true? Is he going to dance again?' the girl asks. 'We read on the internet to meet here at dawn.'

Miguel nods. 'Once the cherries are in, he will dance.'

'I've heard about this place. My grandparents told me about it. I never thought I'd get to see a *peña* here.'

'It's a secret. If the tourists find out, there won't be room for those who truly follow flamenco,' Miguel tells them with solemnity. 'Not a word to anyone.' And they nod excitedly.

Eagerly the young people listen to their instructions and join the other pickers in the orchard. Miguel sets about greeting more disciples of flamenco. My heart spins and dips with excitement and terror. What have I done? Because if Antonio is going to dance in front of all these people, then so am I! I'm so nervous and light-headed I feel like I could take off and fly, join the birds on the wire, as more cars pull into the car park and Miguel tells them the same story. The *peña* must be kept secret. The cherries must be harvested and then the Horse Whisperer will dance again.

I'm dizzy with excitement that our plan has worked. Then I see a big black hire car pulling into the car park, and Uncle Paul and Auntie Rita stepping out. I had almost forgotten about Olivia and her birthday party, and my heart drops like a stone.

Chapter Forty-eight

I watch Uncle Paul pulling his belt up over his pot belly and taking in the surroundings like a vulture scanning the lanes for roadkill. Auntie Rita staggers out of the passenger door looking much the same as Olivia did first thing this morning: bemused and like she's taken a wrong turning, though in her case with fresh hairspray and make-up intact. Then the back doors open and my heart zooms right back up again, like it's on a roller-coaster ride.

'Mum! Dad!' I run over to them, my composure forgotten, and collapse into their arms, letting out all the stress I've been bottling up over the past few weeks. My head falls into my mum's neck, and I breathe in her familiar smell of sunflowers and soap.

'Hello, love,' she says with a crack in her voice. My dad just wraps his arms around both of us in a huge hug, and I know that if he could, he'd swing me round like he used to when I was a little girl. Finally I sniff, rub my nose and stand upright. Olivia has joined us from the orchard; now she steps forward and, in contrast, kisses her parents lightly on the cheek, barely making contact.

'So this is what we've been hearing all about.' Uncle Paul looks around, inspecting the place as though he's a potential buyer hoping to find fault and pick up a bargain.

'Anywhere I can get a sangria?' Auntie Rita asks hopefully.

'More pickers?' Antonio appears, looking less tense.

'Yes, this is the place, Dad. Isn't it fab?' Olivia ignores Antonio. 'I couldn't believe it when I saw it.'

'Antonio, this is my mum and dad.' I zone out from Olivia and Uncle Paul and introduce them. Antonio steps forward and shakes their hands, first Mum, then Dad.

'I thought you were renting a place down at the harbour,' my mum says quietly. 'Where's Will?' She looks around.

'There was a slight change of plan,' I say by way of some sort of explanation. 'I'll explain it all later,' I add.

'You've certainly got yourself a good piece of real estate here,' Uncle Paul butts in, sounding like J. R. Ewing from *Dallas*. 'But it's a long way from the tourist trade. What happened to the place by the harbour? And where's that fiancé of yours?'

'This place is just part of Beti's growing empire,' Antonio cuts in. 'She has worked wonders here. Now, time is against us! We must pick!'

My mum looks bemused but follows Antonio up into the cherry orchard, where they all join the other pickers, happily stripping the trees of fruit. By now there are crowds of people in the orchard: young and old, even families. Everyone is talking loudly. Children are helping. Just like it used to be, I imagine.

'It's a very unusual party,' says Uncle Paul to Auntie Rita.

'Any sangria?' asks Auntie Rita again.

A car pulls up and three young British women climb out, wearing matching floppy straw hats and sunglasses. I recognise them straight away as the girls from the airport, Olivia's friends. 'Wow! This is amazing!' one of them says. 'So . . . authentic!'

'If it's rubbish, we can always go to Gav's party at the beach bar,' says another, and I bristle.

But then my heart fills up again, because behind them come Harold and Brenda.

'Saw Miguel's Facebook message,' Brenda says. 'Sounded like quite an event. Thought you might like some help. I've never been up this far – it's amazing! Look, Harold, real cherry trees!'

And in no time they're in the orchard, mingling with the families and flamenco lovers who have travelled miles to see the dancer they have heard so much about. Despite the building clouds and the darkening sky, there is a buzz in the air, like electricity.

'Bonita!' I call. 'We'll need plenty of paella! As much as you can! And some of your almond cake too.'

She waves her tea towel happily, grinning from ear to ear. '*Sí!* Almond cake! With cherries!' And as happy as a pig in muck, she waddles off back to the kitchen, finally reclaiming her domain. Everyone, even Antonio, looks content, and I can't help feeling that we're nearly there. We're going to do it.

By late afternoon, the orchard is full of people picking and chatting, and then someone starts to sing. Others join in with clapping and shouts of encouragement, the sounds of flamenco, and Antonio freezes.

'What is the meaning of this?!' The town's mayor, the

baker walks into the car park where Antonio rushes over to meet him, and the others with him: his wife and daughters, the man from the taverna, the souvenir shop owner, the schoolteacher and the young priest. 'I heard singing. We all heard singing.' The baker looks around suspiciously. 'We've come to find out what's going on.'

'It's just people singing while they pick.' Antonio sweeps an arm towards the pickers dotted over the hillside, filling crates, buckets and even the folds of their skirts with cherries. Even Uncle Paul and Auntie Rita, finally armed with her sangria, are helping out. And Dad looks to be in his element, picking with the three young people who arrived first. 'Do you have all your cherries in? Before the rain comes?' Antonio asks the mayor, nodding up to the darkening sky.

'Nearly. Myself and the other town councillors' – he indicates the other townspeople – 'are just checking that there is no flamenco going on. We don't want a repeat of last time.' He looks around suspiciously, as if trying to sniff out trouble with his big nose.

'No flamenco,' Antonio confirms with his customary nod. 'Just picking.'

'It's a birthday party, for my cousin,' I explain. 'They are enjoying a taste of Spanish life.' I force a polite and charming smile, learned from my time working at the burger bar. 'You're welcome to join us if you like,' I add with my fingers crossed.

The new arrivals look around, eyes narrowing suspiciously, and then at each other.

'It has been a long time since this town has seen so many people,' the mayor says.

'Papa, we have finished our trees. We could help here,' says his daughter.

Her sister doesn't need asking twice and grabs her skirt, running up the hillside to join in. The rest of the group, seemingly satisfied, turn and leave.

As we watch them go, I glance at Antonio. 'The harvest will happen, don't worry. We will make it.' He attempts a smile back, sending my stomach spinning in somersaults. But he still seems on edge, looking around, up and down the road, as if expecting someone. And I know exactly who. Just as the townspeople leave, a motor home roars through the narrow cobbled streets and swings into the car park of Cortijo Ana. The threatening storm has finally arrived.

Chapter Forty-nine

'So . . . here we are.' Esmeralda gives a sickly smile as she steps out of the motor home, followed by Felipe and another man. She is dressed in a turquoise dress with gold trim and big ruffled shoulders. Felipe is wearing a black outfit with matching blue belt and trim on his shirt and trousers. He even has ruffles around his wrists.

Antonio says nothing. I turn to look at the pickers, who are still working and singing. Bonita has fed them rolls filled with serrano ham and cheese, and provided water and strong coffee all day long, and of course her famous almond and cherry cake. Now the harvest is nearly finished. And not a moment too soon. The sky is as dark as night and matches Antonio's expression.

'This is Gonzalo.' Antonio doesn't move to shake his hand. 'Gonzalo is a cherry farmer like you,' Esmeralda continues. 'He has many farms across these parts.'

'And what business do you have here when there is harvesting to be done?' Antonio lifts his chin towards his orchard. The crates are now being carried to the waiting trailer at the bottom of the field, where Miguel is coordinating getting them loaded.

At first no one says anything; then, licking her red lips,

Esmeralda speaks and Felipe grins.

'Gonzalo wants to buy this place . . . when I win it from you this evening!' She speaks as if she is attempting to stab Antonio through the heart. Gonzalo looks around at the trees and moves to inspect one.

'And what would you do with it?' Antonio says with half a laugh.

'Keep it as a cherry farm, of course,' Gonzalo replies, having given the trees nearby a cursory glance.

'Well, that's something, I suppose. At least the town won't suffer for my foolishness . . . if I were to lose,' Antonio adds. 'Which I won't.' He stands tall and proud and I feel myself do the same. He is much taller than the man in front of him, and broader too.

'But change the cherry variety,' Gonzalo continues with a disapproving downturned mouth.

'What?' Antonio loses his composure, and his poker face falls. Behind him the pickers are dusting off their hands, celebrating a good job done.

'There is a variety I grow that harvests much earlier. Much bigger profits than these older varieties.' Gonzalo tosses his head in the direction of the trees beside him.

I can see that Antonio is trying to absorb this information, and I want to reach out and take his hand, let him know I'm here by his side. That he isn't alone and I'm here to catch him if he falls. But I can't. I'm only here for tonight, then I will be gone. I just hope this place won't follow in my footsteps.

'No!' He raises his voice. 'What about the syndicate, the town? They depend on my cherries to make up the quota we sell to the supermarket. Take away my contribution and they can't meet it. Without me, without these cherries, they will have nothing!'

Esmeralda shrugs nonchalantly, like a cat deciding a mouse's fate, while Felipe smirks.

'You will never get my cherry farm!' Antonio roars.

Inside, I feel cornered, just like when Olivia and her friends used to bully me as a child. But I'm not in the school playground any more. I'm not the girl I was back then. This time I'm going to fight my way out of it . . . or in this case, dance.

Chapter Fifty

Just as the last of the cherries are loaded on to the trailer to take to the packing house on the other side of town, there is a huge clap of thunder and the rain starts to fall in big heavy drops. The crowd all shriek with horror and delight. Miguel joins the tractor driver to see the cherries are delivered safely.

'This way!' I shout, waving my arms, pointing up the path to where Sophia is throwing open the doors to the barn next to my *finca*. 'There's cherry liqueur and sangria for everyone.' I give a thumbs-up to Sophia, who smiles and returns the gesture. 'There will be paella soon!' I tell them as they all make their way quickly up the path, my mum and dad, Uncle Paul and Rita included, all laughing and holding their arms over their heads against the downpour.

I stand in the rain for a moment, shutting my eyes and letting it soak through me.

'So, they're in. Safe and sound.' I open my eyes, feeling Antonio beside me as the trailer bounces its way out of the yard and on to the road. The rain pounds the dry ground like it's beating out the rhythm of my heart, as Antonio looks at me. I tuck a wet strand of hair behind my ear. I want more than anything to tell him what I'm thinking, how I'm feeling.

That when I'm dancing with him, when I'm with him, I feel more alive than I've ever been.

He grabs my hand and runs to the veranda, pulling me out of the rain. He turns to me, holding my arms, as if he's about to say something too. My heart is hammering now.

'You planned this, didn't you? These people aren't just here for the picking, are they?' He nods towards the barn. The storm clouds are rolling in around me, and inside me too. 'You did this! You knew it had to be a secret!'

'I didn't exactly plan it. In fact, you could say this is the least planned event I've ever been part of. I have no idea what's going to happen, and I'm terrified.'

'You are infuriating, Beti! I could lose my business if they realise what you've done here. No one will come to my restaurant.'

'I'm sorry. But like Miguel told me, some things are worth overcoming your fear for. That boy is way wiser than you give him credit for.'

I look over at the motor home where Esmeralda, Felipe and their guest are getting ready for the dance-off. There is an orange glow emanating from inside, and flamenco music is blaring from it. Antonio follows my gaze. Is this the home they plan to take Miguel away in? Is that going to be his life if I lose tonight?

'Tell me exactly what's going on, Beti,' he demands quietly.

I look around, but realise I have no choice.

'The truth!' he says, much louder.

'I . . . Miguel had this idea, and I agreed it was the only way. He wanted to organise a *peña*. A secret dance night. To sell tickets. He wanted to . . .' I pick my words carefully so as not to tell him about the money I gave Miguel for the dance competition. 'He wanted to make up the money we lost on the party. Lots of people want to see you dance again and are willing to pay to do so. Look at how many have turned up.'

'But they came to pick.'

'We said it was a cherry harvest festival.' I sigh, knowing there's no way of hiding any of this. 'We said they had to arrive at dawn and pick, and then there would be a *peña* tonight. Word got out and spread.' I throw my arms open. 'I thought it would help Olivia too, giving her a birthday party in Spain, a truly authentic one. I thought we would get away with the dance-off if we said it was still a party for my cousin, a one-off Spanish-themed party that I had organised.'

He looks at me and my insides melt like an ice lolly in the sun. I wait for him to explode and tell me how much trouble I've caused him.

'You're a remarkable woman, Beti,' he says softly, tucking the wet hair back behind my ear. What's left of my insides explodes like a strip of firecrackers. 'And what's in it for you?'

'Well, hopefully you'll be able to pay me my wages and I'll be able to put down the deposit on my bar.' I swallow again. All I really want to do is reach up and take that kiss that I'm certain was promised to me in the cherry orchard. I want to feel it on my lips, to taste it. I wonder if it tastes as sweet as the cherry, its memory still lingering there.

'And?'

I want to tell him how I'm doing this for him and Miguel. How much they have both come to mean to me for different reasons. Miguel has become like a younger brother, someone to look out for and care for. And Antonio . . . well, he has become so much more than a boss, a dance teacher. He has become—

'Beti!' someone calls, shattering the moment. It's Will, getting out of a battered Transit van. The rest of the band pour out of the van too, including Freya, scowling. 'Beti!' he calls again through the rain.

'Ah, yes.' Antonio lets my arms go as if realising he's handling stolen goods. 'Your errant fiancé.' He looks down and then back at me. 'I remember. This is what's in it for you. So . . . we have work to do,' he says, suddenly my flamenco teacher again, and my head is spinning as if I've been riding the waltzer. 'It is time to dance,' he says. 'It is time for us to get what we both want from this.' He strides off the veranda into the pouring rain.

'Beti!' Will runs up the steps towards me, a broad grin plastered on his face.

'You came?' I manage a smile.

'I got your message. We came.' He gestures to the rest of the band and Freya, her arms folded. 'Thought you might need a band!' he says with that familiar twinkle in his eye.

'Get yourselves to the barn. There's drinks there, and Bonita will be serving food soon. Mum and Dad will be delighted to see you.'

He's still smiling as he and the rest of the band run through the rain up to the barn.

I follow from a distance, returning to my *finca* to get changed. I turn to look back towards the apartment, where I know Antonio is now, but I can't see him. I'm about to get everything I wanted. Will. The bar. Why then don't I feel thrilled with excitement? Why instead am I sick with worry about how Antonio is feeling? Terrified that I'm going to let him down? Why does he fill my head so there's no room for anything else?

Back at the *finca*, as the party warms up next door, I can hear music playing and people chatting. Outside, the thunder rumbles and bangs and the sky lights up with jagged bolts of lightning. The lights flicker on and off. I shower for what may be the last time in my little shower room, and then pull out my dress and hold it to me. Slowly I slip it on and carefully apply my make-up. Finally I open the old wardrobe door to take out my shoes. Just like Dorothy, the shoes that are going to help me find my way home, back to Will and the Butterfly Bar. I bend down for them . . . but they're not there! I search around the wardrobe and under the bed. I look everywhere, panic beginning to rise. I can't dance without my shoes! They're not there! They've gone!

'Antonio!' I shout up at the apartment. I've run through the orchard barefoot, not bothering to take the stony path; my hair is plastered to my head, and my dress is clinging to me as the rain belts down. The sky lights up once more, and there's another crash of thunder. 'Antonio!' I shout again. But he doesn't respond. Where is he? Has he stormed off, cross that I organised the *peña* without telling him? Has he run out on me? Why did his face darken like that when Will arrived? What if this has all been for nothing?

Just then, there is a thundering of hooves from the path through the cherry trees behind the horses' enclosure and

Antonio appears at the side of the *cortijo* on horseback. His dark hair is a mass of springy curls, soaked from the rain, with droplets like crystals hanging from strands around his face.

'Where have you been?' I ask. I know it's none of my business really, but I can't help myself. 'I thought you'd walked out. I thought you were cross about the *peña*.'

'I just needed to clear my head. Get my thoughts together. Work out what to do for the best. The mayor and the others are back. They've heard the music. They've heard rumours, so Miguel says. I've sent him back to tell them I'm on my way. What's the matter? Why are you down here?' He looks at my feet. 'Where are your shoes?'

'They've gone,' I say, throwing my hands up.

'Gone where?'

'I . . . I don't know. I think . . . well I think someone must have stolen them. Someone who didn't want me to dance,' I finish.

He says nothing. His face darkens. 'You'd better climb on,' he says, riding towards me on Suerte.

'Oh, I can't . . .'

'Don't be scared.' He reaches out a hand to me. 'Miguel is right. Some things are worth overcoming your fears for. Like you said, he has more sense than anyone. Let's fight on.' He reaches down and I stretch up. He takes hold of my elbow and I grab his. 'I want to save my farm and home, yes. But I also want to make you happy, Beti. Are you with me?'

Shaking from the rain as it pounds against my face, I nod.

'Put your foot on mine,' he says, and I do what he tells me.

'Let's go!' In one swift movement he pulls me up and on to the horse's back in front of him. His big, strong arms around me. Then he makes a clicking noise to Suerte in the corner of his mouth. The stallion needs very little encouragement to power up the hill towards the fairy-lit barn, and we duck and dip through the branches of the stripped cherry trees. I can feel the rhythm of the horse's hooves beneath us, and it's as if my heart is finally beating its own natural rhythm too.

When we reach the brow of the hill, I hear raised voices. There, standing in the doorway, are Esmeralda and Felipe. She has her hands on her hips and is in heated conversation with the mayor. Will is there too, trying to get into the barn but being prevented by the locals gathered there. As we approach, the conversation stops and everyone turns to look at us.

'Bloody hell!' says Uncle Paul, pushing through the crowd at the doorway.

Will turns to see me sitting on the stallion's back with the ruffles of my dress draped over the horse's shoulders, and his jaw drops, practically hitting the floor.

'I'm sorry, I can't let you in,' says the mayor. He steps forward and holds up a hand in front of the horse. 'I can't let this dance go ahead. We have heard that there is a *peña* here tonight. I can't allow it! I cannot allow any flamenco.'

'Flamenco has been a part of this place for generations. It is time we heard its song again,' Antonio says from up high on the horse's back.

'*Olé!*' A shout of appreciation comes from inside the barn, and the crowd clap and shout in anticipation. I can see my mum and dad and Olivia beaming in expectation. Will can't take his eyes off me.

Antonio dismounts and then takes my hand, helping me down from the horse.

'I didn't even know you could ride.' Will steps forward into the rain, still looking at me in complete wonder.

'Neither did I,' I say. 'You don't know what you can do until you want it badly enough.'

'You look amazing!' he says, his eyes dancing. 'Really amazing, Beti. So this is where you've been hiding out. I've been trying to find you. I went back to the bar but the couple there wouldn't tell me where you were. I wanted to find you, tell you . . . well, everything that's been going on in my head. How stupid I was. How much I love you.'

My heart is thundering, my head giddy with all the words I've hoped to hear. He came looking for me! Antonio, on the other hand, is scowling.

'Beti, you go on in,' he instructs, pointing past Will.

'No!' says the mayor.

'Let her pass!' Antonio's eyes flash, and Suerte swings his rear end left, then right. The men scatter, reluctantly making a pathway for me.

I glance at Will. He's looking at me again with . . . well, frankly, admiration and desire in his eyes. I can't remember ever seeing him look at me like that. It takes all my willpower to lift my head, like Antonio has taught me, pick up my skirt, open my shoulders and walk into the barn.

With shaking knees, I stand in the middle of the space with my skirt ruffles in my hands, showing my bare ankles and feet. Everyone looks down and a whisper goes around the room: 'She's dancing barefoot!' I wish I had my shoes. I know I'd be able to do this if I had them. As Antonio has taught me, I lift one hand to rest on my hip so the skirt lifts above my knee. The room falls quiet, watching me. I get a sudden buzz of terror and excitement.

I lift my head a little higher and feel the power it gives me. The tiled floor is cold under my feet. I really don't know if I can do this without my shoes. I keep my eyes on Antonio, who has handed Suerte's reins to Miguel and is walking into the barn towards me. He is taller than any of the other men in the barn, and very broad in the shoulders – even more so, it seems, in the tight-fitting black shirt and trousers he's wearing. There is a ripple of excitement from the audience who are crowded into the barn, sharing chairs, standing, some sitting on the floor, cross-legged, with small children in their laps. The place is absolutely rammed to the rafters. They are all sipping cherry liqueur or sangria, but there are so many people here, Sophia's friends can barely get round to top everyone up. Olivia and my family look awe-struck. Uncle Paul is taking photographs. The atmosphere is electric.

Not to be outdone, Esmeralda lifts her skirts and slowly walks on to the floor beside me, Felipe following. She doesn't take her eyes off me. Her dark hair is pulled back and tied up with a turquoise feather to match her dress.

'That's my girl!' I hear my dad choke, and I briefly glance round. Will is still looking as if, for once, he's lost for words. Freya digs him hard in the ribs and then storms off with a furious glare to sit with the band. She plonks herself on the bass guitarist's lap, occasionally checking to see if Will has noticed. Will, though, hasn't taken his eyes off me, and I feel my nerves rush back in. But as I look back at Antonio, trying to find my focus and my centre again, the group of local men, led by the mayor, step in front of him.

'Let me pass. I'm warning you,' Antonio says in a low growl. The room is so hushed, we can all hear every word and every raindrop falling on the roof.

'No, Antonio! I cannot let this happen. You know the rules. No flamenco. It is banned. This place was closed down years ago,' the mayor chides.

Antonio looks at him. 'You're right. It was. And now its doors are open again.' He glances at me and my heart gives a little *stamp, stamp*. 'Now if you'll excuse me, you are on my land. Either stay for the *peña* and feel the flamenco again, or please leave.'

'No! I won't allow it! Flamenco is forbidden in the town.'

'By a priest who is long since dead. That was the past. This is now. Things are different.'

'Nothing has changed,' one of the other men in the group pipes up.

'Everything changes.' Antonio sighs, as if weary of the conversation. 'Now let me pass.' But the men are standing like a wall in front of him, refusing to move.

'You know the rules. We don't want trouble like last time. The harvest nearly didn't happen.'

'But the harvest is in! It's safe! No one's livelihood is at stake here, except mine.'

'It's time this farm was sold off and someone new bought it. Someone who doesn't want any trouble,' Esmeralda calls out, butting in.

'*I* don't want trouble!' Antonio's eyes flash with anger and the crowd of men shuffle back slightly.

'What does she mean, "sold off"?' the mayor asks, confused.

Antonio's eyes are still flashing. 'I am dancing for my life here. Fighting for it. As someone wise said recently' – he looks at Miguel, who has returned to the barn again – 'some things are worth getting over your fears for. This place belonged to my grandparents. They brought the passion of flamenco here because they loved it. They loved what it stood for. It is called the fire dance for a reason. It is about people's lives, their passion, their pain and their expression of love!' He looks straight at me, and my heart bangs out a response to his words.

'Bloody hell! What a show! You can forget the Pink Flamingo, this place has got it all,' Brenda says to Harold.

'Absolutely fabulous! I'm putting this on Facebook Live!' says one of Olivia's friends, despite being squeezed in between a large man holding a child on one side and a crowded table on the other. 'Beats any of the other thirtieths I've been to, and Lula Hamilton had waterskiing acrobats. Plus this cherry liqueur is amazing!'

'Sold off? Who is selling up? Why? Who to? Will it be someone who wants to carry on the cherry orchard? Not developers!' the mayor splutters, his voice thick with panic.

'Gonzalo here is a cherry farmer,' Antonio says, pointing to the man in question. 'He would like to buy the farm but rip up the trees and put in new, early-harvesting cherries for a bigger profit.'

There is a collective intake of breath.

'So unless I can take part in this dance competition right

now, my farm will be sold off to the highest bidder. To Gonzalo.'

'I'd like to buy it,' pipes up one of the local worthies, and Antonio practically bares his teeth at him, causing him to step back into the shadows.

'Hang on! This is Beti's place,' I hear my mum say, and my heart sinks. How do I explain this?

'Yeah, her and that Will bloke. Are you telling me she doesn't own this place after all? That it was all a pack of lies?'

'Oh shut up, Paul!' my mum and dad say in unison, taking me by complete surprise. That's the first time I've heard them stand up to him, and I feel a rush of pride. I know what courage that takes.

Antonio pushes through the line of men and walks over to Uncle Paul, towering above him. Paul suddenly looks like a very small man, very small indeed.

'Everything I have right now is because of Beti.' He glances at Miguel, who has followed him. 'She is the richest and most generous woman I know.'

'Do you hear that, Rita? She's earned a fortune! All off the back of that china cow my mother left her, I bet!' he hisses.

Antonio silences him with a dark look, and my uncle shrinks back into his seat.

'Enough!' Esmeralda announces. 'No one cares about the British woman. Let us get on with this. Let us see if you have made her into a flamenco dancer, or just dressed her up to look like a cheap souvenir doll.'

'Is she talking about Beti?' I hear my mum say. 'Don't you

speak about my daughter like that! She's got more guts than you've had hot dinners, by the look of it!' Mum has spent so many years feeling guilty for the happiness she and Dad managed to find with each other. She has been quietly content, never wanting to rub Uncle Paul's nose in it, letting him reassert himself by boasting loudly about his achievements. And now here she is, like a lioness protecting what she cares about the most: her family.

Esmeralda sneers at her.

'Don't you ever, ever look at my mother like that again,' I say coldly. 'Don't look at her, don't speak to her. Do you understand?'

Then I turn slowly to Uncle Paul and lift my chin.

'No, I don't own this place.'

He gives me a 'told you so' smirk.

'But life isn't about what you own, it's about who you are,' I continue, and his smirk slips as all eyes turn to him. 'You may own a house twice the size of theirs, a car bigger than their front room, but my mum and dad are twice the people you'll ever be. Think about whose house you always want to spend Christmas at. Not because it's filled with expensive furniture, but because it's filled with love. They found what we all spend our lives looking for: happiness. It's not in the buildings we own, the parties we attend or the holidays we go on; it's about what's in here!' I hold my hand on my heart. 'Like I say, it's about who you are. And I finally know exactly who I am.'

'God! She's amazing!' I hear Maxine say to Craig. I didn't even see them arrive, and I feel a warm glow at the fact that they've turned up.

'Thought you said your cousin was really drippy?' one of Olivia's friend's says.

'She looks pretty incredible to me,' chips in another.

'Wish I was more like her,' says the third, and Olivia smiles uncomfortably.

'That's my girl!' My dad stands up, clapping, tears in his eyes.

Antonio looks right at me with pride and a glint of his passion in his eyes. I can hear my heart banging out a loud familiar beat. He gives one deep nod.

I hesitate.

'You're scared?' he whispers into my ear. I feel his hot breath on my skin, making me shiver in anticipation.

'What if I make a mess of it?' I say, turning towards him.

'Remember to always listen to this,' he tells me, and places his hand on mine over my heart. 'Listen to it and you won't go wrong.'

'But my shoes,' I say to him quietly.

'Remember when we danced in the cherry orchard. Remember how it felt. It's not the shoes that make you dance. It's you. Remember the feeling.'

I shut my eyes and I'm there, right back in the cherry orchard. Oh, I'm ready to dance! I really am. The fire in my belly is raging. I let my nan down when Will took off with my money. There is no way I can let Antonio down. I can't let him lose this place. I can't let him lose Miguel. I open my eyes and look down at the dress. I'm doing this for Antonio, for Miguel and for Nan, who always believed in me. All around me camera flashes from phones are going off.

'Esmeralda, why don't you go first, show us the fine

dancer that you are?' Antonio says graciously, taking me by the hand and leading me to the edge of the dance space.

'No!' says the mayor.

'I have told you,' says Antonio, 'either you let the flamenco in, or you leave. We have spent too many years in this town shutting out the past. Scared of how it will affect the future. We have denied the young people their heritage. They are leaving, moving to the coast, where people come to see our culture in nightclubs showing cheap *tablaos*. We have fought to keep our cherries alive, to keep the variety alive, because it is part of our landscape, but so too is flamenco! Now do you want to remember what it felt like, or do you want to go?'

'I want to feel it!' says the mayor's dumpy daughter.

'Me too!' says her sister, and they sit down on the edge of the dance floor.

'And me!' says his wife.

'*Sí!*' says his eighty-year-old mother, who attempts to sit on the floor but has to be helped on to a nearby chair.

'You are a good farmer, Antonio. I do not want to see this place sold off to someone who doesn't care,' the mayor says, relenting.

'Then let me save my farm and my home.'

'Any other farmer could do what you do,' says Esmeralda. 'Miguel has had a taste of country life now; he will be ready to leave with me. He will realise that his life will be better on the road, rather than as a mere cherry farmer.'

'Miguel, of course, has the right to choose.' Antonio turns to look at his son, who stares straight back at him. They hold each other's gaze as if forming a bond that won't be broken, whatever the outcome of the dance. Antonio finally turns back to Esmeralda. 'But I will let him have that choice. You won't take my farm! Now, let's dance!'

He nods to Pedro, who is sitting by the fireplace surrounded by heart-shaped fairy lights. The drummer next to him begins to beat out the rhythm on the square box between his legs. *Boom-boom. Boom-boom.*

The crowd falls silent.

Esmeralda raises her head, stepping up to take centre stage, and my heart is thudding so loudly I can hardly hear the drummer as he begins to sing, telling the story of a life, a struggle, a dream, a longing and a passion. I feel every word and note as Esmeralda lifts her elbows and rolls her hands over and over each other. This may be the beginning, but I have no idea how it's going to end.

Chapter Fifty-one

The audience cheer and applaud the fancy footwork and complicated clapping of the dance, far more involved than ours. Esmeralda and Felipe finish with a flourish, then nod and smile as they soak up the plaudits from the appreciative crowd. But the expectation is growing in the room. The Horse Whisperer hasn't danced since this place closed down. The tension and excitement is palpable. I tremble.

'Feel the fire in your heart and in your soul and use it,' Antonio whispers in my ear. I close my eyes, blocking out the faces around me. 'Remember the cherry orchard,' he tells me quietly. 'Feel the energy beneath your feet. Feel the energy here, between us.'

I'm aware of his body right next to mine, and it's like there's a rocket inside me waiting to go off and light up the night sky.

Antonio nods to Pedro and the music begins. He looks straight at me, drawing me into his dark eyes, transporting me back to the cherry orchard, and I begin to dance. I'm not counting any more; I'm dancing and feeling the music and I don't think I want it ever to stop. I hold Antonio's deep gaze, knowing he won't let me fall, and by the time we get to the third verse, I feel alive, I feel like me. I feel more like me than I ever have before, and I realise that I'm happiest here next to him. My heart is thumping in my chest and filling my head. I feel elated, like I'm flying, and I never want to come down.

Then I hear it. The applause. The clapping. The cheering. People are on their feet. My mum and dad, even Uncle Paul. The mayor and his daughters. Everyone is clapping and there are shouts of '*Olé!*' '*Bravo!*' and 'Go, Bet!' from Olivia. I see Will, wearing the look on his face I have wanted to see for years, like I am all his heart desires. He's finally noticed me again. I'm the woman he fell in love with all those years ago . . . and a thought flits through my head, like petals from the blossom caught on the wind. Or am I? it says. And disappears.

Esmeralda walks into the middle of the floor and turns to the musicians.

'So you have seen the dances,' she says, and the room hushes and falls silent. 'I have to say congratulations, Antonio. I didn't think you would be able to get the girl to move, so you are to be commended.'

'Hey!' I hear my mum again, with her new-found voice, being loud and proud.

'But clearly our dance was far more accomplished, so we are the winners of this dance-off,' Esmeralda announces. She looks at the two musicians sitting either side of Pedro, the aficionados he has arranged to be here.

'You wanted me to teach her to dance: one dance. I have done that. I win,' Antonio says.

'Pah! A *sevillana*. It is hardly even flamenco. It is a folk dance!' she spits with disdain. 'True flamenco takes years to learn. It cannot be performed by a beginner. You lose!' She throws up a hand, dismissing him.

Heads start to lean together around the room, debating the argument, murmuring in agreement and disagreement.

Antonio walks over to Esmeralda, lifting his head and chin, making him seem like a giant. The room falls silent again, the atmosphere crackling with anticipation. I bite my lip. I can barely breathe.

'You may have all the technical moves,' he says slowly. 'But Beti has the one thing you will never have . . . she has the *duende*, the soul. You may be able to dance the steps, but Beti feels them. You cannot learn the *duende*, you cannot teach it. You either have it or you don't . . . and Beti most definitely has it. What you saw here was real flamenco.'

Esmeralda's composure suddenly drops, and she lets out a shriek of frustration. Felipe steps up next to her.

'*We* performed true flamenco. Yours wasn't real—'

'Not real?' Antonio cuts him off and raises an eyebrow. 'Ask any one of this audience how real it was, if they felt it in here,' and he puts a hand to his chest, 'in their soul. That is real flamenco!'

The crowd bursts into more cheers and applause and whooping. Esmeralda looks around the room, then points at the band.

'You are aficionados,' she says. 'Tell him! He cannot win over what we performed here.'

'The bet was to teach one dance,' Pedro says with a smile. 'He has done what was asked.'

'But is the *sevillana* flamenco or just a folk dance?' asks the drummer.

'How will the music and dance survive in a modern age if we do not embrace the new?' says the second guitarist sitting on the other side of Pedro. And suddenly the whole room erupts with people throwing in their opinions. Arms are being waved. People are shouting in Spanish. The musicians are up on their feet. Members of the audience surround Antonio and Esmeralda as opinions are aired, loudly and all at the same time.

'I don't understand what's going on!' I shout to Miguel.

'Some are saying it is not traditional flamenco; others are agreeing with Antonio that it is about the soul of the dance, the *duende*, rather than just the steps. No one can decide who is right.'

I can't stand it. The noise, the shouting, arms waving. I couldn't bear it if he lost out now. I suddenly feel hot, really hot and dizzy. I go to make a run for the double doors, pushing my way through the crowds standing there and throwing myself out into the night air.

'Beti, wait!' I hear a voice but I don't stop, running on instead into the orchard. It's stopped raining at least. Everything is wet, but feels fresh. Like the start of a new day. Clean and cleansed. A new beginning. I stand barefoot amongst the newly stripped trees, breathing in the cool air. Getting rid of the fruit has left them lighter, more upright. It's as if they've rid themselves of what's been weighing them down. There are no expectations on them any more. They can simply be trees.

I put my head in my hands. I've blown it. It's all been for nothing. What now? I force myself to look up and open my eyes. The clouds are beginning to roll away, and behind them the sun is starting to set. The stunning colours fill the sky; fiery reds, warm oranges and brilliant yellows glowing on the horizon, reaching out towards the cherry orchard.

Suddenly I hear a rustle behind me and spin round.

'Will?' I say, surprised.

'I called after you,' he says. He smiles. 'You were amazing in there. The Beti I remember, the one I fell in love with.' He walks towards me. His shoes and trouser bottoms are wet from the long grass.

A voice pipes up in my head again. *Am* I that same Beti? Or have I become someone completely different? Someone who doesn't worry about what people think; who does something because it matters to her, not because she thinks it's what she should be doing. Someone who listens to her heart.

'Take them off.' I nod to his wet shoes.

'What?' He looks puzzled.

'Take them off. That way you can feel the earth's rhythm. Everything has a natural rhythm. A natural place, a natural fit. You just have to listen with your heart rather than your head.'

'OK . . .' he says, unsure, but slips off his socks and shoes anyway, bouncing on one foot and then the other. 'Cold, ah!' He hops around some more, and then walks right up to me and takes my hand. I wait for my heart to quicken. Is this it? Did our dance actually work? Does he want me back more than anything?

'You really were amazing in there,' he says.

A smile starts to spread across my face before dropping. But I blew it, I think, and hang my head. He places a finger under my chin and lifts it. I look up, his familiar face now close to mine.

'I know what I did was wrong, Beti. The money and Freya. And I understand now what a fool I've been. I should have stayed. I should never have let you go. I know I've been an arse,' he says, making me laugh through the tears that seem to be rolling down my cheeks, 'but I never stopped loving you. I just got scared. Panicked. And when I blew it, well, I thought you'd never want to see me again anyway. But then when I got your message to come tonight, well, I wondered if you might be feeling the same way as me. The way I've been feeling since I saw you in the Butterfly Bar. I can't stop thinking . . .' he swallows, 'that there might still be a chance for us.'

'Beti?' I hear Olivia's voice from the barn door. 'Your mum sent me to see if you're OK. She's stuck behind a table arguing about true flamenco and can't get out.'

The colours of the sunset are creeping slowly across the sky towards us, pushing the remaining clouds aside.

I take a deep breath, hesitating for a moment. Is this what I really want? Because if it is, I have to grab it now.

'Think about it, Beti, we could still be the dream team. You and me. Here in Spain. We'll find the money somehow. And your mum and dad love me!' he tries to joke.

'Actually,' I look back at the packed barn, the argument still rumbling on, 'I think I might have got the money.' Miguel has sold tickets to almost everyone in there.

'Beti?' Olivia calls again.

Will looks at me, suddenly serious. 'I never did ask you properly, but ever since that night in the Butterfly Bar, I've realised what I need to do.' His eyes are so familiar, but are they filling me with fire and passion? I'm not sure any more. Maybe I'm just a bit unsettled by the dance-off and the row. I should get back in there, check on Antonio and Miguel. I turn to go.

'We'll talk later.'

'No.' He grabs my wrist. 'I have to do this now.' He kneels down in the wet grass.

'Will, are you OK? Are you in pain?' Alarmed, I wonder if there's a doctor in amongst that arguing bunch inside.

'Beti?' He looks up at me, wincing as the wet seeps into his jeans. 'I should have done this years ago. Shown you how much you mean to me. But I'm doing it now.'

'Huh!' There's a sharp intake of breath from Olivia, who has come out to find me. 'He's proposing! A proper proposal! Here! In the cherry orchard! Just like I thought Gav was going to!' she says with a sob for everything she's lost.

'Beti, will you do me the very great honour of marrying me? I love you, and seeing you here tonight, like this, has made me realise how much I never want to let you go.' He reaches into his breast pocket and pulls out a gold ring with a tiny diamond in it, holding it up to me. I can't help but suddenly think about my money he lost playing poker, and wonder how he's been able to afford to buy a ring. But I quickly try and push the thought away. This is everything I wanted. Nan would be happy for me, wouldn't she? This is what Antonio helped me get back. This is what Olivia was desperate for.

I look down at the ring, clearly meant to replace my nan's one I've been wearing all these years, waiting for my heart to jump-start into life and patter away excitedly. But words fail me. I can hear Olivia sobbing gently as she's led back into the barn by one of her friends who's come looking for her.

'Would you mind if I stood up now?' Will says, wobbling on one knee and grimacing ever so slightly at the wet patch spreading up his leg.

'No . . . I mean, of course.' I help him to his feet and he puts his arms around me.

'So is that a "no", or an "of course"?' His smile wavers. 'Let's do it. Let's put all this behind us.' He pulls me close so I'm right up against him. Still I'm waiting for my heart to quicken. 'Let's show everyone we're still Beti and Will. Just like we planned. Running our own place. With your organisational skills . . . I mean, look what you've done here tonight. And with me out front . . .'

'I quite liked being out front,' I surprise myself by suddenly saying.

'Well, yes, of course.' He falters, then smiles again. 'We'll be a team. Please, Beti, let's go back to where we were.'

'And Freya?'

'I've told Freya we're over. We were just passing through each other's lives on the journey of life,' he says expansively. In other circumstances it might have sounded romantic, but here in the cherry orchard it just comes across as a bit cheesy.

'Really? You really want this?' I ask, getting my thoughts back on track.

'More than anything,' and he smiles widely and looks at me just like he used to when we were first together. 'This is the Beti I fell in love with.'

I try and turn my thoughts to the excitement of those

nights: the energy, the chemistry, the lovemaking – or was it just sex, carefree, fun sex before real life kicked in in the form of rent payments, microwave meals and who was doing the washing-up? Did I throw myself into organising our wedding to try and disguise the fact that we weren't in love at all?

'Actually, Will, I don't think I am the same Beti you fell in love with. I think I might be a whole new Beti.'

'I'll happily take the whole new Beti,' he says, and finally he kisses me. His familiar lips back on mine, the way I've dreamed about for weeks. At last I've got everything I wanted. The money for the bar, and Will back at my side, kissing me, desiring me. This must mean we were meant to be together – that he's the one after all.

I wait to listen to my heart, to hear its rhythm. For it to burst into life just like it did in the dance with Antonio. But nothing. I listen again. Come on, fireworks, where are you? That big rocket that was getting ready to take off when I was dancing with Antonio, where are you now? Still nothing. My eyes spring open and I see Will's face, his skin, his eyelashes, and behind him, the fiery red of the sun setting in the sky. So bright it's like a signal, reminding me there is something beyond this, beyond where I am right now.

He pulls away and grins lazily. 'Now can we please get off this wet grass?' He laughs and takes my hand.

'In a minute,' I say, and don't follow as he tugs at my hand. He cocks his head questioningly. 'I'll be there in a minute,' I tell him. 'I'll catch you up. I just need a moment to think, take this all in.'

I look out at the clearing sky, and then turn back and watch him walk away. That casual swing to his walk.

Everything I wanted is right there. Now. For the taking.

'Life isn't about what you own, it's about who you are.' My own words come crashing back to me, and I look towards the barn, where there are still hands flying and voices raised. It's not about the Butterfly Bar, or getting Will back. It was never about that, I realise. It was about finding me. And standing here, right now, in the sunset over the cherry orchard, I think I might have done just that.

I touch my lips where Will's were. They feel cold. Then I put my hand on my heart, and as I listen to its beat, I let the words slowly form in my head. He's not the one, I finally admit to myself, and a fat tear rolls down my cheek for all that might have been. After everything, he's not the one.

I look back at the barn, and it hits me like a sledgehammer. I know who is . . . but will he want me?

Chapter Fifty-two

I pick up the ruffles of my long skirt and run as fast as I can back to the barn. Antonio is standing in the middle of the room, his wild black hair falling over his right eye. His wide shoulders are open and his big hands are clenched like dumb-bells.

'Beti!' My mum waves at me. 'It's terribly exciting!' she says, totally caught up in the drama of it all. 'Better than *Big Fat Gypsy Weddings*!'

'Antonio!' I cup my hands round my mouth and try and shout to him above the uproar. Someone pushes a chair over, and a woman screams. It's turning ugly in here. Is this what happened last time, when they banned flamenco for good? I can't let him lose his farm because of me. I can hear my heart loud and clear, telling me what to do.

'No! Stop!'

Everyone turns to look at me. A corridor in the crowd opens up in response, and I walk through to stand beside Antonio.

'This man has taught me everything in the last few weeks,' I begin. 'Not just the moves to a dance, but to be who I am. Not to worry what other people think. He has taught me that it's not what you have in life that matters, but who you are. And that you can't plan life; you have to just follow the path set out for you, the natural rhythm. I have learned that you have to listen to your heart to discover who is the one for you . . . even if you didn't expect it.' I look at my mum and dad, who fell in love and have paid the price ever since. 'I have discovered that when love does come along, you can't fight it; you just have to grab it.'

Antonio slowly turns to look at me. The fight over the dance is all but extinguished as the room turns its attention on me too.

'I have realised that I have fallen in love with the most annoying, scruffy, hot-headed, unpredictable man ever. And I don't care whether we live on a farm or have to sleep under the stars as long as I am travelling life's path with him by my side. But I know I can't fight this.' I turn to Esmeralda. 'He taught me flamenco, like you asked. He fuelled the fire in my heart to dance and fanned the flames. He taught me to listen to my soul.'

The room stays hushed.

'She's quite some girl, your Bet,' I hear Uncle Paul whisper, shocking me to my core.

'She is,' Dad agrees proudly. 'Always has been, always will be.'

'Very touching!' says Esmeralda with a sneer. 'But still, he should have picked a more traditional dance.' She tosses her head. 'I suggest you keep out of this. This is about family. The farm will be sold tonight.' She throws up a hand with her proclamation.

There is a gasp, and the chattering in the audience starts up again.

'Wait!' comes a shout, silencing them once more.

The crowd at the door separates, and in walks Miguel in his flamenco suit, the new one he bought for the competition. He looks wonderful! So handsome. My eyes prickle with pride. He is holding Sophia's hand high. She is wearing a beautiful blue and white dress, simple yet stunning. Not flamboyant and showy like Esmeralda's. The pair of them look amazing. I hold my hands together over my mouth. Antonio takes a sharp intake of breath, and I hope it's for all the right reasons, but he doesn't move to intervene.

'If this is a family affair, then I am part of this family, aren't I?' Miguel glares at his mother, who suddenly looks momentarily thrown. 'And this farm is as much about my fate as yours. It's about my family's heritage, yes?' He looks at Antonio, whose eyes seem to have filled with unshed tears. He goes to speak, but no words come out. Miguel carries on. 'As a part of this family, I want to dance too!'

Sophia speaks up, beautiful and poised, all her shyness gone. 'Miguel and I have been dancing flamenco. We know we shouldn't, but we could not stop what was in our hearts,' she says, softly but firmly.

'You may not think I am ready to dance,' Miguel continues, 'but I have known hurt and pain and found love and a life I want to fight for. I too have found the fire in my soul!' He looks at his father. Antonio nods slowly, with a smile of acceptance.

'I would be proud to see you dance,' he finally manages with a crack in his already gravelly voice.

'This is not what we agreed!' Esmeralda interjects. 'The farm will be sold and you, Miguel, will come back and live with me. You can dance on tour with us, be part of the act.'

'And don't I have a say in this?' Miguel challenges her.

'No, you must do what we feel best!' She nods to Felipe.

'Let the boy dance!' Antonio roars.

And the room silences.

Miguel looks to Pedro and nods, then he leads Sophia on to the floor and we all move back, making room. The candles flicker as if sensing the atmosphere, setting the stage for the youngsters.

The singing begins, and the beat of their heels starts up, showing the world what is in their hearts. I think mine might burst with pride as I watch the pair with Antonio by my side, feeling happier than I've ever done before.

Chapter Fifty-three

The applause and calls of appreciation are deafening as the dance ends. Antonio steps forward and embraces his son. The pair hug each other long and hard, and it says everything about how they feel about each other. Then he takes Sophia's hand and kisses it, telling her how proud he is of them both. And then he hugs Miguel all over again.

Esmeralda approaches.

'You are a fine dancer. We have obviously taught you well,' she claims. Antonio goes to react, but instead steps back and lets Miguel talk.

'I dance because I listen to my soul,' he says, dismissing her claims. 'And there has been one person who has been there for Sophia and me, encouraging us, supporting us, helping us live out our dreams. Even giving us everything she owned in the world to make this happen.' He runs his hand over his suit. '*Gracias*, Beti, from the bottom of my heart.' He leans over and pulls me into a hug, and I couldn't feel prouder if he was my own son.

The crowds are moving in to congratulate the couple. The rising stars of tomorrow, everyone is saying, traditionalist and progressives alike. Even Gonzalo is clapping Miguel on the back. Cameras are flashing, and I just know that the performance is already out there on every social media site going.

'So, it is agreed,' Pedro shouts. 'Our winners are Miguel and Sophia. And may we see them dance much more in the future!'

'And!' Miguel tries to quieten the applauding crowd, standing on the chair vacated by Pedro to be heard. 'As I understand it, I have just won a farm.'

Antonio looks momentarily shocked, but nods in agreement. 'It was the bet,' he agrees.

Miguel breaks into a big smile. 'I want to give the farm to my father, the Horse Whisperer, on three conditions: that the cherry variety will always stay the same . . .'

'*Sí!* Of course!' bellows Antonio.

'That I can stay here and this be my home for as long as I want it.'

'Of course.' The beam is widening across Antonio's face.

'And that this barn is opened again as a place for flamenco, where people can come and perform and see other dancers, like in my great-grandparents' day.'

This time Antonio is so choked by happiness, he can hardly speak. '*Sí!*' he manages eventually, his whole being full of pride and love for his son. Then he turns to me. 'You made this happen, Beti . . . *Gracias*,' and he looks down at me with a wonderful softness in his eyes.

Suddenly a bell rings out and we all move outside to see where it's coming from.

It is Bonita, standing by the back door, calling everyone to the restaurant: 'Paella!'

Like a trail of fireflies, we pick up candles and lanterns

from the tables and walk down the path to the terrace, where two huge pans of paella are waiting on a long table. We set the candles down around the veranda, and I run in and bring out the fairy lights from the barn, throwing them over the nearest tree and switching them on, while Pedro strikes up all over again.

Esmeralda is standing by her motor home with Felipe. 'If you don't come with us now, you will never have a home with me again,' she is telling Miguel.

'He has a home here, for life,' Antonio says, standing next to Miguel, who is holding Sophia's hand. 'Miguel?'

'I am staying here with you, Papa,' he says, and puts his arm around Antonio's shoulder.

As the red tail lights of the motor home disappear down the drive with a squeal of tyres, Antonio and Miguel walk back towards the veranda together.

'I'm sorry. That must have been hard. Feeling you had to choose,' Antonio says.

'It was never a choice, Papa. It's what's in here,' and letting go of Sophia's hand briefly, Miguel bangs his chest and gives a soft smile.

Guitars are playing and people are eating and mingling. Mum is with Craig, talking about Sophia's dress. Dad is talking to Harold, who is eating a big bowl of paella and declaring he's never tasted anything like it all the time he's been in Spain. I hear him say that he's decided he would now like to be known as Hernando, which makes me laugh. Bonita is offering Gonzalo some of her cherry and almond cake. Olivia and her coven and Brenda are sitting with one of Sophia's friends, a waitress for the evening, who is showing them how to roll their hands, little fingers first, and lift their elbows in an impromptu flamenco class. Then the drum begins and the singing starts and the whole place comes alive with clapping, and Sophia and Miguel take to the dance floor in the middle of the veranda. Even Suerte is dancing about and showing off, trotting and swinging his mane around the paddock with the colt in tow.

'I realise now why you had to do this; my apologies for my objections,' says the mayor, taking Antonio by the hand and watching as his daughters learn the *sevillana* from Miguel and Sophia. Everyone is joining in: the schoolteacher, the young priest. Frank is dancing with my mother, then Rita and Maxine. Bonita beams as she dances with Gonzalo. The boys from the band are finding their way around flamenco too. The whole place is alive and I couldn't feel happier.

'Beti?' I turn. It's Will, come to stand beside me and watch the dancers. 'So I'm guessing it's a no. We're not back on then?' he says with a resigned sigh and slumped shoulders.

'I'm sorry,' I say, because I am. 'I really wanted it to work. I wanted you to notice me. I wanted you to look at me the way you used to. At least I thought I wanted that, but it wasn't right. It's just the natural rhythm of life.'

'Could I try again? Kiss you again?'

'No!' I laugh in surprise as he leans in to me, and put up a hand. 'We might have wanted it, but you can't choose who you fall in love with. You'll find the one.'

At that moment a little red car pulls into the car park and Valentina gets out and stares at the heaving restaurant. She takes in the music, the singing, the smiling faces and the big dishes of paella. Then she walks over towards where I'm standing with Will.

'Who's that?' Will whispers. 'Jeez! Looks spiky!'

'Ssh!' I tell him as Valentina climbs the steps and stands in front of me.

'You! You did this!' It's not a question. It's a statement. 'You had a better feel for it than me. You understood it – and him – more than I ever did.'

'I'm sorry, Valentina. I didn't mean for it to happen,' I tell her.

'I know,' she says quietly. 'Here.' She holds out her hand, and my flamenco shoes dangle from her fingers. 'I took them. I'm sorry too. I thought . . . I thought if you couldn't dance, then you wouldn't fall in love, like he has been falling in love with you from the moment he first set eyes on you. I knew it straight away – the way he looked at you. I couldn't stop it, even though I tried.'

I catch my breath and glance round for Antonio, who looks over at me at exactly the same time.

I take the shoes.

'Thanks, but I didn't need them.'

'Good. I'm glad. You came to Spain and found what you were looking for. It might not be what you set out to find in the beginning, but perhaps it found you. It is what we are all looking for, after all.' She raises a pencilled eyebrow at Will.

'Erm . . . can I get you a drink?' Will offers, his charming self once again, and Valentina accepts. The two of them walk towards the bar, introducing themselves. I wish Will all the luck in the world. He and I just weren't meant to be. Otherwise we'd have made it happen a long time ago. Will wasn't the one, but he was part of the journey, and I wouldn't change it.

The whole town is here, dancing and clapping. The mayor's eighty-year-old mother is a demon at flamenco, dancing like she was eighteen all over again.

'Best party ever,' Uncle Paul is saying as he and Rita attempt the *sevillana* too. 'We should go to lessons back home.'

'I'd like that,' she says. 'We haven't done anything together in years.'

'Hey! Bet!' He calls me over. 'This has been brilliant. I always knew you'd pull something like this off. Reckon it was me giving you a hard time that gave you the push you needed.' He smiles, raising his arms, watching Rita snake around him. Typical Uncle Paul, I think. 'Hope you know that I was just . . . well . . . maybe I shouldn't have really . . .' He trails off, but I think that may just have been an apology. I can't believe my ears! 'You should be proud of Bet,' he calls to my dad.

'Oh we are!' my parents say in unison. 'And Paul?' adds my dad. 'It's Beti; everyone who knows and loves her calls her Beti.' And I know in that moment that the two of them have finally stopped feeling bad about doing something as natural as falling in love.

Mum and Dad dance together as though they have been doing it all their lives, finding each other's rhythm straight away. Their faces burst with pleasure every time they look at me. I tell them the whole story about Will and the money, and how I ended up here. 'Your nan would be dead proud of you,' Dad says, pulling me to him, and I know he's right. I did it, Nan, I think to myself, and I can just picture her smiling face, making me smile too.

The whole sky finally turns a vibrant red and orange as the clouds are banished from the sky, and the town carries on partying. And as they do, Antonio slips his hand in mine and leads me away from the lively crowd up through the cherry orchard back to my *finca*. When we reach the rickety old veranda where Ana the cat is sleeping, ignoring us, we turn and look out at the amazing sunset that is filling the sky over the cherry orchard, enveloping us in its glow. Then he turns to me and touches my cheek, and finally lowers his lips down to mine, and the rocket that was ready and primed to blast off in my tummy finally takes off with bright lights, sparkles and the sound of strumming guitars. I can taste that first sweet cherry on my lips all over again, and I never want it to stop.

Then he opens the door to the *finca*, and with no words needed, he leads me to bed. We make love with the smell of the cherry orchard lingering on the sheets, and I know I am finally home.

Chapter Fifty-four

Antonio and I sit on the veranda of the restaurant counting the takings from yesterday's *peña*. Some of the crowd finally left in the early hours, whilst others slept in their cars and camper vans in the car park.

'It's enough to buy your bar,' Antonio says. 'Not just the rent and deposit, but the whole lease!' and he pushes the money bag towards me across the table, in amongst the coffee cups and pastries, and a big bowl of juicy cherries.

'But I don't want a bar,' I say, thinking about Harold and Brenda and worrying about how I'm going to break it to them, but for the first time ever knowing exactly what I do want. I push the bag back towards him. 'I want a new water pump, and new pipes for a whole orchard too!'

'No, a bar!' He pushes the bag back towards me, his hand over mine.

'A water pump!' I push it back, but he resists and laughs.

'It was your dream, though, you told me, to get a bar in the harbour. Beti's Bar.'

'Things change. Dreams change. What you thought you wanted isn't always what's right for you.'

'How about you get a water pump with a bar thrown in?' Miguel joins in, pointing up towards the barn.

We look at each other and smile, agreeing that Miguel really does have more sense than either of us.

'Are you sure this is what you want?' Antonio asks, his frown returning.

'Yes,' I tell him. I've known ever since I woke up this morning in his arms where I want to be. I have never been more sure about anything.

'Are you going to keep another one of those big notebooks, like for Olivia's party?'

I laugh. 'No. No more mood boards or party planning files. I've learned that you can't plan things in life. I'm going to trust my instinct. How about we agree to just go with what life throws at us . . . live for today, not the plans we make for tomorrow,' I say, and he leans across the table with a slow smile and kisses me with the same softness as he did last night, making me go tingly with the memory of it. I have tried to plan everything in my life to date, even making mental lists about why Will was the perfect partner for me. But everything has its natural rhythm in life; you just have to listen to it.

'As long as there is a flamenco fiesta next year. A celebration after the cherry harvest, remember?' Miguel adds.

'Agreed!' We both smile at him.

'Flamenco may be about a strict pattern and a rhythm, but it is also about feeling free to go with what feels right at the time . . . a perfect combination, don't you think?' Antonio looks at me, and I feel the rocket being lit ready for a rerun.

'Absolutely.'

'Then stay with me. Marry me?' he says suddenly, reaching

for both my hands across the table. 'Esmeralda has sent a text to say she has started the divorce proceedings.'

'I . . . I . . . But we just agreed! No more plans!' I laugh, feeling surprised and excited.

'No, no plans. What more do we need? Everyone who matters is here.' He glances from me to Miguel, who looks like he might burst with happiness, and I feel like I finally have a family of my own. 'I have spent the last three months getting to know you, Beti Winter, and I want to spend the rest of my life with you. You and your mad ideas!' He smiles, and then says more seriously, 'Now I have found you, Beti, I don't want to spend another day without you.'

'But I thought . . . I mean, with Valentina, you never wanted that commitment,' I say, my mouth as dry as if it were full of sand. I can't look at him.

'Maybe that's because I hadn't found the right person. I know in my heart that this is right for me. I can feel it here,' and he holds his fist to his chest and lifts my chin with his finger and looks right at me. My own heart responds by beating its message loudly back. 'I know the joy commitment can bring now.' He looks at Miguel again, and they share a smile. Then he looks back at me. 'Think about it,' he says, suddenly looking worried. But I don't need to think about it. I know it's right. No plans, just the people I care about most here with me when I marry this man; this infuriating, grumpy, loving, passionate man.

'Yes!' I say, quietly at first. Then, '*Sí!*' and we both stand and he hugs me, lifting me off my feet. Miguel is running the backs of his hands under his eyes, and Bonita and Frank come out to see what all the noise is about. Frank produces a bottle of cherry brandy, and as he hands round the glasses, a car pulls up in the car park. It's Uncle Paul, Rita and Mum and Dad. Followed by Olivia. They've come to thank me for a lovely day yesterday. Bonita brings out more coffee and cherry brandy, plus a plate of her cake.

'Thank you,' says Olivia, walking towards us. 'You really saved my skin!'

'You mean I saved your face!' I find I can finally laugh about it.

'The pictures have gone down a storm on Facebook. Look!' She waves her phone at me. 'I've had hundreds of likes already! I owe you.'

'No you don't. I'm just glad you enjoyed it,' I say, smiling at her shallowness and lack of tact once again.

'Do you know, I actually did!' A slow realisation dawns on her face, then she takes a deep breath. 'You always did your own thing, Beti, never followed the crowd. I always admired that.'

'Really?' I say warily. 'I think I wasted far too many years worrying what others thought.' I think about the life I have in front of me now, and feel so grateful for it. I don't know what will be thrown in our path, what the harvest will bring next year, but I know that whatever happens, I'm going to be doing it with the man I love.

'It never seemed that way. And look, about the business with Tom. I am sorry, y'know,' and at least she does look mildly apologetic.

'Thank you,' I say. 'I'm sure we would have realised we weren't right for each other in the end. Maybe you just helped us along the way.'

She reaches out and gives me one of her stiff hugs, her sharp cheekbones jutting against mine as she checks her phone again. I guess that's the closest Olivia will ever get to warmth and affection. She may have lots of likes, but I'd rather be able to feel real love and passion, I think, pulling away from the awkward embrace. And then over her shoulder I see another car pulling into the car park.

'I have to talk to these people,' I say, excusing myself. Suddenly I'm as nervous as I was on my first day here, when these lovely people threw me a lifeline. I have to talk to them and try and explain. I run over to meet them as they get out of the car.

'Cracking do yesterday!' Harold says.

'Hi, Harold.'

'Hernando,' he corrects me, making me smile, but Brenda suddenly looks nervous.

'Actually, love, we wanted to talk to you,' she says, wringing her hands and making her rings spin on her fingers. My heart twists. They want to get a move on. They want me to hand over the deposit so they can start their new life back in the UK.

'I wanted to talk to you too,' I say. I have to tell them as quickly as possible. I hope they won't hate me. 'The thing is . . .' I start.

'It's difficult, but . . .' Brenda is saying.

'I don't want to rent the Butterfly Bar.' I force out the words, then gaze at them like a rabbit caught in the head-lights.

'We don't want to leave the Butterfly Bar,' Brenda blurts out at the same time, and stares at me, wide-eyed and worried.

We look at each other for longer than necessary, digesting what the other has said, and then we both burst out laughing.

'We don't want to leave. We loved being here so much yesterday. After we came back from the UK, we realised we were just unpaid babysitters there. We'd much rather the family came out to stay with us here and made a proper holiday of it.'

'This is our home,' Harold puts in. 'Bugger Brexit. They'll have to carry me out kicking and screaming. I'm more Spanish now than British. And the price of a pint! No, I'm Hernando from now on, and this is where I'm staying.'

And we all agree that that's a perfect name for him, and that he shouldn't be going anywhere.

'Actually, I have some news,' I tell everybody, and as they all shriek and cheer in delight, weary flamenco dancers wake and stretch in their cars and vans dotted all around the car park. Bonita makes more coffee, and the mayor and his daughters bring trays of pastries. Then one of the young men takes out his guitar and gets the party started all over again.

'I'll make more paella, and lots of cherry and almond cake!' Bonita says. 'Just like Antonio's grandmother used to make.'

'I'll help!' my mum calls out, to Bonita's delight. A pupil!

'And I'll help Miguel,' says my dad. Miguel has fetched a cherry-picking ladder and is putting more fairy lights from the barn in the trees down the drive, for later that night when it gets dark, just like I imagined when I first arrived.

As Ana the cat weaves her way around the trees, purring contentedly, Olivia goes to help Frank restock the bar in the barn.

Antonio smiles at me, pulling me close to him. 'I think this is becoming a family affair!' he says. He drops his head and kisses me, and I never want it to stop.

We all pull together, and as word gets out, the fiesta starts up all over again. We dance, drink, eat and celebrate the cherry harvest and new beginnings. Everything I want is right here, right now, and I'm going to savour every minute of it. I finally feel that I've stopped planning tomorrow and am living for today. What's on my mind, Facebook? Me? I'm Beti Winter, I'm going nowhere, and that's exactly where I want to be. *Olé!*

Sunset over the Cherry Orchard

Bonus Material

Tapas

I love tapas! Tapas are little taster plates of Spanish food. When I started writing *Sunset over the Cherry Orchard* I turned to Jamie Oliver's *Jamie Does . . .* recipe book for inspiration. He has a whole chapter devoted to tapas and many of the dishes I've listed here are in his book. Tapas apparently started in Andalucía, where the little plates were used to cover the glasses of sherry drinkers in bars, to stop flies getting into the drinks. These snacks started as thinly sliced bread or meat. The meat was usually ham or chorizo, salty cuts that would encourage a thirst, thereby increasing drinks sales. These little plates began to evolve to become as important as the drinks themselves. Traditionally, tapas can be ordered one or two dishes at a time. You might even move from bar to bar, enjoying a drink and a plate of tapas in each one. It's social and fun, one of my favourite ways to eat. During editorial meetings for this book, we enjoyed many little plates of tapas. It's a great way to enjoy and share food, drinks and ideas with the ones you love. Here are a few of my favourites:

Croquetas
Croquetas are a very traditional Spanish snack. They are often made with leftover meats, cheese or vegetables, mixed with béchamel sauce. They're then covered in breadcrumbs and deep fried. Rich and satisfying.

Fried squid
This dish is so simple but so delicious. Salted squid in bread-crumbs, fried in olive oil and dressed with a good squeeze of lemon juice. Just gorgeous! Or, alternatively, prawns fried in oil with chopped garlic, salt and sprinkled with lemon juice.

Albóndigas
Little mouth-sized meatballs, served in a simple tomato sauce of olive oil, garlic, tomatoes, seasoning and a hint of chilli if you fancy it.

Manchego
I love manchego cheese. I love it served with a bowl of big green olives, but I particularly love it the way Jamie Oliver suggests, drizzled with runny honey and with a sprinkling of fresh thyme on top. Or you could serve it with fresh figs or other fruit. Divine.

Tortilla
A Spanish omelette, made with eggs, onion and chopped potato. Once cooked, this is fabulous served hot or cold in small cubes or slices.

Cured meats

If I'm ordering tapas I love a plate of cold cured meats. Serrano ham and chorizo, sliced thinly, are my favourites. Sometimes they are served with fresh bread and glorious green olive oil. I love the combination of the salt from the ham and the spice from the chorizo. Simple but delicious!

Patatas bravas

And finally *patatas bravas*, just like Bonita makes in the book. According to Jamie, *patatas bravas* means fierce potatoes! Crispy chunks of potato, simply fried in olive oil with herbs and salt. Served with a fiery sauce over the top.

This is just a small selection of the tapas I love. But you could always just follow your heart and have a go at a few of your own with whatever you've got left over in the fridge. It's all about a taste of something lovely to complement drinks and good company, served with love. Enjoy!

Flamenco

I love dancing and the way it makes me feel. But I rarely get the chance to do it these days. Weddings, birthday parties and Friday nights in the kitchen, cooking and dancing to Simon Mayo's *All Request Friday* on Radio 2, that's about it!

When I started coming up with the idea of a Spanish book, I knew I had to include flamenco. I wanted to discover the passion of the dance. Passion and heart are what flamenco is all about. I wanted colour, heat and romance, and I certainly found these in Andalucía, where people express themselves with music and dance, particularly flamenco.

According to the website Andalucia.com, flamenco started with Indian religious dances. These dances reached Spain, when dancers were brought in to entertain the royals. In the sixteenth century, when the Moors, Jews and gypsies were persecuted, the outcasts took their music and dance with them, and this is thought to be where flamenco began.

Today, many holidaymakers who visit Spain, particularly Andalucía, will go and see *flamenco tablaos*; theatrical shows put on to entertain big audiences with colourful costumes and castanets. But away from the crowds and tourist trails, there is another style of flamenco being danced, more authentic and traditional, usually run by flamenco aficionados in small clubs, the *peña flamenco*.

Bryant, writer on Andalucia.com, describes flamenco as a passionate and seductive art form. It is also spontaneous and emotional, and really quite moving to watch. Wikipedia describes the dance as including *cante* (singing), *toque* (guitar playing), *baile* (dance), *jaleo* (vocalisations), *palmas* (hand-clapping) and *pitos* (finger snapping).

But more than this, flamenco is about the *duende*.

When I started researching flamenco, I discovered there are strict patterns as to how dances are performed, with foot-work and clapping. But there is a phrase which says: 'When you learn to dance, you must also learn how to forget it.'

Everything that has been taught must then be ignored. The dancers must rely on the wisdom flowing in their blood. They must feel the rhythm of their own heartbeat and let that guide their interpretation, searching the inner depths of their soul. That is the *duende*. That is the fire dance.

When I started this book, I went to a dance class in Stroud with a friend and learned the basics of flamenco. I loved the way it made me feel. I loved feeling the fire and the passion. It's a dance for people no matter their age, size or background. It made me feel alive. If you have the chance to go along to a class, do. And dance like no one's watching. Embrace the passion and colour it will fill you with. Enjoy how it will make you feel alive, and then dance around your kitchen.

Olé!